WHEN A
HEART STOPS

Books by Lynette Eason

DEADLY
REUNIONS
BOOK 2

WHEN A
HEART STOPS

A NOVEL

LYNETTE EASON

Revell

a division of Baker Publishing Group
Grand Rapids, Michigan

Published by Revell
a division of Baker Publishing Group
P.O. Box 6287, Grand Rapids, MI 49516-6287
www.revellbooks.com

Printed in the United States of America

Library of Congress Cataloging-in-Publication Data
Eason, Lynette.
    When a heart stops : a novel / Lynette Eason.
      p.   cm. — (Deadly reunions ; bk. 2)
    ISBN 978-0-8007-2008-7 (pbk. : alk. paper)
    I. Title.
  PS3605.A79W44 2013
  813'.6—dc23   2012024085

Scripture quotations used in this book, whether quoted or paraphrased by the characters, are from the Holy Bible, New International Version®. NIV®. Copyright © 1973, 1978, 1984, 2011 by Biblica, Inc.™ Used by permission of Zondervan. All rights reserved worldwide. www.zondervan.com

The internet addresses, email addresses, and phone numbers in this book are accurate at the time of publication. They are provided as a resource. Baker Publishing Group does not endorse them or vouch for their content or permanence.

Published in association with Joyce Hart of the Hartline Literary Agency, LLC.

12   13   14   15   16   17   18   7   6   5   4   3   2

—■—

To my wonderful family and friends.
I couldn't do this without you.

And to Jesus Christ,
my Lord and Savior—
and my reason for writing.
I pray people see you on every page!

—■—

1

If she moved, would she die? Serena Hopkins kept her eyes shut and lay as still as possible in the king-size bed, doing her best to keep her breathing even.

Which was becoming more impossible by the second.

As her fear increased, so did the rate of her heartbeat and respirations.

Was he still there?

A slight rustle to her left answered that question. A sliver of moonlight through her window cut a path across the room, allowing enough light for her to see shadows.

A drawer slid open, then closed with a light click.

She opened her eyes into a narrow squint. How did he get in? Where was Yoda, her golden retriever?

Terror made her shudder.

The figure at her dresser paused. Looked around. She felt his gaze land on her.

What should she do? Move and draw attention to herself? Continue to pretend to be asleep?

Please, Lord, please.

Her cell phone lay on the end table, could she grab it fast enough and dial?

Not a chance.

Another chill slid through her. Why hadn't her home alarm gone off? The tremble started in her hands and quickly spread.

No! She couldn't move. Curling her fingers into fists, she did her best to still them.

Her eyes moved back to the figure. His attention had moved from her to another drawer. What was he looking for? How much longer would he look, and if he didn't find what he wanted, would he turn to her? Wake her? Threaten her? Worse? Her mind registered the slender, lanky build of the intruder.

He went for the next drawer. Slid it open. He turned to look over his shoulder at her and she slammed her eyes shut.

Serena's heart thudded in her chest. Surely he could hear it. *See* it. Was he still watching her? She let her eyes crack. No, his focus was on the drawer in front of him. Slowly, inch by inch, never taking her gaze from the person's back, she slid her hand toward the end table.

The drawer slid shut. A whispered curse brushed her ears. He hadn't found what he was looking for. He knelt. She heard a popping sound and froze. His knees. Somehow that simple sound demoted him from terrifying monster to dangerous human.

A low, almost nonexistent grunt filtered to her.

Her fingers brushed the phone on the edge of the nightstand. The phone teetered.

No! It couldn't fall.

Straining, nearly strangling on the need to keep her breathing even when she wanted to gasp in huge gulps of air, she managed to snag the phone with her thumb and forefinger.

She pulled it toward her, slowly, painstakingly silent, until finally, she had it under the covers with her.

Now what?

Would the touch screen light up the room even under the cover of the blanket?

She had to chance it.

And she had to light the screen so she could see the numbers. Right now, she wished she had a phone with buttons one could just feel and know exactly what number it was.

There was one button on this phone she could find by touch. The one that would light the screen. But if she hit the numbers, the rest of the touch pad would make noise. If she'd left the phone on ring instead of vibrate.

She couldn't remember.

Panic nearly smothered her.

He was in the closet. Maybe he wouldn't hear it.

Maybe.

She pressed.

Not a sound. Squinting, still watching his back as he searched, she suppressed a relieved sigh when he never paused.

The phone was on vibrate.

Thank you, Lord.

Her intruder disappeared farther into her walk-in closet.

Now was her chance.

Fingers still wrapped around the phone, Serena pushed back the covers as silently as possible and swung her legs off the edge of the bed closest to the door. She finished dialing 9-1-1 and pressed Send, keeping her hand over the screen to minimize the light.

Even as the phone rang and the 9-1-1 operator picked up, Serena was moving toward the open bedroom door. Her bare feet never made a sound on the hardwood floors.

But she couldn't speak into the phone yet.

She slipped out of the bedroom and into the hall. Her goal was the back door to the garage.

And then she heard him curse.

"Serena, where are you?"

The silky-smooth low voice shot new terror through her as she used a precious second to debate her next move. Getting out of the house was no longer an option. He would be on her before she got the dead bolt turned.

Footsteps—terrifying, unhurried footsteps—came her way. "I'll find you. You can't be far."

She spun on her heel and hurried as silently as possible to the spare bedroom. Hopefully, he would expect her to make a run for one of the doors that led outside.

Serena closed and locked the bedroom door and turned to answer the operator, who was asking, ". . . Is someone there? What's your emergency?"

Serena held the phone to her lips and whispered, "104 Bennett Drive. Someone's in my house."

Her foot kicked something soft. And warm.

"Yoda," she whispered. Grief welled up in her as she placed her hand on Yoda's chest. And felt a beating heart.

Relief replaced the grief, but she didn't have time to do more than offer the unconscious animal a soft pat. She tossed the phone on the bed, the operator still talking. Hurrying toward the closet, she flipped on the light and blinked as her eyes adjusted to the sudden brightness.

Serena pulled out a locked box.

And froze as the bedroom doorknob rattled.

"Serena, I know you're in there. Give it up, honey. If you just give me what I want, I'll leave you alone."

Sure he would. Fingers shaking, she went to the nightstand, opened the drawer, and pulled out the key.

It took three tries, but she finally managed to get the box open.

"I'm running out of patience, Serena. Open the door or I'll kick it in." He did sound irritated. And that made her blood churn. She was an irritant to him. A mere bother.

She had no doubt that if he got his hands on her, she was dead.

How long would it take for the cops to arrive?

A few minutes at least.

"Serena!"

It just registered that he knew her name. So this wasn't some random break-in.

Still, she refused to answer him.

Her fingers worked the magazine into the Glock 17. Her father's gun. The one he insisted she learn how to shoot and handle as well as any police officer.

Her palm racked the slide at the top and the round chambered. The semiautomatic pistol felt comfortable, reassuring. Some of her terror dissipated. Enough that her hands steadied.

Now all she had to do was pull the trigger as many times as it took. Surely seventeen bullets would do the trick. "I have a weapon!" she hollered. "And if you come through that door, I'll use it!"

A pause. Then a low laugh. "Sure you do, Serena."

Gripping the gun with both hands, she lifted the pistol and fired.

The bullet slammed into the door.

She heard a scream, another curse.

Then the sound of sirens filled her ears. Seconds later, through the window, flashing blue lights filled the room.

"The cops are here! Leave now!" she ordered, wishing her voice didn't tremble with each word.

A loud boom hit her ears and the bedroom door slammed open. His slender frame filled the opening and his malevolent green eyes met hers.

Serena felt a cold chill invade her and knew she was going to have to shoot to kill.

"Please, don't make me do this," she whispered.

He lunged toward her and she pulled the trigger for the second time that night.

2

"It's time," he breathed. "Are you ready?"

An anxious longing twisted inside the listener. "I'm ready. I've waited a long time for this. But why now?"

"Doesn't matter why now." Then he laughed and rhymed, "I've missed the game, it's time to play, I have the name, you pick the day."

"What are the names?"

"Leslie Stanton and Kelly Popour."

He reeled off the street addresses. "Call me when it's done."

3

Leslie's hand shook as she stared down the barrel.

Kelly Popour sat at the table, arms shackled at the biceps, effectively holding her in place. She pleaded, "Don't, Leslie, don't!"

But Leslie didn't have a choice. Not if she wanted to live. Her heart shuddered as she looked to the left. To the person who'd brought this nightmare down on them.

"Why?" she whispered. "Why?"

An insane giggle reached her and she knew her life would never be the same. If she even had a life after tonight.

"It's your turn, Leslie," the voice singsonged. "You lost the hand."

Leslie looked at the cards scattered across the table. Nausea welled up, gagging her. The bullet in her shoulder caused it to burn like someone had touched a blowtorch to it.

She couldn't do it. She simply couldn't. Her mind scrambled for a plan, a way to escape. And the only way to do that was to end the life of the person who'd snatched her from her home two days ago.

But she couldn't turn the gun on her captor either. The steel bar attached to the table ensured the gun would point in only one direction.

13

Toward her best friend, Kelly.

And Leslie had been warned. If she didn't pull the trigger, she would die.

The only way to live was to pull the trigger. "God! Help me!"

Her finger tightened and Kelly flinched, screaming as she ducked her head into her shoulder. "Don't! Don't!" The shackles kept Kelly bound to her chair.

Leslie felt the bite of her handcuffs. The ones around her ankle, binding her to her own steel chair that had been bolted to the floor. No shackles this time. The shooter didn't have shackles.

A sharp pain sliced through her shoulder, and her arm convulsed.

"Do it, Leslie. Kelly pulled the trigger on you, didn't she? What's keeping you from doing the same?"

She couldn't do it. Glancing at the one who was now in control of whether she lived or died, Leslie suddenly knew without a doubt she wasn't going to live much longer.

With a deep breath, she set her jaw, determination sliding through to push the terror aside a fraction. If she was going to die, she wouldn't die a murderer.

She dropped her arms, heard the gun clatter to the table as the steel bar fell over. "I won't do it."

She felt something slam into her forehead and knew no more.

4

Dead, dark eyes stared up at her, and Medical Examiner Serena Hopkins suppressed the shiver that slid over her. The feeling was unwelcome—and unexpected—since she saw dead bodies on a daily basis.

Ignoring her odd reaction, Serena leaned in and examined a small package with a bright red bow. It lay on the woman's midsection with her rigid hands grasping it. If she didn't know the woman was dead, Serena would think she was lying there, stretched out on the bench, taking a short nap while waiting on someone to wake her.

Only this woman would never again wake up.

Serena let her gaze move down the body, taking note of the pink hoodie jogging jacket over a white T-shirt, matching pink jogging shorts, skinned knees, and bare feet.

Detective Katie Isaacs cleared her throat. "Well?"

Serena watched as the bomb squad van pulled away. It hadn't taken them long to examine the package and declare it nonexplosive. But Serena wouldn't open it. CSU, the crime scene unit, would take care of that. Her job was the body. "I would say she's been dead anywhere from eight to thirty-six hours. She's cold and stiff. From the hole in her forehead, I'll make a wild guess and say that

15

was the cause of death. But until I do the autopsy, I won't know for sure. I can say for certain that she wasn't killed here, though."

"Not enough blood," Katie stated.

Serena nodded. Head wounds bleed profusely, but this woman . . . "Not *any* blood. At least none that I can see." Serena pursed her lips and narrowed her eyes on the woman's head. "Something's just not right . . ."

Straight dark hair, slender, tall, athletic.

But there was something familiar . . .

"I don't want to move her until Mickey gets here." Mickey Black, the CSU photographer, would get the pictures from every conceivable angle before Serena would move the body. And then he would take more pictures. But she could take in as much information as possible while she waited on him.

As she continued to study the woman's face, recognition finally came like a punch to the gut. "I know her." Stunned, Serena straightened and looked at Katie. "Her name's Leslie Stanton. She was in my graduating class in high school. You were a senior when we were freshmen."

Katie took another look, then shook her head. "She doesn't look the slightest bit familiar to me."

Serena lifted a brow. "Death has a way of messing with a person's looks. I'm sure she would prefer the yearbook picture." She paused. "Where's your partner?" Serena had no idea how Hunter Graham worked with Katie Isaacs. The woman could be crass and downright rude, but she and Hunter had developed a relationship that worked for them.

And Serena had to admit Katie seemed to have mellowed a bit since being shot a few weeks ago.

Katie said, "He and Alexia took a little trip trying to track down her father."

Hunter Graham and Alexia Allen, two of Serena's closest friends, needed the break from the trauma they'd just lived through four weeks ago. Someone had been after Alexia and almost succeeded in killing her.

Fortunately, she'd escaped and Hunter was determined to stick close while she searched for the father she hadn't seen in ten years.

Katie shielded her eyes with her hand and looked at the crowd behind the tape. "Chad's here working with some of the other officers asking questions, trying to find someone who saw something."

Detective Chad Graham, Hunter's brother and a bit of a loose cannon. But likable enough and a good detective. He was going through a nasty divorce, but Serena noticed he was learning to leave his personal life at home while he focused on the job.

Another man caught her attention. Tall, with broad shoulders and reddish blond hair, he was an all-around good-looking man. "Hey, isn't that Colton Brady? What's he doing here?"

Katie looked over her shoulder. "Yes. He was transferred to our department two weeks ago. Word's out that he has his eye on the captain position when Captain Murdoch retires in a few months."

Serena bit her lip. "Huh." She watched him move through the crowd, stop to speak to officers, and then engage in conversation with Chad. He had an air of authority around him. It would be interesting to see if he got the captain's job.

Mickey arrived and, after briefly greeting them, got to work.

Serena stepped back, tilted her head toward Katie, and refocused on her news. "So they found Alexia's father?"

"They think so. With all the feelers they put out, they finally got some hits. A homeless shelter director in Charlotte, North Carolina, said he thinks the man's been staying there for the past week."

Serena continued her observations, making notes and studying the area around Leslie.

When Mickey finished snapping, he said, "We can turn her now. I'll snap while you move her."

After positioning the gurney next to the bench, Serena motioned for one of the CSU members to help her. Together, they hefted

Leslie onto the body bag, placing her facedown. Serena stepped forward and moved the woman's head. The condition of the back of Leslie's head brought Serena up short.

"Bullet went through the back," she muttered to herself. "And he cleaned her up."

"What?" Katie looked up from her notepad.

"Look. The bullet went out the back of her skull, but there's no blood, brain matter, nothing. And her hair's clean, freshly washed—and not by her, I can tell you that."

"Now that's just . . . weird." Katie's nose wrinkled as she waited for Serena to continue.

"Sure is." Serena frowned. "Do you find this kind of creepy?"

"Creepy?" Katie lifted a brow. "You're a medical examiner and you find a dead body creepy?"

Smirking, Serena said, "Cute." Then her frown returned. "By creepy, I mean this is the second classmate to be murdered in the last month." From the corner of her eye, she saw Rick Shelton climb from the white CSU van. It had taken him long enough to get here.

"You're talking about Devin being the first?" Katie asked. Devin Wickham had been killed a little over four weeks ago, starting a weeklong reign of terror for Alexia. When Serena nodded, Katie said, "But Devin's killer was caught."

"True." Serena's mind continued to turn over the possibilities as she gathered evidence and placed it in bags to be delivered to the lab. She would handle the body; CSU would cover everything else.

Rick walked up and Serena asked, "What are you doing here? Don't you have a lab to run?"

Head of the crime lab, Rick didn't go out into the field much anymore. He rolled his eyes. "When you're short staffed, you do what you gotta do. That was one reason it took me awhile to get over here. Had to pull people out of bed. Third-shift workers don't like first shift, so some may be a little grumpy. Just ignore it." He started issuing orders to his team and Serena turned back to the detective.

Looking puzzled, Katie chewed her bottom lip. Walking forward, she stood next to Serena and studied the gift they'd removed from the dead woman's hands.

Serena noticed Katie wince as she moved her left arm. "You're back at work a little soon after being shot, aren't you?"

The detective shrugged with her good shoulder. "Can't stand sitting around doing nothing. I'm on light duty for the next couple of weeks. But I can go to a death scene, write reports, and do a little investigating. I leave when I get tired."

Katie had been shot protecting Alexia from the person who'd murdered Devin and eventually grabbed Alexia. But the shooter had been killed in jail and couldn't have been responsible for this new death.

"What's up with this present? Who is it for? Is it hers? Did someone give it to her? Or was she going to deliver it?" Katie machine-gunned the questions and made Serena blink.

"I don't know," she answered. A chilled sensation crawled up the back of her neck and a sense of foreboding surrounded her. Her eyes scanned the crowd, probing, seeking. Was the killer here, watching her work? Reveling in the chaos he'd created?

Nobody looked out of place. The crime scene photographer snapped shots of the crowd. The cops held the growing masses back, trying to give Leslie the dignity she deserved. Unfortunately, she had been placed on a park bench right along the jogging path. In full view of the gawkers.

And the news media. The Channel 7 news van pulled up followed by Channel 10, and Serena winced. Just what they needed. Fortunately, more police arrived at that moment and would help keep the media and their cameras away. They'd tried to make the crime scene area large enough to keep the body out of range of sight, but the layout of the park made it impossible. They would just have to deal with it.

Turning back to Leslie, she gathered every last scrap of evidence from the poor woman's body and handed everything over to Rick.

He curled his fingers around the handle of the evidence bag. "I'll get this to the lab and see what I can get for you, but until you find the original crime scene, it's going to be a tough one."

"I know. And unless someone tips the cops off," she shrugged, "you know as well as I do that finding where she was killed is a shot in the dark."

Rick nodded and looked at the present Serena had immediately tagged and bagged to avoid any kind of contamination of evidence that might be on the outside of the package. "Want me to take that now?"

"Sure."

His eyes gleamed. "I'll let Christine take care of this one."

Serena bit her lip to hide a smile. Alexia had told her that Rick was in love with Hunter and Chad's sister, Christine Graham. Christine worked in the lab with Rick. "I'm sure she would appreciate that." She tilted her head. "How is Christine doing with taking over the high school reunion planning?"

For a moment Rick's eyes blanked at the change of subject, then he shrugged. "Fine. I think she's enjoying it in spite of Lori dying." Lori, the committee's former leader, had killed Devin Wickham and then kidnapped Alexia. "The committee thought about canceling it but then decided they didn't want to let murder be the theme of their ten-year reunion. If they don't go through with the plans for it . . ." He shook his head. "What are you going to think of whenever anyone mentions their ten-year reunion?"

Serena realized Christine was right. They needed to have the reunion.

Katie and Chad walked up together. Chad said, "We're going to inform Leslie's family and see if they can answer a few questions for us. We need a timeline of her whereabouts for the last few hours. Maybe if we can figure out who saw her last, we'll find her killer."

"Sounds like a good idea. I'll be at the morgue. Just let me know when they're ready to see her."

Chad nodded and, together, he and Katie left.

Serena noticed the frown on Rick's face as he looked to the black and silver package, then back to Leslie. "What is it?" she asked.

His eyes continued their perusal. "I'm not sure. There's something vaguely familiar about this whole scene."

"What do you mean?"

The frown deepened. "Again, I'm not sure. I'll have to think about it, but it's like this crime is ringing some sort of bell for me."

"Something you worked on before?"

"Nope." He shook his head. "Something I read. Maybe. Or heard in a lecture." He shrugged. "It'll come to me. If you get anything else, bag it and bring it to me."

Rick left and Serena turned back to Leslie. Sorrow swept over her and she firmed her jaw. Leslie had been a quiet girl who kept to herself but was friendly and smart. To see her now made Serena furious, sad—even a little shocked. The same way she'd felt when she'd been called to Devin's murder.

Swallowing her emotions, she zipped the bag, stopping at the woman's face. Staring down at the life cut short, she felt sorrow seize her.

"I'm sorry, Leslie," she whispered. "I'm going to find who did this to you."

"Still talking to the dead?"

The quiet voice behind her made her freeze. And her heart gave a startled thud before settling back into a faster than normal rhythm. She finished zipping the bag. "Almost every day."

"Do they ever talk back?" Dominic Allen stepped into her peripheral vision and pushed his sunglasses to the top of the short red curls that lay tight around his head.

"All the time." Serena kept her voice even, hoping the sudden tremor in her hands wasn't noticeable as Dominic took one end of the gurney without her asking. Together, they pushed it to the back of the vehicle where Serena opened the door. "What are you doing here?"

"I've got two more days of medical leave. Supposed to be recovering from my surgery."

Serena knew from Alexia about Dominic's surgery. He'd been a bone marrow donor for his mother, who suffered from aplastic anemia. "Glad to see you're feeling better."

"Pretty much back to 100 percent." A smile crossed his lips. "I'm not here officially. Hunter knew I've been climbing the walls from sheer boredom, so when he got this call, he sent me a text. I'll fill him in once he gets back in town."

She eyed him. "And that's the only reason you're here?"

He paused. "You got me. He said you'd be here and I need to talk to you."

"About?"

"Jillian Carter." Dominic's smile faded. "He wants me to quietly look into Jillian's disappearance. I have access to resources he doesn't have."

Serena felt the tremor ease, but a ball of ice formed in her gut. "Really? Why?"

"Because we want to find the man who got away. The person behind Alexia's kidnapping is still out there and she's not truly safe until he's caught. His main concern seemed to be finding Jillian. When he had Alexia, he questioned her at length about how to find Jillian. When she finally convinced him she didn't know, he left orders for Lori to kill her. Thankfully, Alexia got away. But . . . we still need to find the person behind everything. So . . . we find Jillian, we find our mystery man."

Serena gave Dominic a wary look and said, "Sounds kind of like setting up a trap for Jillian to walk into."

Dominic rubbed a hand down the side of his face. "Maybe, but we were hoping it would be a trap for the guy who had Alexia kidnapped. Not for Jillian."

Still unsure about that whole plan, she said, "And you think I can help?"

"Alexia said you were the last one to talk to Jillian. Everything that happened to Alexia has something to do with Jillian. We just need to figure out what."

"Jillian called me a couple of months ago," Serena admitted, "but she didn't say much. Asked a few questions, then said she was coming home."

"But she didn't say when?"

"No. She said she had a few things to take care of first."

"You said she asked you questions. I need to know what those were." He gestured to Leslie. "After you get her taken care of, will you meet me for a cup of coffee?"

Dominic asking her out. She'd dreamed of this day since she was twelve. Only it wasn't a date. Not really. "I might be able to do that." Proud of the cool tone she managed to achieve, Serena motioned for help to get Leslie into the back of the vehicle.

Dominic offered his assistance once again and together they got Leslie situated and the doors shut after her.

Serena pulled off her gloves and disposed of them in the hazardous waste bag. She finally turned and got a good look at Dominic Allen. He still looked as good as he had the last time she'd seen him. She'd been fourteen, he'd been seventeen.

His red hair and emerald green eyes still made her heart flutter. "Give me a couple of hours to get things wrapped up."

Dominic slipped her a card. "My cell number is on here. I'll be waiting."

———■———

Standing next to his car, one hand on the open door, the other wrapped around his keys, Dominic paused and watched the very competent Serena speak to the coroner. At five feet nine, she looked exotic with her olive skin, flashing blue eyes, and straight black hair. Right now, she wore it pulled up into a ponytail, but he could envision it flowing around her shoulders.

He blinked and shook his head, remembering the feel of her skin as she'd taken the card from his hand. Her fingers had scraped his palm and his heart had trembled at the contact.

Weird. Very weird. But intriguing. She'd been his kid sister's best friend all through grade school, middle school, and high school. Because of his father's penchant for alcohol and swinging fists, Serena had only been over to the Allen household occasionally.

And he had to admit he'd noticed she was a cute kid, then a pretty preteen. And he also had to admit if she'd been older, he'd have been interested. Then everything had fallen apart and he'd fled, doing his best to leave his memories behind him.

Only now he had a feeling Serena would play a prominent role in his thoughts, and it was a feeling he wasn't sure he was comfortable with.

Serena could very easily become a distraction for him and that was something he couldn't afford right now.

Then she turned and gave him a small wave.

And he decided maybe he could live with one distraction.

Dominic slid into his car and cranked it. He wondered how long he'd have to wait before Serena called him.

—■—

The game was off to a rocking good start. Excitement boiled as the killer stood amongst the masses, back behind the newly placed yellow tape, taking delight in the chaos caused by the discovery of Leslie. Leslie hadn't wanted to play the game right. She'd cheated and stolen the fun. When the toys broke or weren't fun anymore, they had to be thrown away and replaced with a new one.

Replacing Leslie would be a challenge.

The killer shifted, twisting fingers that had gently washed Leslie's hair only hours before.

Already, anticipation for the next name burned inside.

Another call would come.

Two more names would be whispered.

Who would it be? Excitement at the unknown churned even as impatience escalated. Who?

Eenie meenie miney moe.

------■------

"She received the package in the mail last week."

"What's in it?" Senator Frank Hoffman tensed as he awaited the answer. He'd been desperate to get his hands on the package they'd discovered was en route.

A brief moment of silence echoed over the line. "I don't know, she beat me to it. When she signed for it, all I had time to see was the return address from California. I checked out the name on the package and had a buddy of mine in law enforcement do a facial scan. Investigative Reporter Julie Carson is definitely Jillian Carter." He paused. "And now she's disappeared again. I think the PI I put on her spooked her somehow. He can't find a sign of her anywhere."

Frank slammed his fist onto the desk. His coffee sloshed over the side of his mug. Ignoring it, he leaned forward, fingers gripping the phone he had jammed to his ear.

"We found her, only to lose her? I thought you said you had this covered."

"I do." The voice never changed in pitch or tone, but Frank still shivered. He might think he was calling the shots, but he had to admit—if only to himself—that the person on the other end scared him a little. The voice continued, "I've found someone to take care of the problem. When the time is right, the problem will be resolved."

"What kind of someone?"

"Someone who knows exactly what needs to be done and will do it without hesitation."

"Does Serena know she's a target?"

Another pause. "She may suspect something after the break-in."

"Break-in? What break-in? Did you have something to do with it?"

"I did. We failed to find what we were looking for."

Frank grunted. "We seem to be having a lot of that lately."

"Serena has a gun and knows how to use it. The guy I hired to get the package is now in a coma in the hospital. Fortunately, his prints aren't in the system."

Fear shot through Frank. "Can he be traced back to you in any way?" If he could, he could be traced to Frank.

"No."

"What makes you so sure?"

"I'm sure."

Frank paused, and regained control. "We need to get her out of the picture, to stay out of her house to give us time to search it. And then when we find what we're looking for, get rid of her."

"I know. And I've got it covered." Satisfaction sounded in the voice and Frank felt slightly better. Slightly.

"And how are you going to accomplish that?" he asked.

"I've already set things in motion." A light chuckle graced the line. "It's amazing how contacts you once wished buried forever can come back to save your skin."

Well, that was good to know. Maybe.

"I want to know what's in that package." Frank forced calm into his tone. "It could lead us to Jillian." Or it could land him in prison.

"I'm working on it."

"Work harder."

5

Serena straightened and stretched, her back aching, her thoughts whirling. She examined the gunshot wound one more time, content that her findings were correct. "The gunshot in her shoulder didn't kill her. Slowed her down and hurt like crazy, I'm sure, but it didn't kill her. The one to the forehead did the trick."

Paul Hamilton, her assistant, nodded his agreement. Serena made the Y-cut and they started on the organs. Serena talked as she worked, recording her findings to be sure she didn't forget anything when it came time to write the report.

Paul took the liver from her. He would weigh it, record it, and then move on to the next organ.

They worked in a practiced synchronized harmony that came with doing this many times. When she finished with the internal exam, she did another external one on Leslie's legs. As she did, her thoughts went to the man she'd shot in the head and who now lay in a coma four floors above her.

The 9-1-1 call had confirmed the fact that Serena had acted in self-defense. No action would be taken against her. However, she wanted the man to wake up and tell her why he'd targeted her. It was no random break-in. He'd called Serena by name.

27

"You okay?" Paul asked.

She glanced at the handsome young man in his late twenties. His dark hair set off his light blue eyes, and the dimple in his left cheek had charmed just about every woman he'd come into contact with at the hospital.

Serena found him to be a top-notch assistant who'd also become a friend in the year that they'd worked together. At first she thought he might have some romantic feelings toward her, but when she didn't encourage him, he backed off and now seemed content with a good friendship. "I'm fine. Just thinking."

"About the man you shot?" His dimple flashed at her.

She lifted a brow. "You're getting pretty good at that mind reading stuff."

He grinned, his blue eyes twinkling. "It's called spending a lot of time with someone and getting to know her."

"Hmm. I suppose."

"Ready for me yet?"

Paul jumped and Serena gasped, startled at the sudden question that came from behind her. She whirled to see Dorie standing in the doorway.

Dorie laughed, then sobered. "Oops, sorry, didn't mean to sneak up on y'all."

Heart still thumping with the adrenaline surge, Serena placed a hand on her chest and gulped. "It's all right. We're just about finished here."

Dorie King, the morgue janitor, was about fifty pounds overweight, but she moved her pear-shaped body easily, never seeming to tire while she worked. The woman could have been anywhere between thirty and fifty with straight auburn, chin-length hair, and dark brown eyes.

Even though Dorie was a recent hire, Serena had come to appreciate her unique sense of humor and cheery outlook on life. Working a swing shift wasn't easy, but Serena had never heard the woman complain.

Which was a miracle in itself considering what she had to clean up sometimes.

"Can you tell me about her?" Dorie asked, pointing to Leslie.

And Dorie had an insatiable curiosity about all of Serena's patients, as she hoped one day to have Serena's job. A fact Dorie had told her with gleeful satisfaction. Then laughed. "Well, not your job, but I do want to be a medical examiner one day. What better way to get there than from the ground up?"

So Serena did her best to teach Dorie every chance she got.

Looking at the clock, she gasped. There would be no time for teaching today. "Oh Dorie, excuse me, I'm sorry, but I have something I have to do today. Paul can fill you in if he has time." No names would be mentioned and nothing about the crime. When she taught, she kept to the facts of the autopsy. And Dorie knew better than to ask for anything more.

Paul clicked his tongue with regret. "Sorry, Dorie, I'm off to a dentist appointment."

Dorie shrugged. "Oh well, maybe next time."

"You bet." Paul smiled as he shrugged out of his lab coat.

A knock sounded on the door and Serena turned to see a man in a blue business suit, matching tie, and black loafers.

She asked, "Can I help you?" Then she frowned. "How did you get in?"

He shuffled his feet a bit, then looked at Leslie still stretched out on the table. Serena felt unease slide up her spine. Glad she'd covered Leslie to her shoulders, she looked at Paul and Dorie, who stared at the intruder.

"Sir?" Serena questioned.

"Um, yes, I'm sorry." He blinked his gaze away from Leslie, then focused on Dorie and Paul. His eyes narrowed as he seemed to shake off whatever had distracted him and said, "I saw it on the news. About Leslie. I wanted to come see her. Come see if it was true."

Compassion stirred. Had this been Leslie's boyfriend? "I'm sorry. We usually use the viewing room. I just finished up her autopsy."

"How did she die?"

Serena's uneasiness returned. "Again, I'm sorry, but unless you're family, I really can't reveal anything about her death or medical information."

"It's all right." He shook his head. "She was shot, wasn't she?"

"I believe that information was on the news."

He nodded. "Along with the picture of her laid out on the park bench holding a gift."

Serena winced. "Yes. I didn't realize that made it on the news." She remembered the media trucks that had pulled up and her anger at their intrusion. She was still mad about that.

Again, his gaze bounced between Serena and Leslie, then back to Dorie and Paul. Serena said, "I think it's best if you contact Leslie's family about anything you'd like to know about her."

He backed toward the door. "Yes. Yes, I'll do that."

"Sir? I didn't catch your name."

But he was gone.

She looked at Paul and Dorie. "That was weird."

Dorie shuddered and blinked. "Definitely. We really need to talk to security about this. He shouldn't have been allowed down here."

"He probably said he was family or something and got one of the orderlies to let him in." Serena pursed her lips and then glanced at the clock again. She nearly shrieked as she snatched her cell phone to dial Dominic's number. It rang once.

"I wondered if you'd forgotten me." Dominic's deep voice rumbled in her ear.

"Um . . . well . . ."

His laughter followed. "I get it. I lose track of time too when I'm involved in work."

"Sorry." She knew she sounded sheepish. And she was. She hadn't meant to forget him. Normally, she set her phone alarm to remind her when she had an appointment. "I can meet you now. You have someplace in mind?"

"The Java Stop?"

"That's around the corner from here. I can walk over there in just a few minutes." The hospital morgue was in the basement of Palmetto Hospital in downtown Columbia.

She hung up. Slipping off her lab coat, she made a mental note to call Rick Shelton on her way to meet Dominic. She really wanted to know what was in that package. She grabbed her purse, then opened a desk drawer and pulled out an envelope that held a special gift for the girls' home she volunteered for. She smiled as she thought of the surprise and joy the check would bring to those who needed it.

"Want me to mail that for you?" Paul asked.

"No, that's okay. I need stamps anyway. But thanks." She would stop at the post office on her way back from lunch. "See you later, Dorie," she called. She waved to Paul, who was gathering his stuff to leave.

He waved back. "Bye."

Slipping her phone from her pocket, she dialed Rick's direct number as she walked down the hall.

Voice mail picked up and Serena left a message for Rick to call her.

Pushing through the heavy glass doors, she exited the hospital and made her way to the sidewalk, busy with the lunchtime crowd. People passed her, walking shoulder to shoulder, jostling, nudging. "Excuse me's" and "sorry's" abounded. She moved toward the outer edge of the crowd and stuffed the envelope into her purse.

Horns honked, cars roared past. The smell of exhaust burned her nose.

The café was just ahead.

A tug on her purse, then a hard hit to her right shoulder made her cry out as she stumbled on the edge of the curb, twisting her right ankle.

31

Her purse slid from her shoulder and she felt herself falling, falling.

As though in slow motion.

Right into the path of an oncoming city bus.

Brakes screamed, voices cried out.

Serena felt panic choke her as she did the only thing she could think to do.

Keep moving.

Scrambling on all fours, the asphalt scraped her palms, tore at her knees through the fabric of her pants.

Wind rushed past her as the bus missed her by a mere inch.

Horns blared, tires squealed. And Serena came to a trembling halt in front of another car that managed to stop centimeters from her.

"Are you all right?"

"Ma'am?"

"Can you stand?"

The voices echoed in her ears. She couldn't speak, couldn't move, couldn't stop shaking.

In the back of her mind, she registered the symptoms.

Shock.

A hand slid under her arm and gently helped her to her feet. She winced at the stinging pain lancing through her hands and knees and right ankle, but miraculously enough, she decided she was otherwise unhurt.

Grateful for the helping hand, she limped her way back to the sidewalk.

Her rescuer turned concerned eyes on her. "I think someone tried to steal your purse but dropped it when you didn't let go right away. Are you all right?"

"I think so. Thanks." She took the purse from him and winced at the sting in her hands.

He left and people continued on their way.

Serena stood still, leaning against the building until the worst of the trembling ceased. People once again hurried past, anxious to get to wherever they needed to be.

"Serena?"

Her head snapped up to see Dominic pushing his way through the crowd, heading toward her, the frown on his face communicating his concern.

Reaching her, he stopped and looked down. At her hands. She hadn't realized she'd been holding them palms up. Gently, he grasped her wrists for a closer look. "What happened? I saw all the commotion out here and thought I'd find out what was going on."

Offering a slight shrug and a shaky grimace that she hoped passed for a smile, Serena said, "You might say someone just tried to throw me under a bus."

———■———

Dominic had the crazy urge to offer comfort. "What do you mean?"

She shook her head, but the fear remained in those blue eyes.

He pulled her into his arms, wishing he could always be close enough to help.

Mild shock ran through him when she didn't protest.

For a good minute, they stood huddled up against the side of the building, her face buried against the crook between his neck and shoulder. The scent of her shampoo wafted up and he inhaled. Then he got himself together and wrapped a hand around her upper arm. Clearing his throat, he said, "Come on, let's go to the café and you can get cleaned up a little bit." He paused. "Or would you rather I take you home?"

"No." Her voice sounded husky. "I'll be okay. Let's go to the café. You're right, I can clean up there. I want to hear what you have to say about Jillian."

A few minutes later, Serena came out of the restroom, limping slightly, favoring her right ankle. She had wet paper towels pressed to her hands. "I think the bleeding is stopped." She bit her lip and frowned in disgust. "And I tore a hole in my best pair of pants."

He looked. "Ouch. Are you sure you don't want to go home?"

"And do what?" Another slight lift of her shoulders and she said, "I took some ibuprofen—that should kick in soon." She slid into the seat opposite him.

The waitress came over and they placed their order. Then Dominic asked, "So what did you mean, someone tried to throw you under a bus?"

"I'm not sure exactly what happened. One minute, I was going with the flow of the crowd, the next, I felt someone tug on my purse, then a hard shove against my shoulder. I fell into traffic and looked up to see a bus heading my way. I rolled and—" she swallowed— "somehow made it out of the way in one piece."

A shudder racked her and Dominic felt his protective instincts kick in. "You could have been killed."

"Believe me, the thought had crossed my mind," she said softly.

He frowned. "And you don't think it was an accident."

Their coffee and food arrived. She sighed. "I don't know what to think."

Dominic picked up his cup and took a sip. "Well, if it's not an accident, then that means you have someone who wants to hurt you."

She fiddled with her fork, then her napkin, then picked up her water and took a gulp. "It's possible, I suppose."

"You have some enemies?"

"Maybe."

He lifted a brow. "You want to tell me about it?"

"Someone broke into my house last week while I was asleep."

Dominic frowned. "What? How?"

"Good question." She took a bite of her salad. "I had the alarm armed and it never went off. My dog was drugged before she could warn me." She shrugged. "Then again, she's not really a good watchdog so I don't count on her for that."

"What was the intruder looking for?"

She shrugged. "I don't know. I shot him before I had a chance to ask him."

Dominic choked on his tea and grabbed a napkin before he could spew the liquid everywhere. Finally, he asked, "Excuse me?"

Her eyes flicked to his, then back to her food. "I had my dad's gun in a closet. I managed to get to it, and now my intruder's in a coma on the fourth floor of the hospital. The bullet entered his skull and did some damage, but he's still alive." She took another bite. She sounded blasé about the incident, but he could tell she was deeply disturbed by the fact that she'd shot a man. Before he could try to think of something to say that didn't sound patronizing or just plain stupid, Serena said, "Tell me about Jillian, please."

Dominic hesitated. Serena looked worn out, tired, and stressed. He wanted to protect her, comfort her, and tell her everything would be fine. But his gut said she wasn't the type to believe it if it wasn't true. He reached over and gripped her free hand. "I'm sorry you had to go through that."

Tears formed for a brief moment before she blinked them away. "Tell me about Jillian. Please."

Dominic hesitated again, trying to get a read on the woman across the table. The beautiful woman with the shadowed eyes. She was hiding something and didn't want to confide in him. Yet.

He could understand that. He had a few secrets of his own. But he still made a mental note to look into the shooting. He gave her fingers a light squeeze and reluctantly withdrew his hand. "We know she left town on the night of graduation. She must have used the cash you and Alexia gave her."

Serena poked at her salad. She winced at the movement, her hand obviously in some pain, but continued with the details of that night. "I gave her several hundred dollars." A slight smile crossed her lips. "I had all my graduation money in my wallet. I'd planned to go to the bank that day, but there wasn't any time. Between us, we gave her almost a thousand dollars."

She didn't say it, but Dominic knew Serena had given the bulk of the money to Jillian. Alexia hadn't had much, and what she had, she'd needed for her own plans. "What was her emotional state?"

"She was frantic, scared, desperate to get away. So . . . we helped her."

"And you don't have any idea where she is now?"

Serena met his eyes. "None."

He believed her. "I've talked to her father. She hasn't contacted them one time since she left. Even missed her mother's funeral six years ago."

"She wasn't particularly close to her parents." Serena took another small bite of her salad and chewed. She swallowed and said, "But I'm sure she didn't know about her mother or she would have found a way to come to the funeral."

Dominic leaned back and tried to assess her. She was cool and composed even after almost being run over, possibly killed. And then he had caught the slight tremor in her fingers and figured she wasn't quite as together as she portrayed. "What did you find out about Leslie?"

"The autopsy showed mostly what I thought it would. The gunshot to her forehead killed her. Without the bullet, however, I can't tell you exactly what kind of gun it came from, but the small hole suggests a small caliber. Probably something like a .22 or a .32, but that's just a guess. There's no way to determine the caliber without the bullet. I can rule out some of the larger caliber bullets, of course, but . . ." She shrugged and Dominic understood. Simply put, without the bullet, they wouldn't know what kind of weapon they were looking for. Serena continued, "Marks on her wrists suggest she was tied up. Bruise around her left ankle looks like some kind of restraint was used there. No sign of sexual assault. The scraped knees could have happened before her attacker grabbed her. Or while she was trying to get away from him. They're pretty recent scrapes, though." She set down her fork and frowned. "But there's no way to really tell."

"But why her?"

Serena lifted a brow at him. "That's your area of expertise, not mine." Her phone rang and she pulled it off the clip at her side. "Hello?"

She listened, frowned, and nodded. He sat up straight and studied her as she said, "Okay. Thanks for letting me know." She hung up and slowly put the phone back on the clip.

"What is it?"

"That was Rick. He said when he couldn't reach you, he tried me. He has something he needs us to see right away."

6

In Rick Shelton's office, Serena stood next to the man and listened as he said, "I was in a meeting all morning and didn't get to this until just now."

With gloved hands, Rick lifted the top of the box. Serena felt dizzy and realized she was holding her breath. Letting it out slowly, she focused on deep, even breaths while Rick drew out a miniature doll.

Dominic shifted beside her and the musky scent of his cologne drifted to her. For some reason it comforted her.

"It's beautiful—blue eyes, black hair, distinct features. Almost more like a sculpture," she said.

"But that's not all," Rick said. "There's a note to go with the gift." He reached behind him and pulled a plastic baggie from the shelf. Inside, a 4 × 6 index card stared back at them.

"What does it say?" Dominic asked.

Rick glanced at Serena, then read in singsong fashion: "Eenie meenie miney moe, a killin' I will go. But it's my game, it's my fun, the next to die, someone you know."

"Someone *who* knows?" Dominic asked.

Rick shrugged.

"And look at the outfit . . ." Serena leaned closer.

"Dressed in a pink jogging suit just like our victim," Dominic said.

"Right," Rick said. "Of course I'll go over all of this with a fine-tooth comb looking for prints, hairs, fibers, whatever I can find." He paused. "Actually, for fingerprints, I'll use an EDAX Eagle II XPL MXRF instrument with a 40 W rhodium anode—" He broke off at Dominic's yawn.

Crestfallen, Rick whined, "You too? Hunter influenced you, didn't he?" Suspicion darkened his gaze and Serena grew confused.

"What does Hunter have to do with anything?" she asked.

Rick pursed his lips. "Because Hunter is an old fogey at the ripe old age of thirtysomething. I try my best to explain how this new technology works and he tunes me totally out." He turned his attention back to the man at her side. "He got to you, didn't he?"

Dominic raised a brow, the picture of pure innocence. "No, man, I'm just tired. Been a long day already."

With a beleaguered sigh, Rick laid the doll flat on the evidence examination table. "I did some research while I was waiting on you two to get here." He lifted his gaze to Serena. "You know how I said something seemed familiar about this killing?"

"Yes."

"I started looking stuff up. Past crimes where a doll was left behind."

A bad feeling started in her gut. "And?"

Rick motioned them over to his computer. He wiggled the mouse and the screen lit up. "Here."

Serena leaned in to read. "The Doll Maker Killer." She frowned. "I don't remember this."

"That's because it was before your time. You're a few years younger than I am. You're what? Twenty-eight?"

"Just turned twenty-nine last week. Why?"

"This guy was killing people back from '92 to '95. You would have been a child."

She quirked a brow at him. "As would you. You're only three years older than I am."

"Yes," he conceded with a nod, "but I generally remember just about everything I read and I remember reading about this guy a couple of years ago. Drake Lindell. He was trying to get parole, made a plea that he'd been rehabilitated, found God and all that jazz."

"How many did he kill?" Dominic's quiet question made her jerk.

Rick rubbed his eyes. "The FBI says nine that they know of, but they suspect more."

"How did he get his victims?"

"Some just wouldn't come home. Others left to go to lunch from work and were never heard from again. Several were snatched from their homes. There didn't seem to be a pattern. Two of the women reported they thought they were being stalked. Notes left in their mailboxes, dead flowers delivered, et cetera." He scratched his nose with the back of his wrist, then said, "But really, the only connection between the victims that anyone could find was the doll and the note." He looked over his glasses. "Really bad poetry most of the time, mocking the police, saying he was going to kill again and the police, the FBI, could do nothing about it. He was on a real power trip for a while there."

Dominic winced and Serena felt her skin crawl. Dominic shook his head. "I should remember this one. We would have studied it at the academy."

"Maybe." Rick shrugged.

She looked back at the article and asked, "So is this killer back? Could he have killed Leslie?"

Rick shook his head. "Can't be him. He's still in prison." His lips twisted. "Trust me, I checked."

"Then we have a copycat," Serena said.

"Looks like." Dominic blew out a breath. "I need to call my boss."

Serena looked at him. "Will the FBI get involved after one killing? Doesn't the FBI usually wait until after the second death before they will identify the killer as a serial?"

He nodded. "Usually, but if this is a serial copycat, and it's definitely looking like it, I'm going to ask to be assigned this case. Now." His eyes narrowed. "I don't want to wait for a second death to happen. We have to catch this guy before he goes after his next victim." His attention zeroed in on the doll and the note. "The killer's made it clear. There's going to be a next victim."

———■———

Who would get to play next? Waiting on the phone call was annoying. But necessary. Only HE had the names. Only HE would know who would be the best players.

Waiting was necessary.

Waiting could be fun. Anticipation of the coming game caused shivers of delight to dance up and down the killer's neck.

Eager eyes roved over the names in the book. So many to choose from. Who would it be?

Was it her? Beth Hollister? Or maybe Stacy Hathaway?

The killer shut the book with a snap and placed it back on the shelf.

It didn't matter.

The phone would ring soon.

And the game would begin again.

———■———

Dominic hung up the phone and felt a grim satisfaction. Local authorities had agreed to let the FBI take this one and run with it while offering their cooperation.

His boss, Deputy Director Zeb Tremaine, had given Dominic the go-ahead to take over the case as the lead investigator. A task force was being assembled and would be dispatched to the Columbia office within hours.

He walked back into Rick's office and said, "We're treating this as a copycat killer. The package, the note, everything indicates the killer is out there right now stalking his next victim. We're going to jump on this and try to stop him before he strikes again."

Serena looked at him, then back at the doll. "Why would he leave a note? Why taunt us?"

"It's part of his game," Dominic said.

"I don't like this game and I don't want to play."

Dominic tilted his head. "Not sure we have a choice."

Rick said, "If he's a copycat—and it's sure not Drake Lindell—he's sticking to the MO, an MO the FBI and police never could figure out."

"What do you mean?" Dominic asked.

"With each body, the Doll Maker Killer would leave the doll, but it was never determined who the doll was supposed to represent. Sometimes she was dressed like the victim. Sometimes she looked completely different. There wasn't any pattern, nothing to pull from the dolls to help figure out who the next victim would be. The authorities were sure it was a message, but they couldn't decipher it."

Dominic saw Serena's lips tighten. Then she asked, "But what kind of message and *who* was the message *for*? In the note he said 'someone you know.' Someone *who* knows? Who is the *you* in that statement? You?" She pointed to Dominic. "The investigating officer? Me? The medical examiner?" This time she jabbed a finger against her chest. "Or the person who found her and called it in? How are we supposed to know *who* the message is for?"

"All good questions," Rick said. "Unfortunately, they've all been asked before and no one could come up with an answer. Another question that needs to be asked is, how does this person know all the details of these killings?"

"I've already been asking myself that. I don't have an answer to that yet." Dominic pointed at the doll. "We know one thing for sure. If the Doll Maker Killer has a copycat, the copycat's only getting started." His jaw tightened. "Which means, so are we."

—■—

It was crazy. Totally crazy. She'd never come across anything like this before. A serial killer sending a message to the people working the murder? Okay, so it had been done before, she supposed, but never anything she'd worked on.

Serena watched Rick, then bounced her gaze to Dominic, who was engrossed in something that had just come across his phone.

She thought about the break-in at her home last week. About the man she'd shot.

She shivered. She hadn't been some random homeowner who woke to find an intruder in her house. She racked her brain, trying to figure out who was targeting her. Had possibly pushed her in front of a bus.

Were the incidents related?

God, I think I've had enough excitement to last me awhile. Boredom would be nice at this point. Seriously, God, what's happening? Why is my life suddenly spinning?

She added a prayer for protection and for wisdom to find Leslie's killer as she watched Rick testing for fingerprints.

She couldn't help but think about her intruder and wonder why the man she'd shot hadn't just killed her while she lay in bed. Why search her bedroom? Because he'd planned to take her alive when he found what he wanted? Or force her to tell him what he wanted to know when he didn't find what he was looking for?

Whatever his intentions, she'd interrupted his plans. Rick's phone rang and Dominic said, "You get that. We'll be in touch."

"Sure." Rick waved and turned his attention to his phone.

Dominic took Serena by the arm, and she couldn't help the small thrill that invaded her at his touch.

"So, Katie and Hunter are the detectives on this one, along with Chad Graham and Colton Brady," Dominic said.

"Colton Brady, huh?" She mulled over what she knew about the man. Not much.

"Yep, he's back."

"I'd noticed that."

"Sounds like a great team."

"It is."

"Katie's at Leslie's house, looking for something—anything— that might give us a clue as to how and why this killer picked her. Colton and Chad are questioning family and co-workers. We'll have a pretty good picture of her life soon. Maybe there'll be something we can work with."

They made their way out of the building and Dominic said, "Are you in the mood to do a little research?"

"On what?"

"The Doll Maker Killer."

Serena swallowed hard. "Yes, I suppose. But you don't need me. I'm sure you can find what you need without me being in the way."

"True. I don't necessarily *need* you there. But . . . what if I *want* you there? And you won't be in the way."

Her mouth formed a silent "Oh." He wanted her there because he wanted to spend time with her? The thought made her stomach dip and swirl. She snapped her lips shut. "Well, I suppose I could lend a hand." She smiled. "Could put my FBI clearance to good use again."

He lifted a brow. "FBI clearance?"

"I handled a pretty sensitive murder. As a result, I was going to be exposed to a lot of information about this particular victim in trying to figure out how he died. He was in the witness protection program and died right before the trial. The US Marshals were fit to be tied—as well as the FBI agents working the protection detail."

Dominic's brow furrowed and she could almost see the wheels turning. Then he let out a low whistle. "The Sandino case."

"Yes. The FBI wanted everything I did on the case to be top secret. I had to pass all kinds of background checks and basically go through everything you guys do when you first apply to become agents. Anyway, I passed. So now, when the FBI needs something pertaining to a case and they need it top secret, they come to me. I'm an FBI consultant."

Admiration glowed. "You're amazing."

Serena let out a self-conscious laugh. "Not really. It's just the way things worked out."

"Then you really could help me out here. I won't have to be too careful what I say around you."

"I can help."

"Great. You want to follow me?"

"Where?"

"Back to my office. I'll pull everything I can find on Drake Lindell and we'll go through it."

Serena bit her lip. She would love the excuse to spend more time with him, but she had two more autopsies to do before she went home. "I said I can help. And I can, but I really need to get back to work. How about you pull the info and call me. I'll meet you somewhere."

"Deal."

He placed a hand on his door handle, then turned back. Serena waited, wondering at the frown he wore.

"Be careful," he said. "There's no proof that the message was for you or anyone else associated with the crime scene, but I do find it odd that someone broke into your house last week and now you're a victim of a purse snatching gone wrong. And you're the ME for this death?" He shook his head. "That's just too many

45

things in a short period of time to be a coincidence. And I'm not a big believer in coincidences."

"I know. I'm not either." She paused. "Although, I have to say that the more I think about it, the more I think the purse snatching *was* just a purse snatching gone wrong."

"What do you mean?"

"I remember I felt the tug on my purse, but I had a good grip and reacted reflexively by pulling against the tug—" she licked her lips and said— "and then I was in front of the bus, so now I'm doubting whether the person was really trying to hurt me. I think he was just trying to grab my purse and when I resisted, he let go and I ended up falling in front of the bus."

Dominic frowned. "That's a reasonable argument, but we don't know that for sure, and I have to admit I'm still a little hesitant to leave you alone."

A puff of air escaped her in a humorless laugh. "Well, there's not much we can do about that. We both need to work."

Still, his hand hovered above the handle of his car door. "Just . . . be on your guard."

He was truly worried about her.

"I will be, I promise." A shiver shuddered through her. The doll's oval face and pink jogging suit danced at the forefront of her mind. She would definitely be careful. And she wouldn't be jogging through the park again anytime soon.

"You have my number," he reminded her. "Promise you'll call if you need anything at all?"

"Promise."

He gave her a warm smile, his eyes lingered on hers a moment longer, then he was in the driver's seat and backing out of the parking space.

Serena climbed into her Suburban and cranked it.

On the drive back to the morgue, she considered everything that had happened to her in the last week. Receiving the package, the break-in, the dead classmate, the attempted purse snatching—and now a possible serial killer copycat with a victim who was found on her watch. Something was going on in this town and it seemed to be revolving around her.

She still didn't understand how the man had managed to get into her house without setting off her alarm.

And Yoda hadn't barked, but she wasn't exactly a watchdog. If someone paid her the slightest attention, she was a friend for life. All her intruder had to do was bring her a treat, and if she could have, Yoda would have thrown the door open with a welcoming lick.

Chewie, her cat, would have found a place to hide.

No, getting past her animals wouldn't have been an issue.

Before she had a chance to think about it further, she arrived back at the hospital. She pulled around to the back and parked in her reserved spot.

She thought of spending more time with Dominic, and liked the thought. The man had gotten under her skin before she was old enough to realize what the phrase meant. Now, as an adult, she got it. She was attracted to him. And she wanted to explore that attraction.

Maybe.

As she walked into the morgue, she waved to Dorie. "What time do you get off today?"

"I leave at five." Today Dorie's hair was a light brown, and she had it pulled back with two pins on either side of her temples.

"Meant to tell you this morning, nice hair color."

"Thanks. I was ready for a change."

"You're ready for a change about once a week, aren't you?"

Dorie laughed and shrugged in agreement, then rolled her cart toward the office at the end of the hall.

Serena stuck her head in her boss's office. "Hey, Daniel, I'm back."

"What's up with the girl you brought in?" He consulted his notes. "Leslie Stanton?"

Serena filled him in on the murder and the doll. She didn't bother to mention the doll's resemblance to herself. "Now I've got that cardiac patient, Gary Hanson. The family still insists someone at the hospital was responsible for his death."

"Any chance of that?"

She shrugged. "He had a history of heart problems. He had his first attack at the age of thirty-eight. I'd say he was probably lucky he made it to sixty years old."

Daniel grunted. "Well, glad it's you doing the job. At least I know it'll be done right."

Serena lifted a brow. "Something wrong?"

"Naw." He grimaced and waved her away. "Go do your thing. I'm just ticked about the funding issues that are popping up everywhere I turn."

"Oh." Serena wrinkled her nose. "More cutbacks?"

"Looks like it."

"I'm sorry. Anything I can do?"

He shrugged and sighed. "Nope. Get outta here."

She did, but she couldn't help the ping of anxiety that ran through her. She felt pretty sure her job was secure. But there were those she worked with—the tech, the cleaning staff, and others—whose jobs could be on the line. She prayed as she walked to her office and slipped into a gown.

Just as she released the brakes on Mr. Hanson's gurney, her phone rang. Pausing, she pulled it out and looked at the number.

Camille. One of the girls with Adopt-a-Sis, a program Serena tried to volunteer with at least once a week. Camille had wiggled her way into Serena's heart. Unfortunately, she lived with a father Serena felt sure was emotionally and verbally, if not physically, abusive.

She pressed the button to answer. "Hello?"

"Hi."

Then silence.

"Camille? Are you all right?"

Sniffling.

"Darling, what's wrong?"

A long sigh filtered to her. Then Camille cleared her throat. "My dad kicked me out of the house."

Serena flinched. "I thought you two had kind of worked out your differences in counseling."

"Well . . . um . . . yeah . . . we did. Sort of. But . . . "

"But?"

"That was before he found out that I'm . . . p-pregnant." Loud sobs came from the girl.

"Ohhhh."

"Yes." Camille's sobs faded to a whisper and Serena had to strain to hear her.

"You need a place to stay?" Serena asked.

"No, but . . ."

"You need some money?"

Weeping once again filled Serena's ear. "Okay, honey, it's going to be all right. I have to do an autopsy. It's going to take me about an hour, but I want you to go to the address I'm going to give you and wait for me there. Can you do that?"

More sniffling, a long sigh, then, "Yes."

Serena closed her eyes and gave her the address. "See you there." After Camille hung up, Serena stayed still a moment longer, praying for the girl.

She continued praying even as she rolled Mr. Hanson under the light.

7

Dominic sat at his desk and dialed a number he knew by heart. The office hummed with busy agents, but Dominic tuned them out.

Hunter Graham picked up on the third ring. "Hello?"

"Any luck on finding my father?" Dominic didn't bother with a formal greeting.

"Nope. The man's gone. If it was him—and we think it was—he left about three hours before we got here."

"Bummer."

"Yeah."

Dominic could hear the weariness in his friend's voice. "So what are you going to do?"

"Head home. We've both got work to do." He paused. "You hear anything about Jillian?"

"No. I've got Terry O'Donnell working on it. I should hear something soon. One way or another."

Hunter grunted. "The woman has disappeared from the face of the earth."

"So it appears." Dominic pushed a paper across his desk searching for his pen that had gone missing. "How does Alexia like working with the Columbia Fire Department? We haven't really talked a lot about it since she got the job." He found the pen under the next set of papers.

"She loves it. Thrilled to be back working fires. I'm not crazy about it. Scares me to death. I live for our days off together so I know she's safe."

"Yeah." Dominic worried about his little sister fighting fires too, but that was what she'd chosen to do, and there wasn't a thing he or Hunter could do about it. Except pray.

Which he found himself doing on a regular basis. For a lot of people. "Bet you can think of better ways of spending those days off than tracking down a deadbeat dad." Silence on the other end. Dominic said, "I'm sorry, shouldn't have said that."

"Dom, you know—"

"I'm working the case now."

The abrupt change of topic didn't faze Hunter. "Which case?"

"The one you talked me into checking out."

"The dead girl in the park? My take-pity-on-Dominic case?"

Dominic allowed himself a small smile. It was more the other way around—Hunter had his hands full to overflowing with all of his cases. "That would be the one. It's now an official FBI case. I think we've got a serial killer running around our city and I aim to catch him before he kills again."

"Fill me in."

Dominic did, and when he finished, Hunter said, "We'll be back before lunch tomorrow. We'll catch up then."

"Count on it." Dominic hung up and turned to his computer. Before he could type the first letter, his phone rang.

He smiled when he saw the caller. "Hi, Serena."

"Hi, Dominic." Her husky voice jangled his senses. In a good way. "I'm finished for the day here, but I have to run an errand. How much longer are you going to be in your office?"

"At least another couple hours. Why?"

"I thought I'd offer to help and join you in your research. That is, if that's what you're still planning on doing."

"It is. I'll have to get you clearance to get back to my office. It'll just take a few minutes," Dominic told her.

"Great. I'll call you when I get there."

His brow lifted and he couldn't help the smile that spread across his face. "I'll be waiting."

<hr />

Serena flashed her ID to the security guard and walked into Covenant House, a shelter for homeless teens—or for teens whose home wasn't worth living in. Like Camille's. It gave the girls a place to regroup, decide what they wanted to do and a way to develop a plan. Serena became interested in the place after she did the autopsy on one of the residents who had been killed by an abusive uncle. The man had broken in, kidnapped the teen, slit her throat, and tossed her in a dumpster. She'd been found a couple of days later. She'd had Covenant House's card in her pocket.

Serena scanned the occupants and spotted Camille curled in the corner of the couch, sound asleep.

Biting her lip, she hesitated, hating to wake the girl, but she'd promised. She walked over and lightly touched Camille's shoulder.

Camille blinked and got her bearings. When she saw Serena, her eyes filled again, but the tears didn't fall. Surprise flickered in her gaze for a moment. "Hey. You really came."

"I said I would."

"I know, but . . . never mind."

The people in Camille's life didn't keep promises. Serena dropped to the couch beside her and looked the girl in the eyes, studying them. Even pupils, direct gaze. She wasn't using. But then that wasn't Camille's way, thank goodness. "What are you going to do?"

"I don't know. I . . . I'm seventeen years old. I can't believe I was so stupid." A tear managed to escape and slid down her cheek. She lifted a hand to give it an angry swipe.

"Who's the father?"

Shame filled Camille's eyes before she lowered them. "Bobby. My boyfriend." She scoffed. "I guess I should say ex-boyfriend now."

"He dumped you?"

"As soon as I told him." Bitterness flashed, taking the place of the shame. "I should have known."

"All right, here's what we're going to do if you want to do it. Mrs. Bea Lamb is the director here. If you're willing to stay, you're welcome to do so. But, there are rules."

Camille's upper lip began to curl. Serena lifted a brow and the lip settled.

Camille gave a slow nod. "I met her when I first got here. She was really nice and didn't ask any questions. Just told me to have a seat on the couch and to wait for you." A low sigh filtered out. "I don't have any other options, Serena. I . . . want to stay if she'll let me."

"She will, but I'll be honest with you. If you mess up and don't follow her rules, the rules of the house, then you're out. You understand?"

Camille seemed to think it over, then nodded. "Yeah."

Would the girl follow through? Did she believe it when Serena said the director would tell her to leave if she didn't comply?

Only one way to find out. "All right, let's go get you settled in your room. Did you bring a bag?"

Camille pointed to the bag on the table behind the couch.

Serena snagged it and pulled the girl to her feet.

"What if my dad shows up?" The fear in Camille's voice and eyes was unmistakable.

"They have security here. They won't let him in."

"But—"

"And the guard will call the cops if necessary."

Camille swallowed hard. "He would be so mad about that. You can't do that. Promise me, you won't call the cops on him."

Serena bit back the things she'd like to say about Camille's father. Bashing the man wouldn't do Camille any good. "I can't make that promise if he shows up here causing problems. But let's not worry about that right now. Let's just take it one day at a time, all right?"

Another slow nod from Camille. Serena motioned for the girl to follow her and together they walked down the hall to one of the empty bedrooms. Serena stepped inside, then turned to watch her young friend's reaction.

Camille's eyes went wide as she took in the soft pastels and thick comforter on the twin bed. "It's nice." She looked at Serena and gave her a tremulous smile. "Thank you."

"You're welcome, honey." She gave Camille a hug and let the girl cling to her for a few moments.

Finally Camille let go and drew in a deep breath. "Okay. I can do this."

Serena gripped Camille's hand. "We'll do this. Together."

An hour later, after making sure Camille had what she needed and with promises to return soon, Serena headed back toward Dominic's office, her mind back on the case and the information she and Dominic might learn.

Once inside the building, she rubbed her bare arms in the air-conditioned office. As she waited, she let her eyes scan the walls. Plaques, awards, honors . . . fallen heroes.

"Ready?" Dominic's voice rumbled in her ear from behind her.

"Sure." She followed him through security and through a weave of desks. Feeling eyes on her, she smiled at those she passed, then found herself in a corner in the back. A desk, a computer, and a stack of files greeted her.

Dominic smiled. "It's temporary but it's home base for now."

He grabbed a spare chair and pulled it up to the desk next to him. Serena slipped into the seat and leaned in. She drew in a deep breath, his woodsy-smelling cologne drawing her like a fly to honey. The man smelled good. He turned and met her gaze. She was helpless to stop the flush she could feel forming on her cheeks. He gave a slow smile as though he knew exactly what was going through her mind. Then he let her off the hook.

"All right," he said. "Let's see what we have on Drake Lindell."

A few clicks of the keyboard brought forth a man's picture.

Serena stared. "He looks so . . . normal. Approachable. Like my next-door neighbor."

"Yeah. Scary, isn't it?"

"Definitely."

A few more clicks brought up the man's entire history, transcripts of the trial, and everything else they could possibly want.

"What about his family?" she asked.

More taps on the keyboard. "Hmm," Dominic said, "he's left a lovely legacy. He's fathered four children all with the same mother. He's got a son who's in jail for murder." She watched his eyes scan the screen. "Looks like Trey Lindell got in a bar fight that went really wrong. He ended up killing a guy not long after his dad's trial. Two more sons, Pete and Nate. Pete's location is presently unknown." He glanced at her. "Which can mean dead, but not necessarily. Nate, who is the oldest at forty-two, is a lawyer here in town. Interesting." Back to the screen. "And finally, we have a daughter. Gwendolyn Lindell, age thirty-nine. Location also unknown."

A young woman's face appeared. Serena sighed. "She's pretty even without makeup. Very natural looking." Slender, with hair so blond it looked almost white, blue eyes, clear skin. "She has sad eyes."

"This was taken at her dad's trial. Apparently she was the only family member in attendance."

"Then I guess she has a reason to look sad."

"After the guilty verdict, she said she never wanted to have any-

55

thing to do with him again. Here's her quote. 'I can't believe this. He's betrayed me and I hope he rots in prison.'" Dominic shook his head. "Pretty bitter."

"Do you blame her? Poor thing. I can't imagine."

A few more clicks brought up the photos of the shed containing the evidence. He said, "The shed was soundproofed as was the room below it."

"Guess that explains why no one in the neighborhood heard anything out of the ordinary." As he scrolled through the photos, she narrowed her eyes. Blood spatter covered the wall behind a poker table. Cards littered the table and the floor next to the table. A roulette table backed up against a wall.

A length of chain with handcuffs attached to the end lay on the floor beneath a steel chair. Serena could see the bolts holding it in place.

"What's that?" she pointed.

"I don't know." A piece of steel that looked to be about fifteen inches long lay on the poker table. "Says they didn't know what it was for. But some of the victims' DNA was found on it."

"Poker. So, he was a gambler."

"Looks like."

He pressed print, then leaned over and grabbed a manila folder from the bottom drawer.

Placing the stack of papers inside, he said, "One more thing." A few more clicks of the keyboard. "Okay, the case agent on the Doll Maker's case was Howard Bell."

"Then we need to talk to Mr. Bell."

"He retired four years ago, but I bet he's the perfect place to start." Dominic sent the man's contact information to his phone.

Serena said, "I wonder how Chad and Katie are coming with Leslie's investigation."

"I'm sure they've notified the family by now. I guess the next step will be releasing the body to them."

She nodded. "Yes. And I'm not ready to do that yet."

He frowned. "I thought you were finished with the autopsy."

"With the preliminary stuff. I want to go over a few more details before I let her go."

"Like what?"

"The Doll Maker Killer's victims. I want to look at their autopsies."

"And compare them to Leslie?"

"Exactly."

8

Howard Bell agreed to talk to them at ten o'clock. Serena had slept fitfully the night before, waking often, hearing the echo of her gunshot in her dreams. Only the Glock in her nightstand and Yoda's comforting presence at the foot of her bed kept her from pacing the floor all night.

She looked with satisfaction at the reports she'd finished, the result of the last two hours. Mr. Gary Hanson had definitely died of heart failure. The tox screen came back clean of any suspicious drugs. His heart had simply stopped and no amount of drugs or procedures had been able to get it started again.

The family wouldn't want to accept that. They were a noisy lot and Serena wasn't looking forward to sharing her findings with them. Maybe she'd pass them off to her boss. She smiled at the thought. He would tell her she was a wimp and she'd agree.

Camille had called in the midst of the report writing and grudgingly admitted, "It's not so bad here."

Serena prayed the girl would stay put. The home would allow her to continue her education during the school year, attend parenting classes and even an optional Bible study. Serena fully believed God needed to be in these kids' lives, but she wouldn't shove him down their throats.

58

Serena set the folder on the edge of her desk. She'd drop it by Daniel's office when she left.

A glance at the clock said she needed to get a move on. Dominic had asked if she wanted to go with him to meet the retired FBI agent, Mr. Bell, and Serena did.

Gathering her things and the folder, she headed to Daniel's office. She left the folder where he could find it easily and made her way up the stairs and out the door into the parking lot.

Dominic was waiting for her. She slipped into the passenger seat. "Good morning."

"Morning." He offered a smile and a cup of coffee. "Sweet with cream, right?"

She took a sip and sighed. "Perfect. Thanks."

Dominic pulled from the lot and made a left. "Howard can be a crusty dude, but underneath the gruff, I think he's a decent guy. He's not happy to have a copycat of the Doll Maker Killer walking the streets and is willing to answer questions and share information."

"Good." Serena sipped her coffee and thought about the case. "Thanks for letting me come along."

"Sure."

They continued the small talk until they pulled up to the front of Mr. Bell's house and climbed out of the car.

Serena took in the details. Middle-class neighborhood with a quiet street. The two-story white house with green shutters looked well taken care of, but Serena was surprised by the yard. It didn't look like anyone ever did anything with it. Overgrown and neglected, it was obviously the eyesore of the neighborhood.

Mature trees lined the streets, some grouped in clusters for maximum shade and privacy, others were spread out.

She drew in a deep breath, the peaceful ambiance striking a chord within her. Dealing with what she did every day, she'd gladly take a measure of peace wherever she could find it.

Dominic knocked on the front door.

It swung inward and a man in his late sixties with bushy gray brows and sharp blue eyes greeted them. "See you found it okay."

"Yes. Thanks for seeing us." Dominic shook hands with him, then Serena had her turn.

With a look up the street, then back down, keeping the door between him and the outside world, he waved them in. "This is a first."

Seated on the love seat next to Dominic, Serena shifted and tried not to be distracted by his nearness. Pretty soon the clutter in the room took her attention away from Dominic's cologne.

The word "hoarder" came to mind. But just on every available surface. At least she could see the blue shag carpet under her feet. And the place smelled musty and probably dusty, but nothing that indicated anything was dead underneath the piles of . . . stuff.

Dominic handed Howard the file he'd compiled on the current killing. "Leslie Stanton. Can you tell us what you think about this?"

—■—

The killer hunkered down on the roof of the empty house. Not exactly the prime spot for a clear shot, but it would do. Fury burned at the realization that everyone was already inside. Too late. "Well, make the best of it and get this over with."

The killer looked through the scope of the McMillan Long Range G-30 hunting rifle. The 7mm bullet would do the trick as soon as the target stepped into view.

—■—

Howard took his time looking through the folder. As he read, his face paled and Serena saw him swallow at least three times. When he finished, he broke the silence. "It's not Lindell."

"We know that, sir," Dominic said. "Lindell's still in prison."

Howard still seemed to be engrossed in the file in his lap. He didn't respond to Dominic's statement. Instead, he muttered unintelligibly under his breath and Dominic shot Serena a questioning look. She shrugged her own confusion.

Then Howard said in a louder voice, "It's got to be a copycat."

"Yes sir." Dominic nodded. "We realize that. Any idea who would want to do that?"

Howard shook his head and visibly gathered his thoughts. "No. But you know there are the crazies out there. People who are fascinated with serial killers. Women fall in love with them and marry them even though the killers will never get out of prison. Men want the fame of being the copycat. Of garnering national attention. They study the transcripts of trial cases, get all the details just right, and then they strike." Howard grunted. "But you know all that. So what do you need from me?"

"I guess we need to know about Lindell's family. Only his daughter sat in on the trial. Apparently she's had nothing to do with him since. Changed her name, her address. So far, we haven't been able to pin down her location."

A gray brow rose. "Yes. Gwendolyn. His daughter. I remember her well." Howard rubbed his chin, got up and paced to the window. He pushed the curtain to the side and looked out, keeping his body well away from exposure. Serena realized he was a prisoner in his own home.

Which was probably why the yard looked like it did. Howard looked at the floor, then back up as he returned to his seat. "Do you blame her for wanting to disappear?"

"Not at all."

Howard settled back against the antique armchair. "As for the sons, they're mostly a greasy lot. Only one of them turned out decent if I remember correctly."

Dominic nodded. "Nate Lindell. He's a lawyer here in town. We plan to speak to him too."

"Nate. Right. Kind of a quiet fellow. I think I remember him. He didn't come around much. Avoided the media and tried to stay hidden." Tapping the folder against his palm, Howard said, "This guy, Drake, he owned a janitorial business, made good money and lived in a nice neighborhood." He pursed his lips. "He was crazy. Certifiable. But you'd never know it looking in from the outside. He came from a good home as a kid, was a great dad from all that we could tell. His kids were crazy about him. Had a wife that doted on him." Shaking his head, he raised a hand to rub his chin. "Nothing about his behavior made sense. Why start killing people all of a sudden? It just didn't add up." He met their eyes. "His wife killed herself the day they found him guilty."

Serena felt a chill wrap around her.

Dominic lifted a brow. "That wasn't in the report."

Howard shrugged. "I read about it in the paper the day after it happened. By then the case was closed and we'd all moved on to other ones. You know how it is. When it came time to testify, I had to study my notes for days to make sure I had all the details straight in my head again."

"I know."

Serena watched as Howard stood and paced from one end of the room to the next. He never stopped in front of a window. And he kept his back to the wall. Or he walked between the stacks of . . . stuff . . . papers, newspapers, furniture.

She felt sure her initial observations about Howard being trapped in the home were accurate. She'd been hanging around cops too long to think she was imagining things. Her father, a former cop turned lawyer, had trained her well, and she found she enjoyed the company of those in law enforcement over "the normals," as her dad used to call those not in law enforcement.

She and her cop friends shared the same weird sense of humor.

And Howard was a retired cop. Old habits died hard, she supposed. And yet . . . it seemed to be more for Howard. "Are you afraid of something, Howard?"

He jerked, sighed, and looked toward the kitchen, then back

at them. "There's a lot about this case that just . . ." He shook his head.

"Just what, Howard," Dominic pressed.

"Still bothers me."

"Like what?"

Another shake of the gray head. "They said he killed nine."

"Yeah."

"But in that shed, there were unaccounted-for hair fibers, trace evidence that didn't link to any of the known victims."

"And you think it came from some of his other victims?"

A shrug. "Who else would it come from?" He rubbed a hand down his face and shuddered. "All I can tell you is that if you have a copycat, you'd better find him fast. He'll keep killing until you put him away."

"That's the goal. Is there anything else you can tell us to help us figure this out?"

———■———

Howard Bell stood to the side of the door, his expression thoughtful, troubled, as Dominic led the way back to the car. Something about the man's expression made him want to turn and force him to say what he was thinking. Instead, Dominic opened the door for Serena and she slid into the passenger seat.

Without looking toward the house, he said, "He's thinking hard about something."

"What do you mean?"

"He talked a lot and told us very little. He left something out. Something that could be important but he was reluctant to share for some reason," Dominic said as he shut her door.

When he'd climbed in and buckled his seatbelt, she looked at him. "Why didn't you confront him?"

"He's the kind of guy that has to chew on something before he spits it out."

She nodded. "You think he'll come around and call you with whatever it is?"

Dominic quirked a smile at her. "Exactly."

Serena tapped her lip. "I think we need to talk to Drake Lindell."

Dominic started the engine, then looked at her. "I can talk to him. I don't want you anywhere near that psycho."

Her right brow lifted and she simply stared at him.

Dominic cleared his throat. "Not that I have any right to tell you who you can talk to, but . . ."

She laid a hand on his arm. "Don't apologize. I know why you said that, but it's really my decision. I can't say I'm crazy about the idea of talking to him face-to-face, but maybe he could give you a name or an idea of who might be behind Leslie's murder."

"I've already asked for copies of every letter he's ever received and a list of all visitors since he's been incarcerated."

"Really?"

"I'm on this, I promise."

She flushed. "Now I need to apologize. Of course you are. Sorry, I didn't mean to try and tell you how to do your job."

He shook his head and offered a smile. "Hey, brainstorming is a great thing. I don't always think of everything, so it's nice to have input."

Dominic started to pull away from the curb, then stopped as Howard came rushing toward them, hand held high, motioning for them to stop.

Dominic put the car back in park and rolled down Serena's window.

"Wait a minute," Howard said. His eyes darted left, then right. He stopped his forward momentum now that he had their attention and backpedaled toward the open front door. "Come back inside. It's time I told someone—"

Howard Bell jerked and fell to the ground, his chest pumping bright red blood.

9

Serena let out a scream as time fell into slow motion. She felt Dominic push her down into the seat, then slam his body over hers.

No more shots followed in the next few seconds. Serena pushed out from under Dominic and her hand groped for the door handle.

She had to help Howard.

Shoving the car door open, she noticed Dominic's weapon in his right hand and his gaze scanning the street through the windshield.

She tumbled from the vehicle, Dominic right behind her screaming, "Shots fired! Man down. I need an assist!"

The car was parked at the bottom of the front walk so that the walk and the car formed a T. Scrambling, heart thudding, fear shaking her, she started toward Howard.

And felt a hard hand yank her back even while his voice barked their location and that of the gunman.

Then Dominic's voice echoed in her ear. "I know you want to check on him, but I can't let you get in the way of a bullet."

"But I might be able to help him!" She jerked on her wrist, but Dominic held tight.

"Or he might already be dead and you could be next if you expose yourself."

She looked at Howard, the blood covering his chest. And saw no movement. She tried to see his face, but it was turned away from her.

Dominic gripped her arm. "Stay put. I think I know where he was shooting from."

"There he goes," she said as she pointed. A flash of white blinked at her as something moved through the trees to her right. "Dominic, look."

He turned. "It's him. Stay here, I'm going after him."

"But—"

He took off before she could voice her protest. Serena offered up a quick prayer for his safety, then moved toward Howard. If Dominic was chasing the shooter, surely she'd be safe enough to check Howard.

Sirens reached her ears. Help was on the way.

Even so, she couldn't help feeling like she had a big red target on her back. She reached Howard and his eyes blinked, his chest gave a sudden heave as his mouth moved.

Knowledge hit her. There was nothing she could do for him. Even if he were seconds away from a hospital, he would die. Grief slammed her. She whispered, "I'm sorry, Howard."

His mouth moved again. He was trying to tell her something. She leaned over. "What did you say?"

"File . . . Look . . ."

And then he was gone. That vacant stare of death that Serena was so familiar with looked back at her. With a sob in her throat, she whispered again, "I'm so sorry."

And closed his eyes.

———■———

Dominic followed the rustling trees. Soon the guy would have to come out into the open and he'd get a shot. "Freeze! FBI!"

The figure kept moving. Dominic couldn't get a good look at him but thought he had a ball cap and a white T-shirt on.

Where was he headed? Had he had this all planned out? But how? It had to be a spur-of-the-moment thing.

But why? Why now? Why Howard? Why today?

The questions tumbled through his mind as he moved, ever watching. One comforting thought. If Dominic was chasing the shooter, the shooter wasn't shooting anyone else. But if a neighbor was out in the yard, the fleeing person could take someone hostage.

The shooter was almost to the tree line. He'd have to expose himself to continue running and there was nowhere else to go except straight ahead.

"FBI! Stop! Now!" he called again.

Dominic waited, his weapon ready.

Then heard the roar of a motorcycle.

—■—

Serena dropped her hand from Howard's neck, unable to keep herself from checking his pulse one more time. But the man was dead and there wasn't anything she could do to change that. Shoving back the tears that kept wanting to fall, she forced herself to focus.

Shock and bone-deep sadness mingled with the fear as she crept back toward the car just as the first police vehicle pulled up. She kept her hands visible to the approaching law enforcement.

The officer exited and drew his gun. "Show me some ID."

"It's in my purse in the car."

Keeping the gun trained on her, he pulled her purse from the front seat and dumped the contents onto the floorboard. He handed her the wallet and she flipped it open. "I'm a doctor, I was trying to help him."

The officer didn't lower his weapon. He wouldn't until he'd proven her story. He nodded at her hospital ID but said, "Stay down, ma'am, and keep your hands where I can see them." She had no intention of lifting her head too high, although the precaution seemed silly in light of the fact that she'd just exposed herself by trying to help Howard. The officer's badge read J. Tullis.

"Dominic Allen, an FBI agent, went after the person who shot this man," she said. Her gut churned. Had Dominic caught up with him? Was he okay?

He seemed satisfied but didn't relax his stance.

She kept her eyes peeled in the direction Dominic had disappeared.

Officer Tullis spoke into his radio. Serena couldn't understand him, but got the response that more help was on the way. Officers had started going door to door checking on the residents, warning them to stay inside.

Then Dominic appeared in her line of sight, his gun held at his side.

"Freeze!" Officer Tullis yelled, raising his weapon to train it on Dominic. "Put the gun down now!"

Dominic froze, held his arms out to the side, and knelt to place the weapon on the ground.

Serena said, "He's an FBI agent. He's the one who went after the shooter."

Her gaze locked on Dominic's and she could see the frustration there. The shooter had gotten away.

Officer Tullis hollered, "Show me some ID."

Slowly, Dominic reached into his back pocket and pulled out his ID, flipping it open with the smoothness of someone who's made the move often.

Tullis relaxed a fraction and lowered his weapon. Dominic picked his up and slid it into the holster under his arm.

Serena breathed a little easier. "Howard's dead," she told Dominic.

He nodded once, his tight jaw and granite features telling her this hit him hard. And she thought she knew what he might be thinking.

Had their presence today gotten Howard killed?

"He whispered something before he died," she said. "I think he said, 'File. Look.'"

Dominic frowned. "'File. Look'? Wonder what he meant by that?"

"That we're supposed to look in a file for whatever it was he decided at the last minute that he wanted us to know?"

"Sounds logical to me."

◼

The killer blew out a harsh breath. Killing Howard had been easy. And it had been a long time coming. But HE might not be pleased with this new development. Howard's murder wasn't in the plan. At least not HIS plan.

Learning that Serena and Dominic were going to visit the man who held explosive secrets had necessitated quick action. But they'd spent nearly an hour with the man before the shot. What had he told them? Watching the man chase after the FBI agent and Serena, it had been obvious he was going to say something more.

No doubt about it. He'd had to die.

Now, to make sure all of his secrets died with him.

It was time to visit HIM again, to fill HIM in on the latest developments.

◼

Crime scene tape now fluttered in the slight breeze that almost offered a respite from the glaring heat of the sun. An Attempt To Locate had gone out and officers logged each and every person who entered the area. Mickey Black, the crime scene photographer, snapped a constant stream of pictures. Hunter Graham and Katie Isaacs arrived on the scene twenty minutes later.

Dominic saw the car pull up as Serena crouched over Howard, collecting whatever she could from the deceased man. Although he and Serena had seen what happened, they still needed to collect trace evidence from Howard. If the killer had ever been in the house, there was a possibility the lab could match the evidence up with . . . something.

Assuming they caught the person and the lab had something to work with. Nevertheless, they'd cover all their bases.

Officers still canvassed the neighborhood and Dominic was ready to begin searching Howard's house. He'd already spoken to the lead crime scene team member. Part of the team was already working, determining the exact place Howard had been standing and the position of his body, the direction he'd been facing, when he'd been shot. This would allow them to figure out the angle and path of the bullet, which would lead them to the exact spot the killer had chosen to wait for his target.

Hunter waved Dominic over while Katie engaged the nearest CSU member who'd just arrived.

"Fill me in," Hunter said.

Dominic did, then said, "Backup didn't get here until the shooter had ridden off on his motorcycle. There was no way I could catch up with him."

"I've got the description from the ATL you put out. You got anything else to add?"

Dominic pursed his lips in disgust. "Not much to add to 'Slender person in a white T-shirt with a baseball cap.'"

"Right." Hunter smirked.

"Like I said, slender build, probably around five feet nine or ten. Fast as a jackrabbit. Only saw the back of him." Dominic shook his head. "You going to help me go through the house?"

"Sure." A pause. "Katie's with me."

"I saw her."

"Are you going to be okay working with her?"

Dominic lifted a brow. "Sure. I'll be fine, why?"

"She's still got a thing for you, you know?"

"Katie?" He didn't have to fake the surprise. "That was years ago." Although she *had* been his hometown contact when he'd needed information about his family. Had she read more into that than he thought?

"Maybe so," Hunter said, "but she hasn't let it go."

Uncomfortable with the thought, Dominic glanced at the woman he'd known from high school. The woman he considered a good friend but didn't have any romantic interest in. At least not since he'd left home. They'd dated once, but now . . . his gaze steered itself to Serena. He cleared his throat. "Okay. Thanks for the heads-up."

Hunter nodded.

"Are you any closer to finding my father?"

Frustration stamped Hunter's features. "No. You don't have any more ideas, do you?"

"Nope. I even had Terry try and track him down, but when someone doesn't have a job, uses cash, and travels from shelter to shelter, it's like looking for a needle in a haystack. Last time I saw the man, he was behind bars. He told me what happened with Alexia and his intention to kill Mom, Karen, and Alexia the day of the fire." He swallowed hard, annoyed that thinking about his father's words still left a bitter taste on his tongue. "I went back undercover for a long time after that and wasn't even aware when he was released from prison until just recently."

"When you came home into the middle of Alexia's troubles."

"Yes."

"Alexia's becoming obsessed with this." Worry coated Hunter's voice. "She still thinks it's possible he had something to do with that week of terror we lived through."

It was hard to believe it had only been four weeks ago that Alexia had been kidnapped. "The man who questioned her and escaped—" Dominic rubbed his jaw—"I know she was blindfolded most of the time, but is she sure it wasn't our father?"

Hunter went silent for a moment. "She says it wasn't, but sometimes she second-guesses herself. It's been a long time since she's seen the man, Dominic." He lifted a shoulder in a helpless shrug.

"Wow, that's helpful."

"Exactly."

Serena came up to them, pulling her gloves off and stashing them in the hazardous materials bag on the curb. "What now?"

"Now, we search the house and see if we can find a file . . . or whatever we're supposed to look at."

———◼———

In the living room of Howard's house, Serena looked at the area where she'd sat less than an hour before. Her heart twisted at the sudden demise of a man she hadn't known, but might have liked to had she been given the chance.

Dominic and Hunter began searching, sifting through Howard's life. Dominic took the den area while Hunter headed down the hall. Serena watched from a distance, listening, absorbing the details. Soon, she would need to leave and get back to the morgue. But she didn't want to miss a word of the discussion about this case.

The Doll Maker Killer's accomplice or his copycat had killed Leslie, a woman who'd graduated with Serena and one she'd called friend ten years ago. Serena was going to be an active participant in figuring out why Leslie was targeted. And someone had killed Howard because of what the man knew about the Doll Maker Killer and didn't want him talking to law enforcement.

Possibly. Probably.

She pictured Howard trying to get their attention as they were leaving the house. He'd had something else to say.

But what?

Dominic walked over to her. "He was going to tell us something."

"I know, I was just thinking about that."

"Hey, Dominic." Hunter stuck his head out of a room off the hall. "Come here. I think I found your file—or one of them."

Serena followed Dominic as he stepped into the room to find Hunter in front of an open closet, staring at a stack of files as tall as Serena.

"Wow," she said.

Dominic walked over and picked up the top file. His gloved hand flipped through it. He looked up and said, "It's a case from twelve years ago."

Hunter shook his head. "I've been going through these for the past twenty minutes trying to see if he's got them organized a certain way. But as far as I can tell, they're random. No sense of order that I can find."

Dominic pulled another one, then another. "I want these in the office. I think we need to go through these one by one."

With a muffled groan, Hunter said, "That's a lot of reading."

"Yeah."

"I'll help," Serena offered. "Poor Howard didn't deserve to be cut down like that."

"I agree. And I want justice for him. One way to get that is to find the person who shot him." Dominic raised a hand to his head and looked back at the files. "So," he said, "my place, six o'clock? I'll provide the pizza."

Serena barely managed to suppress a shudder. "Takeout pizza? I'll bring my own dinner, thanks."

Dominic looked at her. "You don't like pizza?"

"Only when I make it."

He lifted a brow. "You're a food snob."

"Of the worst kind," she drawled. She shrugged, unapologetic.

Hunter looked at Dominic and asked, "You want to bring Katie in on this?"

"Sure. Another set of eyes is great."

Serena wasn't sure how she felt about that idea but kept her mouth shut. She refused to be jealous.

Hunter went to find Katie and let her in on the plan while

Dominic still stared at the stack of files. "There was something he was going to tell us." He spoke low, almost as though talking to himself.

"And you think the file he was talking about is in that stack?"

"I think there's a good chance. I think we're looking for anything that has to do with the Doll Maker Killer's case. If we find that file—"

"You mean the needle in a haystack?" Hunter asked from the door.

"What do you mean?"

"I mean every closet in the house has files and folders in it. This is going to take forever to dig through."

Dominic blew out a sigh. "Then I guess we need to get started."

10

Senator Frank Hoffman leaned back in his leather chair and looked at the guns hanging on his wall. Each one had a story behind it. Some stories were more interesting than others.

His eyes focused in on the antique revolvers. His collection. His pride and joy. Guns like the 1894 Colt Bisley. Or the .44 caliber Wild Bill Hickok's "Dead Man's Hand" 1851 "Aces & Eights" Black Powder Revolver. Thirty-four different weapons in all. He'd invested a small fortune in them.

He looked at his desk, clear of everything except the piece of paper with the words.

IT'S NOT OVER.

"Sir?"

Frank jumped and looked up to find Ian, a faithful employee of two decades, standing in the door. "What is it, Ian?"

"You asked for the car. It's ready."

"Oh, right. Thank you."

"Do you wish me to drive you somewhere?"

Ian, always ready, always available. "No thank you, not today."

Ian inclined his head in acknowledgment, turned on his heel, and left.

Frank reached out and picked up the note one more time. Simple block letters. A simple message that he more than understood.

Time was of the essence as the election crept closer.

As he slipped the note into his drawer, he stood and grabbed his suit coat from the back of his chair. When his phone rang, he paused, debated whether to answer it or not, then sat back down and grabbed the handset. "Well?"

"The plan is in motion."

Frank paused. "What is the plan, exactly?"

A low chuckle reached his ear. "I don't think I'll share that. I'm not sure you would approve."

"Will this plan find Jillian?"

"Of course. That's the goal, is it not?"

"Then I approve."

11

TUESDAY, 6:04 P.M.

Serena juggled the grocery bag into the crook of her left elbow, reached up with her right hand, and knocked on Dominic's door. Her eyes scanned the surroundings behind her.

Driving over here, she could have sworn someone had been following her. But now, with the sun still shining and children playing catch in the yard across the street, she felt silly, paranoid. Still jumpy after what had happened to Howard. Sadness invaded her. She wished she could have saved him.

The door opened and Dominic grinned down at her. "Welcome."

Shoving the sadness away, she smiled. "Thanks."

Dominic took the bag from her and motioned her in. "What's all this?"

"We're going to have a little contest." She followed him into the kitchen.

"A what?"

He started pulling items out of the bag and Serena suppressed a smile. "A pizza contest."

"Ah," he said as realization dawned. "You're going to make a pizza and we're going to see what's best—takeout or Pizza à la Serena, right?"

"Yes."

77

He chuckled. "There's about an hour backup on pizza delivery tonight. You get yours ready and I'll set the oven to heat up when you need it."

"Good. That'll be a fair and square win." She grinned as she gathered the supplies and got to work. She'd already prepared the dough, so it only took a few minutes to spread the sauce, cheese, and toppings and then pop the concoction in his oven.

Dominic set the oven to turn on in half an hour, then cast a sideways glance at her. "You're crazy."

She smirked. "We'll see who's crazy when you taste my pizza."

Still laughing, Dominic herded her into the den area.

Surprise hit her as she entered. Comfortable and bright, thanks to the large window on the opposite wall, it wasn't the typical bachelor home.

Tasteful curtains, classy oriental rugs, and comfortable navy blue furniture filled the room. The flat screen television mounted on the wall opposite the couch told Serena how he spent some of his downtime. But the thing that caught her attention was the train circling the perimeter of the room just above her head.

The scent of fresh mint filled the air. "Alexia helped you do this, didn't she?"

He laughed. "A little. It's not fancy, but the rent was right and the air-conditioning works great."

"It's really nice," Serena said. "Love the train." She watched a few seconds and said, "The detail is incredible. Even down to the little puff of smoke from the engine. Amazing."

He smiled, a gleam of pride in his eyes. "Thanks."

She could see Katie sitting on the couch, her nose buried in a file. At Serena's entrance, she looked up and said, "Hey."

Hunter had the recliner and Alexia had made herself at home on the floor in front of the fireplace.

Serena looked around her and lifted a brow. "It looks like a dozen filing cabinets exploded in here."

Dominic returned to the den area and nodded. "I got permission to bring this home. I have more room to spread out and it's more convenient if I want to work on it in the middle of the night."

Serena wondered what that last comment meant. Did he have trouble sleeping? It wouldn't surprise her considering his line of work. Sometimes her job kept her up nights too.

"And this is only about half of the files," he was saying. "The task force is working on the other half."

"Howard didn't believe in keeping stuff on the computer?"

"Our IT guy is going over the desktop we found, so we'll see if he comes up with anything. In the meantime . . ."

Alexia rose and gave Serena a hug. "Good to see you."

"You too."

Footsteps sounded from the hallway and Serena looked up to see Colton Brady enter the den. He offered her a small smile that didn't quite dispel the shadows in his eyes. "How are you?"

"Hanging in there. You?"

He shrugged. "The same."

"So," Dominic rubbed his hands together as he took a seat on the couch, "the task force is assembled. They're going through the other half of the files and doing everything they can to find this guy before he kills again." He looked at Serena, who grabbed a handful of files and took a seat on the floor beside Alexia. "I've already filled everyone in on what we learned about him. Now, we just need to figure out what it was Howard was going to tell us before he was shot. I don't know if the answer's in here or not, but it looks like a good place to start, based on what he said before he died."

He reached over and pulled a handful of envelopes from a file. "But before we keep going on the files, these are the letters Drake received while in prison. I've gone over all of them and can't see anything that jumps out at me." He flapped them back and forth. "Drake was not happy about giving these up, but if there's something incriminating in them, it's in a code I can't decipher. The

79

letters are repetitive. The writer just talks about admiring Drake. Wanting to know how he thinks. What it felt like to kidnap and kill his victims." He looked up. "A lot of questions about how he felt when the victims died. Our handwriting analyst came up with an interesting analysis of the fifty letters written by the same person. He first identified the writer as a woman." Dominic pulled those from the top of the stack. "Then he says, 'The writing is small, which indicates a detailed, technical personality. In conjunction with that, we have tight upright strokes which says the person is motivated by factors other than people.' He also says this person is childlike and self-centered, wants attention and will do anything to get it."

"Including writing to a serial killer," Colton said. "But it doesn't mean she wants to copy him and start killing people."

"Maybe not, but it might be a really good way to get his attention, don't you think?"

"Indeed."

Dominic said, "So, I'd like to track this woman down and just check her out."

"What's her name?"

"Allison Kingston. I've got our computer specialist tracking her down as we speak. And ballistics is working on the guns we pulled from Howard's house." He pulled a file from the stack beside him. "But for now, we concentrate on these."

As Serena opened the first one, Dominic said, "When you're finished, just make a stack of the ones you've been through. We're looking for any reference at all to the Doll Maker Killer."

For the next half hour, they worked, mostly in silence, occasionally making small chitchat. They were all intent on finding something before the killer struck again. The amount of information was nearly overwhelming, but they were making steady progress.

Katie broke the silence. "Hey, what's the name of the oldest son? Nate, right?"

Dominic looked up. "Yeah, he's the lawyer here in town. What do you have?"

"Maybe nothing, but this file is different than the rest." She held it up. Inside was a photograph of a young man sitting at an outdoor café, staring off into the distance. "He looks to be in his late thirties or early forties."

"Looks pretty recent," Dominic mused. "How old are all the kids again?"

Serena sat down and looked at the notes she'd made when she and Dominic had gone through Drake's information. "Nate's forty-two. Then Gwendolyn is the next in line at thirty-nine. Trey, the one in jail, is thirty-five, and Pete, the missing son, is the youngest at thirty."

"Anything else in there?" Hunter asked.

"Yeah, phone records, banking information, a schedule of places Nate likes to go to," Katie said. "And a note saying, 'It's only a matter of time before she contacts him.'"

Colton asked, "'She' who?"

"It doesn't say."

Dominic held out a hand. "Give me the phone records and I'll have the numbers checked out."

Katie handed him the papers. "There's a yellow sticky note on it that says, 'Dead end.'"

"Looks like Howard already traced the numbers and they didn't lead him to the person he was looking for."

Colton let out a low whistle. "Check this out." He held up a picture of a dead cop. "Shot in the middle of his forehead."

"What's his name?"

"Billy McGrath."

"Wait a minute," Katie said. "I know that name. He was Howard's partner. I came across a newspaper article about his death and set it aside because I couldn't figure out why Howard kept it." She pushed aside some files and came up with the yellowed piece of paper. "It's about his death. He went missing for a few days right after Drake Lindell's trial started and was found murdered the same day Mrs. Lindell committed suicide."

Dominic stood and began to pace. "I don't understand how all of this seems to have been swept under a rug. Why didn't any of this come up when I put Drake's name through the system?"

Hunter shook his head. "Weird. Let's keep looking."

Alexia said, "I may have something." She held up a folder. "A stack of pictures of women. With dates on them and DMK written in the corner."

"DMK," Colton mused. "Doll Maker Killer?"

Alexia nodded and Hunter asked, "But who are they and how are they related to the Doll Maker Killer case?"

Dominic frowned and asked, "How many are there?"

"Nine."

"Nine," Dominic muttered. "The same number of women he killed, but *not* the ones found." He looked at Alexia. "Does it say whether these women are dead or alive?"

"No. Just missing."

Serena saw Hunter, Dominic, and Katie exchange a look. Katie grunted. "After all these years? Probably means they're dead."

"Probably," Dominic agreed, "but let's see if there's anything that connects these nine to the Doll Maker Killer. Keep your eyes open to the possibility."

Silence reigned as they went back to their reading. Dominic took the file folder from Alexia and started making notes from it.

A buzzer sounded from the kitchen. Serena stood. "I'm going to check on the pizza." Her stomach growled at the tantalizing aromas coming from the kitchen.

As she headed in that direction, the doorbell rang. "I'll get it." Dominic hopped up to join her.

When she reached for the knob, he laid a hand on hers and pulled her to the side. He pushed the curtain slightly to the right, then nodded.

Serena opened the door to find the delivery guy there, four large pizzas in hand. Dominic paid the man and Serena turned her nose up at the boxes as she left him and entered the kitchen.

His low laughter reached her ears as she grabbed potholders and opened the oven. She couldn't help the smile that curved her lips. Cheese bubbled and the meat sizzled.

She breathed in. "Perfect."

Dominic leaned over her shoulder. "Wow. I have to say that looks awesome."

"Tastes even better, I promise." Sliding the pizza from the round stone onto the platter Dominic handed her, she set it on the counter to cool.

He leaned over to inhale. "Ahhh. I think you're going to convert me."

Serena smiled. "Do you have a pizza cutter?"

"Um . . . no. My pizzas always come sliced."

She smirked. "Right." Wiping her hands on her shorts, she said, "That's all right, I can use a knife."

"Hey, guys," Hunter called. "We're starving. Bring the food in here, will ya?"

Dominic grinned and grabbed two pizzas in the cardboard boxes from the counter. Serena quickly sliced hers with a knife and together they returned to the den.

Katie stood and tossed her file to the side. "I'll get the drinks."

"Cans are in the fridge," Dominic said.

"I know where they are." Katie moved toward the kitchen, tossing an unreadable look in Serena's and Dominic's direction. Dominic missed it, but Serena didn't.

Katie was jealous. Great. Pushing aside the unsettling knowledge, Serena set the pizza in the middle of the quickly cleared coffee table. Dominic handed out paper plates and napkins while Katie returned with sodas and bottled water.

Serena snagged a bottle of water, a plate, and two slices of the homemade pizza.

"Hey, this is good stuff," Colton exclaimed.

Serena flushed as Dominic agreed.

"Where'd you learn to cook like this?" Dominic asked.

Serena gave a shrug. "Mostly trial and error." She grinned at Alexia. "Alexia and I used to cook a lot at my house on the weekends. She was my guinea pig."

Alexia, mouth full of pizza, nodded and swallowed. "I gained fifteen pounds that summer between our junior and senior year when Serena went on a cooking frenzy."

Serena laughed, then sobered as she slid another file in front of her. But even while she joined in with the others' laughter and much-needed lighthearted conversation, she found her thoughts drifting.

Her mind had been subconsciously working on a problem all week, and Serena allowed herself to let it surface while everyone became absorbed in the food and files. Conversation eventually stalled.

Her phone buzzed. Frowning, she pulled it out, praying there were no dead bodies to call her back to the morgue.

No dead bodies, just a text message from Camille. DO I HAVE TO STAY HERE? CAN I STAY AT YOUR PLACE?

Serena closed her eyes and said a prayer. Then texted back, I'M SORRY, HON, U HAVE TO STAY THERE FOR NOW. I'M NOT HOME RIGHT NOW. I'LL TRY TO COME SEE U TOMORROW.

I'M GOING TO LOOK FOR A JOB TOMORROW.

I'LL TEXT YOU OR CALL. WE'LL WORK SOMETHING OUT. JUST STAY THERE FOR TONIGHT AT LEAST, OK? PROMISE?

At least two minutes passed before Camille's response came through.

OK. BYE.

She set her phone aside and sighed. Camille had found a special spot in Serena's heart, but she refused to let the girl manipulate her. Covenant House was a great place and Camille would learn to adjust. She would.

With that comforting thought, knowing that for now Camille was safe, Serena was able to turn her mind back to present business.

The man she'd shot still hadn't been identified.

And her questions still remained unanswered.

Who was he? Why had he been in her house? And what was he looking for?

She had her suspicions about the answer to that last question but no way of knowing whether or not she was right. But if she was, then she had no doubt that this wasn't the end of it just because her intruder was now in the hospital in a coma.

If someone was after the package that Jillian had sent her, she needed to figure out what to do with it. Because there was no way she could allow that information to fall into the wrong hands.

12

From the street, the killer watched. The pizza delivery man had come and gone. Laughter echoed from inside and the killer lifted a brow. What were they doing? Having a party? Indignation rose. There was a killer on the street and the cops were partying? How apropos.

A giggle escaped. Then full-fledged laughter.

Continuing the game was going to be so easy. Dumb cops. They never figured out much of anything if you didn't want them to. Throw them a few crumbs and they never really looked past the obvious.

Dominic munched on the pizza and watched Serena from the corner of his eye. She was with them, but she wasn't. She stared at the file in front of her, but from the pensive look on her face, he had a feeling the words weren't registering with her.

The others continued to pore over the files in between bites of homemade pizza. The delivered pizza was the last to go and Dominic had to admit Serena's pizza had spoiled takeout for him. He studied her and thought about what it would be like to have her

86

around all the time. Yeah. He wouldn't mind that kind of spoiling. She looked up and caught his eye. He didn't look away, and after a few seconds, she flushed and ducked her head.

Dominic allowed a small smile to curve his lips as he watched her.

Her flush faded as she turned her attention back to the stack of files in front of her. She grabbed one and set it on the floor in front of the fireplace to read through it. Dominic simply watched her. When she finished, she placed it on the stack labeled "nothing" and reached for the next one, her movements smooth, fluid, graceful.

Dominic moved to sit next to her.

Katie stood just as he sat down and said, "I'm sorry, guys, I've got to call it a night. I have to be up and at a meeting in the morning."

Dominic hopped back to his feet and said, "Thanks for your help."

"Wasn't much help that I could see," she grumbled. "Thanks for the pizza, though."

"Sure."

She looked at Serena and said, "I see why you make your own."

A real grin slipped across Serena's face. "Thanks."

Serena shot Dominic a teasing glance but was too classy to say "I told you so." At least not out loud. The words were written all over her face, though. Dominic bit his lip on a grin.

Hunter and Alexia followed Katie's lead, with Colton a few minutes behind them, and soon the house was empty—and quiet.

He returned to the den to find Serena immersed in yet another file. She finally closed it and looked up. "Another nothing." She slapped it on top of the stack and stood. Stretched and yawned. "I guess I'd better go too." She glanced at the clock on the mantel and gasped. "It's ten-thirty already? I didn't realize it was so late."

He didn't want her to go. "Do you want some coffee?"

She paused. "I wouldn't mind a cup. Even in the dead of summer at ten-thirty at night, I like my coffee. Decaf, though, okay?"

He nodded. "I'm right there with you."

"And do you have any flavored creamer?"

"Vanilla or mocha."

Delight lightened her pretty eyes. "Mocha."

———■———

While he rummaged around in the kitchen, getting the coffee brewing, Serena straddled a stool, placed her elbows on the bar, and settled her chin in her hands.

And studied him. It wasn't a hardship.

Tall, with the same fiery red hair that he shared with his sister, Alexia, and gorgeous green eyes. Serena sighed.

He looked up. "What's wrong?"

Mortification filled her. Sighing over him like a lovesick teen. Again! She cleared her throat. "Um. Nothing. Just thinking."

"About?"

She couldn't help the small smile that lifted her lips. "You really want to know?"

He paused and looked at her. "Yes. I really want to know."

"It's kind of silly, actually." Serena forced herself not to fidget. "I was thinking how much you've changed since the last time I saw you. You know, when I was a kid."

A light went on in his eyes. And he grinned as he gave her the once-over. "I could say the same about you."

She bit her lip, then blurted, "I had a big old crush on you when I was twelve."

His face softened. "I know."

The heat of embarrassment hit her. "You do? You did?"

"Yes. Which is why I did my best to avoid you."

Serena winced. "I was that annoying?"

"No." His somber expression grabbed her. "I knew I wasn't any good. And I didn't want to hurt you."

That made her heart flip. "Oh."

He shrugged and turned back to the coffee. "You were too young for me anyway. But it didn't stop me from noticing that you were going to be an incredibly beautiful woman one day."

"Oh." She couldn't seem to find any other word in her vocabulary.

Dominic chuckled, stepped closer, and pushed a strand of hair behind her ear. "I was right."

Serena felt the breath leave her as his gaze dropped to her lips. The musky scent of his cologne surrounded her. In the blink of an eye, a thousand thoughts raced through her mind. Finally, her tongue got back in touch with her mind. "I'm not twelve anymore." As soon as the words left her, she wanted to recall them. While she'd found other words, apparently she'd lost her filters.

He froze. Tender fingers lingered on the fragile shell of her ear as he stared down at her. "I know." He paused as he studied her closer. "Trust me, I've noticed."

Her lower lip trembled. Her heart thumped, threatening to rupture through her chest.

His head lowered.

Her eyes closed.

And the doorbell rang.

13

Dominic flinched and pulled back, his heart racing at the interruption. He'd almost kissed her. And regretted that he hadn't. Clearing his throat, he said, "Excuse me a minute."

He noticed the red in her cheeks and hoped she wasn't thinking he was trying to move too fast with her. That certainly wasn't his intention. In fact, he really didn't have any business thinking about her romantically.

Did he?

Then again, why not?

Like she said, she wasn't twelve anymore.

He left her in the kitchen and walked to the front door. Out of habit and self-preservation, he stood to the side and peeked out the window.

No one stood on the porch.

Uneasiness tightened his gut.

His hand reached for the weapon that was never too far from his fingertips.

"What is it?" Serena asked from the doorway.

"I'm not sure. Some kids playing around maybe." Dominic reached for the doorknob, then hesitated. He walked into the den and pulled back the curtain that would allow him to see the front porch.

The porch light illuminated the area. No one stood on his porch.

He looked down and his eyes landed on a package sitting on the top step.

Closing the blinds, Dominic said, "Stay here."

"Why?"

"Someone left a package for me on the step. I'm going out the back door and around the side of the house."

He wasn't about to open the front door and expose himself. Dominic hesitated, his fingers hovering over the speed dial number. Then he looked at Serena. He wasn't going to place her at risk. He called for backup, then said, "I may be jumping the gun here, but right now I only know one person who's been leaving packages that look like that. If he's around here, I want this area searched."

"Do you think he's still out there?"

"One way to find out."

"You're going after him?" Worry creased her forehead.

"Yes."

If the person who left the package wanted to play sneaky, Dominic would oblige him. "You have your phone?"

"Right here." She pulled it from the pocket of her shorts, her eyes troubled, scared, yet determined to help him.

"Call my number."

She did and he answered. "Now stay on the line. Do you mind standing off to the side here and watching the porch? If you see anything that looks suspicious, any movement or whatever, let me know, but don't open the door or move in front of the window."

She took up her position next to the window. "Okay."

Dominic whirled and headed through the kitchen to the back door. After a look through the window, he checked the lock and backtracked, passing a curious—and worried, if he was reading her eyes right—Serena to find himself in his bedroom. No way was he using a door right now.

He went to the window, opened it, and climbed out.

He never kept a screen on his bedroom window simply for speed's sake. He never knew when he might need to get out fast. Or quiet. Like now.

Landing on the soft earth, he crouched, weapon ready.

◼

Nerves jumping, Serena peered out the window and kept her eye on the porch and the area illuminated by the light that stretched a few feet beyond.

Where was Dominic's backup?

She saw nothing, but that didn't stop her blood from humming a little faster in her veins. And then a shadow passed just on the outer edge of where the light reached.

Serena brought the phone up, her heart thudding a little faster. "Dominic, I think someone's still out front. Beyond the light, back in the shadows."

"Heading that way."

"Be careful," she whispered. "Please be careful."

She kept her eyes on the spot where she thought she'd seen something, then scanned beyond. Nothing else caught her attention. Had it just been her imagination?

Serena bit her lip and said a prayer for Dominic's safety. Then considered her options. Did she stand here in wait-and-see mode? Or did she do something to prepare herself for . . . for what?

For an attack? Was there anything she could do to help Dominic? She shivered as she listened for his voice to come over the line. So far, just quiet stillness echoed in her ear.

◼

Dominic scoured the area, probing the darkness, examining each shadow. And still he had nothing. He'd investigated the area where Serena thought she saw movement, but by the time he arrived, if someone had been there, he was gone, leaving Dominic no way to track him in the dark.

He stopped. Stood completely still, kept his back to a tree, and closed his eyes. And listened.

Night sounds. The flap of a bird's wings?

A branch snapping to his left?

He spun, started toward the sound.

But heard nothing more.

His nerves shivered and the hair on the back of his neck lifted.

Feeling exposed, he stayed in the shadows, but that didn't settle his uneasiness, his belief that someone had been there watching his every move.

The half moon illuminated the area away from the shadows pretty well. Dominic approached the porch, glancing over his shoulder with every step. Through the trees, in the direction of the street that ran behind his backyard, he thought he saw flashing blue lights headed his way.

Within seconds the first car pulled into the drive. Colton climbed out, weapon drawn. "Heard your call on my radio. Where is he?"

"Out here somewhere." He motioned toward the area. Three more cruisers parked on the curb and Dominic flashed his badge at them. "He could be long gone by now—then again, he might be nearby. Keep your guard up."

The officers dispersed and Dominic waited for the last vehicle. The bomb squad. The dark van crunched to a stop and a large German shepherd led his handler out. Dominic saw Jessica Goode follow, the dog's leash wrapped around her left hand. "Where is it?"

"On the porch."

Jessica led the dog to it and said, "Search, Buddy."

Buddy sniffed, walked around the package and back, but gave no sign that anything was going to explode. Jessica looked at Dominic. "He didn't sit, it's clear."

"Great. Thanks." Jessica and Buddy disappeared back into the van and Dominic walked up the steps to rap on his front door.

Within two seconds, the knob turned and the door opened. Dominic told Serena, "Will you grab me a pair of gloves from under my bathroom sink?"

"Sure." She turned and within seconds was back. He took the gloves from her and pulled them on. Then he grabbed the package and slipped inside. Serena shut the door behind him.

Dominic carried the package into the kitchen and set it on the counter.

Serena tilted her head and looked at it. "It's not a bomb, is it?"

He shook his head, studying the package. "No, the dog cleared it. But I didn't really think it was a bomb anyway. I also figured the person who left it here had to carry it a pretty long way, because I didn't hear a vehicle leave." Or footsteps or anything else that indicated someone had been near his front porch.

"Which means the person came in on foot—or bicycle—and left the same way. Why?"

"Because he didn't want to take a chance on being seen in a car. Too easy to identify it." He shrugged. "But who knows?"

Another rap on the door sounded and Dominic opened it to let Colton in. "Ready to join the party again?" he asked.

"You going to open it?" Colton jutted his chin toward the box in Dominic's hands.

"Yep."

"Have at it then. The officers are still searching, but I think your gifter is long gone."

Dominic reached for the edge of the tape on the box and paused. "I know it's not going to explode, but I'd feel better if I knew what was in here before opening it."

"I would too," Serena said.

He looked for a return address.

Blank.

94

Colton shook his head. "You think it's from the killer?"

"I don't know. Could be some kind of prank, but I'd still like to X-ray it before I open it. Just to be on the safe side."

Serena tilted her head, still studying the small box. "It looks just like the one left by Leslie's killer."

A shiver crept up his spine even though she was only confirming what he'd already observed. "Yeah, I'd noticed that. It's a different color, but it's the same style and material. A smooth, almost plastic feel. And the corners are rounded."

"We can take it to my office to X-ray or take it straight to Rick and let him do it. Whichever you prefer."

Troubled, he rubbed his head, feeling the stiff curls against his palm. "I could send it off and have it done or call the bomb squad back, but that takes time and I want to know what's in here. Now." He never was very good at waiting. He did it when he had to, but if there was a way around it . . . He nodded. "Okay, let's go."

Colton agreed to stay until the officers were finished and call with a report.

━■━

Within minutes, Serena and Dominic were in his car, heading toward the morgue. Once there, Serena used her key and led him to the room containing the X-ray machine. Dominic settled the package where she indicated. In moments, she was finished. "Now, I'll just put these here." She slid the large black slides into place and clicked the backlight on.

The contents appeared in milky white form.

Serena drew in a deep breath. "Another doll."

Dominic's mouth pulled, his gaze still on the picture on the wall. "But why send it to me?" His eyes met hers. "The killer's connected us. Put us together on this."

"But why?"

He went still and lifted a hand to rub his chin. He looked at her. A look that made her uneasy. "What?" she pressed him.

"Somehow he knows we're working together. He knows you're the ME working on the body and he knows I'm the lead investigator. And for some reason, he wants *us* to know that *he* knows and that he's watching." A frown pulled his brows down.

Serena gulped. "He followed us today, didn't he?"

"Yes." Dominic nodded. "I'm sure he did. And he waited until everyone left before he put that package on my front porch. I need to warn the others." He reached for his phone.

"Why?"

"Because they were with us tonight. They need to know they might be receiving interesting packages on their front porches."

Serena left him to make the phone calls and turned back to study the X-ray, but it was too hard to tell what the doll looked like, other than long wavy hair.

Curling her fingers into a fist, Serena forced herself to be patient.

For the next few minutes, Dominic made calls and Serena checked her email on her phone. When he hung up, she asked, "Anyone get anything suspicious?"

"Nothing."

"So, you were just the lucky one."

"Hi, guys, what's going on?" Dorie King pushed her cleaning cart into the room. She squinted as she saw Serena and Dominic's serious expressions. "Everything all right?"

"Just working on something," Serena said. "This is Special Agent Dominic Allen with the FBI. Dominic, meet Dorie King, a future medical examiner."

The two exchanged greetings. Dorie started emptying the trash, and Serena asked Dominic, "Should we call Rick?"

He nodded. "I did. He's on his way. Said he'd be about ten minutes. I offered to bring the box over to the lab, but he said he didn't want us handling it any more than necessary."

"So, what's in there?" Dorie eyed the box, a gleam in her eyes.

Serena bit her lip on a smile. Dorie was going to make an excellent ME one day. With her insatiable curiosity and an eye for details, she had a great career ahead of her.

"Evidence for a case, we believe." Serena paused. She exchanged a look with Dominic, who gave a slight shake of his red head. Serena said, "I don't think this is something we can share right now, Dorie. Why don't you give us a few minutes?"

Dorie's face dropped, but she said, "Sure, sure. I understand. I've got the rooms down the hall to take care of." She spun the cart and headed toward the door. Turning back, she asked, "Will thirty or forty-five minutes work?"

"That should be perfect." Serena smiled her thanks and looked at Dominic. "Coffee?"

"Please."

Serena walked into her office and pulled out the decaf. As she got the coffeemaker going, Dominic said, "We still haven't talked about Jillian."

His words made her pause. Hoping he hadn't noticed her hesitation, she said, "What do you want to talk about?"

"You said Jillian asked you some questions the last time you talked to her. What kind of questions?"

She pulled two mugs from the cabinet above the coffeemaker and handed one to Dominic. "She wanted to know about her family. She also wanted to know if I'd seen Colton Brady lately. And she wanted to know about the reunion." *She wanted to know if I had a safe place to keep some precious information.*

Serena debated whether or not to say anything about the package Jillian had sent her and decided it wasn't her place. Jillian trusted her to keep her confidence and Serena would do it as best she could.

Dominic nodded. "And you answered all those questions."

"I did."

"Why did she want to know about Colton?"

Serena frowned. "I don't really know." She tapped her finger against the mug as she thought. "But the summer of our junior year, Jillian was acting . . . weird."

"Weird? How?"

"She just wasn't around much. Always had an excuse why we couldn't hang out or go to the movies. And then senior year rolled around and she was almost back to normal."

"What was normal?"

Serena shrugged. "Just always ready to have fun, hang out at my house, go shopping, whatever. Then she got a job and we just never saw her that much unless it was at school."

"A job doing what?"

"Waiting tables at Mac's on Main Street. Her mother was helping raise Jillian's cousins because Jillian's aunt had been diagnosed with cancer."

He grimaced. "Ouch. Sorry to hear that."

"Yes, she died about three months later. So money was tight for them." Serena rubbed her nose. "And after that, things were different, but still good, you know? Jillian seemed moodier than usual, but that was understandable when you thought about everything her family was going through at the time. Then there was graduation and the party . . ." She shook her head and poured the coffee that had finished dripping. She added her creamer and took a sip. Then said, "I don't know what happened that night, but it had to have been something of mammoth proportions to send her running like she did."

A knock on the door startled them. Serena turned to see Rick standing there.

She stepped out of her office, Dominic right behind her. "Hey, thanks for coming. I know it's late."

He yawned, then shrugged. "It's what I do."

Dominic led them over to the table where they'd left the box. Serena offered Rick a pair of gloves, which he pulled on with a snap. He set his bag on the table and Serena handed him a scalpel to use on the tape.

She reached for the digital camera. "I'll do the pictures."

"That's fine," Rick said. "I'll guide you through it. Don't forget to get every fold and document the way the tape was applied."

Opening the box, Rick reached in and pulled out the doll. Dominic leaned in from the opposite side of the table and Serena shifted to make room for him.

Rick laid the doll on the table beside the box and simply looked at her. "Does she resemble anyone you know?"

"No. She doesn't." As Serena snapped pictures from every angle, she took in the doll's curly brown hair and green eyes. She thought the black dress with the pearl necklace looked expensive. "She looks like she's dressed for a party." Serena bit her lip. "If she's supposed to represent someone, I don't have a clue who it could be."

Dominic sucked in a harsh breath as he ran a hand over his short red curls. "I'm meeting with the task force first thing in the morning. I'll share this information with them and get some feedback. Debbie Sanchez is our profiler. She's amazing. I'm sure she'll have something to say about all this."

Rick nodded. "Good, I look forward to getting an update from you." He bit his lip, then pushed it out as he thought.

"Is there a note?" Dominic asked.

Rick looked back in the box, then examined the flaps.

"Yes, right here." He slipped the note from the tape and opened it. "'Eenie meenie miney moe, try to catch me, you're too slow. I saw you once, I'll see you again. Until next time, she's all mine.'"

Serena looked at Dominic. "Does that make any sense at all to you?"

"No. Just sounds like bad poetry to me, but I'm sure there's a message there somewhere. For someone." He pinched the bridge of his nose and went quiet. She didn't know if he was thinking or praying. Probably both.

"Okay," Rick said. "We know he's not the original Doll Maker Killer. That's obvious. We're trying to catch him and he's telling us it's a waste of time to try, because we're too slow. And he's saying he'll see us next time. So, what's his goal? Why leave the notes? Does he want some kind of fame from this?"

"Some people will take fame any way they can get it," Dominic muttered.

"I know. But if the Doll Maker Killer has a copycat, the person taking over the killings is putting a new twist on things."

"We know there are some discrepancies, but what have you found?" Serena asked.

"Thus far, if this Doll Maker Killer sticks to his MO, he leaves a doll, a bad poem, and a dead body. This time we have the doll and the poem, so where's the body?"

14

That question had haunted Dominic the rest of the night. Rick was right. Where *was* the body? Because as sure as he knew his own name, he knew in his gut there was a dead girl somewhere. If the killer followed the same MO as Leslie, then the doll would look like the victim.

"Eenie meenie miney moe," he muttered in disgust. Who did he know that had curly brown hair and green eyes?

A lot of people.

He rolled onto his back and did his best to rub the weariness from his eyes. Then he swung his legs around to let them hang off the edge of the bed. For a brief moment, he let his head droop. *God, let me end this day with more answers than I'm starting with, please.*

Rising, he grabbed his workout clothes, and headed for the small one car garage he'd turned into a mini weight room. He did his best thinking—and praying—here.

An hour and twelve minutes later, he walked out of his house and headed for the office where he would meet with the task force.

His mind spun with everything they needed to discuss. As the case agent on this, he had to have his facts straight and his A-game on.

Pulling into the station lot, he parked and bowed his head once

101

more, got his thoughts together, and headed inside the building. As he walked inside, his phone buzzed with an email from Oliver Cook, the IT guy who was going over Howard's computer.

He read, "Computer is from the midnineties and I don't think Howard used it. The hard drive is missing. There's nothing on any of the other drives. And I do mean nothing. They'd never been used. Everything must have been on the hard drive that Howard got rid of. Nothing I can do with this one."

Dominic frowned. No hard drive? They hadn't found one in Howard's house. What had he done with it? Tossed it in the nearby lake? Buried it? And when? Last year? Whatever he'd done, it was no use looking for it now.

Dominic found the task force team assembled in the conference room. "Good morning, everyone."

A round of replies greeted him.

He glanced at the clock. 7:45.

Standing at the front of the room, he looked out to see Hunter, Chad, Katie, and his FBI team members. The profiler he'd requested, Debbie Sanchez, sat to his right. A stack of files from Howard's house lay sprawled across the table in the back, spilling onto the floor.

"Here's the latest. So far we haven't come across the Doll Maker Killer's file. Those of you assigned to the files, keep looking. Ballistics stated none of the guns found in Howard's filing cabinet had been used recently, but had been cleaned to the point of perfection."

"Which means we really don't know if any have been fired recently," Chad grunted.

"Right."

"He was ready for trouble?" Hunter asked.

"And expecting it?" Katie chimed.

"Possibly." Dominic nodded. He looked at Debbie. "You've studied this killer. What do you have?"

Before she could answer, the door opened again and Colton

Brady stepped inside. The beginnings of a beard and faint shadows under his eyes betrayed his recent long hours and little sleep. He looked at Dominic and smiled. "Sorry I'm late. Made a bust about an hour ago and was trying to finish the paperwork."

"No problem. Thanks for coming."

Dominic nodded to Debbie. "Go ahead, please."

While Colton took a seat in the back of the room, Debbie straightened, her dark ponytail swinging behind her. She glanced at her notes and said, "I know about the Doll Maker Killer. I've interviewed him on several occasions. However, I've not had a chance to talk to him about the recent killing that resembles his work. I have an appointment to see him later today." She drew in a deep breath and looked at Dominic. "Do you know if he took any trophies, like a body part or a piece of jewelry? Anything?"

"We're not aware of anything at this time, no."

She nodded. "With only one killing to work with, it's hard to say at this moment."

"Two killings," Dominic said.

"Two?" Hunter asked.

Everyone straightened at this news. Dominic rubbed the back of his neck and told them about the doll left on his doorstep. Then he read them the note. "I feel sure there's another body out there, we just haven't found her yet." Murmurs echoed across the room as they processed this new information. Dominic looked at Debbie. "Anything else?"

"No, I'll keep you updated. Right now, I'm in stage one of this investigation. Gathering the information." She shrugged. "And to be honest, you haven't given me much to go on."

"I know." He tapped his chin and asked, "Hunter, what do you and Katie have on the victim, Leslie Stanton?"

Katie took the lead. "Chad and I notified the family. They were shocked, devastated, of course. The mother became hysterical at one point. Finally, after she calmed down a bit, she said she wasn't aware of anyone in Leslie's life who was upset or angry with her. She said she'd seen Leslie the Thursday before and they'd had dinner together. When they left the restaurant around seven o'clock, Leslie didn't say whether she was meeting someone later or not."

Chad said, "But Leslie's father said that she called him around 9:00 to confirm a lunch date for the following week."

Dominic nodded. "Any cameras in the park?"

"No." Katie took over. "Not in that particular area. We've viewed what footage we have and at one point, two people on a motorcycle drove past, but were soon out of sight."

"And around 2:00 a.m. there were some partiers that park security had to chase off, but they weren't near the bench where Leslie was found."

Dominic wrapped up the meeting with more instructions and the order to keep him in the loop.

As everyone filed out, Colton passed him, slapped him on the shoulder, and said, "When you get some time, I need to talk to you."

"Something about the case?"

"No, personal."

"You have my number. Give me a call and we'll set something up."

Dominic and Colton hadn't been exactly friends in high school simply because they hung out with different crowds, but Colton had always been friendly, with a level head on his shoulders. At least that was how it seemed to Dominic.

Colton nodded and Dominic asked, "Wait a minute, while I have you, I want to ask you a question."

"Sure."

Dominic motioned Colton back into the empty conference room. The detective lifted a brow but followed without question. "What is it?"

"I talked to Serena and she said that Jillian Carter, one of her old friends from high school, called her a few weeks ago."

Colton went rigid, his jaw tightening, nostrils flaring. Then his face went blank. "And?"

"She asked about you."

The blank expression never changed. "Why would she do that?"

"That's what I'd like to know." He considered the man before him and knew he was one of the best detectives on the force. An outstanding one. He was also a man of integrity with a high work ethic. "One thing we've managed to keep from the press is that in the midst of this serial killer mess, the person after Serena is really after Jillian."

Worry flashed in Colton's eyes. "He is? Why?"

"We don't know. Alexia couldn't figure it out and now Serena's puzzled. They both agree it probably had something to do with whatever happened graduation night that sent her running scared."

"Wait a minute." Colton lifted a hand. "What happened graduation night? I thought she just . . . left town."

"She did, but before she left, she told Serena and Alexia whatever she saw could get her killed. And if she told them, they would be targets too. They gave her some money and she bolted."

Colton's face went white. He pulled out a chair and dropped into it. "I didn't know. I thought . . ."

"What?"

"It's been ten years and I still can't forget her." Colton fisted his hand and slammed it onto the desk in front of him.

Dominic leaned forward and placed his hands on the table. "What are you talking about? Give me details."

Colton lifted his eyes and Dominic winced at the pain glittering in them. "I was in love with her in high school. I wanted to marry her."

"Serena didn't tell me that."

A harsh laugh slipped from the detective. "That's because Serena didn't know." He closed his eyes and drew in a deep breath. "Jillian and I kept our relationship a secret because of my family.

They never would have approved of her." He shrugged. "I didn't care about her background, but she did. Said she didn't want to embarrass me." He gave a wry smile. "I promised her I wasn't embarrassed and that my family would come around. But she said she wouldn't date me if there was any chance that it would mess up my relationship with my parents."

"Your parents expected you to date someone more fitting of their social class? People still have those kinds of hang-ups?"

"Yeah. At least my parents did." Colton shrugged. "My parents were very clear about their expectations. I was to go to law school and join my father's practice. I was to only date or marry someone they approved of. Very . . . old school, they would say. I just call them snobs."

Dominic lifted a brow. "I see how well that plan worked out."

"Yep." A glimmer of a smile reached the man's eyes, then faded. "I love them, but I'm my own man, and if they don't like it, I'm sorry, that's just the way it is." He rubbed his head and his gaze hardened. "Unfortunately, they don't like it much." He blew out a breath. "Jillian left town and I haven't heard from her in ten years. No goodbye, no letter, nothing. I was afraid she'd been killed or kidnapped or something. But when I went to her house looking for her, her mother showed me a letter Jillian left. It just said, 'I have to go. I love you.'"

"That's it?"

"Yeah. So, I decided to find her on my own. I went to college, started walking the path my parents had laid out for me, but I . . . became obsessed with finding Jillian. I quit school, went to the academy, and became a cop." He smirked. "Much to my parents' horror. Then I became a detective." He shut his eyes and rubbed them. "And I still haven't found her."

Dominic blew out a sigh. "Well, that explains why she would ask Serena about you."

Colton stood, a determined light now shining in his gaze. "You don't have to call me now. Jillian was what I wanted to talk about, but sounds like I need to talk to Serena."

"I can tell you right now, she doesn't know where Jillian is. She said Jillian called, asked a few questions, and said she'd be coming home soon, that she had things she needed to take care of."

The light dimmed. "Tell Serena I want to know the minute she hears from Jillian. I have a few things to take care of myself."

Colton turned on his heel and exited the conference room. Dominic watched the man go, then noticed Hunter and Katie lingering in the hallway. "What's up?" he asked them.

"Any word on the package left on your doorstep?" Hunter asked.

"No, Rick said he'd call me if he found anything he hadn't already told me. The dolls are handmade, carved, sanded, painted, and dressed with handmade items."

Katie's brows drew together. "Is it a special kind of wood or . . . ?"

Dominic shook his head. "It's a soft balsa wood. Very common and found at any home improvement store."

"So the killer may fancy himself as some kind of artist." Katie pinched the bridge of her nose and closed her eyes.

Dominic touched her shoulder, concerned. "You okay?"

She grimaced and dropped her hand. "Yes. Just a bit of a headache."

"You need some time off? It hasn't been that long since you were shot."

She straightened her shoulders, her posture defensive. "I'm fine. What else needs to be done?"

Hunter said, "This guy may have some artistic talent, but all the handmade stuff could be that he just wants to make sure he's not leaving a trail behind. Common wood, no store-bought clothes."

Katie nodded. "But store-bought fabric. He has to get the fabric from somewhere to make the clothes, right?"

Dominic rubbed the side of his nose. "True. That might be a

good place to start. Katie, you want to talk to Rick and see if he can come up with some ideas of where the fabric may have come from? You know, is it fancy stuff sold only in upscale fabric stores, or is it something we can't trace because it came from a local chain?"

"Sure. I'm on it."

"Thanks." She headed off and Hunter glanced at his watch. Dominic asked, "You need to be somewhere?"

"Not yet." Hunter rubbed his hands together, then shoved them in his pockets.

Dominic frowned. "You're nervous about something. What is it?"

Hunter blew out a deep breath, looked up the hallway, then back down. He leaned in close. "I'm meeting Alexia for lunch."

"Yeah? So?"

"And . . . uh . . . we're going to . . . uh . . . a store."

"A store."

"Right."

Suspicion hit him. "And what store would that be?"

Hunter rocked back on his heels, then grinned, nervousness fading to be replaced by glee. "Reed's."

"Reed's. As in . . . ?" He tapped his ring finger on his left hand.

"Yep. As in."

"She's not a diamond kind of girl," Dominic said.

Hunter pursed his lips. "I think I'm aware of that, thanks."

"Go with a pearl engagement ring and you'll nail it."

"She said a small one, nothing fancy."

Dominic hesitated. "I'd go somewhere in between."

Hunter let out another breath. "Yeah, that's what I was thinking. Thanks."

Dominic slapped the man on the back. "Now let's go see if we can find this killer before your lunch date."

All nervousness fled Hunter's face as his eyes hardened with determination. "Let's do it."

15

Once they found the body, the cops would swarm the crime scene like ants on a discarded candy bar. Well, they could look all they wanted, but they'd never find what they were looking for.

HE always said cops were dumb.

And of course, HE'd been proven right. But sometimes cops got lucky. It might be best to tread carefully regardless.

Tension slithered through the killer as the prey came into sight. The hunt for the next player in the game was almost as exciting as the capture—and the kill.

Kelsey Nicholson exited the doctor's office.

Hunkering down in the backseat of Kelsey's Subaru, the killer popped the plastic cover off the needle.

—■—

Serena's nerves hopped as she pushed the half-finished cup of coffee aside. She was antsy, restless. And not just from all of the caffeine she'd inhaled over the last few hours. She still couldn't stop thinking about the fact that she'd been so close to kissing Dominic.

And the fact that she wouldn't mind an instant replay of the moment in the kitchen.

Minus the ringing doorbell and the package left on the porch and Dominic's mad dash into the night to chase after a possible killer and . . .

Focus. Focus. Focus.

She'd pulled the files on all of the victims of the Doll Maker Killer. All nine. Nine missing women. Ranging in age from twenty-two to thirty-eight. All Caucasian. All very pretty. All killed in Columbia, South Carolina, over a three-year period—1992 to 1995. And then the killings just stopped.

Or the killer started hiding the bodies instead of placing them where they could be found.

Nevertheless, all was silent for a year, then Drake Lindell was arrested after authorities received an anonymous tip, along with a picture of two of the victims alive and in the room the caller said needed to be searched. That had been enough to get a search warrant for a room below a shed on the man's property.

They'd searched the area and found more than enough evidence to put Drake away.

Serena took each of Lindell's victims' files and laid them on the counter space she'd cleared for this purpose. She wondered if these nine could possibly have any connection to the nine missing women mentioned at Dominic's house the other night. She made a note to ask.

"What are you doing?"

Serena turned to see Paul standing in the doorway. "Hey there." She turned back to the files. "I was curious about something, so I'm looking for some answers."

"We've got a light workload today. Want some help?"

"Possibly." She waved him over. "Take a look at these. All of these girls were murdered by the same guy. His signature is all over the murders."

"And?"

"And someone is copying him. But who? Who would have inside

110

knowledge into how he worked? The details of the scenes?" She thought about everything she knew. "Was there any detail the cops didn't release to the media?"

"You're talking to yourself, aren't you?"

She jerked. "Yes."

"Good, because I don't know any of the answers." Paul picked up the nearest file. "Cause of death—gunshot to the forehead."

"Right."

"And he left a package with a doll in it," he muttered.

"Right again. According to the authorities, the original Doll Maker Killer was indiscriminate about what the dolls looked like. This time around, we're not sure yet if the killer will use the dolls to represent his next victim."

"What do you mean?"

"This new killer is taking a lot of the Doll Maker Killer's modus operandi and using them, but he's also coming into his own."

"As a killer."

"Unfortunately."

"But there's only been one person killed," Paul pointed out.

"We have one body," Serena corrected. "One body and two dolls." She told him about the special delivery Dominic had received last night. "The first doll looked like Leslie, with blue eyes and straight black hair. The doll found on Dominic's porch had curly brown hair and green eyes. But this time, unlike the original Doll Maker Killer, this killer didn't leave a body with the doll."

"Sick." Paul shook his head. "And I don't mean 'sick' as in 'awesome.' I mean that's just sick."

Serena gave a short nod. "I know. Definitely a very twisted person."

Her assistant nodded. "Right." His frown deepened. "That's kind of scary, Serena."

"Tell me about it. Rick brought up a good point. If the Doll Maker Killer left a doll, there should be a body somewhere." The more she thought about it, the more she knew that was right.

"So where's the body? The one that goes with Dominic's package."

She sighed. "He could have killed her and buried her anywhere. We won't find her unless he wants us to."

Paul's lips twisted. "You'll find it."

"You sound awfully sure of that."

"Well, think about it. Why leave the gifts if he's not going to give you the body? Isn't that the whole point?" He shook his head. "She'll turn up."

Serena had a feeling he was right. "But this is another aberration. The original Doll Maker Killer never sent his packages ahead of time. They always came with the body. So, I don't think we can predict what this killer *will do* based on what the first killer *did*."

Paul asked, "Where were all of these girls found? Were they spread out or in the same general area?"

"I don't know. I'm just getting ready to pull out the corkboard and a city map and make me a little diagram."

Paul grinned at her. "Isn't that the cops' job?"

Serena lifted a brow at him. "Yes, and they're doing it, but I'm curious. I've hung around enough cops to know how this works."

He set the file down. "I'll get the board for you."

"Thanks."

Five minutes later, she had her map pinned to the 3' × 5' corkboard and was ready to start using her pushpins.

A knock on the door interrupted her. She turned and looked to see Dominic standing there, watching her. "Hi."

"Hey there." He nodded at the board. "What are you up to?"

"Playing detective."

One of his brows lifted. "Hmm. How's it working for you?"

"Well, I've only gotten started. You want to help?"

"Of course. I've played that game a time or two. Seem to have a knack for it, as a matter of fact."

She smirked and handed him a file. "Funny. Dominic, meet Paul

Hamilton, my assistant. Paul, meet FBI Special Agent Dominic Allen." The two men shook hands. Dominic opened the file as Serena said, "Victim number one. Cori Hale." She paused and looked at Paul. "Will you mark the victims' addresses on the wall map? I have some pushpins in the tray. Use the red ones if you don't mind."

"Sure." Paul snagged a few of the red pins.

Dominic read the information as Serena filled in the chart on the white board and Paul pinned the addresses. Dominic looked up at her and said, "You know we have computer software that will do this for us."

"I know, but I don't have access to that and I'm a hands-on kind of girl. Humor me, will you?"

He smiled. "Of course."

By the end of the ninth victim, Serena studied the map and frowned. "They're from all over the place."

"No obvious pattern there," Dominic murmured. "How about use a different color pushpin to mark the places where they were found."

Serena nodded. "Good idea."

"Got it," Paul said.

Dominic started back with the first victim. Nine blue pushpins soon dotted the map.

"Where did the Lindells live?" Serena asked.

Dominic pulled out his iPhone and tapped a few keys. "Near the Five Points area." He picked up a white pin and pressed it into the map. "Right about there."

"You really think this is going to help anything?" Paul asked.

Serena lifted a brow at him. "I have no idea." She stacked the files. "And you know Rick said there could be more. They just knew about the nine." She sighed and looked at their work. "So, we really might not have a complete picture of everything."

"True." Dominic nodded as he studied the map. "What if we connect the dots?"

"Well, that was the plan, but," Serena frowned, "I'm not seeing a pattern here."

"If we used the latest technology, it would be a simple matter of pressing a button. But if you want to do it the old-fashioned way, I'll need some string. You have some?"

"Yes." She walked over to a metal drawer and pulled it open. "Kite string."

"That'll work." Dominic took it from her.

"Need some scissors?" Paul asked.

"Yep."

For the next thirty minutes, the three of them did their best to come up with some kind of pattern linking the deaths. Dominic finally sighed. "I give up." Lifting his iPhone, he snapped a picture of the map. "I'm going to give this to the geographic profiler and ask him to enter it into the computer. We'll see what he comes up with."

Serena nodded. "Good idea. We're just wasting time here." She studied the map. "Just one more thing." She snagged two yellow pushpins. "Let's add Leslie to the map." She pushed one into the area containing Leslie's address and one into the park where she'd been found.

Paul snagged a few more of the pins. "Might as well add Dominic's house."

"What?"

He shrugged. "That's where you found the last package, right?"

Serena exchanged a glance with Dominic, who shrugged. "Why not? At this point, it's not a bad idea."

"Are you sure the body isn't somewhere on your property?" Paul mused. "Seems like all the bodies were found in close proximity to the package."

Dominic shook his head. "We searched every square inch of that property last night. There's definitely no body there."

Paul frowned, then shrugged.

Serena asked, "Was there any detail about the killings that the police didn't release to the media?"

Dominic pursed his lips. "Yeah. The fact that the killer cleaned them up."

"And some of the victims had more than one bullet hole. I mean besides the one in the forehead."

"Right. Some were in the shoulder, one was in the throat."

"But always the upper torso."

He gave a slow nod. "Yes. Why?"

"Just an observation. Leslie was the same way," Serena said.

Dominic snapped several more pictures. "I'm going to start tracking down Drake Lindell's kids."

"I want to go with you. When are you going and who are you going to talk to first?" Her heart thudded. That was out of the ordinary. The ME didn't usually go with the FBI agent while he investigated a case. But maybe Dominic would make an exception for her.

When he didn't immediately say no, her hopes rose. Spending more time with Dominic was definitely high on her want-to-do list.

She could get excited about that.

"Right now. And probably Nate, since he's the easiest one to find."

Her hope deflated like a stuck balloon.

Work came first.

Serena did a quick mental inventory of her caseload for the rest of the day and winced. It was practically nonexistent. Like Paul said, she only had one, a hit-and-run victim. Another woman about her age.

And she was finished with her.

She would have her phone with her if they needed her. But the paperwork she still had . . .

"I can come if you don't mind. I may have to work a little later tonight, but I want to go with you." She hardened her jaw. "By leaving that package on your porch, the killer's made this personal."

"That's the way I feel about it." His phone rang.

Serena helped Paul put the supplies away while Dominic put the phone to his ear. "Dominic here." Silence while he listened. Then, "I'll be right there."

At the grim tone, she turned. "What is it?"

"I think we've found the body that the doll from my porch belongs to."

"Where is she?"

He swiped a hand over his eyes and looked at the multicolored pinned map, then at Paul. "In the storage shed in my backyard."

16

"I just came to borrow the lawn mower like you said I could, and when I opened up the door, there she was!" Mr. Eric White exclaimed with a wave of his wrinkled hand.

Dominic patted his seventy-year-old neighbor's shoulder to calm the man down, which was an effort considering his blood hummed through his own veins like a current out of control.

But he'd had a lot of practice hiding that. With confidence, he said, "It's all right, Mr. White. We'll take it from here."

"But I don't understand." Mr. White's red-rimmed blue eyes flashed his worry. "Why would she be sitting in your shed, dressed like she's going to a party?"

Dressed like she's going to a party?

Dominic's head snapped up and he shot a look at Serena. "Just like my doll?"

"Let's find out," Serena said.

A uniformed officer took over questioning Mr. White while Dominic led the way to the shed. Another officer handed him a pair of blue booties to slip over his shoes. Serena took a pair too. He heard her snap on gloves, then felt her shove a pair into his left hand.

He gripped them, balling them in his fist. "She wasn't here

117

last night. This place was thoroughly searched after I found that package."

"I know." Serena's soft agreement echoed around him.

The sliding door was open, the light was on. And a young woman sat on the wooden bench he'd nailed to the wall to support himself when he worked on his hobby.

He built trains as a stress reliever. Loved to watch them come together and run around the track. The meticulous detail work let him push every other thought from his head.

Now the dead woman looked like she might snatch the rod of styrene he'd set out a couple of nights before and pick up where he left off.

Dominic stepped inside, careful to stay along the edge as he didn't want to disturb anything. He looked at the CSU team. "How long have you guys been here?"

"Just about three minutes," one of them said.

Tyrone Johnson, his badge read. He introduced himself to the man, then pulled out his phone and texted Hunter the details. Then he sent a quick text to Katie, Chad, and Colton.

All but Colton would be here soon. Colton was involved in something related to the case and couldn't get away. He said he'd explain later.

Then Dominic sent a text to the rest of the task force to let them know about this latest development.

Serena stepped closer, looked at the floor around them, and shook her head. "She wasn't killed here."

"Same as Leslie," Dominic muttered.

"Yes."

"Gunshot to the head?"

A sigh slipped from her. "Yes. I'll check for more wounds in a minute." Serena knelt and looked all around the body without touching or moving her. "Look at her hands and fingers. No defense wounds there."

"Anything under her nails?"

Serena picked up one hand and examined it. "Nothing. She's been thoroughly cleaned, just like Leslie." Serena tested her shoulders. "Her upper body is stiff. Lower extremities are not. Taking in the fact that this building is air conditioned, her body temperature would drop pretty fast. She also has cloudy eyes and this happens around twelve hours after death. I'll be able to get a better time frame back at the lab, but I'd say twelve hours is a good estimate."

She reached down and cut through the stocking. "Look. Lividity in her lower legs and fingertips. She died sitting up with her hands hanging down. It looks like he shot her and positioned her this way. At some point, he cleaned her up."

"What a sicko," Dominic muttered.

"Definitely."

Serena leaned closer. "There's a bruise around her left ankle."

"From a restraint?"

"Probably." An odd look crossed her face and Dominic asked, "What is it?"

"She matches the doll sent to you."

Dominic nodded. "I noticed that right off. She's even wearing the same clothes."

She nodded.

"And yet there's another package." The silver box with the bright red bow glared at him, as though daring him to open it to discover the secrets trapped inside. "I hope this doesn't mean there's another body to be found."

A young woman stepped from the shadows, slipped an instrument into her bag, and said, "It's not a bomb."

Serena shook her head. "No, he doesn't send bombs."

Dominic looked at Tyrone. "Is Rick coming?"

The man shook his head. "He's got enough field coverage for now. He's at some conference learning about machines that can see through walls." Tyrone smirked. "I'm sure we'll hear all about it when he gets back."

"I'll look forward to it," Dominic muttered. He looked up from the package and asked Tyrone, "I want to open this here. Can you do it so we don't mess anything up as far as contaminating the evidence for court? I mean, assuming we get that far."

"Can do. After all, there may be something in there that leads to another clue around here, something that would lead us to her killer, right?"

"Absolutely." Dominic liked this guy. He spotted Mickey off to the side talking to one of the uniformed officers who'd been the first on the scene. "Hey, Mickey, did you get all the pictures you need for now?"

Mickey gave him a thumbs-up and went back to his conversation.

With a glance at Serena, who nodded her permission, Tyrone reached out his gloved hands and picked up the box. The dead woman's hand stayed rigid, but the box slipped easily out from under it.

Serena grabbed her bag and started the evidence-gathering process. She kept shooting glances at the victim's face and Dominic frowned. "What is it?"

"Just wondering about her. Who she is, where she's from, what kind of dreams she had for the future." She paused and bit her lip. "She doesn't look familiar, but remember the note? He said it would be 'someone you know.'" She looked up at him. "Do you know her?"

Dominic leaned in a little closer and took a good look. "No, I don't think so."

A small sigh slipped out as she went back to work. Something more was going on inside her head.

"Come on, what is it?"

Serena shook her dark head. "Nothing."

He laid a hand on her shoulder. "Something. Tell me."

Her eyes met his. "I just . . ." She cast a glance around the scene, at Tyrone who was taking the top off the box, and dropped her voice. "Do you ever get tired of it?"

Dominic didn't have to ask her what she meant. "Yes. I do. Then I catch another bad guy and realize I'm making a difference. That—and God—gives me the strength to keep going."

A slight smile pulled at her lips. "It's funny how life has a way of spinning in a direction you never expected it to go."

"What do you mean?"

The slight flush on her cheeks intrigued him.

"Well," she drawled, "I sure never expected to be working on a case with Dominic Allen."

Before he could respond to that interesting statement, Tyrone said, "Okay, folks, we've got a 4 × 6 index card with writing on it."

Dominic and Serena turned their attention to the man.

"What's it say?" Dominic asked.

Tyrone read, "'Eenie meenie miney moe. I have a mission, I have a plan, I'll finish it soon, you know I can. I left you one, I left you two. Three's the charm, this game's not new. Stay out of my way or it'll be the last thing you do.'"

"He's threatening *us*? Telling us to stay out of *his* way?" Serena said with a frown.

Dominic matched her frown. "Threats don't bother me. Him using my shed to send a message? Yeah. That bothers me. Leaving the doll on my porch? That too." He rubbed his head, weariness rushing over him. Shaking it off, he wondered out loud, "He has a mission, a plan, but will finish it soon. Finish what? How many have to die before he's done?"

"'The game's not new.' What does that mean?" she wondered aloud.

"He's played this game before? With the original Doll Maker Killer?"

Serena rubbed her nose and closed her eyes as she shook her head. "I can't wrap my mind around it all. He's just crazy."

Dominic clicked his tongue and planted his hands on his hips. "Maybe."

Serena opened her eyes and looked at him, brow raised. "Maybe?"

"I'm not saying it doesn't take a twisted person to do this kind of thing, but . . ." He shook his head. "He doesn't have to be crazy to kill. It could just all be a game for him. What if he's not really crazy? What if he just wants us to believe he is?"

"Then that's just even crazier."

"Excuse me, I need to talk to you." Chad's voice came from behind them.

The look on his face sent worry shooting through Dominic. "What is it?"

Chad pulled him outside the shed and said, "Stephanie was in a car wreck."

Air punched from his lungs. Stephanie was Chad's ex-wife. "Is she all right? Was Michelle with her?" Six-year-old Michelle, Chad's daughter.

His face drawn, Chad nodded. "Yes, Michelle was with her, but she's fine, thank God. She came out without a scratch. But . . . ," his voice hitched, "they don't think Steph's going to make it. I've got to go get Michelle and keep her until Stephanie . . . until we know . . . until—" his eyes filled and he turned away, clearing his throat. "I've got to go get her. Stephanie's mother has a heart condition and her dad's not in the picture. I've got to go."

"Of course you do. Don't worry about this case. Get Michelle and do what you've got to do. Your mom and dad, Hunter, Alexia, they'll all help, you know."

Chad nodded. "I know." He man-hugged Dominic and turned to head toward his truck.

Dominic called after him, "Keep me updated."

Chad lifted a hand in acknowledgment, climbed in his truck, and sped off.

Dominic returned to Serena, his heart heavy for his friend, but he knew he had to keep his head in the investigation.

She was still working. The coroner had arrived, ready to transport the body whenever she was finished. Officers still held the neighbors behind the tape.

The tip of Serena's tongue poked between her lips as she probed, took samples from skin, clothing, and everywhere she deemed necessary.

"Is Chad all right?"

"Not really."

Serena stopped and looked up at him. "What's wrong?"

He told her and sympathy flared in her eyes. "I'm so sorry to hear that."

"Yeah, me too."

"Is there anything I can do?"

"Just pray," he said softly. "Pray for Chad and Stephanie and for Hunter too. He's got enough on his plate dealing with Alexia's hunt for our father. And now this . . ." He shook his head.

With a nod and a frown, she went back to the victim. She also went back to their previous conversation. "I never would have thought you'd wind up catching bad guys for a living."

Dominic forced thoughts of Chad, Michelle, and Stephanie to the back of his mind as he watched Serena, fascinated with her thoroughness. He gave a short laugh at her statement, though. "Yeah, well, at the age of seventeen, I wouldn't have thought it either." He shuddered at his remembered youth. He'd been on the fast track to either prison or death when his arresting officer, Marcus Porter, stepped in and took the angry teen under his wing.

Thanks to Marcus and his wife, Dominic had learned that dads weren't supposed to beat their kids or drink until they passed out. Marcus and Rayleen had modeled what a Christ-centered marriage looked like. Sure, they had their disagreements, but they were also determined to work through them without violence or intimidation.

123

"Hey, you in there?" Serena's quiet question jerked him from his thoughts.

"Yes, yeah, sorry. Are you finished?"

"Almost."

Dominic looked out of the shed to see Katie and Hunter working the crowd. Hunter caught his eye and broke away to walk over to Dominic. "I just got a text from Colton."

"What is it?"

"Those nine pictures of the women in that file?"

"Yeah?"

"He's got some info he wants to share with us."

Dominic frowned. "Like what?"

Hunter looked around. "You have a minute?"

"For this? Yeah."

"All right. When Howard put that file together, he neglected to let anyone know what was in it."

"Why?"

"He was taking payoffs."

Dominic stilled. "From who?"

"We don't know. Yet. The money was very skillfully routed to a bank account in his name. Over $300,000 worth of payments since 1996."

"That's the year Lindell was sent to prison."

"I made that connection too."

"What else?" From the corner of his eye, Dominic could see Serena talking to one of the CSU team members. The man smiled and leaned toward her, and Dominic found himself tensing up. He relaxed when Serena stepped back.

Hunter was saying, "So Bell knew more about the Doll Maker Killer than he was letting on."

"Right. We already figured that out the day we talked to him. So, what was he taking money for? Did he gamble?" He glanced sideways at Serena again. She'd moved away from the man and Dominic breathed easier.

"No. His wife was dying from Alzheimer's. Medical bills were eating them alive. Then all of a sudden, the bills started being paid. Howard moved his wife to a high-dollar assisted living home and the search for the killer came to a screeching halt."

"This doesn't make sense. If Howard was covering up and taking payoffs, why would they start in 1996? If Howard had figured out who the killer was, confronted him, then cut a deal, wouldn't that have started prior to Lindell's arrest? Isn't that the whole point of paying off a cop? So you *don't* get caught and go to prison?"

Hunter frowned right along with Dominic. "I know. The timing doesn't make a lot of sense."

"Why start paying a cop off *after* you've been arrested?"

"To buy fake testimony at the trial?"

Dominic shook his head. "Maybe. But Howard testified that they'd definitely arrested the right guy and provided the evidence to prove it, so the money wasn't to buy his silence."

"Maybe not on that score, but what about something else?"

"Like what?"

"Silence about a partner?"

"Lindell didn't want anyone to know someone was working with him?" Dominic nodded. "Okay, that makes sense. But who?"

"I don't have the answer to that one. However, the nine girls in those photos? They each had a best friend."

Dominic stilled as his mind jumped ahead. "Let me guess. Each of the victims that were found."

"Yep."

"And those other nine girls? They're still missing?"

"They are."

"So Howard was covering up information about nine missing girls linked to the victims that were found."

"Exactly."

"Then we need to put all this together and figure out why he would do that."

Hunter nodded. "And why would his partner go along with it when there was nothing in it for him?"

"Did you check Billy McGrath's bank records?"

"Sure did. No sign that he was taking payoffs."

Rubbing his chin, Dominic thought as Serena consulted with Tyrone once again. "Howard could have been giving him his cut on the side."

"Well, if he was, it was cash and the man stashed it in his mattress because there's nothing on his bank records."

"We've got to find this killer," Dominic said.

"I know."

"Because he probably already has his next victim picked out."

———■———

Frank watched his wife button her blouse, straighten her collar, and slick back a nonexistent stray hair. She'd just changed from her navy blue suit, white shirt, and matching navy pumps. She turned and drilled him with her gaze. "It didn't take long for your numbers to slip."

"I know."

"It was that comment you made about abortion." Ice down his back would have been warmer.

"Elizabeth, you know where I stand on that issue. Everyone knows where I stand on that issue."

She snorted. "You know how to play both sides. What made you say such a stupid thing?"

He sighed and rubbed the back of his neck. In his stressed state, he'd made a blunder. One that might hurt him terribly. At the reporter's question, Frank had bristled, let his tight control slip. "That's not what I'm here to discuss. Why does my stance on abortion matter today when we're talking about capital punishment?"

Wrong thing to say.

The temperature had dropped considerably as the stunned audience stared before whispering behind their hands. Even his wide smile and attempt to smooth over the awkward moment with a joke didn't thaw the chill in the room.

Elizabeth walked past him without looking at him. "I'm going shopping. Ian will be taking me."

Frank sighed. He went after her and caught her arm before she reached the door. Turning her to him, he said, "There are things you don't know. Things I'm trying to take care of—" He broke off. Things she didn't need to know. "I'm under a lot of stress right now. I'm sorry, Elizabeth."

Her ice melted a few degrees. "Me too, Frank."

And then she was gone.

17

Serena would be home soon. Watching the house over the last several weeks had proven interesting . . . and frustrating. Serena really had no set schedule. She came and went at all hours, and just when it looked like she might be in for the night, she left again.

How did one learn the routine of someone who didn't have one? This would take some more thought. Serena could wait for now. Lights flashed in the rearview mirror. What was *he* doing here? This cat-and-mouse game was rather fun. Having him show up at the strangest time was interesting—and annoying. What was his plan? Asking him was out of the question. For now. Right now, there was a mission to accomplish and the mission had to come first.

Which meant, right now it was time to find another toy.

Serena stopped in her driveway and opened her garage door. She watched a nondescript blue sedan pull away from the curb a few doors down. Had she noticed that vehicle before? Seemed like she had. Maybe one of her neighbors had gotten a new car?

She shrugged. Then turned back to watch it drive away. With all the weird things happening to her and Dominic, though, maybe she should pay more attention to her surroundings.

Serena shivered although the sun peeked through the dark clouds overhead. She still had about two hours of sunlight left and she planned to use them to work in her small garden out back—if it didn't rain.

Or should she stay in the house? The image of the first doll left by the killer wouldn't leave her. And while it looked an awful lot like Leslie, it occurred to her that it could pass for her too.

She looked to the sky as though she could see straight into heaven by doing so. "I need your help, Lord. I feel like I'm spinning my wheels. Help me leave work behind and take a break from it. I'm weary and really need to recharge."

She pulled into the garage and closed the door behind her, then looked over at her boat. She hadn't used it all summer. Sadness hit her. It seemed all she did lately was work.

Maybe she should invite someone to take a spin around the lake this weekend.

Dominic's handsome face immediately came to mind and she grinned. Yeah, maybe she should do that. Then she frowned as she remembered Lyle Ames. The man she thought she'd marry. The man who'd wanted her to be someone else. She shook her head. Where had her judgment been?

But Lyle had been so different from her father. Or so she'd thought. Not that she really had anything against her father, except the fact that he'd never been home. Never had time for anything she was interested in. He'd been passionate about his work at the law office and she'd been passionate about school and her friends.

And yet, she loved her father. Very much. She looked up to him and admired what he did.

But she didn't want to marry a man like him.

So why was she so attracted to Dominic? A man who seemed

to be very much like her father when it came to being in control and thinking he knew best about almost everything.

She sighed and let out a small groan.

Maybe she was wrong.

She felt her muscles relax a little. She pulled out her phone and sent Dominic a text, asking if he'd like to join her on the lake Saturday. Just for a couple of hours. They needed a break.

She felt slightly guilty even thinking about going out and having a good time, because she felt quite sure the killer wasn't taking time off. But if the ones chasing him burned out, what good were they going to be to the investigation?

Walking into the den area, Serena felt peace wash over her. Even though someone had breached her security system, with the added features and a new code, she felt safe in her home once again.

Yoda nudged her hand and she gave her silky ears a scratch. Moving to the window, she looked out into her backyard. The garden took up the right-hand corner.

The sky darkened and thunder rumbled.

"Well, Yoda, I don't think we'll be pulling weeds this evening."

Yoda padded to her bed in front of the fireplace and settled on it, never taking her big brown eyes from Serena's face. She smiled. "Okay, we'll read a book."

She walked to the bookshelf, her mind still on the events of the day. A gentle rain began pattering against the window as she considered her options.

Her doorbell rang and she spun. "Who . . ." Uneasiness slithered through her. She walked to the front door and peeked through the side window.

Camille.

Serena cut the alarm off and opened the door. "Hey, get in here out of the rain. What are you doing here?"

Camille swiped water from her eyes and stepped inside the foyer.

She looked pale and drawn, her teeth chattering in spite of the warmth of the evening.

"I went home to get some things. I thought my dad would be working. But he got home earlier than I—" She shrugged and tears welled up. She blinked them back and set her jaw. "You might say he's still not happy with me."

"Come on in the den. How wet are you?"

"Not too bad." She shook her head and a few raindrops flew from her short blond strands.

Serena shut the door and pulled the girl into the den. "Have a seat. You need a towel?"

Camille sat and twisted her fingers together in front of her. "No, I'm okay. I'm sorry. I probably shouldn't have just shown up here."

"It's all right," Serena reassured her. "But the best place for you is Covenant House."

Camille dropped her eyes. "Maybe. I just didn't feel like being surrounded by a bunch of girls right now."

So she'd sought out Serena. "What do you want me to do, darling?"

Shaking her head, Camille swiped at a stray tear. "There's nothing you can do. I just . . . miss my mom," she whispered. "And I think you remind me of her a little bit."

Serena's heart clenched. "I'm so sorry."

Camille swallowed hard and shrugged. "It is what it is." She sniffed. "But what's really hard is that I didn't just lose my mom that day, I lost my dad too. He changed overnight. It's like he hates me because I survived the wreck and she died."

Serena didn't bother to try to offer reassurances. She'd only met the man one time and noticed how he could barely stand to look at Camille. "Do you look like your mom?"

"Yeah. I know that's part of the problem. I'm a daily reminder of what he lost."

"Instead of a daily reminder to be thankful for what he has," Serena murmured.

At her words, Camille broke down. Sobs wrenched from the girl's throat and all Serena could do was hold her.

Pounding on her front door caused them both to jerk. Camille shot to her feet and Serena followed.

"Oh no! That's my dad. He must have followed me. He's going to kill me for coming here."

Alarmed at the words, Serena grabbed Camille's arm. "Has he ever hit you?"

"No, but . . ."

That didn't mean there wouldn't be a first time.

Serena thought about the gun in her end table as she walked to the front door, forcing a calm she didn't feel. "Who is it?"

"You got my girl in there!" Fists beat against her door.

"Mr. Nash, stop pounding on my door, please. You're scaring us." Camille cringed to the side.

The racket ceased, but Serena kept a hand wrapped around her cell phone just in case. "Now, before I open the door, would you please tell me why you're so angry?"

"You're stealing my kid!"

"I'm doing no such thing. Camille just came for a visit—"

Camille reached around her and opened the door before Serena could stop her. "I just came to talk to her, Dad."

Red-faced, unshaven, with rage still glittering in his eyes, the man before them snarled his disbelief. "You're going to leave me too, aren't you? Just like your mother."

"Dad, you told me to leave!"

"My presence. Not the house. Now come on." His rough hand reached out to snag his daughter's wrist, but Serena stepped in between them before he could get a good grasp. He lurched back in surprise, uttered a few choice words, and glowered at her. But he didn't come at her or make her feel like he planned to attack her.

"Don't manhandle her." Serena kept her voice low and even. "Please. She needs your help, not your anger."

He paused and narrowed his eyes. Serena shuddered at the look in them. "You telling me how to raise my kid?"

"No sir, I'm telling you . . ." Serena stopped. She didn't want to make things worse for Camille. "No. I'm not."

"I didn't think so," he growled. Then he turned his attention back to Camille. "Get home. Now."

Camille slid around Serena with an apologetic—and fearful—look. "I'm just going to go now."

"You can stay here," Serena blurted.

"No, she can't," he answered for Camille and shot both of them a threatening glare.

He started to walk away and Serena whispered to Camille, "You call me if you need me. Or 9-1-1, you understand?"

The girl nodded, then was gone with her father. A father who was so lost in his grief and bitterness that he couldn't see the damage he was doing to his child. A child who'd gone looking for some love and affection and found herself pregnant.

Serena's heart broke for both of them as she shut the door and rearmed the alarm. What could she do? What *should* she do?

Should she call the police? And tell them what? She was afraid a father was going to hurt his daughter, but wasn't sure?

Right. That would go over well.

Finally, after thirty minutes of agonizing, she decided there was nothing she could do at the moment. She'd offered Camille shelter in a secure place at Covenant House and Camille had chosen not to stay.

Still . . .

Serena pulled out her phone and texted, ARE YOU ALL RIGHT?

Relief filled her at the immediate reply. YES. HE'LL GO TO SLEEP AND IGNORE ME. I'M FINE. SORRY FOR THE TROUBLE.

YOU'RE NO TROUBLE. I PROMISE. CALL ME IF U NEED ME.

I WILL.

With a sigh and prayer for Camille's safety, Serena tucked her phone away and turned her mind back to her original plan, hoping to relax and forget her world for a few moments.

Which brought her attention back to the books.

A good suspense? She grimaced. No way, the last thing she needed was more suspense in her life. She needed some comic relief. Serena looked over at Yoda who still watched her. "How about some laughs?"

She wondered if she'd find any laughter, though. Camille's situation still weighed heavy on her heart even though the girl had promised she was all right and would call for help if she needed it.

Yoda cocked her head and lifted an ear.

Serena reached for the pink covered book and froze as her gaze landed on the shelf above.

Her high school albums.

She whispered aloud, "Eenie meenie miney moe, a killin' I will go. It's my game, it's my fun, the next to die is someone you know."

Someone you know.

First Devin, then Leslie.

Both from her high school graduating class.

As though in a trance, she settled her hand on her senior year album and pulled it from the shelf. As she walked to the couch, she opened the album. Serena sat down and flipped to the first page of student photos. Not even Chewie's sudden appearance distracted her.

Frozen in time, the faces of smiling classmates from ten years ago stared up at her. One by one, she studied their faces, then turned the page. She'd graduated from a large high school with about five hundred students in her senior class. But as her eyes ran over each face, memories washed over her.

And there was Jillian Carter. Blond curly hair and sky blue eyes. Her porcelain features always made her seem so fragile. Breakable.

She and Alexia both had felt the need to protect her, shelter her whenever they could.

But they hadn't been able to protect her from whatever had sent her running from the graduation party.

Serena's eyes strayed to the mantel. To the three bricks just below the oak wood. "What are you hiding from, Jillian?" she whispered.

With a sigh, she went back to the album, continuing her perusal of the faces. And then she stopped.

There she was. The one Serena had been searching for.

Patricia Morris.

The girl from the shed.

"And that makes three from my class," Serena said aloud. Chewie stopped cleaning her front paw and cocked her head at her. Yoda's ears perked and she gave a low woof before going back to her nap. "Devin, Leslie, and Patricia." But Devin's killer was dead. His death had nothing to do with these two girls. Did it?

She tossed the album onto the couch beside her and hurried into the kitchen to grab her cell phone from her purse.

Punching in Dominic's number, impatience had her pacing the floor as she waited for him to pick up.

When it went to voice mail, she said, "Call me when you can. I know who our shed victim is. And I think I see a pattern emerging. The killer seems to be targeting my classmates from my senior year. We need to warn them."

Hanging up, she continued to pace, her thoughts whirling. Back and forth, back and forth.

At the next turn near the window, a masked face popped up. Serena screamed and stumbled back.

━■━

Dominic hung up the phone and dropped his head into his hands. Hunter was concerned about Chad and rightly so. *God, help Chad.*

He's come a long way in a short time. Don't let him fall back on alcohol to numb the pain. Show me what to do to help him.

Hunter had talked with Dominic about Chad drinking himself into a mind-numbing stupor. Not because he wanted to make Chad look bad, but because he needed an extra pair of eyes on the man in case this car wreck involving his ex-wife and daughter sent him over the edge.

Dominic wasn't sure what else he could do except let Chad know he was there if he needed him. And he could pray.

The buzzing of his phone reminded him someone had beeped in while he was midconversation with Hunter.

Amen.

He entered the code to get his voice mail as he stood at the kitchen counter and sorted the day's mail. File folders awaited him in his den area, but he wanted to take a moment to unwind before he worked several more hours.

Dominic paused when Serena's voice filled his ear. He straightened as he listened, his full attention now on her message. When it finished, he hung up, then dialed her number.

She answered on the first ring, her voice breathless. Scared. "Someone's outside my house."

He grabbed his keys from the counter and headed for his car. "Where? What'd you see?"

"A face in the kitchen window. He has on a mask." He could hear the strain, the toll it was taking on her not to give in to the panic. He slid into the car, cranked it, and backed out of his drive.

"Did you call 9-1-1?"

A left turn and he was out of his subdivision, heading toward Serena's.

"Yes, I have them on the other line. My landline."

"I can be there in five minutes." Fortunately, he didn't live far. No answer. He tensed as he made a right turn.

"Serena?"

"I'm here, I was just checking the locks again."

"Do you see anything else? Hear anything?"

"No, but the cops are here." Her relief echoed through the line.

"I'm almost there."

"I've got to go let them in. I'm fine now."

But I'm not, he wanted to say. *Stay on the line with me until I get there.* But he didn't. "Okay, I'll be another couple of minutes."

A small pause filled the line, then she said, "Thanks, Dominic."

A thought occurred to him. "Are you holding a gun? The one you shot your intruder with?"

"Yes."

"Go put it up before you answer the door, okay? Don't answer the door holding a weapon. Cops don't like that, all right?"

"Right. I knew that. The dispatcher said the same thing, but I wasn't ready to let go of it yet. I'll do that now." He heard her footsteps tap across what he assumed were hardwood floors. Then she came back on the line. "All put away."

"Good. Now hang up and talk to the officers. I'm thirty seconds away."

"See you in a few."

She hung up and Dominic turned into her subdivision, taking in the substantial homes and manicured lawns. He made his way to 104 Bennett Drive and pulled behind a cruiser. Making sure his badge was visible, he climbed out of his car and walked toward the front door.

If the cops did their job right, one officer would be inside, the other sweeping the perimeter of the house for the reported intruder.

Dominic knocked on the door and the officer inside opened it. With a glance at Dominic's badge, his brows raised. "FBI?"

"He's a friend," he heard Serena say as she stepped into the foyer.

The officer whose name tag read "Trask" stepped back and let him in.

Serena looked pale, drawn, and stressed. He walked up to her and pulled her into his arms. She melted against him and let him offer comfort in the only way he could right now. Then she gathered herself together and pulled back.

He glanced at Officer Trask. "What happened?"

"She was just getting ready to get into that."

Serena lifted her chin and motioned toward the den. "Let's go sit down, please."

Dominic and Officer Trask followed her into the tastefully decorated area. He took in the leather couch and matching love seat and recliner. The dog bed in front of the fireplace and the mantel full of photographs.

Homey. Comfortable. Welcoming. A pang hit him. Not for the first time, he wondered why he couldn't have grown up in a house like this with parents who loved him and—

Shutting that line of thought off, he sat beside Serena on the couch. On the coffee table, he noticed the open high school album.

She took a deep breath and said, "I was in the kitchen, and when I looked at the window, this face with a mask popped up." She shuddered. "Scared me to death."

The door opened and closed. The other officer entered the room. Tall with dark skin and hard eyes, he looked like he'd seen a few years with the force. His name tag read "Taylor." Dominic introduced himself and asked, "Find anything?"

"Footprints under the kitchen window. The ground is soft from the rain and it's obvious someone was out there. But he's gone now."

"Can you get a cast of one of the prints?"

"There wasn't a real clear one." Officer Taylor shrugged. "Probably someone looking to see if anyone was home before he broke in to rob the place."

Serena looked at him, her protest almost visible on her lips. Dominic gave a slight shake of his head and said, "It's possible Serena has a stalker. Do you think you guys could ride by a little more often tonight?"

The officers exchanged a glance. "Sure, we can do that, but it might be better if she finds another place to sleep tonight."

"No." Serena's voice was low and tight. She looked at the men in her den. "I'm not going anywhere. I may not sleep as well, but he's not chasing me out of my home."

"Serena—" Dominic started to protest and she cut him off with a shake of her head.

"I'm not doing it."

And the stubborn set of her chin said she wasn't. "What if you have someone come stay with you?"

Serena pinched the bridge of her nose, then rubbed her eyes. "Maybe."

"What about Alexia? Just for the night?"

"I suppose that would be all right." A ghost of a small smile appeared on her lips. "Actually, that would be nice. I'll call her in a minute." She bit her lip.

"What are you thinking?" he asked.

"I work with Adopt-a-Sis, and I had a rather scary confrontation with a girl's father tonight."

He frowned. "What? When?"

Officer Trask leaned in, his attention fully on Serena.

"Right before the person with the mask appeared in my window." She told them the rest of the story.

"You think it was him?" the officer asked.

She shrugged. "I have no way of knowing. I wouldn't think so, though. He strikes me as the type of man who wouldn't bother with a mask."

"We'll check it out," Officer Trask said. "You have his name and address?"

Serena gave it to him, glad someone would be going to Camille's house, but . . . "Can you be real subtle? I don't want him to think I sent you out there because of him coming to my house. I'm afraid he might take it out on Camille."

"Sure. I know this address. We get called out to that neighborhood on a regular basis. A cop car riding by won't set off any alarms."

"Okay, thanks." She looked at Dominic. "I want to show you something."

Dominic saw the officers to the door, then walked back into the den to see Serena holding her yearbook. "Look." She held it out to him and pointed to a picture. "Do you recognize her?"

His heart thumped as he snatched the book for a closer look. "The woman in my shed."

"Yeah. She was in my graduating class."

His eyes locked on hers. "That's what you said in your message."

"We have to find them—each and every one—and warn them. And not just the women, the men too. Because while he's only killed women, it doesn't mean he won't branch out and start killing males."

"We just need to contact the local ones," Dominic said, his mind already on the almost impossible task. "I'll give this to the task force. We'll pull in a few more people who can do this grunt work. We'll also run a segment on the news, warning the class of 2002 to be on guard."

"But won't that warn the killer that you've picked up on at least part of his MO?"

"Yes, but I don't think he cares about that. He had to know we'd figure that part out pretty easily."

"I know a few people still living in town that I can contact. We need to warn Alexia and Christine and . . ." Her hands twisted together and he covered them with his own.

"You did great, Serena. You caught this much earlier than I would have. Call Alexia and let me worry about this."

She nodded, squeezed his hands, then picked up the phone.

And Dominic prepared himself for a sleepless night. Serena didn't have to know it, but he'd be parked outside on the curb, watching—and getting permission to take this case a step further with the media.

———■———

The handcuffs snapped into place. Kelsey stirred and murmured, eyelids fluttering. The killer already had the other girl situated at the table opposite Kelsey.

"What . . . ?"

"Wake up, Kelsey, it's time for the fun to begin."

Kelsey blinked, and the killer watched the girl try to focus.

The killer looked at the one seated across from Kelsey and saw the confusion written in her eyes. Soon that confusion would clear. She would be a good player. She had put up a good fight when she had realized what was happening, the fury in her eyes sparking the killer's interest, spiking the anticipation for a good round of play.

18

Frank Hoffman sat at his desk, staring out the window. The tension was getting to him. He'd lost weight and the bags under his eyes attested to his lack of sleep. Even Elizabeth had said something to him this morning about his haggard appearance.

Thankfully, she hadn't brought up his blunder at the last debate again. His campaign manager, Elliott Darwin, had managed to smooth things over, but warned Frank to keep his head on straight and his mind in the game. Frank promised he would.

His phone rang and he ignored it, his mind spinning with ideas, plans to find Jillian without jeopardizing his political career.

He shuddered to think the outcome lay in the hands of someone else. But his contact had promised to take care of it. Only the fact that his contact had as much to lose as Frank kept him from taking over and expanding his options.

But he couldn't.

He had to keep his hands clean.

He couldn't do anything that would lead back to him.

Something he'd managed to do until Jillian had been in the wrong place at the wrong time. He still found the whole thing

142

surreal. One moment out of thirty years in politics could ruin his entire future.

Frank picked up the phone and pressed speed dial for the one who was supposed to be taking care of this problem.

He answered on the third ring. "Hello?"

"I think we need to change our strategy."

A pause. "Really? How so?"

"I think we just need to get rid of her."

"What about the package?"

"In the chaos of her death, we'll plant someone at the house who can look for it." The more Frank thought about it, the more he thought that was the thing to do.

"Assuming she hasn't told anyone about it."

Frank considered that. "I don't think she has. If she was going to say something, I have a feeling there would have been cops on my doorstep by now. But I can't take a chance or count on her being quiet forever. She may be weighing her options."

"Or keeping quiet to protect her friend."

"Or that." *Or figuring out if she wants to blackmail me.* Frank saw his secretary pass by his office and waited until he was sure she was out of earshot. Rising, he walked over and shut the door. Phone still to his ear, he said, "But we need to act fast and it needs to look like an accident."

"I already have a plan in motion. If you can be patient a few more days, she'll be dead and no one will think anything more of her death other than she was just another tragic victim."

"Victim? Of what? And how can you be sure?"

The voice on the other end hardened. "I'm sure. Let me take care of it."

Frank rubbed his eyes. "All right. A couple more days. But either find the package or take her out. Or both. Both would be best."

"You hired me to take care of this. Stop thinking and let me do it. You focus on the election. I've got your back."

"Right. You've got my back." He just hoped one day there wasn't a knife sticking out of it.

———■———

Serena smelled coffee. Her stomach rumbled and she looked at the clock on her end table.

A gasp escaped her and she threw the covers off. She needed to be at work by 9:00 for a meeting and it was already ten after eight. She gave a quick glance at her phone and found a text from Dominic. ALL QUIET LAST NIGHT. HAVE CRUISERS DOING DRIVE-BYS. CALL IF YOU NEED ME. WILL SEE YOU SOON.

She frowned. How did he know it was quiet last night?

He'd stayed, watching the house.

Warmth invaded her heart and she felt herself staring into space thinking about the man. His goodness, his protective instincts, what it was like to kiss him . . .

Her eyes strayed back to the clock and she jerked, muttering, "Quit mooning over the man and get moving."

After a record-breaking quick shower, she dressed and walked into the kitchen to find Alexia sitting at the table, sipping a cup of coffee and watching the morning news on the 17" flat screen television Serena had recently mounted in the corner.

"Morning."

Alexia's green eyes slid from the screen and she smiled over her cup. "Good morning."

"How long have you been up?" Serena asked as she moved toward the carafe.

"Just a few minutes. We stayed up way too late last night talking."

A grin curved Serena's lips. "Tell me about it. But I have to admit, I'm glad. I needed the girl time."

Alexia's red curls bounced on her shoulders as she nodded her agreement. "I'm sorry it took you getting scared to death to get me over here."

Sadness took over. "I know. I'm sorry. It seems like we're all so busy, there's never any time for fun and relaxation anymore."

"Especially with a serial killer stalking the streets."

"Stalking our classmates," Serena murmured.

"Are you sure it's not just some crazy coincidence?"

"No, I'm not sure at all, but I'd rather play it safe by warning as many people as possible than ignore the possibility."

"I agree. I'll see who I can get in touch with too."

"That would be great. Keep a list so we don't duplicate our efforts."

Alexia nodded to the television and picked up the remote to up the volume.

The announcer was saying, "Authorities report that a serial killer seems to be targeting the Columbia High School class of 2002. Already, Leslie Stanton and Patricia Morris have been identified as victims of this killer, both graduates in 2002." He looked at his coanchor. "Coincidentally, the class of 2002 is working on their ten-year reunion to take place at the end of September."

The pretty woman shook her perfectly styled dark hair. "I have to say I'm glad I graduated in 1998. This is simply a terrifying time in our city right now. If you know these victims and think you might have anything relevant to add to the investigation, we urge you to call our hotline at 1-800-TIPACOP."

Serena frowned at the television. "I can't believe they released those notes. What were they thinking?"

"That they're smoking out a killer?"

"Maybe." She smirked at Alexia. "*Smoking* out a killer?"

Her friend shrugged. "I can't help it. It's in my blood."

Serena glanced at the clock. "I have a meeting at 9:00. I need to go." She rounded the table and gave Alexia a hug. "Thanks for coming over."

"Anytime." Alexia paused. "Hunter said something about preferring I stay over here anyway."

"He's still worried the guy that kidnapped you is going to come back and try again?"

"Yeah." She shivered and frowned. "I can't say the possibility hasn't occurred to me."

"Hunter's staying close to you, isn't he?"

"Real close." Her frown slid into a soft smile. "I'm not complaining."

Alexia sighed and Serena grinned. "You sound positively sappy."

Her friend laughed. "I am. You want me to come back tonight?"

Serena cocked her head as she gathered her keys and purse. "That depends. How's your mom doing?"

"Better. She's home resting. I'm getting ready to head over and check on her."

"Are she and Michael getting serious?"

Alexia grimaced. "I think so." The fact that Alexia's mother had been dating the pastor at her church when Alexia had come home several weeks ago was a shock to her friend.

"Why the screwed-up face? I thought you liked him."

"I do. I just . . ." She shrugged. "I don't know. It's just still weird, that's all."

Serena smiled. "You'll get used to it."

"Yeah, I think I'd better. I think he's going to ask her to marry him just as soon as she's recovered well enough to handle it."

Serena gave her friend a pat on the shoulder. "She could do worse."

This time Alexia's look was heated enough to fry eggs. "She *has* done worse."

"True." Alexia's father had been a real loser when she'd been growing up. Serena was afraid if her friend found him now, nothing would be different. Once a loser, always a loser?

True, God could change a person, but still, the man she remembered was the stuff of nightmares. She wasn't sure anyone could change that much. Keeping her opinion to herself, she said, "I've got to run. If you want to come back tonight, I would love it, to be honest. You check your schedule and let me know."

"Sure. I've got to go too." Alexia gathered her purse and overnight bag. "I'll see you later."

She watched Alexia drive off and closed her eyes briefly to offer up a prayer for the law enforcement officers working this case. *Please let them catch this guy.*

In the garage, Serena opened the back door of her SUV and dropped her purse and briefcase on the backseat. She shut the door and climbed into the driver's seat, her mind clicking like crazy.

She started to crank the car when something caught her eye. She turned and saw the doll sitting there on her passenger seat.

She gasped, gaped.

Then ordered her mind to function.

Bolting from the car, she raced out of the garage, looked around the surrounding area, and saw nothing that alarmed her. Nothing to indicate someone had been near her car.

Shock and fear making her legs weak, she stumbled back to her car to grab her phone from her purse. She punched in Dominic's number and waited. He answered on the first ring.

"Hello?"

"I need you to come over to my house. The killer's been in my garage."

"What!" His shout stung her ear and she grimaced. Before she had time to explain, he said, "I just left there two hours ago. I'm on my way."

"I'm calling Rick. Then I've got to call Alexia and tell her. She was here when the killer was, she needs to watch her back."

"I'll get everyone else."

Hands shaking, she dialed and lifted the phone to her ear once more.

Rick answered on the second ring. "You need something?"

"Yes, I need you to process the evidence sitting in my car."

"What do you mean?"

"I mean bring your kit and come on over to my house."

"Okay, see you in a few." Rick sounded puzzled, but it would all clear up for him once he got over here.

Ten minutes later, Dominic pulled into her driveway, jaw tight, eyes flashing.

"Show me."

———■———

Dominic stared at the doll sitting in Serena's car. She looked completely different than the other ones. Straight light brown hair, hazel eyes, two little hoop earrings pierced through the ears. Dressed in a pair of jeans and a short-sleeved T-shirt.

And the 4 × 6 note card with the cryptic little message.

Serena read aloud, "'Eenie meenie miney moe, now you see her, now you don't. The game is close but the clock ticks on. King me, checkmate, or are you just a con? Look close, look near, she's calling your name. It's your move, it's your play in this cat-and-mouse game.'" She licked her lips and repeated, "Look close, look near, she's calling your name."

Dominic grunted. "He references checkers with the 'king me' thing. And chess with the checkmate statement." Pursing his lips, Dominic blew a disgusted raspberry. "He's a really bad poet."

Serena shook her head. "He may be a bad poet, but he's good at confusing me. There's no dead body again, just the note."

"Yeah, no package either, just the doll." Dominic pursed his lips and looked at the doll again. Then he met Serena's gaze. "Was your car locked?"

"No, it was in my closed garage. I didn't even think about locking it in here."

For the next ten minutes, they bounced ideas off one another as to how the person who had left the doll had gained access to her garage.

"I was here all night," he muttered and paced. "The windows are tight. Locked," Dominic noted as he looked around the area. "I tested them the other day and it doesn't look like they've been touched."

He nodded to a door. "I assume that leads to a storage area?"

"Yes, but I keep it locked." She walked over and tested the knob. "Still locked."

He nodded. "All right."

"Hey guys, what do you have for me?" Rick called as he walked up the drive.

Serena waved him over. Mickey trailed behind him, camera ready for action.

Rick looked in the car and let out a low whistle. "Well, this makes things even more personal, doesn't it?"

"Just a little," she agreed, not bothering to filter the sarcasm.

Rick examined the door. "I'll see if I can get some prints off the handle, but if you've already touched it, I'm not sure what I'll get."

"I touched it to open it. I didn't see the doll sitting there until I was already in the car."

"Well, the doll's in the passenger seat, maybe he used the other door."

Colton walked up. Serena greeted him. He said, "Dom filled me in when he called. Hunter's got someone tailing Alexia today." He looked at Serena. "I'm sure he would be grateful if you wouldn't mention that to her."

Serena shook her head. "I won't say a word. Whatever works to keep her safe."

Colton nodded, then jerked his head at the doll. "Does she look familiar to you?"

"She could be anyone." Serena paused. "If the dolls are actually supposed to represent real people. And it's beginning to look like that's the intent."

"All right," Rick said. He walked around to the back of the vehicle. "Can you pop the back?"

She clicked the button on the remote and the back hatch lifted as though in slow motion.

"Um, Serena? I think I know what the message means."

She walked around to the back and sucked in a deep breath. A young woman stared up at her with dead milky hazel eyes. The bullet hole in her forehead gaped.

Serena looked at Rick, then Dominic. "He's not wasting any time upping the body count, is he?"

"Do you recognize her?"

"No, but that doesn't mean she's not in my yearbook." She swallowed hard. "Is the task force making any headway on contacting the class?"

"Yeah," he said, sounding subdued, "but this one obviously didn't get the message soon enough."

An hour and a half later, Serena slipped off her gloves and blew a stray hair from her face. Sorrow snagged her and wouldn't let go. Three women dead now. Plus Howard.

Because of what?

What was this all about?

"We've got the pictures, so let's get this stuff bagged. We'll need to keep your car, Serena."

Serena grimaced. "I don't like it, but all right."

"You'll like it if we get a print or two that gives us a hit and leads us to the killer."

"True," she sighed.

"Need a ride to the rental car place?" Dominic asked.

She looked into his eyes. His kind, concerned, bright green eyes. "Looks like I do."

"I'll be happy to volunteer for taxi duty." Those eyes crinkled at the corners as he offered a sympathetic smile.

"And I'll let you." Exhaustion swept over her and she realized how long they'd been diligently working the area. It felt like she'd been up twenty-four hours straight. But it was only 11:00 in the morning. This case and being stalked by a serial killer was wearing her down.

Serena stood. "Why is this sicko leaving a doll and a dead body in my car?"

"He left a package on my front porch, a dead body in my shed, a doll and a dead body in your car. He's leaving messages all over the place," Dominic murmured.

"Yes, but what do they mean?" she asked. "I don't understand what his messages mean other than I'm—we're—targets." She sliced her hand through the air to emphasize her point. "Okay, I get that. I'm tired of his games."

Dominic nodded. "I am too, but we can't stop now. He's already planning his next move."

Serena allowed Dominic to usher her out onto the driveway. The sun still beat down and she broke into an instant sweat.

Rick was just finishing up. He looked at her. "She's on her way to the morgue."

"Thanks."

After getting what she needed, she climbed into the passenger seat of Dominic's F-150. Once she'd gotten her rental, she said goodbye to Dominic and headed to work.

She'd called Daniel, her boss, and explained that she was going to be late but hadn't told him why. When she walked into her office, she saw Paul on the computer. He looked up at her entrance. "Hey, everything okay?"

"I'll explain later. What'd I miss in the meeting?"

"Nothing. It was postponed. Daniel was called into a meeting with the bigwigs first thing this morning and said we'd meet later."

"So what time are we meeting?"

Paul glanced at the clock on the wall. "In thirty minutes. They're serving us some kind of cheap bag lunch thing from the cafeteria." He stood and nodded toward the body on a nearby table. "Patricia Morris. I'll have her prepped for you before the meeting."

Thirty minutes later, Serena slipped into her lab coat, then into the chair in the conference room for her hour-long meeting. As she munched on the chicken salad sandwich, chips, and apple provided, Daniel discussed cutbacks and what he was doing to try to preserve everyone's job.

Paul leaned over and whispered, "If they'd let us buy our own lunch, that would save a few bucks."

Serena smiled. "I don't think it's going to matter in the long run."

Paul didn't smile back. "If I lose this job, I'm toast."

Patting his arm, she whispered back, "I know, Paul. That's why Daniel's doing everything he can to make sure that doesn't happen."

He gave a slow nod, but the furrows over the bridge of his nose told her he was still worried. Then Daniel called for her report.

She gave an update on the autopsies she'd performed and got her assignments for the rest of the day and tomorrow.

After the meeting, she walked to her office, her mind spinning with everything going on. She had two autopsies today. Patricia Morris and the Jane Doe who'd been placed in the back of Serena's car. She was anxious to get to them and see if she could get some answers that would help the authorities find the killer.

Then she would catch up on her paperwork. And at some point, she really needed to touch base with Camille. Serena sent the girl a text asking her to meet her for an ice cream at the park later this afternoon.

Paul strode along beside her. "We only have two today."

"I know."

"That's not good." At her lifted brow, he hastened to assure her, "I mean, not that I want people to die, but what if Daniel sees that I'm not very busy? He may think you can handle everything on your own."

Serena walked into her office, motioned Paul inside, and shut the door. "Paul, you're a great assistant, one of the best I've worked with. You're insightful, smart, and seem to know more about diseases, drugs, and death than I do." His lips quirked at that statement. "In fact, I've often wondered why you haven't gone on and become an ME." He shrugged and looked away. Serena said, "You've had wonderful evaluations and I know for a fact that Daniel thinks very highly of you. We both want you here and we'll fight for you, okay?"

His blue eyes met her gaze once more. Some of the tension left his shoulders and his jaw relaxed. "All right. Good enough. Thanks."

"You're welcome. Now, let's go see what Patricia has to tell us."

Unfortunately, Patricia didn't have a lot to say. And so far, neither did Jane Doe. Serena had called Daniel in for help on the autopsies in order to finish them and get the results for the police fast. With his and Paul's help, they'd discovered nothing new, but at least they were finished. Daniel left after telling her to call him if she needed anything else.

Everything Serena had deduced while at the crime scene was just reinforced by Jane Doe's autopsy. Dominic had arrived toward the end, ready to take Serena over to the prison for their meeting with Drake Lindell.

Looking up, she told Dominic, "The bullet in Patricia's forehead killed her. There's no trauma, no defense wounds, no sign of sexual assault, nothing." Her gaze bounced back and forth between Dominic and Paul. "She's been cleaned up—post-mortem. I haven't even found a stray hair. There was some residue from the shed, of course, but nothing that will lead us to the killer. At least nothing obvious. Maybe the lab will find something more." She sighed and frowned. "Jane Doe's results are pretty much the same. I'm stumped and I don't like it."

"What about the tox screens?"

"I'm waiting on them."

"What about Leslie's tox screen?"

"Still waiting on that too. I called about it before I started Patricia's autopsy and Christine said she'd have it to me ASAP." Serena removed her gloves and threw them in the red hazardous waste bin to her left. She walked to the computer in the corner and with a few clicks saw the information in her inbox. "And Christine was as good as her word. It's back."

Serena pulled up the document and read while Dominic stood behind her, leaning over her shoulder. "She had some alcohol in her system, but it's about the amount you'd have if you had a glass of wine with dinner. No red flag there." She scrolled down. "But here. Wait a minute. What's this?"

"What?" Dominic moved closer. Crowding her. She inhaled a whiff of his spicy cologne and decided she didn't mind his close proximity. Blinking, she focused back on the screen.

"Scopolamine."

"What is that?"

"A drug." She drew in a deep breath. "Well, that's interesting."

"I know it's a drug. What kind?"

"I don't know a lot about it, but—"

"I can tell you about it," Paul said.

Serena's fingers halted on the keys as she said, "Okay, fill us in."

Paul slipped his gloves off and tossed them in the red biohazard materials bin. "It's used to render victims helpless, docile. And it's not like the common date rape drug, Rohypnol, better known as roofies. With scopolamine, the drug blocks any formation of memories, so victims don't have a memory of anything they do or anything that happens to them while under the influence of it."

"What about hypnosis?" Dominic asked.

Paul shook his head. "Nope. Hypnosis isn't even an option, because with hypnosis, you're looking for a repressed memory. Unfortunately, with this drug, the way it works on the mind, there's no memory to bring forth."

"And you know this, how?" she asked.

154

Paul pursed his lips. "I was in pharmaceutical school for two years before I dropped out."

Dominic shook his head. "Scopolamine. I'd never heard of it before this case, but now that you say the name, I recognize it from seeing it in one of Drake's files. Where does the drug come from? Where would someone like this killer get it?"

"It comes from Bogota, Colombia, mostly," Paul said. "That's where the tree grows. But most people who want to use it illegally don't bother harvesting the drug from the seeds that are scattered all over. They just get it from Ecuador already in drug form. It's used for human trafficking, robbing people blind, all kinds of rotten things."

"Is it available in the States?"

"Yes, just not very widespread as it is in Bogota."

Dominic rubbed a hand down his cheek. "Why is the fact that this drug was in Leslie's system so interesting?"

Serena exchanged a look with Paul, then turned her gaze to the white board with the nine known victims of the Doll Maker Killer. "Because it was found in the systems of every one of those girls."

19

Dominic eyed the chart. "Okay, I think it's beyond time to pay Mr. Drake Lindell a visit."

Paul stepped around and said, "I'm going to leave that stuff to you guys. I have another appointment I need to get to if you don't need me anymore."

"Sure, go on," Serena said. Then she looked at Dominic. "I guess it's just you and me then."

"I guess." He smiled. That worked just fine for him.

"I'll need to take my car, though. I might be meeting a friend later."

"Oh." Hoping he sounded casual, he asked, "So, who are you meeting? Alexia?"

"No. Another friend."

"Ah." She didn't want to tell? She was meeting a guy? The dart of jealousy took him by surprise.

Then she sighed. "I'm working with some girls, troubled girls who've been kicked out of their home, runaways, et cetera. One particular kid who has a grip on my heart seems to need a little extra TLC. And I find myself wanting to give it to her." She looked at Dominic. "It's Camille, the one who showed up at my house last night. She really needs to know someone cares about her, and I told her I'd meet her today at the park."

Relief swept over him. It wasn't a guy. Then the rest of her words registered and admiration filled him. "When do you find time to do that?"

A smile curved her lips. "I don't find it, I make it."

As he walked Serena to her rental car, he picked up his phone and called Terry O'Donnell at BSU, Quantico. Although Terry's main job with the Behavioral Science Unit was as a research analyst, he spent a lot of his time tracking down missing people. "Hey, I want you to check on the Lindell family."

"Lindell? Drake Lindell? The Doll Maker Killer?"

"That's the one. See if there's any connection between them and Ecuador or Bogota, Colombia, will you?"

"Sure."

Thirty minutes later, Dominic stepped into the prison and felt Serena behind him.

He couldn't believe she'd insisted on being there. But he supposed the doll on his doorstep and the one in her car had freaked her out enough that she took the threat personally.

He didn't blame her.

If the tilt to her chin said anything about the way she felt, he figured it might be in his—and Drake's—best interest to stay out of her way.

Or be honest and tell her what she needed to hear.

"You okay?"

"Just fine, thanks."

The metal door clanked shut behind them and Serena flinched. She composed herself fast enough, but her moment of vulnerability touched him, made him want to protect her.

He squelched the feeling.

For now.

———■———

Walking the corridors of the prison made her nervous. Like she'd done something wrong. And when they were ushered into a small visiting area, her pulse rate accelerated and she felt like the walls were closing in on her.

Claustrophobia.

"Is he going to be in the room with us?"

"Yes. We'll also have a guard in the room and one outside the door."

"I thought he'd be on one side of the glass and we'd be on the other." The thought of coming face-to-face with the man who'd killed those women turned her stomach. And made her mad.

Dominic shot her a glance. "Are you going to be all right?"

She nodded. "I'll be fine. I've just never really come across anything like this in all my days of working as an ME." She'd had some doozies but had definitely never walked into a prison to confront a killer.

"You don't have to stay. I can do this, and I promise I'll tell you everything."

Serena shook her head. "For some reason, I feel compelled to stay." At his raised brow, she said, "Don't worry, it's not because of some weird fascination. The killer has made this personal. He's made this about me—and you. I'm hoping Mr. Lindell will have some answers about that. And I might have a question or two for him I need to be here to ask. To see his face when he answers."

Dominic didn't have a chance to respond. The door clanked open. One guard entered followed by the prisoner and another guard.

She was rather relieved to see he had chains on his hands and feet but was surprised when she looked into his eyes. A light blue, they didn't hold the hardness she'd expected. They landed on her first.

"Hello, Mr. Lindell," Serena said with a nod.

"You must be Dr. Hopkins." His low, gravelly voice vibrated through the room.

"I am."

Dominic said, "And I'm Special Agent Dominic Allen with the FBI. Thanks for agreeing to meet us."

Drake settled into the chair opposite her and Dominic and rested his hands on the table. The chains gave a loud clank, but the man didn't seem to notice. His once blond hair was now gray. He shrugged and offered a wry smile that reached into eyes. "My schedule was pretty open today."

Dominic gave a low chuckle and Serena leaned back in her chair, allowing her shoulder muscles to relax a fraction.

This man was a cold-blooded killer?

She continued to study him while Dominic took the lead. "We have a few questions for you concerning the women you killed back in the nineties."

Drake's eyes didn't change, but a subtle thread of tension ran through him. Serena saw it and felt her own muscles respond in kind. Then Drake let out a low sigh as he lifted both hands to scrub his face.

Then he looked at them. "So you still think I'm the one."

"And you're still protesting your innocence."

Drake nodded. "I am. My attorney is in the process of filing another appeal."

"I know." Dominic shifted. "I hear you've changed, found the Lord."

A soft smile crossed Drake's lips. "Indeed. The church service here is one of the highlights of my week."

Serena wasn't so sure about his claim of being saved. While that was between him and God, something just didn't ring true. Something in his eyes . . .

She leaned forward. "Mr. Lindell, I'm the medical examiner working with the FBI and we've had three murders that mimic your . . . ," she paused, then reworded, "that mimic the Doll Maker Killer's MO."

He stilled. For a moment he didn't even blink. "Oh?"

Dominic took over. "You keep saying you're innocent. Okay, let's say that I believe you for a moment. Do you have any idea who would want to frame you for the murders? Any idea who the real killer is?"

Lindell let out a slow breath and shifted in his seat. His eyes lifted toward the lone barred window in the room. "No. I just know I didn't kill them."

Serena watched his body language. His fingers remained clasped together, but she didn't see them flex. His gaze remained calm even though his nostrils flared. She found herself wanting to believe the man.

"Have you ever heard of the drug scopolamine?" Serena asked.

"Of course. It was the drug used by the killer to incapacitate those women before he killed them." Drake shifted, his eyes bouncing between her and Dominic. "It was mentioned at the trial, but I hadn't heard of it before then."

"And do you have any connections from Ecuador?"

"Ecua—" He broke off and shook his head. "That's a new one. No."

"Bogota, Colombia, or Ecuador is where the drug originates. Most people who use it for nefarious purposes generally get it from there. I looked up your trial transcript. I'm amazed no one questioned you about that. Apparently, they just assumed that you got the drug from somewhere here in the States."

Serena glanced at Dominic, wondering what he was thinking. His furrowed brow told her his mind was working, mulling over each and every nuance the man gave off.

"The evidence was found on your property," Dominic said, changing the topic.

"In a secret room under the shed in my backyard. Yes, I'm aware of all of that."

Dominic spread his hands, palms lifted. "Well, if you didn't put the evidence there, who did?"

Lindell's lips tightened and he shook his head. "I don't know. I never went out there. It was an abandoned shed that I dragged home one afternoon. I was working all hours because the cleaning business had taken off. That shed sat there for two years without me ever paying it the slightest attention. I haven't a clue how that stuff got there." His eyes lifted to meet hers.

Serena cocked her head. Nothing about him said he was lying. No nervous twitch, shifting eyes, or defensive body language.

"You're protecting someone," Serena said softly.

The man jerked and narrowed his eyes at her soft statement. For the first time since they'd entered the room, he showed emotion other than calm, cool, and collected.

She'd nailed it, she knew she had. "Who are you protecting? One of your children?"

He stood abruptly and she froze. The guard stepped forward, ready to intervene, but Drake waved him off. "I'm not going to do anything." To Serena and Dominic, he said, "We're done here."

Serena didn't say anything more or try to stop him from leaving. Neither did Dominic. One thing she noticed before the guard led him away.

Drake's eyes.

They resembled hard chips of ice.

20

"What do you think?" Dominic asked Serena as they left the prison.

"I don't know if he killed those women or not, but I think he knows who did."

Dominic nodded. "And I think you were right when you said he was protecting someone. Possibly one of his kids?"

"Yeah."

"The question is, which one?" Dominic pulled his car keys from the front pocket of his khakis.

"Well, it's not the one in prison. He's been there almost as long as his father, right?"

"Right. That gives us three others to choose from."

"We have to find them first."

"We know where one is." Dominic glanced at his watch. "What time are you meeting your friend?"

Serena frowned. "She was supposed to call me if she was going to make it." Serena wanted to go with him to see Nate. But she really needed to check on Camille. Torn, she hesitated.

Dominic offered, "Why don't you come with me to the law office? It's only about five minutes up the road. If Camille calls, I'll run you back to your car."

"Okay. That sounds great."

Her phone buzzed. Camille? No. A text from Paul. She read aloud to Dominic. "Tox screen on Patricia shows scopolamine. No other drugs indicated."

Dominic looked at her. "You're not surprised, are you?"

"No. Unfortunately, it's what I expected."

"Come on then, let's go."

They climbed into his car and made the little jaunt to the law office where Nate worked.

When they pulled into the parking lot, Serena shook her head. "Five minutes away from his father and he hasn't seen him in almost twenty years."

"If your father had done what Nate's had, would you go see him?"

Serena bit her lip. "I don't know. If I was the one he was protecting, maybe." She looked at the sign near the door: THE LAW OFFICES OF JAMISON, LINDELL, AND CRAINE. "He's done well for himself," she murmured. Four cars were scattered in the parking lot and a black Lexus sat in one of the reserved spaces.

Inside, cold air blasted and Serena shivered but was grateful to be out of the heat.

A receptionist who looked to be in her early sixties greeted them with a professional smile. "May I help you?"

"Dominic Allen and Serena Hopkins. We're here to see Mr. Lindell," Dominic said.

Serena noticed that he didn't flash his badge or give their credentials. Interesting. He wanted Nate to feel at ease.

"Of course," the woman said. "He's expecting you." She glanced at the phone on her desk. "He's on a call right now. Just have a seat and he'll be with you shortly."

Serena sat in the nearest chair. Dominic chose to pace the floor.

Five minutes later, a tall man with a military-style haircut, piercing blue eyes, and blond hair appeared in the doorway. His eyes landed on Dominic and Serena. Nate stepped into the waiting area and held out a hand. "Nathan Lindell. You can call me Nate."

Dominic shook the proffered hand. "Thanks for agreeing to see us."

"No problem. Come on back to my office."

Serena stared at Nathan Lindell as she tried to figure out her first impressions of the man whose father had murdered at least nine people. She thought he looked a lot like a younger version of Drake, short blond hair, intense blue eyes. Nice looking but not overly so. He would blend in with the crowd.

And yet she thought she'd seen him somewhere before. "Do I know you?"

Nate gestured for them to sit in the two comfortable chairs facing his desk. Instead of sitting behind the desk, Nate pulled a chair up so they all faced each other. "I don't think so. What can I do for you?"

Dominic said, "We wanted to—"

"You came to the morgue," Serena blurted with an apologetic look at Dominic. Then she turned her gaze back to Nate. "Right after Leslie was killed. That was you."

Nate blinked. "Oh, the morgue. Right. Yes, that was me."

"Did you know Leslie? You left in such a hurry . . ."

Nate let out a sigh and shook his head. "No, I didn't know her. I'd seen the news report and," he gulped, "it sounded so much like . . ."

"What your father had done twenty years ago?" Serena asked.

"Yeah." He rubbed his hand across his lips. "Seeing that just brought everything back. I found myself in my car, then talking my way into the morgue. I couldn't believe it. She'd been found with a package on her and she had a bullet hole in her forehead. The news said she'd been missing for several days before they found her." He lifted his shoulder in a helpless shrug. "It all added up."

Dominic said, "And that's why we're here. We're investigating this recent killing that appears to be following the MO of the Doll Maker Killer."

Nate flinched. "It's been awhile since I've heard that name."

"Do you think your father killed those women?"

"Yes."

His quick, without hesitation, answer took Serena by surprise. Dominic merely blinked. "We do too."

"But," Nate said as he lifted his left ankle to rest it on his right knee, "my father maintains his innocence."

"Why don't you believe him?"

"Because of what I saw the night I called the police to report what was in the shed in the backyard."

Dominic leaned forward. "You were the anonymous caller."

"Indeed." Nate's eyes were shuttered and Serena imagined that he hated to dwell on whatever it was that he found that night. "Three girls have died now. I heard about the notes on the news. Have you figured out who they're for?"

Dominic shot a look at Serena, then said to Nate, "No. Do you know who the killer would target?"

Nate rolled his eyes. "How would I know?"

"Right," Dominic said. "I don't guess you would. Well, the last one we find pretty interesting. It seems to be a threat directed to the officers."

Dominic pulled the copycat's latest message from his pocket and handed it to Nate, who studied it. "Hmm. Yes, it does, doesn't it? Seems to be. But sometimes things aren't always what they seem." His brow furrowed and he seemed to lose himself in deep thoughts.

"What do you mean?" Dominic asked.

Nate looked up. "I don't really know what I mean. My father always seemed to talk in circles. If his note says one thing, it probably means something else."

"But your father didn't write this note," Serena said.

"I know."

Dominic said, "So . . . you think the note was meant for . . . who?"

The lawyer shrugged, then grimaced. "I have no idea. I'm just . . . not thinking straight right now."

Serena spoke up. "We think your father was protecting someone. That he may not have actually done the killing, but maybe had a partner that helped or planned the kidnappings and murders."

Nate blinked as though shoving off unpleasant thoughts. Then as her words registered, he frowned. "That's something new. Why would you think that?"

Dominic explained about the copycat killer. "The thing is, though, he's not following the Doll Maker Killer's MO exactly, but enough to make us believe these new deaths are by someone who was also involved in the deaths almost twenty years ago."

Nate tapped his hands on his knee, his expression closed, while Dominic talked. When Dominic finished, Nate rose and walked to the coffeepot sitting on the side bar. He poured himself a cup and offered each of them one. Serena accepted. Dominic shook his head. "No thanks."

When Nate handed her the mug, she said again, "I think he was protecting someone."

Again Nate's expression didn't move. Serena tried again. "Do you have any idea who could have been his partner?"

Nate sat once again. Took a sip of his coffee then said, "No, I don't. I've done my best to forget those years and rehashing it isn't going to unearth anything new. If you've got someone out there killing using my father's MO, then you've got a serious problem on your hands." He set his coffee on his desk. "Unfortunately, there's nothing I can do to help."

"Nothing?" Serena blew on the hot brew, then sipped. Surprise hit her. Nate liked good coffee.

The man let out a sigh. "Have you talked to my sister? Gwen?"

"No. We haven't been able to locate her."

"Hmm. Well, I haven't seen her since the trial, but she might be able to help you more than I can. She and Drake were tight."

"You call him Drake?"

"I'm certainly not calling him my father," Nate spat, contempt dripping from him.

Serena didn't blame him.

"You said they were tight," Dominic said. "Tight how? What kind of relationship did they have?"

"One that was exclusive. No one else could come between them. My father had his girl." A glimmer of something Serena couldn't identify flashed in the man's eyes. Hatred? "He was big on the idea of having a 'Daddy's girl.' Being the hero, the god that his little girl looked up to. He got all that with Gwen. From the time she was born, my father lavished her with gifts, elaborate toys, trips to theme parks." Bitterness laced his voice.

"And he didn't do any of that for you, did he?" she asked.

At the sympathy in her voice, Nate sighed and rubbed a hand down his face. "No. He didn't. And he didn't do it for my two younger brothers." He shrugged. "Drake and Gwen were always together when he was home, secretive, laughing at some private joke." Another shrug. "It was weird, not incestuous or anything like that—it was just like they were in their own little world when they were together, with no room for anyone else. And if you tried to wedge your way in, or if you did something Gwen didn't like, well, trust me, you paid for it."

"You were afraid of her?"

"Yes." He didn't elaborate, but Serena caught the slight shudder that went through him.

"Do you know where she is now?" Dominic asked.

"Not a clue and I don't want to know. After Drake was found guilty, she was a basket case for weeks, crazy, talking to herself, yelling at shadows. Then one day she just disappeared."

Serena frowned. "What about that statement she gave to the

167

newspapers about how he'd shamed their family and she never wanted to talk to him again."

Nate gave a short humorless laugh. "He got caught." At Dominic's confused look, Nate said, "She was angry he was in prison. He'd failed her because they could no longer be together. At least that's my theory."

"And yet she never went to visit him?"

Nate lifted a brow. "Really? I find that hard to believe."

"There's no record of her being there," Dominic said.

Nate shrugged. "Like I said, I don't have anything else to add."

"So," Dominic said slowly. "You think she was involved in the killings?"

Nate paused, glanced out the window, and shrugged. "No. I don't know. When he was caught, I think she was genuinely surprised, horrified, and . . . hurt. Hurt that he would do the things he did, devastated that he could hurt our mother the way he did. Betray us the way he did." He shook his head. "It was— unfathomable."

Dominic nodded, sympathy emanating from him. Serena could tell he felt for the man. Dominic's own father, while not a serial killer, had contributed to his sister Karen's death, had a heavy fist with his family, and was basically a horrible man. Fortunately, Dominic had had Marcus Porter to show him the way a man was supposed to behave, believe, and *be* on the inside. It didn't sound like Nate had ever had that.

"Have you ever heard of a woman named Allison Kingston?" Serena asked, breaking the silence.

Nate cocked his head. "The name's not familiar. Why?"

Dominic said, "She's been writing your father, talking about how she admired him and is so sorry he's in jail. How unfair it is that he was found guilty and how she'll be waiting for him when he gets out."

Nate snorted. "He's not ever getting out."

"No, but we're not sure that this woman is fully in touch with reality to realize that fact."

"I would say not."

"So you're sure you don't have any idea where your sister is? A wild guess would even help us out."

"No, and I'm happy to keep it that way. The less I even hear her name, the better I feel. And I really don't want to discuss this anymore. Like I said, I've spent the last twenty years trying to forget everything related to the man who contributed to my existence." His revulsion spoke much louder than his words.

Serena cast a glance at Dominic who nodded and frowned.

"Please. Just a couple of more questions. Do you have any connections with anyone in Bogota, Colombia, or Ecuador?" Dominic asked.

"Bogota?" He tapped his lips as his brows drew together. Shaking his head, he said, "No. But if I remember correctly, we had some cousins, distant family that lived in Ecuador." He gave a short laugh. "Haven't thought about them in years."

"Really? Because your father said he had no connection to either place."

"Well, technically, he doesn't. They're my mother's family. However, he lied if he said he didn't know anyone there."

"Was your sister close to them?"

He shook his head. "Not that I recall." He shrugged. "Then again, they could have visited them on one of their little father/daughter trips and I'd never know it."

Dominic handed Nate one of his cards. "If you hear from her, will you let me know?"

The man hesitated and Dominic rushed to reassure him. "You don't have to tell her we came looking for her."

Nate gave a slow nod and reached out to take the card. He slipped it into his right front pocket and said, "All right. But I really don't think I'll hear anything from her." He laughed, a short sound that reminded Serena of something more like a cough. "I mean, I haven't heard from her since she disappeared. Why would you think she'd surface now?"

Serena sighed as she thought about the gifts. "Call it a gut feeling."

"Could you give me the names of your relatives in Ecuador?" Dominic asked.

The lawyer shook his head. "I think Rafael Perez was the name of a cousin or a second cousin who was around my age." He shrugged and held up his hands. "I'm sorry, I can't think of anyone else. It was a very long time ago and I never met them, just overheard conversations."

Dominic stood and Serena took that as her cue. Standing, she held out her hand and Nate shook it. Dominic already had his phone in his hand and, after a quick handshake, said to Nate, "Thanks so much. We'll be in touch."

"I hope you find her." He sounded dubious, as though he didn't believe they'd be successful.

"We will." Dominic's tone left no doubt that *he* thought they would.

Serena wished she had his confidence. Her head ached and muscles she knew existed, but hadn't thought about in a while in relation to her own body, throbbed.

Once outside, Serena and Dominic walked to his car. She noticed his tight shoulders, his roving eyes. Always alert. "You think the killer's watching?"

"It wouldn't surprise me." He opened the car door for her and looked around. "Do you feel like you have a target on your back?"

"Nope. My forehead."

Dominic flinched at the thought of Serena with a bullet in her head. "No more joking about being targets. Gives me the creeps."

She dared to laugh. "What? The big bad FBI guy has the creeps?

I thought you guys joked all the time in morbid fashion. Like it's some kind of ritual."

"We do." He slid into the driver's seat and cranked the car. Serena slammed her door and fastened her seatbelt.

Morbid jokes were the norm around the office. He participated in the fun most of the time, but when it came to joking about Serena and death, he didn't want to think about it, much less joke about it.

He dropped the subject and dialed BSU again. He hoped his computer forensics buddy was working today.

Terry O'Donnell picked up on the second ring. "What can I do for you, Dom?"

"I need you to track down a Rafael Perez. Last known location, Somewhere, Ecuador. He's a relative of Fanny Correa Lindell. Do a search for her, you'll probably find him."

"Any more info?"

"Yeah. If you come up empty in Ecuador, try Bogota, Colombia."

"Okay, got it. I'll find him and get back to you."

"One more thing."

"Shoot."

"Gwendolyn Lindell. I need you to find her too. Last known location, her home address in Columbia, South Carolina." He rattled it off for Terry.

"That it?"

"For now."

"Sit tight. I won't be long."

Dominic hung up. "We'll know something soon."

"I thought you already looked for Gwendolyn and couldn't find her."

"Yep, but we now have some new information. Terry may be able to put out new feelers, check old ones, and come up with something that'll give us an indication of where she is."

"I sure hope so." She remembered her text. Should she bring it up? Maybe he wasn't interested in spending a few hours on her boat. She bit her lip, then blurted, "I'm taking the boat out Saturday. Are you interested in going with me?"

Dominic nodded. "Sure. That would be wonderful."

"I'd already planned to take tomorrow off to run errands and work around the house, get my mind off all of this craziness. Soaking in the warm sun will feel good regardless."

He reached over and took her hand in his and squeezed her fingers. "A couple of hours in the sun will do us both some good. I'll make sure Katie and Hunter are still running down the leads Saturday morning and offer to switch off with them another time. I don't want this case sitting idle for one second."

"I understand, and I also understand if you don't want to go. I almost feel guilty even asking."

"Don't. We're human and we have to recharge or we'll fall apart. I didn't answer your text right away because I wasn't sure I'd be able to go. My mother's friend, Michael, wanted Alexia and me to go eat with him and my mom Saturday morning." He gave a brief smile. "I think he's trying to get to know us a little better. Anyway, they've decided to do dinner instead. So, all that to say, yeah, a couple of hours on the water sounds great. We've been going nonstop on this case. Some downtime is needed or we're going to crash and burn."

Relieved he hadn't just been ignoring her invitation, she felt silly for even thinking he had. But she really wanted him to go with her. The more time she spent with him, the more she wanted.

But was it because he made her feel safe—or because she really wanted to be with him? "How is Stephanie doing?"

His jaw tightened. "She's still hanging in there. Michelle keeps asking about her, of course, but the docs said she shouldn't see her yet."

"I'm so sorry."

"Me too." He took a deep breath. "So, early?"

"Early's fine."

"I'll be at your house around 8:00?"

"Perfect."

In the prison parking lot, he pulled up behind her rental, and she got out of the car. "Thanks for the ride."

"Anytime."

As she reached for her car door, Dominic called out, "Serena."

She turned to see his window rolling down as he leaned across the seat toward her. "You hungry?"

She lifted a brow. "Always, why?"

"Would you want to go to that little café around the corner from my office and grab a bite to eat?"

Her stomach flipped. "Sure." Spend more time with Dominic or go home to Yoda and Chewie? A no-brainer. "I'll follow you over there."

"Parking's probably tight right now and we go right by the hospital. How about you leave your car there and I'll drive us over?"

A relieved smile spread across his face. Had he thought she'd turn him down? Did she look stupid?

Serena climbed back in the passenger side and shut the door. She smirked at herself, thinking how much her feelings for him had changed since childhood. She'd gone from schoolgirl crush straight into an adult longing to get to know the man better.

As Dominic pulled out onto the street, she glanced in the side mirror, wondering if someone else was following them. Seeing no one there, she still couldn't help the shiver that danced across her skin or the feeling that this string of dead girls was just getting started.

21

THURSDAY, 7:17 P.M.

Dominic held the door open for her and she stepped into the refreshing cool of the interior. An assortment of smells assaulted her and she breathed in deeply. Baking bread, parmesan, cinnamon, sizzling steaks. Her stomach rumbled.

"Are you sure you have time to do this?"

"Hey, a man's gotta eat, right?"

She laughed. "Absolutely. So does a girl. But I know things are crazy with this investigation . . ." She shrugged.

"I asked you, remember? Besides, I wasn't sure you'd say yes. Now that you have, you can't back out."

"If you're sure."

"Well, it's either eat with you or grab something at the drive-thru. I'd rather eat with a beautiful woman." At her lifted brow, he paused. "Let me clarify that. Not any beautiful woman. Just you." Serena smothered a grin as he sighed. "I think I'm going to stop talking now. I just keep shoving my foot deeper down my throat."

Serena let out a genuine laugh. Seeing this side of him was a treat. He always seemed so self-assured, confident, like he had control of the world and everything in it. This not-quite-secure, little-bit-awkward Dominic was intriguing.

And he thought she was beautiful.

That was good to know. She knew that a lot of men liked the way she looked, but the only man's opinion that mattered right now was Dominic's.

Some of the day's weariness slid from her shoulders as Serena slid into a booth. Fifteen minutes later, as she speared a bite of salad, she said, "You think you'll hear something from Terry soon about Gwendolyn Lindell?"

"I think so. He's one of the best when it comes to tracking down someone." He paused a moment, took another bite, then asked, "So, why did you come home?"

His abrupt question made her jerk and he laughed. "Sorry. My mind's jumping from one topic to the next."

She gave a low chuckle. "It's fine." Then a small sigh escaped her. "I left Spartanburg because . . . it was time."

"Alexia said she was a little surprised you'd come home because you had some good friends in Spartanburg."

"I had some very good friends. And I miss them, but . . ." Did she really want to get into it?

"But?"

He wasn't going to give her a choice but to scrape at the scab that had started to heal over the gaping wound. "I was dating a guy and I knew he was getting ready to ask me to marry him." Dominic froze and Serena saw wariness enter his eyes. "Hey, you asked."

The wariness receded and he nodded. "Yeah. I did. Go ahead."

She shrugged. "He wanted to get married, settle down, have a few kids."

"And you didn't?" A frown played around the corners of his lips.

"I did. He just expected me to quit my job."

"Ah . . ." Realization danced across his face.

"Yeah," she said softly. "Ah . . ."

"So you broke it off?"

"I had to. I want a family, but I love my job and I'm not ready to quit. Yet."

"Yet?"

"Maybe one day. For a few years until my children, if I end up having some, are in school. But he didn't agree to that. He meant quit my job. Period. And I couldn't see myself doing that."

His brows drew together at the bridge of his nose. "I can't see it either. Sorry."

A slow smile curved her lips. She couldn't help it. She really liked this man. Flashes of her childhood, the times in his home, turned the smile into a frown. "Tell me about what happened to you after you left home. Alexia thought you hated her."

Dominic went quiet and Serena wondered if she'd stepped over the line with that question. Then he nodded. "I did hate her for a while. But now I know her actions probably saved my life. There's no telling where I would have ended up if she hadn't done what she did."

"Alexia said you'd forgiven her for calling the cops on you and having you arrested for the drugs, but she hasn't said a whole lot about your background and how you came to work with the FBI."

He shook his head as he sipped his tea. "It's really quite amazing. God gave me another chance. Fortunately, I was smart enough to recognize it before I destroyed it."

Serena watched him, took in each expression that flitted across his face. She knew he was letting her see a part of him he usually kept closed off. "Dad was there when Marcus responded to Alexia's call. As you can imagine, Dad showed up and started beating on me. Alexia tried to jump in, but Dad knocked her out cold. Marcus intervened and arrested Dad and me."

"Wow."

"Yeah. Anyway, Marcus made some kind of deal with the judge, got the charges dropped, and took me home to live with him and his wife." She thought she saw moisture spring to his eyes just before he looked away. Clearing his throat, he said, "They taught me what it means to be a God-fearing man. One with integrity and ethics and compassion for others. Marcus became the dad I always wanted but never had."

"Why would he do that?" Serena thought about her own father. While he was a good and generous man in a lot of ways, he'd never take a chance on bringing home a juvenile delinquent. If he did and the kid broke the law or caused trouble, it could tarnish the man's good name.

Dominic wiped his mouth with his napkin. "I asked him after I graduated from the academy."

"What'd he say?"

"He showed me a picture of a kid who was about fourteen years old. It was their son, Joe, who'd been killed in a car wreck about three years before. Marcus said when he arrested me, he was viciously angry. He saw me, a kid throwing his life away on purpose, whereas his son's life had been snatched from them. He railed at God about the unfairness of it all. And he said God just told him to help me."

"So he did."

"Yeah. So he did." The last sentence was so soft, she almost didn't catch it.

"But he had to have seen kids your age doing that almost every day in his line of work. Why would he react that way with you?"

Dominic shook his head. "I have no idea. I think I just happened to be his breaking point, the one he had to make a difference with. So I went to the police academy, but moved on to the FBI. I found out that my background, my years of living on the streets when Dad's drinking raged out of control, my drug knowledge, all of that made me a really good undercover cop."

Serena gazed at him, saw the determination in his eyes and the goodness lurking underneath. "I'm glad you're the one working this case."

His gaze snagged hers and he offered her a slow smile. "I am too." Then the smile disappeared. "I'm sorry that it took a serial killer to bring you back into my life." His hand reached out to grasp her fingers. "But I have to say, I'm glad you're in it."

Senses and pulse all aflutter at his words and the look in his eyes, Serena pulled in a steadying breath as she searched for the right response.

Her phone buzzed, causing her mind to blank. His lips pulled up at the corners and he let her hand go. "You need to answer that."

"Probably." Still, she didn't move to do so.

The phone buzzed again.

He smiled wider and the dimple in his right cheek flashed at her. "Go ahead. I'll wait."

Serena snagged the phone from her pocket. "Hello?" She couldn't help the small twinge of irritation that made her voice sharper than usual.

"Serena? This is Colton."

"Colton? What's up?"

"Just wanted to let you know that the man you shot is waking up. I'm on the way to the hospital now. If he has anything interesting to say, I'll give you a holler."

"I'll meet you there."

Dominic's eyes rose to meet hers. He'd finished his salad and downed the last of his tea. She hung up and he asked, "What is it?"

"He's waking up."

"The guy you shot."

"Yes." She rose and placed a twenty on the table. "I could catch a cab."

"I'll take you." Dominic stood with her and added another bill to the table. She was grateful he didn't try to insist on buying her dinner. This wasn't a date. Yet.

"Are you sure?"

"I'm sure."

"I'm sorry to be so much trouble."

He took her hand. "You're no trouble, trust me."

And she did. Trust him.

Without another word, he led her back to his car. She glanced at the clock on her phone.

8:02.

It had been a long day and didn't look like it was going to end anytime soon.

Wishing she'd snagged a coffee for the drive, she forced her mind to focus on what lay ahead. She was finally going to get to confront the man who'd broken into her home, terrorized her, and ended up on the floor with a bullet in him.

A bullet she'd delivered.

She gulped back her fear and glanced at the man beside her. Thank God that he was with her. She hated to admit it, but he made her feel safe. Safer. And that made her frown. She'd always been very independent, mostly relying on herself—and God—to get her through the tough times.

But this was turning into one of the toughest things she'd ever come up against, and having Dominic in her corner felt good.

Her phone vibrated. She glanced at the caller ID, forced her mind to switch gears, and answered it.

"Camille's back and said she desperately needed to see you." Mrs. Lamb, the director of Covenant House, spoke softly, her words causing Serena to bite her lip.

"She was supposed to let me know if she wanted to meet in the park."

"She said she didn't want to be out in the open. Afraid of her father. They had another fight."

"How is she? Appearance-wise?"

"Scared, underweight, fidgety, and looking over her shoulder."

Serena frowned. "Have you seen her father anywhere on the premises?"

"No. I haven't noticed him and no one has come asking about her."

Dominic looked at her and raised his brow, silently asking if everything was all right. She mouthed, "Camille."

He nodded.

To Mrs. Lamb, Serena said, "All right. Keep an eye out for the man. I'm in a tough spot right now and I don't think I can get there tonight. Did she say she'll stay there?"

"Yes, she's too upset to go home and asked if she could stay tonight. I'll tell her you'll talk to her in the morning if you don't get a chance to call tonight."

"All right. Thank you."

Serena ended the call and laid her head back on the headrest, exhaustion nearly overwhelming her. She felt Dominic's hand on her arm and looked over at him. The concern on his face stirred something deep within her.

"I feel like I'm being pulled in a hundred different directions," she said.

He gave her arm a gentle squeeze. "I'm here for you. You don't have to do this on your own."

His words wrapped around her and lifted the weight from her chest, replacing it with a warmth that held more than just gratitude. "I know." She smiled at him, her throat tightening with emotion. "That means . . . a lot."

At the hospital, Dominic pulled into a spot reserved for the police. Several other cruisers were parked, lights flashing. "I wonder what's going on?" he asked aloud.

They climbed out and Serena led the way, anxious to see the man and grill him with a few questions.

180

Like what he was after in her house.

As they rushed toward the door, they were stopped by a uniformed officer. "You can't come in here right now."

Dominic flashed his badge. "What's all the commotion?"

"A missing kid. We've got the hospital on lockdown."

"We need to get up to the fourth floor."

The officer's radio crackled. He listened, then said, "Ten-four." He looked at them. "Found the kid. Go on up."

As they headed for the elevator, a mental picture of the package Jillian sent shot through her mind and she wondered how her intruder would know about that. "Hey, slow down a bit, will you? I just about ran a little old lady down."

She turned to see Dominic rushing to keep up with her and slowed. "Sorry, I guess I'm so used to dodging people in this place that I forget others don't have the art form down."

He laughed and stepped up beside her. Serena found the elevator and pressed the button.

"I hope he's able to answer a few questions," she muttered, and tapped her foot impatiently.

"Did Colton say whether they'd managed to ID him yet?"

"Not yet."

The elevator doors slid open and Serena waited for the people to unload. A young mother with two toddlers took her time ushering them into the hall. A slim figure in a baseball cap and ripped jeans brushed past her, nearly knocking her off balance.

Serena grumbled under her breath at the rudeness of some people and thought about taking the stairs when the elevator was finally empty. She rushed inside and jammed her finger on the button that would take them to floor number four.

When the doors opened once again, Serena hurried off the elevator to rush to the nurses' station—and found it empty. "That's odd."

Dominic looked around. "The place is deserted."

Serena rounded the desk and started pulling charts until she found the one she was looking for. "John Doe. Room 423."

Together, she and Dominic headed down the hall. Heart thumping, she found the room on the opposite side and came to a halt. "I think we found where everyone is." Nurses and security hovered outside the room. Looking inside, she saw one head she recognized.

"Colton?"

The detective turned, his expression fierce. "He's dead."

22

All the air left her lungs.

Dominic's voice rumbled in her left ear. "What?"

She pushed past everyone to stare down at the man with a small hole in his forehead. To match the one that had entered above his left ear. The one that she'd put there defending herself. The one in his forehead said murder.

His empty eyes stared back.

When her gaze landed on the small gift box sitting on his lap, his hands neatly folded around it, she gaped. "Dominic? Do you see this?"

"I see it." He looked at Colton. "What have you done so far?"

"CSU is on the way." Colton rubbed his chin and studied Dominic. "Looks like this case and yours are connected in a big way. If you want to take the lead, I'll step back."

Dominic nodded. "I would appreciate it."

Colton planted his hands on his hips, ready to take direction. Serena admired the man who was so confident in himself. He knew how to lead but was willing to follow when the situation called for it.

"All right," Dominic said, "we need everyone to clear the room."

He looked at the nearest nurse. "Do you mind calling security? I'll need video from every camera with an angle on this room along with hospital entrances, elevators, and parking lots. I want to know what this guy was driving."

Serena saw the woman's hands still held a fine tremor, but she nodded and made her way back to the nurses' station.

Next Dominic addressed Colton. "Where's the cop assigned to guard the room?"

"Haven't seen him. Been too busy to look for him."

Dominic nodded to another officer. "See if you can track him down." He then looked at Serena. Shaking his head, he rubbed his chin. "This is going to throw Debbie's analysis off the chart."

The profiler.

"Why?"

"Because this isn't the serial killer's MO. I mean, it is, but he's never killed a male before." He paused. "Other than Howard. But we know why he killed Howard."

"Because of what he knew," Colton muttered.

"So," Dominic pinched the bridge of his nose, "he had to get rid of this guy too." He blew out a breath. "I need to call Katie and Hunter. And Debbie. Excuse me for a few minutes." He looked at Colton. "Let me know when security gets here."

Dominic got back on the phone, discussing the new killing with Debbie. Serena stared at the man on the bed. Who was he? Why had he been in her house? Why did the serial killer want him dead?

Questions swirled, but no answers followed. She just knew that somehow she was suddenly *very* connected to a killer and it scared her spitless.

"He's only been dead for a short time," she said.

"I just checked on him about forty-five minutes ago," a soft voice said from the door. "He buzzed the nurses' desk saying he wanted more water but was too weak to get it." Serena and Colton turned to find the same nurse who'd called security standing there.

The woman took a deep breath. "I'm Hannah Grant. I am . . . was his nurse."

"So he was killed sometime between . . ." Serena looked at Colton. "What time did the call come in saying he was awake?"

"I noted it on his chart," Nurse Grant said. "But I remember. It was 7:13. I was in here changing his IV bag and he grabbed my hand." She pressed a hand to her stomach. "Nearly scared me to death."

"And he asked for water," Colton said.

"Right. Actually, he gestured. He couldn't talk with the tube in his throat. I checked his vitals and called the doctor who came immediately and took him off the ventilator."

"And I received the call at 7:33," Colton said, then looked at Serena. "I made a couple of other calls, wrapped up a few things, then called you."

Serena frowned as she studied the machinery. "No alarms went off?"

The nurse shook her head. "No."

"So whoever killed him knew exactly which buttons to push to make sure the alarms didn't sound."

"Which was why I came back to check on him this last time," Nurse Grant said. "I noticed the heart monitor wasn't reading up at the desk. I walked back here and found him." Tears welled in her pretty green eyes. "At first I just stood there staring at him, I couldn't believe it, then I called the police."

"Who called me," Colton said. He shrugged. "It was my case."

"Yes," Serena drew in a deep breath. "Your case that's now tied in with a serial killer."

A knock on the door made her turn. "Hi, Rick. Short staffed again?"

"Unfortunately." He nodded to the body. "Looks like he made someone mad."

"Indeed."

He handed her a kit and said, "I'm guessing you don't have your bag or you would've already started collecting evidence."

"You would guess correct."

He moved to the package. "I'm also guessing you want to know what's in here."

"You win the big prize." Dominic returned, followed by Hunter and Katie. She looked at them. "You're just in time for the big reveal."

With gloved hands, Rick grasped the box lid and pulled it off. Looking in, he shook his head. "No doll this time, just a note."

"What does it say?"

Rick read, "'You lose. I win. She's mine.'"

Serena immediately felt Dominic's tension spike. He said, "This is the guy who broke into Serena's house. The serial killer took him out because he thought he was trying to take something that didn't belong to him?"

Hunter frowned and Katie lifted a brow as she looked at Serena. "So, the killer thinks that Serena belongs to him?"

Serena felt her insides start to shake.

"Oh boy," Katie said. "I wouldn't want to be in your shoes."

Dominic shot her a black look and Serena just shook her head. Katie didn't use her filters most of the time, but she was harmless. Serena didn't have the energy to even get upset at the woman's unprofessionalism. She had a feeling Dominic might say something to her later, though.

Serena asked, "Why leave a note? Why taunt me?"

Dominic and Hunter exchanged a glance, then Dominic said slowly, "Because he wanted us to know exactly why he killed this man. He's saying flat out that you're a target. Not that we didn't already know this, but this just makes it irrefutable."

Fear started in her belly and spread north until she felt suffocated. Spinning on her heel, she pushed her way from the room, away from the man who tried to kill her and the note that a serial killer had left her.

Heavy hands landed on her shoulders, spinning her around. "It's going to be okay, Serena. I promise. I'm—"

She shrugged him off. "You can't promise that, Dominic. I appreciate it, but you just can't."

Fire lit his eyes. "Nothing's going to happen to you. Not unless it's over my dead body."

"Don't." She lifted a hand. "Just don't."

"We'll get you some protection, we'll—"

"There's not enough manpower or money for that."

"We'll see. I also have friends. Don't be stubborn about this."

She closed her eyes for a brief moment. When she opened them, Dominic's handsome features blurred into a shapeless blob. "This is what happened to Alexia," she whispered. "This is exactly what she went through when that woman was after her, trying to kill her just a few weeks ago."

Dominic frowned and she could see his mind spinning. He paced in front of her. "Okay, so a few weeks ago someone terrorizes Alexia and finally kidnaps her because they want to know where Jillian is. Now bad things are happening to you. Someone breaks into your house looking for something, tries to steal your purse, and now a serial killer targets you. Why? You think all of that could be related?"

A sobbing, humorless laugh escaped her. "No. I don't know. I don't think it's just that I've had some really bad luck lately." She waved a dismissing hand. "That's not what I meant anyway when I said this is what Alexia went through. I just meant I now understand so clearly exactly how she felt. Helpless, afraid, and very, very angry." The rage simmered just below the surface. She kept a lid on it, refusing to allow it to boil over. "He's not going to do this to me."

Satisfaction glinted in Dominic's eyes. He said, "That's right. Get mad. Get really, really mad. And fight back."

"How?"

"With my help." He paused. "We need to warn those closest to you about this. So far he hasn't gone after family members. Then again, he hasn't warned his victims they were targets either."

Her parents. The air rushed from her lungs. She bit her lip and walked to the end of the hall and back. "Do you know who my parents are?"

"Of course."

"My father is running for the senate. He's not a shoo-in, but he's got a good chance of winning. This . . . this would not be a good thing for his political . . ."

Dominic pulled her to him and she let him. He cupped her chin. "Your life is more important than any political race."

She blinked. "How did the killer get past the cop?"

Dominic switched gears as easily as she did. Knowledge filled his eyes. "The missing child." He turned to the passing nurse. "What floor was the child on when he disappeared?"

Her eyes widened. "This one."

Dominic's lips tightened. "It was a distraction." He snapped his attention back to those in the room. He asked Colton, "Has anyone located that cop yet?"

"No."

"What about video?"

"Security's pulling it up now," Colton answered.

He looked at Serena. "I know you have to take care of things here. I'll be back."

"Fine."

"Are you going to be all right?" he asked her, concern written on his face.

"I guess I'm going to find out."

———■———

The video showed the officer standing in front of Serena's attacker's room. Then a distraught young woman with a panicked

LYNETTE EASON

expression on her face approached the officer. He placed a hand on her shoulder, looked around, then spoke into his radio.

Dominic saw uncertainty cross his features, then he followed the woman down the hall with a glance back toward the room he was supposed to be covering. "There he goes," Dominic said.

Nurses scrambled in the halls, going in and out of rooms. Chaos reigned for the next several minutes.

Which was all the killer needed.

"Look," Dominic pointed.

A nurse exited John Doe's room. Another person appeared on camera and entered. Colton grunted. "You can only see that one from the back. Is it a man or a woman?"

"Can't tell. Whoever it is, he or she is tall for a woman, short for a man, thin, maybe five eight, five nine? I'm trying to judge seeing where the person's head hits the height of the door. He walks with a confident stride in spite of the bent head."

Colton said, "Lab coat, head down, but short brown hair with a baseball cap."

"Okay, wait. Here he comes." The door opened—and the person backed out of the room. "He knows where the cameras are," Dominic slapped a hand against the table in disgust as he watched the probable killer walk down the hall toward the stairwell, passing the cop and the young woman clutching a toddler who looked to be about two years old. The officer, who was now returning to his post, spoke into his radio.

"Look," Dominic pointed. "There's our cop. He came back, so where is he now?"

"In the ER," a voice said from behind them.

Dominic turned to find the officer he'd sent to track the missing cop down. "What do you mean?"

"Someone found him out cold on the steps. He's got a serious knot on the back of his head. Maybe even a fractured skull. Doc said he's going to be unconscious for a while."

Dominic winced and turned back to the video.

"Bet if we back up, we'll see this guy snag the kid from the hall and put him in the stairwell," Hunter said. "And the officer will disappear again too at some point."

"It was all over in less than thirty seconds," Dominic murmured. "No one paid any attention. As soon as the commotion with the kid starts, our killer's in and out."

The head of hospital security turned and said, "There. I've got him grabbing the kid. Hold on. Watch." He reversed the video.

They turned as one to watch as the person backed from the stairwell door. When he turned, he tugged the baseball cap low, leaned against the wall, and pulled a newspaper out from under his arm. He kept his head down.

And then he waited.

Katie said, "If you didn't know he was watching everything going on, you'd never know he was watching everything going on."

Thirty minutes passed before the toddler appeared in the hall. Quick as a snake on a mouse, the killer snatched the child and was back behind the stairwell door.

"He was just waiting for something to give him the opportunity to create a distraction," Colton said. "The cop's back was turned too. He didn't see a thing."

"You don't get any better than a missing kid to stir things up," Katie agreed. "And the timing of everything just fell right into this guy's plans. I hate it when that happens."

The stairwell opened once more and again, the killer pulled out his newspaper and casually leaned against the wall. The cop shifted, glanced down the hall, didn't see anything amiss, and resumed his bored stance.

Hunter said, "Kid's in the stairwell. The door's heavy enough there's no way he could open it."

"Wouldn't someone hear him crying?" Dominic asked.

"Not if he was having a good time playing on the steps," Katie said. "And besides, this hall's basically empty. Who's around to hear him except the cop?"

A harried woman appeared from the end room and looked both ways, up and down the hall, like she was getting ready to cross the street.

When she didn't see her child, fear flashed across her features. Then she searched the hall, talked to the cop, stopped a nurse, then was back to the cop who spoke into his radio. And then it picked up where they started earlier.

"Look, he comes back to his post after he finds the kid, then goes back into the stairwell."

"He suspected something and went to look."

"Should've called it in."

"The killer was still there and caught him by surprise?" Dominic asked.

Colton nodded. "Looks like it."

Dominic sighed. "Well, we know what happened, we just don't have a clue who did it."

Colton shook his head. "This dude is smooth."

"All right." Dominic looked away from the screen and into Colton's always shuttered eyes. Then he let his gaze bounce from Hunter to Katie back to Colton. "I want to see video of all of the entrances and parking lots *now*. This killer's made this highly personal when it comes to targeting Serena. I want to know which door he came in, where he parked, everything."

"We're on that. And yes, Serena needs protection." Colton's flat statement said he caught on quick.

"I can talk to my boss and the local chief of police, but you and I both know what they're going to say," Hunter said.

Colton nodded. "No money, no manpower."

"I'll talk to my boss too," Dominic said. "Because of Serena's father, he may be able to pull a few strings and get some extra coverage."

Colton grunted. "I know her father. He and my uncle Frank are going head-to-head in this election coming up."

"Is working this case going to be a conflict of interest?" Dominic asked.

"No way," Colton snorted. "I have no use for politics. This is my job. Serena's a great girl, she doesn't deserve this."

"I'll be glad to do whatever you need," Hunter volunteered. "Alexia won't have a problem with that, considering what she just went through a few weeks ago."

Colton said, "I can help."

Katie tightened her lips and Dominic raised his brow at her. She rolled her eyes. "All right, I can donate a few hours. I mean, it's not like I have a life or anything."

"Thank you." Dominic didn't worry about Katie. She had a wicked wit and spoke mostly in sarcastic phrases, but she was professional and would do the job to the best of her ability.

Even if it meant taking a bullet for someone.

"All right, folks, let's catch us a killer before he strikes again." Dominic turned and walked back into the hall.

＊

Serena paced from one end to the other, head bowed, deep in thought. She startled as Dominic stepped in front of her, grasped her upper arms, and pulled her to a stop.

She let him, looked into his eyes, and said, "Okay, we're targets, no doubt about it."

Dominic tapped his chin. "I agree—to a point. Or he's being really smart and just wants us to think we're targets."

She frowned. "That doesn't make sense. What does that gain him?"

"I have no idea. It's just a thought."

She considered that. "If we're targets, and I think we've established that, what kind of police protection can we expect?"

Dominic grimaced. "I was just discussing this with some of the team and here's the deal. About you, not me. The sheriff could put a protective detail on you for the short term, but I hate to break it to you, no one has the manpower or the money for a long-term deal."

"I see. So I'm pretty much on my own."

Shivers rippled through her when he reached over to grasp her fingers. "Hey, no way you're on your own. I told you I was just discussing this. Whatever the sheriff can't cover . . . well . . . let's just say I've got friends." He snorted. "And trust me, after that 'gift' left on my property, I've asked a few to watch my back for me."

Serena bit her lip. "That's good to know." She firmed her jaw. "Maybe it's nothing. Maybe he's just taunting us, telling us that we can't catch him. Like this is all part of his stupid game."

Dominic's brows pulled together at the bridge of his nose. "Maybe." His expression said he didn't think so.

"So why is he picking on *us*? Why is he making this so personal?"

"What if it just happened to be you and me? What if it's not us per se? What if we're now targets because we're the ones who're working Leslie's case?"

"What do you mean?"

"I mean, maybe he was watching to see who found her. Watching to see who responded to the call. And it happened to be you on the time clock."

Serena wrinkled her nose. "So I'm just lucky. Is that what you're saying?"

"Maybe. Who knows? It's just a theory and probably not even a good one."

"Well, until we have a better one, I'd say let's work with that one."

"Then again, the note pretty much makes it clear that this guy thinks you belong to him."

Serena shivered. "I know."

Even Dominic's warm hand covering hers couldn't chase the chill of terror invading her.

———■———

Serena's house was lovely. The killer stood in the den and looked right . . . then left. Where to start? Golden green eyes peered around the edge of the recliner, causing the killer to jump. Heart pounding, a little laugh escaped. "Hello, kitty. Not much of an attack cat, are you?"

The dog, Yoda, sniffed the gloved hand and decided she'd found a new best friend. Serena should have chosen her pets more wisely. But then she had no reason to.

The instructions had been clear.

Get the information before getting rid of Serena.

But that had been much harder to do than originally thought. The woman didn't scare easily. And with her schedule so wacky, getting inside and feeling comfortable that Serena wouldn't be coming home anytime soon was impossible.

The killer sighed and ran a gloved hand over the mantel, looking at the pictures of the perfect family.

Resentment swelled.

The perfect family didn't exist. At least not the one that—

"Stop it."

Saying the words aloud derailed those unpleasant thoughts.

"Get back to it. Find the package and get out."

But before the search could begin, the front door slammed and the alarm blared.

23

Serena stood at the sink in the morgue and watched John Doe's blood swirl down the drain. The clank of Dorie's cleaning cart passing her door registered at the edge of her thoughts. She'd texted Camille an hour ago, but she still hadn't heard from the girl.

Worry niggled at her.

Why wouldn't the girl text her back? Was her phone dead? Serena had paid the bill for two months' worth of time, so an unpaid bill wasn't an issue. Plus, the phone rang four times before going to voice mail. If it had been turned off or had a dead battery, it would go straight to voice mail.

The phone was on and working.

But was it in Camille's possession?

She glanced at the clock. There was something to be said for being too wound up to think about going home and sleeping. At least she could take the day off tomorrow. Have a long weekend. Take the boat out on the lake.

Quit stalling, she ordered herself.

She needed to call her parents. Her father was going to flip. Her mother would probably cry and beg Serena to move home so she could live behind their gated security walls.

It was tempting.

No, she couldn't call yet. She needed to be stronger, prepare herself more for their reaction.

Then again, there was a serial killer out there with a bead on Serena—and maybe those she loved.

She had to push past her own silly issues and call.

After peeling the blue gloves off and trashing them in the red biohazard bin, she grabbed her cell phone from her pocket and hit the speed dial.

Serena's father answered on the third ring. "Serena, love, so glad to hear from you. It's been awhile."

She grimaced at his tone. Gentle enough, but with subtle undertones of disapproval. "How's Mom?"

"Wondering when she's going to get to spend some time with her daughter."

Right.

"Dad, I have something I need to tell you."

A pause. Then a cautious, "All right."

Serena lifted a brow. He sounded awfully calm. "I need you to be aware that I may . . ." How in the world did she put this? Just say it. "I may have a serial killer targeting me."

Another pause. Then, "What! I don't think I heard you right because I thought you said you had a serial killer targeting you, but that can't possibly be what you said."

There he was. The dad she knew and loved. She almost smiled.

Before she could respond, he said, "Are you talking about the one that's all over the news? The one killing these young women?"

"Yes."

"Okay, hold on a minute while I try to breathe." She heard him take a deep breath. "Explain yourself, please."

She filled him in, starting with the first 9-1-1 call to finding Leslie in the park to the latest death of the man who had broken into her house.

For a moment, her father didn't say a word. Then, "Pack your bags. I want you here where we have a state-of-the-art security system. I'll hire a bodyguard."

"Dad, you can't afford a bodyguard," she reminded him softly.

He went silent. "I'll take out loans, I'll mortgage the house. Whatever it takes. I want you safe."

Her father was running for the senate seat. What most people weren't aware of—yet—was due to a few bad investments over the last couple of years, her father was now about to lose everything.

"I have a friend, an FBI agent, who is working to keep me safe. I'm not moving in with you and Mom because if I do, it may draw his attention to you. And I absolutely won't do that."

"Serena—"

"Dad, don't you understand? I simply can't do that. Please take precautions to protect yourself and Mom. I'm doing the same."

For a moment he didn't speak. Then he said, "I have friends in high places. I'll see what I can do about having someone on your house and at work 24/7."

This was exactly why she hadn't wanted to call him. He would take over, think he could control everything. She clamped down on her tongue and tried to understand the situation from his point of view. He was worried. Had every right to be worried.

She asked, "How's the financial situation?"

He sighed. "We're hanging in there. I've taken on a couple of extra cases, putting in some long hours, some weekends, but we're doing all right."

"And the donations for the campaign?"

"That's the good news. Those are rolling in pretty steady."

Relief swept over her. "Let me know if there's anything I can do to help."

"Just concentrate on staying out of this killer's path." He paused again. "I've had a hard time watching you grow up, Ser, but I suppose I have to admit . . . you are grown. I want to demand that you get yourself over here and stop playing around, but after the humbling experience of borrowing money from my daughter—"

"That was a gift, Dad."

"*Borrowing* money from my daughter, I've lost a little of my arrogant attitude."

"Good," she smiled into the phone, "you needed to."

"Humph. If it wasn't for your mother . . . so anyway, I'm not going to make any demands or make you feel guilty for not locking yourself away here at the house." His voice lowered. "But please, please, be careful and listen to your FBI friend. Do exactly what he tells you to do when it comes to security. If something happened to you . . ."

Wow. Did she hear tears in his voice?

"I promise, Dad. I love you."

"Love you too, darling."

After she hung up, the conversation swirled through her brain. Her father, the know-it-all, arrogant criminal lawyer who'd faced death threats and turned down bribes, had been brought to tears over her safety. She wasn't quite sure what to think. She knew her dad loved her, she'd never really doubted that, but . . . well, wow. This was a side she'd never seen before.

One that would take a little more processing than she could handle right now.

Her phone buzzed and she glanced at the ID. Dominic.

"Hello?"

"Are you ready to go home?" his deep voice rumbled in her ear.

"Almost. Where are you?"

"Turn around."

She did. Dominic stood at the opposite end of the room, the phone pressed against his ear. She hung up. "You're silly."

"Sometimes. Not very often." He walked toward her.

True enough.

"It's late," she said. "What are you doing here?"

198

He reached up and pressed a hand to her cheek, then ran a finger down it. "Making sure you get home safely."

Warmth flooded her. Along with relief. Before he could see how his touch affected her, she turned on the pretense of putting away the last of her instruments. "I was going to ask security to walk me out to my car."

"But who would make sure you got inside your house without any problems?"

"Hmm . . . good question." She slipped her lab coat off and tossed it into the bin to be washed. "I'm ready."

Serena followed him down the hall and out the back entrance to the employee parking lot. She found her rental. A blue Chevy SUV. Just what she'd asked for. Serena didn't like small vehicles, especially if Yoda decided she wanted to come along.

"I'll follow you," he said.

Once in the rental, she adjusted the rearview mirror and the seat. Looking behind her she saw Dominic's headlights.

Grateful for his attention to her safety, she drove home, her mind racing. Just as she pulled onto her street, her phone buzzed. She answered, "Hello?"

"This is ADT security, we have an alert at 104 Bennett Drive. We need to speak to Serena Hopkins."

"This is she. An alert? My alarm's going off?" Her heart thudded and fear spiraled through her.

"Yes, ma'am, could we have your password, please?"

"It's . . . Yoda."

"Thank you. Officers are on the way to the address."

Serena parked in her driveway, phone still pressed to her ear as her alarm blared. Her neighbor across the street stepped out onto his porch, a frown on his face.

She opened the garage door and waited for Dominic to pull in beside her. She saw realization cross his face as he got out of the car and drew his weapon from his shoulder holster. She started to follow, but he turned and said, "Stay back."

"You need the code. It's 2582."

He nodded. "Now get in your car and lock the doors."

"Be careful."

Three city police cars pulled up to the curb. The officers got out of their vehicles.

One approached Serena, hand on her weapon. The other pulled his gun as his gaze landed on Dominic who had his weapon in one hand and ID in the other.

The officer relaxed at the sight of the FBI badge.

Dominic said, "Cover the rear." He looked at the first male officer. "You come with me to clear the house. Serena, you wait in the car with the door locked." He glanced at the third officer.

The woman nodded before he had a chance to say anything. "I'll stay with her."

The men entered the garage and then disappeared into the house. The alarm went silent.

The officer who'd stayed behind with Serena pulled her to the police car and opened the passenger door. "Let's just wait out here until we know everything's all right. If anything starts, I don't want you caught in the crossfire." Serena looked at the pretty female officer whose badge read "Hudson."

"What happened?" Officer Hudson asked even as her gaze darted toward the front of Serena's house. No doubt, she was worried about her partner.

"I got a call from the security company that my alarm was set off." She watched her neighbor head her way and wondered if he'd seen anything.

Officer Hudson said, "So you just got home."

"Right."

Mr. Randall Barnard walked up to the police car.

Serena said, "I'm so sorry, Mr. Barnard."

"No problem." The older, graying man scratched at his five o'clock shadow. "I was just worried about you. Everything all right here?"

"I'm not sure. It looks like someone tried to break into my house."

"Might have been that scraggly teenager I saw hanging out around here earlier today."

Some of her fear faded. "Scraggly teen?"

"Yeah. Skinny little thing. I heard the alarm go off and saw her take off running across your front yard."

Camille. It had to be.

But what had the girl been doing trying to get into Serena's house?

The officer and Dominic came out the front door. Serena's heart filled with relief at their safety.

Dominic waved them in. "It's all clear." He no longer held his weapon.

Serena looked at Mr. Barnard. "Thanks for your help."

He headed back toward his house with an "anytime" tossed over his shoulder. Serena and Officer Hudson approached the men. Dominic led them back inside and Serena filled them in on what Mr. Barnard said about a "scraggly teen."

He promptly called in an Attempt To Locate with Mr. Barnard's description.

Yoda padded in to greet her, her tongue coming out for a quick swipe of her hand. She scratched her ears, then watched her turn and head out through her doggie door to the backyard.

Dominic said, "You need a better watchdog."

"That's not why I got her," Serena said, defending her beloved pet. She looked around her house, the kitchen, into the den, and out into the glassed-in porch area.

Something niggled at her. She frowned and looked back toward the kitchen, then gave the den another sweep with her eyes.

"What is it?" he asked.

"I'm not sure. Something just feels . . . off."

"Off? Could you be a little more specific?"

"Just . . ." Her eyes landed on the sofa. "The afghan's thrown over the wrong end of the couch."

The officers exchanged a glance as Dominic lifted a brow. She flushed. "I know. It sounds crazy, but I always stretch out with my feet at that end. So I keep the afghan on the same end to make it easy just to pull up." She waved a hand. "Trust me, when I left this morning, that afghan was on the other end of the couch."

Dominic reached up and rubbed his chin, his eyes thoughtful. "Anything else seem off?"

Serena walked back into the kitchen, her eyes scanning the area. "No, I don't guess so." But her gaze kept going to the sink. She stepped over to it. "Yes, I left a mug in here this morning and now it's gone."

This time he frowned. "Look in your dishwasher."

She opened it and saw the mug. "Well . . . how'd that get in there?" Shutting the dishwasher, she simply stared at Dominic and the officers. "This is totally weird. I don't understand. Why would someone come in my house and move things around?"

Officer Hudson's radio crackled. She listened, then said, "We have another call. If everything's all right here, we'll leave you to it."

Serena blinked and gave an absent nod. "Yes, fine. Thanks for your response."

"Anytime, ma'am."

The three officers left and Dominic looked at her alarm panel. "This time the person tripped your alarm. Just out of curiosity, who has your code?"

"Just Alexia and Hunter."

"What about your parents?"

She blinked. "Oh. Yes, they have it. But none of those people would give it out to anyone. They would have no reason to. And now you know it."

"And now you're going to change it once again."

She walked over to the panel and punched the sequence of buttons that would allow her to change the code.

Dominic said, "I think the question we're not asking here is, What do you have that someone wants?"

Serena jerked. "What?"

"It's the only thing I can come up with. Someone is determined to get in your house. For what reason? It's either to hurt you or get something you have. You said that when you woke up, the intruder, who had ample opportunity to shoot you while you slept, was looking for something."

Jillian's package.

Ever since she'd signed for it at the post office, she'd had trouble stalking her.

He must have picked up on her stillness. "What is it, Serena? What do you have?"

She sighed and closed her eyes, then opened them. "I'm not even sure if it's what I'm thinking of."

"Which is?"

"I . . . made a promise to someone to keep something safe. Whoever's after me must know that I have it."

His eyes narrowed. "And you're just now telling me this?"

"I made a promise," she said. "I don't take that lightly."

"Serena, there's someone who has access to your house, someone who—"

"I know! I know!" Frustration made her words sharp.

He simply stared at her. She reached up with both hands to grab hunks of hair on either side of her head. "Argh! I'm sorry. I don't mean to take it out on you."

His face softened, but not the determination in his eyes. "Show me."

"I can't."

"You have to," he pushed.

She dropped her hands. "You don't understand. *I* haven't even looked in it."

That made him frown. "Why not?"

"Because in her letter that came with the package, she asked me not to. I was only to open it if I received word of her death. Otherwise I was to keep the package until she asked for it." Serena felt tears choke her and swallowed them back. She didn't have time for tears, but she was exhausted and needed sleep. "Look, I'll think about this, pray about it. I can't just open it without really . . . figuring out if that's the right thing to do."

At first she thought he would argue with her. Instead, he clamped his lips shut, then pushed out a sigh. "This has to do with Jillian, doesn't it?"

She simply stared at him, refusing to betray the trust of her friend.

"Fine," he finally said between clenched teeth. "But you need to decide soon. Whatever's in that package could lead us to whoever is after it. And we definitely need to stop that person before he succeeds in his mission—and hurts you in the process."

She nodded. "I know. I'll . . . try to come to a decision soon."

Dominic hesitated and she waited, knowing he had something else to say. "Look, Jillian was one of your best friends in high school. Think about this. She wouldn't deliberately put your life in danger, would she?"

"Of course not."

"Then when she sent that package, she had to believe that it wouldn't bring danger with it. But it did. That kind of changes things, doesn't it?"

Serena groaned and rubbed her eyes. Everything he said made sense. "Let me sleep on it."

He looked around. "All right, the animals are taken care of. Why don't you pack a bag and stay in a hotel room for tonight?"

She wrinkled her nose. "I thought you had someone watching my house."

"I do, I just think you'd be safer at a hotel." A cunning light entered his eyes. "In fact, I think that might be a really good idea. See if we can catch whoever's been sneaking in your house."

"You mean set a trap?"

"So to speak. You'll be tucked away safe and one of my buddies will be watching the house."

She thought about it. And knew she'd sleep better in a hotel. "But what about my animals?"

He frowned. "So far the killer hasn't seemed interested in harming them. I would think if he'd wanted to kill them, he wouldn't have bothered with feeding Yoda sleeping pills. He would have just killed her."

Serena shuddered at the thought. "But—"

"And no one may even try to get in. But if someone does, Brett will be there to nab him."

She glanced at the clock and caved. She needed rest. "I guess that's a good idea . . . but I'll be back first thing in the morning. I'm taking the day off tomorrow to get errands done. Let me grab a bag."

His gaze softened and he pulled her into a hug. "Thanks."

She rested against his broad chest, reveling in the security he represented. Then she pulled back and said, "If you'll feed my fish, I'll be back in just a few minutes."

———■———

That had been close. The killer shut the car door and thought about the figure who'd run from the house. Who was she? Someone important to Serena?

She looked to be about seventeen or eighteen, thin as a rail, but fast on her feet.

The fact that the girl had found a way to access Serena's house without setting off the alarm made the killer smile.

The fact that this girl had interrupted the search turned the smile into a frown. There'd been no time to hide, to figure out the next step.

With the alarm blaring, there'd been no point in sticking around and getting caught by all the cops who had descended on the house.

No, getting out had been easy. Getting back in might prove a problem because Serena would be on guard even more now. She might even move out of her home. Which would be a good thing.

Unless the cops monitored the activity around the house. Then getting to Serena would prove extra difficult. The killer spied a shiny object in the grass, slid out of the car, and snatched it up. Shrewd eyes glanced in the direction the teen had gone.

And the killer felt satisfaction flow as a plan formed.

24

Dominic hung up the phone. No one had tried to get in Serena's house last night, so the trap had been a bust. But at least she was safely ensconced in her hotel room overnight.

This morning, an officer would be waiting at her house when she got there and provide protection for her throughout the day.

He reached for the next file in the stack retrieved from Howard Bell's house and opened it.

As he bent his head to read, his phone buzzed. Geographic profiler and Special Agent Regina Gaines said, "I put together that information you sent me."

"Were you able to get anything from it?"

"Maybe. Even though you said we may not have all the victims, the software is prioritizing a specific area. I'm sending the information to your phone. The nine girls that disappeared and turned up dead over the three-year period of time the Doll Maker Killer was killing don't seem to have a lot in common. They're pretty much scattered all over. And yet, we have this area Dragnet is giving us." Dragnet, the profiling software.

"Great."

207

"I did manage to find one thing that connects some of them. Drake Lindell's cleaning business."

"Some of them?"

"Seven out of the nine worked in buildings that Drake's janitorial service covered."

"Why wasn't that in the file?" Dominic ground out. What had Howard done with this investigation? From all the information he had on Howard, the man had been a topnotch cop. But this missing information . . . "What about the other two?" he asked.

"I'm still searching for a connection, but I'm guessing Drake knew them somehow other than through his business. Could have been through his kids' school, church, a chance meeting in the grocery store. Who knows? But I don't think a geographic profile is going to help you much. His home was over in the Five Points area. But his work took him all over the city. Which is probably why you have victims from those areas."

"All right, thanks for the update."

Dominic hung up and processed the information he'd just learned. The man had access to the victims because he had keys and alarm codes to businesses. He would have had no trouble choosing a victim, learning her routine, getting her home address, and snatching her when the moment presented itself.

Rubbing his eyes, he focused back on the file in front of him. Just as he was about to start reading, his phone buzzed again. "Yeah?"

"You're sounding a little distracted, big brother."

He smiled and gathered his thoughts to focus on Alexia. "Sorry. What's up?"

"I just checked on Mom."

"How's she doing?" He read as he listened. Nothing. He tossed the file on the "nothing" stack. His eyes fell on the next file and he pulled it toward him.

"She's doing really well. Gaining some weight and getting better every day. The doctors are optimistic—and so is Michael."

He stilled, then leaned back in his chair. "Her pastor."

"Right."

"The one you say is in love with her."

"Uh-huh."

Dominic stared at the file, not seeing it now. "I'm surprised she would even consider a relationship with someone else."

"I know. And . . . there's something she never told us about her and Dad."

The hesitancy in her voice set his senses on alert. "What's that?"

"They're still married."

His heart flipped and he swallowed hard. "What?"

"Apparently Dad left but never filed for divorce. And neither did Mom."

That was crazy. He'd just assumed . . . "Well, she can file for divorce based on his desertion. There's not a judge in town who wouldn't sign off on it. Dad hasn't been around in what . . . eight years?"

"Yes." More hesitation. Then a rush of words. "She's not sure she can do it."

"What?" Disbelief crowded through him. "File for divorce? You're kidding me."

Tears now clogged his sister's voice. "She said when she married, she married for life, and that if Dad didn't file, he must have had a reason."

"Yeah, he was too cheap to pay for it!" Two nearby officers looked up and Dominic made an effort to control his temper and the volume of his voice. "You've got to be kidding me," he snapped.

"No, I'm not. Dominic, I just got back into her life. If we find Dad, and she wants a reconciliation with him, I . . . I don't think I can be a part of her life anymore. The only reason I want to find him is to find out if he's the one who tried to kill me!"

Dominic did his best to slow his racing thoughts. "All right. Tell you what. Let's not borrow trouble. Take it one step at a time. How close are you to finding him?"

"We've tracked him to another homeless shelter. We're waiting on a call to see if he's still there, then we'll take off to find him."

"What state this time?"

"He's still in North Carolina. Charlotte."

"What does Michael have to say about all this?" Dominic asked.

"He's handling it well. I was surprised. He said if a reconciliation was what Mom wanted, he would refer them to a counselor and step out of the picture." She sighed. "But the pain in his eyes is awful to see, Dominic."

"He loves her."

"He does." He thought she had more to add, so he waited. Alexia said, "And she loves him, but I think she's scared. When she was so sick, she didn't have to worry about the relationship going anywhere. She was in a safe place. But now, she's getting better and Michael's dropping hints about proposing. I think this is a defense mechanism of some sort. She wants Michael, but she's scared. And this is her way out."

"A big way out. If they're really still married . . ."

"Exactly."

"Then I guess we need to find Dad and bring this to a closure—one way or another." He paused. "What does Hunter think about all this?"

Her voice softened. "He's doing this to help me. I think he wishes I would leave it alone, but since that's not going to happen . . ."

Dominic gave a low chuckle. When his sister put her mind to something, she was like a dog with a bone. Hunter was probably wise to keep tabs on her if only to keep her out of trouble—and safe.

"All right. Tell Mom I'll be by to see her soon. And I've got a buddy at the Bureau. I'll have him put some feelers out and see what we can come up with. Although, Hunter's got good contacts. If Dad's still slipping through your fingers, I don't know how much good my friend will be."

"Just try. It can't hurt."

"All right."

He hung up and dialed the number of his friend at headquarters. Special Agent Jeff Brown promised to help out and be in touch.

After Dominic hung up with Jeff, he steepled his fingers and stared at the wall. He didn't want to find his father again. He'd found him once and it hadn't been pretty.

And now his mother was thinking about a reconciliation? He shook his head. There was no way he'd let that happen, he just wasn't sure how he would stop it if it came down to it.

But he'd figure out something.

Even if it meant bribing the man to stay gone forever.

After he filed for divorce.

———■———

In the accommodating deer stand some kind neighbor had built in the copse of trees right across from Serena's house, the killer lifted the scope to an eye and focused it on the French doors leading into Serena's den.

Taking her out would be as simple as pulling the trigger. When the time was right. A grim smile crossed the killer's face as Serena stepped into the den.

———■———

9:02 A.M.

Serena dropped her overnight bag in the hallway and walked into the den. Yoda hadn't greeted her when she came in, so the dog was probably out in the backyard.

She pulled out her phone. Where was Camille? The girl had all but disappeared, refusing to answer texts or calls.

Frustration and worry set in.

She was going to have to find Camille.

And that meant starting with the girl's father.

It may be her day off of work, but she had several things she needed to get done. She felt bad about leading her shadow around on all the errands she needed to run, but it couldn't be helped. A peek through the window confirmed the officer who had spent the night was being replaced by her daytime shadow.

She wandered through the den to check the backyard. Yoda chased a squirrel up a tree, then sat down to watch the critter dance across the limbs. While she wasn't the best watchdog—okay, she was probably the worst watchdog *ever*—at least she didn't seem worried about any potential intruders . . . or new friends to greet . . . and Serena breathed a little easier.

After the safety fiasco with Alexia when she'd stayed at Serena's house and the intruder had gotten inside, Serena had had a six-foot wooden fence installed around the back of her property. She had felt more secure, but knowing someone had once again breeched her home had her wondering if anyone was ever truly safe. If someone wanted to get to her, she had a feeling it was only a matter of time.

Not exactly comforting thoughts.

Walking to the mantel, she ran her hands over the three bricks. Then moved one to the left and two to the right. Reaching into the small exposed area, she pushed aside some valuable jewelry left to her by her grandmother and pulled out the manila envelope with her name on it.

Serena slid Jillian's letter from the package, leaving a second sealed envelope inside. On the outside of that envelope, Jillian had written DO NOT OPEN. On the letter Serena now held, Jillian had written READ FIRST.

Serena had followed her directions, honoring Jillian's request for privacy.

Only someone seemed intent on getting it from her. One way or another.

The hair on the back of her neck lifted and she glanced toward the French doors that led to her glassed-in porch. The porch overlooked the fenced yard. Beyond the fence, oaks and maples offered shade and privacy.

Only, it felt more isolating than private right now.

Shivering, she looked back at the letter.

Ser,

*It's been a long time and I know I probably have no right
to ask this, but I need a favor from you. My life's in danger.
It has been ever since graduation night, but I've managed to
hide under a false name and identity. I've been running for
so long, I don't know if I know how to stop. But I have to
try. For more reasons than one. I've built quite a name for
myself as an investigative reporter, but there's one crime I've
been too afraid to face. The one I witnessed. So, it's time.
I've been working for over a year to arrange to come home
before it's too late. I know that's vague, but I don't want to
go into details here. I'll see you soon. But if you should hear
that I've died, please open the other envelope and give it to
the person I've specified. BUT ONLY IF YOU KNOW FOR
SURE THAT I'M DEAD.*

I've missed you and Alexia.

*Looking forward to more than a high school reunion, I'm
looking forward to exposing the truth about that night. I'm
just trying to stay alive while I figure out how to do that.*

> *Love and hugs,*
> *Jillian*

For the hundredth time since receiving the letter, she refolded it
and slid it back into the envelope.

What had Jillian seen that night?

Serena stared at the unopened envelope. Did she have the right to
look? There was no doubt in her mind this was what her intruder
had been looking for.

She should really put this somewhere safer than her house. Like a safe deposit box. Serena shot a glance at her briefcase, then looked back at the envelope.

Then out the French doors one more time. If she left now, she'd have time to run by the bank before going to the girls' home.

Grabbing her briefcase and everything she needed, she prioritized. She'd go by the bank later. She needed to see if she could find Camille.

Serena exited the house into the closed garage and stilled. The echo of the door closing behind her rang in her ears. Her pulse pounded. Fear clogged her throat.

And she took a deep breath.

Was someone hiding in the spacious area?

Inside the boat under the tarp?

In the backseat of her car?

If so, she couldn't have this package on her.

As the blood thrummed through her veins, she whirled and fumbled with her keys, finally getting the lock open, then the door. Then she slammed it shut, twisting the dead bolt as her keys fell to the floor with a clank.

With dread in her stomach, she grabbed her cell phone. Should she call the police?

911?

Dominic?

The cop sitting outside watching her house?

As she watched out the window, her nerves started to calm. There was no one there. She was being silly.

"There's no one out there," she whispered aloud. "Get in the car and go. Camille might need you."

But the thought of opening the door and walking out of the house terrified her.

And some small part of her realized what was happening. He was gaining control of her life, her thoughts, her actions—and she was allowing it.

Oh Lord, help me. I don't want to let fear rule me.

For another few minutes, she just stood at the door, looking out into the garage. Nothing moved.

"Get in the car, Serena," she told herself. Putting the package back where she thought it would be safe, she thought about her nerves and the fact that the killer had done everything in his power to keep her off balance and constantly on guard. No doubt, a tactic meant to exhaust her and make her careless.

With determination, she unlocked the kitchen door dead bolt and stepped back into the garage. With jerky movements, she opened the SUV door and shot her gaze to the passenger seat.

She was almost surprised to find it empty. She slid into the driver's seat and slammed the door, locking it in one quick motion. She pressed the button on the garage door remote.

As the door behind her rose, her phone rang and she grabbed it from the cup holder. "Hello?"

"Hey, pretty lady. How are you this morning?"

Dominic. She backed from the garage, her heart picking up even more speed. She smiled, although she couldn't help the nervous glance at the covered boat.

"I'm doing great. I actually slept last night." Should she say anything about her nervousness? About the feeling that someone was in her garage?

Before she closed the garage, she waited at the end of her driveway for one last, long look.

Still, nothing moved.

"You feel like going to a meeting with me?" Dominic asked.

"Nate?" she guessed.

"Yep. I'm meeting him at 11:00. I know this is your day off, but—"

"No, I want to go." She tapped the steering wheel. "I need to go see Camille first at the girls' home, but I can meet you there."

"Okay." He paused. "You sound funny. You sure you're all right?"

She breathed a laugh. "I'm fine. Just my imagination working overtime."

"Are you sure it's your imagination?"

Serena bit her lip. Was she? "Probably."

"You don't sound so sure."

"Yeah. I know. Never mind. I'm just jumpy."

"With good reason. Is your shadow with you?"

She glanced in her rearview mirror. "Yes, he's there."

"Great."

Serena pulled up to the four-way stop and pressed the brakes. Her shadow hugged her bumper. A car to her right seemed to be traveling fast as it approached the stop sign, so she waited to be sure the driver planned to stop. When it seemed like the vehicle slowed, she pressed the gas.

But she was wrong. Heart in her throat, she realized too late that the driver planned to run the stop sign. The other vehicle plowed into her passenger door.

25

Dominic heard the screech of metal crunching metal, Serena's terrified scream. The roar of a motorcycle.

Then seconds later, the sound of a gunshot.

"Serena!" Panic clawed at his throat, helplessness spinning his mind. "Serena! Answer me!"

Dead silence echoed back to him.

Was she dead? Terror streaked through him as he pressed the gas pedal. *Oh God, please no.*

Where was the officer who was supposed to be protecting her?

Heart thudding, he spun the wheel of his car to race back toward Serena's house. They hadn't been talking long, so she couldn't be very far from her home.

His adrenaline flowed, free and easy. He took in a deep breath and forced himself into cop mode, emergency response instinct. It terrified him that the person involved was Serena, but emotions had no place in his response.

He realized he still had the phone pressed against his ear, but no sound penetrated. He looked at the screen and saw the call had been disconnected. He pressed redial.

No answer.

He dialed the officer who was supposed to be watching out for her.
No answer.

His gut tightened and sweat broke out on his forehead.

If he knew her location, he'd call for backup.

But he didn't.

Quickly, he called in the wreck, giving what information he had—which wasn't near enough.

He just prayed he could find her before he was too late.

———■———

Serena groaned and pressed a hand to her aching head. She'd whiplashed, the impact jerking her head toward the car that hit her, then slamming back against the driver's window. A motorcycle rumbled. She heard what sounded like a car backfiring twice, then someone cursing behind her, followed by an angry "What are you doing here? Why'd you shoot that cop?"

She lifted her head to see two figures, blurry and distorted. She closed her eyes, pressed her finger to the lids, tried to gather her scattered thoughts. When a hand reached in to grab her by the upper arm, she looked over, thankful for the officer who'd been behind her.

But her eyes didn't land on the officer.

A black masked face stared down at her. A scream bubbled in her throat even as dizziness made her head spin.

"Where is it?" the low voice hissed.

"What?" Serena blinked against the dark spots swirling before her eyes.

The hand on her bicep tightened and gave her a shake. "The package from Jillian. We know you have it. Where is it?"

Where was the officer who'd been following her?

She squinted through the throbbing pain and ignored her attacker.

Then the person leaned over and snatched Serena's briefcase from the passenger seat and brought a gun to her head.

"Is it in here?"

Serena brought her hand up in a quick defensive move, knocking the gun to the ground. Her attacker let loose a string of curses. A fist connected with her already aching head. From the corner of her eye, she saw him bend down. As she fought the encroaching darkness, she heard the other person say, "I'll see you soon." A low chuckle sounded. "And I shot the cop because I couldn't let the game end before it's even begun, could I?"

A gunshot sounded, then all went black.

———■———

Through the windshield, Dominic saw the figure leaning over Serena and at first thought it was the officer who'd volunteered to protect her. Then he saw the man on the ground beside the un-marked Escape. Dominic recognized the officer as the one who'd been following Serena and grief stabbed him as he wondered if the man was dead.

As his mind pieced together the scene at mach speed, the person near Serena turned at Dominic's approach, lifted his right hand, and fired a shot.

Dominic swerved as the bullet slammed into the side of the car. Keeping his head low, he yanked his weapon from his holster and grabbed his radio. "Officer needs help! Intersection of Dove Park and Spring Ridge at the four-way stop sign." He tossed the radio down after receiving notification that help was on the way. Dominic noticed a bag clutched in the person's left hand.

The killer bolted toward the car parked behind Serena's, leaped over the officer, and dove into the driver's seat.

Through the open window, Dominic aimed his weapon and pulled the trigger. The bullet shattered the windshield, but the person slammed the Escape into reverse, whipped the steering wheel around, then sped off.

Dominic pulled his vehicle in as close as possible to Serena's and climbed out, keeping low. Into his radio, he said, "Suspect is going east on Spring Ridge in a Blue Ford Escape. License plate Delta-William-Victor Zero-Two-Four."

Hating his inability to be in two places at once, Dominic abandoned the idea of giving chase and turned to check Serena's pulse.

It pounded beneath his fingers strong and steady.

He went to Officer MacDougall, who lay on his back, eyes wide and staring. Blank. Dominic checked on him even though he knew the man was already gone. No pulse.

And a bullet to the center of his forehead.

Nausea rolled. The loss of life. A good man with two children in their teens. Teens who needed their dad. Fury grappled with grief as the ambulance and other law enforcement arrived on the scene.

Dominic held up his badge.

Hunter and Katie bolted from their vehicles, worry stamped on their features.

"Serena?" Hunter asked as another ambulance pulled up behind the unmarked car.

"Alive, but unconscious."

Paramedics headed toward them and Dominic waved them over to Serena. There was nothing they could do for the dead officer. Katie was already next to the body. The other officers shut down the intersection, rerouting traffic.

Dominic watched paramedics work on Serena. Anxious, he tried not to hover, but from the slanted looks the younger one kept shooting him, Dominic had a feeling he wasn't doing a very good job of staying back.

As they placed her on the gurney, her eyes fluttered and a moan slipped from her lips. "Dominic?"

He stepped forward and snagged her hand. "Right here, Serena."

"What happened?"

"You got hit."

"It was him, wasn't it?" she whispered.

Dominic nodded. "Yeah."

"The officer behind me . . ."

"Dead."

Grief flashed. "I'm so sorry."

"Me too." Dominic clenched his jaw against the fury that raged in him.

She tried to sit up and he eased her back. "Go to the hospital and get checked out."

"I'm all right."

"Don't argue." He hadn't meant to sound so harsh.

She flinched. "Right." Serena lay back and licked her lips.

The fact that she *didn't* argue worried him. "Sorry, I'm not upset with you."

"I know," she whispered.

"You have an escort to the hospital. I'll be there as soon as I can." He paused. "Anyone you want me to call?"

"Yeah. I want my mom." She gave him the number and his heart clenched when a tear slid down her cheek to disappear into the delicate shell of her ear. He leaned over her and looked into her eyes. "You're going to be okay."

She sniffed. "I know." But Dominic didn't see any belief in the statement.

One of the paramedics nudged him and Dominic stepped back. "See you soon."

"Wait!" She winced and held a hand to her head. The paramedics paused again. "He stole my briefcase."

So that's what the guy had been holding.

"What was in it?"

"Just work stuff."

"Go get checked out. We'll worry about that later."

The paramedics rolled her away and loaded her into the back of the ambulance. Dominic made sure Hunter and Katie were on its tail.

The coroner's vehicle pulled up followed by a black SUV. A man Dominic had never seen before stepped out of the SUV just as his phone rang.

He heard the man introduce himself as Ralph Newton, the medical examiner on call. Dominic punched the green button to answer. "Hello?"

"Colton here."

"I'm kind of in the middle of something, can I call you back?"

"This is important. Hunter just texted me and said he didn't have time to talk to you at the scene. If you can spare me a couple of minutes, I think you need to know this."

Dominic watched Ralph Newton lean over the body of Officer MacDougall. "Sure, what is it?"

Colton said, "We've uncovered some things related to the Doll Maker Killer copycat."

"Go on."

"We've got a possible for the latest dead girl. Kelsey Nicholson. Her prints were in the system when she applied to be a day care worker. But she was picked up on a shoplifting charge a couple of years ago. We're waiting on the parents to come ID her and talk to us."

"All right. Keep me posted. Serena's on her way to the hospital to get checked out and I want to be there for her."

"I'll check with Alexia and see if she remembers Kelsey."

The ME said something to the officer standing next to him, and the officer cursed and turned away to gain control of his emotions.

Dominic said goodbye and walked over to see what the commotion was. "I'm Special Agent Dominic Allen. What's the problem?"

Ralph Newton gently turned the officer onto his side and pointed at a bloody area on the man's upper right torso beneath the shoulder blade. Dominic blinked as he realized what that meant. He looked at the ME. "He was shot in the back?"

"Yep. That's an entry wound. No exit wound."

Dominic felt his stomach churn. "So our serial killer had some help. The only way MacDougall could have been shot in the back is if he were going to help Serena. One drove the car into Serena's, the other waited until the officer got out of his car and shot him." He dropped his head for a brief moment of dread. When he looked up, he said, "There are two of them working together, which means our workload just doubled."

<hr />

1:20 P.M.

"She's in the hospital? I thought you were going to kill her," Frank said.

"Not this way. I still need her alive for a little while longer."

"That makes no sense! She's already had Alexia spend the night. What if she's talking to her?"

"Alexia doesn't know anything," the voice said. "I've already established that. Besides, she's so busy looking for her father, she doesn't have time to worry about anything else. Regardless, Serena's not talking to her. That doesn't mean we're not still keeping tabs on her, but Serena's the one with the package."

"A package she's keeping secret even from her closest friend, Alexia?" Frank couldn't help the sarcasm.

The voice on the other end of the line went silent, then came back a good fifty degrees cooler. "Exactly. Because she knows if she tells Alexia what's in the package, that will mean Alexia's death for certain. Serena's not the type of person to risk that."

Frank thought about that. "How do you know this? You seem so certain."

"I have my sources."

Sources Frank probably didn't want to know about. "Okay. What about that FBI agent she seems to be getting so chummy with?"

"Ah yes, Alexia's brother."

"Right."

"I've been thinking about him a lot. I think he may have to meet with an unfortunate accident."

"As long as it can't be tracked back to either of us. That's the most important thing to remember," Frank said. A sharp shooting pain down his left arm elicited a gasp.

"What is it?"

"Nothing. Just some pain in my arm. Stress."

"I told you I have it under control. Don't go and have a heart attack on me."

"I don't have time for a heart attack. I have an election to win." The pain had faded, but Frank's worry had tripled.

"I've got it covered. After all, Dominic's tracking a serial killer, right? I'm sure that the killer doesn't like the fact that he's got one of the best FBI agents in the country on his tail."

Frank felt a small smile slip across his lips. "Right. I wouldn't think he'd like that at all."

26

At the hospital, Serena sat on the edge of the bed and pondered her next move. Her attacker had taken her briefcase. She thought about the feeling of being watched as she'd stood in front of the mantel in her den. Somehow, he'd seen her put the package in her briefcase.

Obviously he hadn't seen her remove it a few minutes later.

How had he been watching? Binoculars?

Or through a scope attached to a high-powered rifle. Like the one that killed Howard. She shuddered.

First thing, she needed to ask Dominic to escort her to the bank to put that package into the safe deposit box. After they read the contents.

Maybe. The package contents had to do with Jillian. Not Serena.

Of course, if Jillian hadn't sent the package, then the creeps wouldn't be after her, right? She would have shaken her head if she'd been able to do so without pain. So, she had something someone wanted and was willing to kill to get. She was also the target of a serial killer.

This was turning into a really bad week.

She turned her thoughts to Camille.

225

She'd already called Mrs. Lamb and told her to be on the lookout for Camille in case things went south with her father. The fact that the girl hadn't shown her face didn't mean all was well. In fact, Serena was quite concerned since she hadn't heard from the girl in two days. That was very unlike her.

Serena grimaced as worry for Camille mingled with worry for herself and those she was close to.

Her head still pounded, but fortunately, she'd escaped the wreck and the attack without a concussion. She'd be moving slowly for a while, but at least she would be moving.

The memory of the man standing over her sent shudders through her.

"Serena?"

At the soft voice, she looked up to see her mother, Portia Salazar Hopkins, standing in the doorway. For some reason she couldn't fathom, tears climbed into Serena's eyes and she blinked. "Hi, Mom."

The tall, slender woman, who still had a head of hair so black it shimmered blue in certain light, walked over and wrapped her arms around her.

Serena breathed in the comfort of being in her mother's arms. Her mother's suddenly tight arms.

"Hey, you're smooshing me."

Her mother loosened her grasp and pulled back. "That FBI agent called and said you'd been in a wreck." The soft Spanish accent soothed Serena's nerves.

"A car ran a stop sign and rammed into me." Unsure what her father had shared with the woman, she left out the rest of it.

"Oh darling, I'm so glad you're all right." Her mother dropped to the bed beside her.

"Where's Dad?" Surely he wouldn't leave her mom by herself after Serena's news that a serial killer may target those close to her.

"He said he had something to take care of." Her mother pursed her lips and shook her head. "Your father has been acting very strange over the last day or so."

"Strange how?" By not telling her mother about the conversation he'd had with Serena? And the extra protective measures he'd be making? Or was it the fact that her father had also been keeping their financial issues a secret? While Serena didn't agree with him on that particular score, it wasn't her secret to tell.

"He dropped me off with orders not to leave the hospital or talk to strangers. And this morning, he decided he needed to go grocery shopping with me. To make sure I got everything." An indignant look crossed her face. "Suddenly he's treating me like a two-year-old."

So, her father hadn't said anything about what had been going on with Serena and the serial killer. She wasn't so sure that was the wisest thing to do, but bit her lip. She'd honor her father's decision.

For now.

A knock on the door grabbed her attention and she looked up to see Dominic enter, followed by Paul, her lab assistant.

Paul shot her a sheepish grin. "Hope you don't mind me popping in. I ran into Dominic while he was talking to Daniel about what happened to you."

Serena lifted a brow at Dominic, unsure whether to be perturbed about that or not. "You talked to my boss?"

"Just to let him know what happened and to see if Jane Doe's tox screen had come back."

She supposed that was all right. "Had it?"

"Yes, I'll fill you in a little later." Dominic held a hand out to her mother who shook it. "I'm Dominic Allen, the one who called you."

Serena looked back and forth between the two of them. "Have you two never met before?"

Dominic shook his head. "I don't think so. You were in and out of my house a few times when you were a kid, but I don't think I ever met your mother."

Serena's mother eyed Dominic. "I appreciate you calling me."

"And this is Paul Hamilton, my assistant in the lab. Paul, my mom, Portia Hopkins."

The two shook hands then Paul said, "I've got to go back to work. Just wanted to make sure my favorite ME was going to be okay."

"Who was the ME who responded to the officer's death?" she asked, the guilt flooding back as she thought about him.

"Ralph Newton." Paul gave a little grimace.

Serena gave him a small smile. Ralph was a fantastic ME, but brusque and almost rude to those he considered beneath his station. Such as Paul.

Paul said, "I've got to go, but I'm glad you're all right. I'll talk to you soon."

Serena smiled at her friend and grimaced as pain shot through her head. "Thanks, Paul."

He left and Dominic said, "I've got a phone call. I'll be outside."

After the door shut behind Dominic, Serena asked, "So everything's all right? Nothing else weird going on?"

"No, nothing. Well, nothing other than our alarm system seems to have a glitch in it. They're supposed to send someone to come fix it sometime tomorrow, I think. Your father insisted on someone coming out as soon as possible."

"Oh good." Serena breathed a sigh of relief that her father was being as diligent about their security as he'd promised.

2:27 P.M.

Dominic answered his phone on the third ring. "Hey, what do you have?"

"Nothing on the guy that slammed into Serena. But the ME says that the bullet hole in the back of the officer came first. Then the execution-style one to the head," Colton reported.

Dominic felt no surprise at this. "So we were right. There's two of them. He's got a partner."

"Sure looks that way."

"What about the identity of the girl from the trunk? Anything more on her?"

"Yep. It's Kelsey Nicholson. The parents are devastated. Apparently she'd been going down a bad path since the shoplifting incident, she just hadn't been caught with anything since. They found drugs in her backpack and in her car and said they figured it was just a matter of time before she was caught. The fact that she's dead really hit them hard, though."

"Was she in the high school album?" Dominic tensed waiting for Colton to confirm his suspicions.

"Nope. I looked."

His tension dissipated. "Then there goes our theory."

"Actually, she went to school with Alexia and Serena, she just wasn't in the album. Turns out she cried sick that day. Her mother remembered because Kelsey refused to have her picture taken. She had a scar under her eye from a car accident the year before. Hated having her picture taken."

"But she graduated with them."

"She did."

"So our theory's back on." And so was the tightness in his gut. Dominic nodded to himself. "All right, I've still got to go talk to Nate. I called and let him know what happened and he said he could still meet later today."

"Want me to go with you?"

"That's all right, I've got it covered."

"Good deal."

———■———

Serena was more than ready to leave. While her mother stood off to the side speaking into her cell phone, she slid off the bed and got up and moving. Dominic was hanging up his phone as he came back into the room.

"Shouldn't you be in bed?" he asked.

"I'm getting out of here. I don't have a concussion, just aching muscles and a headache. I took some meds for that, so I should be good to go in a little while."

Dominic gave her a look that said he didn't believe her. "Yeah? You're moving a little slow."

Snagging her purse, she touched the swollen side of her face with the other hand. "I look like a clown, don't I? Or a domestic violence victim." She grimaced.

"You look like you went a round with Mike Tyson. But you can take pride in the fact that you look like . . ." He winced. "Well, maybe not like you won, but like you put up a good fight." He smiled.

"Ha. Smooth, Dominic, smooth." But she couldn't help the small smile. She knew the bruises would heal in time, but the fear this person had instilled in her would take longer to fade.

Her mother slid her cell phone in her purse and said, "Your father is on his way up here. Do you need a ride home?"

Serena thought about the man who rammed her car and killed the officer behind her. "No thanks, Mom. I'm good. Dominic can take me wherever I need to go." Then again, maybe she shouldn't assume. "Right?" she asked, hoping he understood why she didn't want to be in the car with her parents.

"Sure. We need to talk anyway." The look in his eye said he got it.

A knock on the door captured her attention. "Come in."

Her father stepped into the room and she introduced Dominic. "This is my dad, Joel Hopkins."

The men shook hands and her dad turned to her and said, "Sorry I wasn't here when you woke up."

She hugged him. "It's all right. Where'd you go?"

He shot a look at her mother, then back to Serena. "I had a little business with the bank."

"Oh." She frowned, wondering if there was more to it than he was telling. Probably.

"Dominic is going to take me home. But I appreciate you guys coming to see me."

Serena's mother hugged her. Hard. "I'm so glad you're okay. You scared us."

"I know, but I promise, other than a few bumps and bruises, I'm all right." She patted her mom's back and her dad slipped over to wrap her in his arms and press a kiss to the top of her head.

"You scared us, darling," he said, voice low, slightly shaky.

Serena inhaled the scent she'd known from childhood. Old Spice and . . . Dad. It gave her comfort. He stepped back and cleared his throat. "You know we're here if you need us."

"I know."

Her father nodded and took her mother's arm. "We'll be checking on you."

They left and Dominic moved toward the door. "You get your discharge papers?"

"I did."

"Did you let your boss know you were down for the count?"

"I thought you said I could take comfort in the fact that I looked like I won." She shot him a mock frown and he grinned.

She shrugged. "I called him. The other ME will cover any emergencies."

He held the door for her. "So, where should I take you?"

"Home, I guess. Until my headache calms down, I don't think I'd better attempt anything that requires thinking."

Together, they walked out of the hospital to the police parking area where Dominic opened the passenger door to his unmarked car.

Serena slid into the seat and leaned her head against the headrest. *Please make this headache go away.*

"Are you all right?"

She lifted her head and looked at him. "I'm fine. I'll let you know if I'm not, okay?"

"Tired of hearing that question?"

"Beyond tired," she laughed. "But thanks for caring."

He shot her a warm look, then focused on the road.

She leaned her head against the headrest again. "You still want to take the boat out in the morning?"

"Sure! If you think you're going to feel up to it."

Pleasure centered itself in her midsection. Along with a good measure of relief. She'd begun to wonder if all of this drama would cool his interest in her. But if he hadn't wanted to go, he could have made up some excuse about not being able to take a break from the case instead of finding a way to cover it.

"Great. We'll head out around 8:00?"

"I'll be there."

"I have another question for you."

He lifted a brow. "Sure."

"Will you check my house and garage and make sure no one's there?"

His smile immediately morphed into a frown. "Of course."

She told him about her weird experience in the garage right before she got slammed by the car.

He lifted a brow. "And you're just now telling me this?"

"Sorry. I kind of had other things on my mind. And I really don't think anyone was there. I'm just jumpy and scared."

"With good reason," he reminded her.

Dominic pulled into her driveway. After a thorough search of her garage and house, he pronounced it intruder free. "But there will be an officer outside all night."

"Great. Thanks."

He lifted a hand and pushed a strand of hair back behind her ear, then curved his palm around the back of her neck. Shivers danced across her skin and she didn't move.

He leaned forward and she stilled. Waited. Hoped her eyes conveyed the fact that she would welcome his kiss. His phone rang and he stiffened. Let out a disbelieving snort, then tapped her nose with a forefinger and said, "I'll be here bright and early."

Serena let him out of the house, bolted the door after him, and set the alarm. Frustration nipped at her.

Her heart still pounded with the knowledge that he'd planned to kiss her goodbye. She grimaced and figured there'd be another opportunity.

With a sigh of longing and a groan of pain at the throbbing in her head, she reached for the painkillers she'd had filled at the pharmacy, cut a pill in half, and popped it.

There was no way she was taking a whole pill that would knock her out. She needed to sleep, but she also needed to be able to wake up if someone tried to get in her house again.

27

Saturday morning dawned clear and hot. Serena rose and dressed in her swimsuit, blue jean shorts, and a hot pink tank top. Matching pink flip-flops completed her ensemble. Yoda's nails clicked on the hardwood floors as she walked behind her.

She definitely felt better. And knowing another officer was still watching her house added to that feeling.

In the garage, she pushed aside the tarp that had covered her boat before Dominic pulled it off last night to check the inside. She opened the garage, pulled the rental Suburban out, and maneuvered the vehicle until she could hook the boat trailer up to the hitch.

Just as she was finishing up, Dominic parked in front of her house. He hopped out of the car and waved to the officer, who waved back and drove off.

"Hey," Dominic called. "I could have helped you with that."

She smiled, ignoring the pull of sore skin stretched tight over the swollen area her attacker had hit yesterday. The pain medication had allowed her to fall into a fitful doze. She'd only gotten up about four times to check the window and make sure the cop was still watching her house.

234

"It's no problem. I've done it a million times."

He planted his hands on his hips and shook his head. "Impressive. You're quite the independent woman, aren't you?"

She cocked her head and shrugged. "When it comes to some things, yes."

He nodded toward the Suburban. "Nice rental. Looks familiar."

"Very funny." She shook her head. "At this rate, the rental place won't have any vehicles left by the end of next week." Serena opened the driver's side door. "My dad had it dropped off for me late last night."

She motioned for Dominic to get in. "If you're comfortable towing a trailer, it'd probably be better if you drove. You know, pain meds and all."

He grinned, walked passed her and around to the passenger door, and opened it. "Your chariot awaits, my lady."

She laughed as she came around the car, took his outstretched hand, and climbed in. He jogged to the driver's side, slid in, and pulled out of the driveway.

He expertly navigated the vehicle on the road, dividing his attention between the side mirrors and the road. She appreciated his vigilance. "How's Michelle's mother doing?"

He glanced at her for a split second before turning his gaze back to the road. "She's hanging in there. They did surgery on a ruptured spleen. She also had a head injury and is still in a coma. Right now, it's just wait and see."

"I'm so sorry for them."

He said, "I am too. Even though Chad and Stephanie have their problems, Alexia says she's a good woman and a great mom to Michelle."

"I've been praying for her."

He shot her a warm glance. "You're a good person, you know that?"

Serena let out a little laugh. "I'm not sure about that, but I believe God can do amazing things if his people will take the time to pray about them."

Without taking his eyes from the road, Dominic reached across and entwined his fingers with hers. "Thanks. I believe that too." He drove in silence for the next minute or two while she relished the feel of his calloused palm against hers.

"Did Rick say when he'd be done with your car?" he asked.

"Sometime tomorrow, or first thing on Monday, I think. I'm not holding my breath."

"I understand that. Everything always takes longer than we're told."

The thirty-minute drive out to Lake Murray passed quickly with small talk and anticipation of a quick two-hour escape. Maybe they'd be able to stretch it into three or four hours.

Once they got the boat in the water, Serena took the wheel and steered them out into the middle of the lake. After cutting the engine, she opened the glove compartment to put the key inside for safekeeping and gasped.

Dominic moved next to her. "What is it?"

She pointed. "Wrappers."

He lifted a brow. "You either have major junk food issues or . . ."

" . . . or someone's been using my boat as a trash can."

She flashed back to the feeling of someone being in her garage. "Who would *do* this? *How* would someone be *able* to do this?"

"Do you have some kind of bag you use for trash?"

"Yeah, lift up that cushion, there should be several in there."

Dominic did as she instructed and pulled out a plastic bag. "I'd prefer paper, but this'll have to do." He gathered the plastic wrappers and placed them in the bag. "I'll have Rick run them for prints."

Serena frowned and sighed. "I don't want to let that ruin our morning. We can't do anything about it at the moment. Let's just enjoy our time out here, okay?"

He gave her a lazy smile and lifted the cushion to put the trash bag back into the storage compartment. "I love that idea."

Serena felt her heart lift and climbed from the helm to the bow where there were two bolted lounging chairs. She slipped into one and Dominic claimed the other. She said, "The sun feels good on my face. It's not as swollen as I thought it would be."

"It looks pretty sore."

"Oh it's sore all right." She reached up to touch her cheek and the puffiness under her right eye. Thankfully, it would fade in time.

Dominic pulled a bottle of sunscreen from his bag. "Want some? I can do your back." He grinned and the glint in his eyes made her stomach flip.

She'd already sprayed sunscreen on this morning before getting the boat ready. She stood and grinned back. "I'd love some."

Dominic stood, keeping his balance easily on the gently rocking boat. But instead of spraying the liquid right onto her skin, he lathered up his hands and placed them on her bare shoulders. She'd shed her tank top the minute she'd stepped on the boat. The modest one-piece black suit she wore covered everything it was supposed to, but she knew it was flattering and Dominic was enjoying the view even though he acted like the perfect gentleman.

Glad the sun gave her an excuse for pink cheeks, she slid the sunglasses down to hide her eyes.

"Turn around."

She did and his hands slid over her shoulders to rub the lotion in. His touch sent tingles rippling up her nerve endings. Serena cleared her throat and said, "You know, that's spray sunscreen. You didn't have to get your hands all messy."

He gave a low chuckle under his breath. "Then what would I use as an excuse to touch you?"

When he finished her back, she turned and looked up at him while he kept his hands on her shoulders. "You don't need an excuse," she whispered.

His eyes darkened and he lifted one hand to push her sunglasses back up on her head. "That's good to know because I've been trying to figure out how to do this since I saw you."

He lowered his head and she froze as she waited for something to happen. A phone to ring, lake security to pick this moment to do a life jacket check, a speeding boat to send waves rocking their way. Something.

Instead, she felt his warm lips cover hers in a light exploratory kiss. When she didn't pull away, he wrapped his arms around her waist and tugged her closer.

He didn't have to ask twice. She lifted her hands and settled them on his sun-warmed biceps.

The kiss seemed to last forever—and then it was over. Her heartbeat tripled and her blood hummed through her veins at warp speed.

And she noticed all the tension had seeped from her tight shoulders.

Dominic lifted his head and looked at her for a long moment. Then he touched his forehead to hers. "I care about you, Serena. A lot. You're an amazing woman and I'm . . . I want to get to know you. More." He swallowed. "Especially when this case is over and we don't have all this craziness going on."

Serena bit her lip, flashes of her father's domineering, controlling ways snagging a corner of her mind. But while Dominic seemed to have some of those characteristics, he didn't use them to further his own agenda. At least he didn't seem to.

Uncertainty crossed his face and she slid her hands up to cup his cheeks. "I'd like that."

Relief made him slump and then he pulled her close again for another heart-stopping kiss. When they parted, he said, "You scared me when you hesitated. Don't do that again, okay?"

Serena laughed, feeling the pull in her injured cheek, but not caring as her heart felt light and carefree for the first time in . . . forever. "Okay."

For the next two hours, they played like children, letting the cares of the world fade while sunning themselves on the cushions at the front of the boat, then diving into the lake to cool off.

Finally Serena wrung the water from her wet hair and said, "I'm starving. Do you want to eat at the marina?"

"Sure. Sounds good." He patted his flat belly. "I'm running on empty myself."

She pulled two bottles of water from the cooler and tossed him one. After taking a long swig, she cranked the boat. Over the hum of the motor, she heard Dominic's cell phone ring.

———————

Dominic groaned as he snatched it and Serena cut the motor.

"Hey, Colton, what's up?"

"Thought you might be interested in this little piece of information I just got."

"What's that?"

Dominic hit the speaker button as his eyes met Serena's. Colton said, "Leslie and Patricia both had their alarm systems worked on in the last month."

Dominic stilled. "Okay."

"We think that's how he's getting in without setting off the alarm."

"So, he's messing with the alarm system, then posing as a representative of the alarm company, getting the homeowner's passcode, sneaking in at night, drugging the victim and carting her off to kill her."

"Possibly." He thought for a moment. "And they're single women who live alone. At least these two have been."

"Serena's alarm went off Thursday night. Hold on a second." He looked at her and asked, "Have you had any trouble with your alarm system in the last few weeks?"

She frowned. "No." She snapped her head up. "Wait a minute,

someone from the alarm company came by to do a survey about two weeks ago."

"A survey?"

"Some customer satisfaction thing."

Dominic spoke into the phone. "Did you get that?"

"I'll check it out. See if it was legit," Colton said.

But Dominic had a feeling in the pit of his stomach that it wasn't. "She changed her code Thursday."

"And the alarm went off."

Dominic nodded even though Colton couldn't see him. "Right. So, the killer didn't realize she'd changed the code when he went back to get in? Only she wasn't there and he didn't know how to turn off the alarm."

"Maybe."

"But that doesn't explain the teenager the neighbor saw running from the house."

"Maybe she didn't have anything to do with anything. It was just a coincidence? Or she was coming to see Serena and got there just as the alarm went off."

Serena lifted a brow and mouthed, "Camille?"

He nodded, then said to Colton, "That's a good theory. Or, it wasn't the killer at all, but a teenager trying to break in, didn't realize the windows were wired too, and set the alarm off."

"Or that," Colton agreed. "Still, I think it's more than just co-incidence that these two had their systems worked on and ended up targets of a serial killer."

"I agree."

Dominic saw Serena pale as though she'd just thought of something that scared her. Tucking the phone under his chin, he said, "What is it?"

"My mom said something was wrong with their alarm system and someone was coming out today to fix it."

28

Serena listened to the phone ring while Dominic hitched the boat to the trailer and the trailer to the Suburban. "They're still not answering." Fear bit at her. A fear like she'd never experienced before. When she'd thought the killer was just after her, that was one thing. But to go after those she loved . . .

She hit redial. "Please, please . . ."

"Colton should be there by now. He'll call as soon as he knows anything."

She'd been ready to leave the boat in the water, jump in the car, and head to her parents' house. Fortunately, Dominic was thinking more clearly. He'd still had Colton on the phone and filled him in. Colton promised to call Hunter. Dominic explained they would be able to get there faster.

She looked at him, realization upping her fear to terror. "You're stalling me."

"What?"

"You sent Colton and Hunter out there so they could warn you in case—" She bit off the thought, but Dominic's guilty flush told her she was right.

"I didn't want you rushing over there to find something you don't need to see." His quiet honesty stilled her rising anger.

"You had no right to do that," she whispered.

He narrowed his eyes. "I thought . . . I was just trying to protect you. I thought maybe it would be best to make sure Hunter and Colton got there first."

Serena went silent, her thoughts churning, gut swirling.

That was something her father would have done. And something she would have to consider later. After she found her parents safe.

She turned her attention back to the ringing phone now going to voice mail. Hanging up, she redialed.

He looked up at her as he opened the door for her. "Anything?"

"No." She clenched her jaw against the worry surging through her. "Answer the phone," she muttered as she hit redial.

Then she tried her father's office, remembered it was Saturday, and hung up. She dialed her mother's number once again as Dominic started the car and took off.

Dominic's phone rang and he snatched it from the cup holder and put it on speakerphone. "Hello."

"Colton here. We're at the Hopkins residence. There doesn't appear to be anyone home nor any sign of foul play."

Relief nearly made her weep. She'd pictured their dead bodies sprawled out on the den floor with bullet holes in their foreheads. But . . . "Then where are they? Why won't they answer their phones?"

"Wait a minute, I've got a gray BMW pulling up."

"That's my dad's car."

Serena and Dominic were still almost twenty minutes away from her parents' subdivision.

"He's pulling into the driveway now."

"Go easy, don't alarm them," Dominic said. "But don't let them go into the house without checking it out first. I'm about fifteen minutes out."

"Got it."

Dominic hung up and Serena leaned her head back against the seat, uttering prayers of thanks to God that her parents were safe.

The next fifteen minutes seemed to last a lifetime, but they finally were waved through by the guard at the gate when Dominic flashed his badge. When they pulled up at her parents' house, she saw her father standing next to the police car.

Dominic parked and Colton walked over to greet them. Serena bolted from the car to her father. "Are you all right?"

His pale face said he'd gotten the details about what Colton had learned. He nodded. "I'm fine, but I can't seem to get in touch with your mother." He raked a hand through his hair, an action Serena had never seen him do before. "She was supposed to be waiting on the alarm company rep, but Colton here tells me they don't have any record of a troubleshooting report."

"Did you call them or did they call you?"

"They called us." Her father's quiet words echoed around them.

"What do you mean?" Serena asked.

"The alarm was flashing trouble on the pad. A few minutes after I noticed it, the phone rang. I took the call and the person identified herself as a representative with the alarm company."

"Herself? A woman?"

"Yes, I believe so. She had me give the password and then told me a few buttons to push to reset it. Walked me through the entire process and said they would send someone out to make sure it was working properly."

"Today."

"Right."

"And did someone come?"

Her father looked helpless. "I don't know. I had a meeting this morning with my campaign manager and was just now coming home."

"Why didn't you answer your cell phone?" Serena demanded.

He blinked and pulled the phone from his front shirt pocket. He shot her an apologetic glance. "I had it on silent."

Outraged, Serena stared at him. "After what I told you about being stalked by a serial killer? And the fact that you and Mom might need some extra protection?" Tears of anger welled in her eyes. "How could you?"

He narrowed his eyes, his body stiffening defensively. "Serena, I had everything under control. This was an extremely important planning meeting. I didn't want to be disturbed."

"Didn't want to—" She chomped down on her tongue. She would not say anything she'd regret later.

This was her father.

She'd thought he was changing, becoming more open to the fact that things wouldn't always go the way he thought they should.

And he still thought he had everything under control.

"Where's my mother?"

The defensive posture slackened. "I don't know." He looked at the house. "She was supposed to be here."

"Well, she's not and she's not answering her phone."

Dominic looked at Colton. "Let's start canvassing the neighborhood. See if anyone saw Mrs. Hopkins this morning." He switched his gaze to Serena's father. "Sir, could you give us her cell number? We'll put a trace on it and see if we can get her location."

"Sure. Yeah, but she probably forgot about the alarm company coming and went to meet a friend for lunch."

"Give us a list of names of friends."

While her father passed on that information, Serena walked over to her father's car and pressed a button on the remote.

"She didn't go meet anyone, Dad."

"Why not?"

Serena pointed to the garage. "Her car is still here."

"We tracked her cell phone," Hunter said.

"Where is it?" Serena asked.

244

Hunter's eyes shifted to Dominic, then back to Serena. "Your house."

Dominic couldn't quell the dread that rose up in him. With a glance at Colton, he said, "Get someone over there." He grabbed Serena before she could get back in the Suburban to go racing over to her house. She pulled out of his grasp. "I have to get to her!"

Dominic saw Serena's father heading for his BMW. There wasn't going to be any stopping him. The man roared off and Dominic motioned for Serena to go ahead and get in. She'd be safer with him than trying to drive in her upset state.

"Hurry!" she urged. Then closed her eyes, her lips moving silently. He joined her in her prayer, pleading for God to spare Serena's mother.

If the killer had her.

And he suspected he did.

Serena's home finally came into view and she grabbed the handle, ready to throw the door open. Dominic snagged her wrist and held her in place even as he brought the vehicle to a full stop.

Police cruisers arrived, one after the other.

"Mom," she whispered.

"Stay here," Dominic ordered.

Tearful, pleading eyes lasered into him. "I can't."

Dominic ground his molars. "You have to. We have to clear the house. I'll let you in as soon as I can."

He could see Colton and Hunter racing for the front door. Serena climbed back into the vehicle and pressed the button on the remote to raise the garage door.

Colton kept going for the front door. Hunter changed direction and went for the garage. Serena's father pulled behind the nearest cruiser and headed for the house. An officer grabbed him and pulled him back. The man struggled until the officer said something. The man stopped his attempts to escape and swiveled to turn his attention to the action going on in front of Serena's house.

Once Dominic was certain Serena would stay put, he took off toward the garage to follow Hunter. Hunter was already in the den when Dominic heard him yell, "Clear!"

Serena's animals were nowhere to be seen.

Colton hollered, "In here!"

Dominic exchanged a microsecond look with Hunter before they both rushed out onto the glassed-in porch.

They came to a screeching halt.

Mrs. Hopkins sat tied to a chair, eyes closed.

With a bullet taped to her forehead.

"Mom!" Serena gasped from behind them.

Dominic turned and grasped her by the upper arms. "I told you to stay outside."

"I'm a doctor, remember?" She jerked from him to rush to her mother's side. "Mom," she whispered.

"She's alive," Colton said. He held up his phone. "Ambulance is on the way."

Serena flashed him a grateful look. She ran her hands over her mother, placing her fingers against the side of her neck, relieved to feel her pulse beating and strong. She lifted an eyelid. "She's been drugged."

"But she's alive. Let's get that bullet into a bag and let's get it to Rick," Dominic said. "And anything else on her clothing that might lead us to the person that did this to her."

He leaned over, concern written all over him. He snapped on a pair of gloves that one of the other officers handed him, then pulled the bullet, tape and all, from her mother's forehead. He placed the items in the paper bag that also materialized from one of the officers.

She lifted her eyes to Dominic. "Will you let my dad know what's going on?"

He turned to the officer behind him and relayed the request.

Serena watched as Hunter cut her mother's arms free, careful not to touch the ropes with his hands. Serena used a now gloved hand to place the rope pieces in another paper bag.

Then Dominic lifted her gently from the chair to carry the woman into the den and place her on the sofa.

Serena dashed into her spare bedroom where she kept her kit from med school. Racing back into the den, she pulled out her stethoscope and slid to a halt next to the couch. Dropping to her knees, she placed the end of the device on her mother's chest, closed her eyes, and listened. "Lungs sound clear." She continued with the checkup, then sat back in relief. "I think she's okay. Whatever he drugged her with hasn't affected her heartbeat or breathing."

She grabbed the tweezers from her kit and pulled every scrap of hair, fiber, and speck of evidence she could see from her mother's clothing. She checked her mother's pulse once more, relieved to find it still unchanged. "It's like she's in a really deep sleep."

The wail of the ambulance reached their ears. Serena looked at the note now held in Hunter's gloved hands. "What does it say?"

She didn't really want to know, but she had to.

Hunter glanced around the room then said, "It's blank."

"What?"

He shook the card. "There's nothing on it."

Dominic lifted a hand to his aching head. "Really? So what's that all about?"

"I just photographed it and sent it to Debbie."

Colton's phone rang. He stepped aside and answered it. His face paled as he listened and Serena wondered what bad news he was receiving now.

A commotion near the door grabbed her attention. "That's my wife! Let me in! Serena!"

Colton motioned for the officer to let him in. He tucked the phone under his chin. "She's all right, sir."

Her father stumbled into the room, saw his wife on the couch, and gave a small cry. Paramedics followed on his tail as he rushed over to drop beside Serena and take his wife's hand in his.

"What happened? Is she all right?"

"I checked her over. She's been drugged but seems to be all right." She nudged his shoulder. "Let the paramedics through."

He moved, but not far. Serena gave the paramedics a rundown of what she knew, then watched them take her mother's vitals, load her onto the gurney, and push her out the door with her father trailing. He looked over his shoulder, his expression curious to her. "What is it, Dad?"

"I want to go to the hospital with your mother, but I don't want to leave you with this crazy—"

"Go," she said with a glance at Dominic and Hunter. "I'll be fine."

He didn't need any more encouragement. Her father gave her a short nod, but the look in his eye promised they'd talk soon.

Serena stood and dropped onto the couch, weariness flooding her. And she realized she was starving. And nauseous at the thought of eating. Then she sat straight up. "Where are my animals? Yoda? Chewie?"

Dominic frowned. "The house was clear."

"They're not here?" she shrieked.

"Hey, calm down. We'll find them."

Serena raced through the house, calling her pets but getting no response.

An officer entered through the front door and Serena rounded on him. "Did you see a dog and a cat out there?"

"I didn't see a cat, but there's a dog in the backyard."

Frowning, she raced back through to the sunroom door and opened it. Yoda nearly tackled her. Relief brought tears to her eyes and she blinked them back. "Hey girl, why didn't you use your doggie door?"

Now that she knew she was all right, she pushed Yoda out of the sunroom and shut the door. She barked her displeasure, but Serena ignored her as she examined the dog's opening.

Someone had slid the hard piece of plastic into the holder, which effectively shut the door to keep the animals inside or outside. Her intruder had banned her animals from the house so he could go about his business unfettered.

She shuddered and walked down the hall to the guest closet. Opening the door she normally kept cracked, she spied Chewie in her favorite spot. On the top shelf of the closet organizer. Breathing another huff of relief, she turned to go back down the hall to the den.

Another thought hit her. The alarm hadn't gone off. Not when the intruder had brought her mother here, nor when the authorities cleared the house.

She walked back to ask Dominic. "Why didn't my alarm go off?"

"It wasn't on."

"What do you mean? Of course it was on. I never leave without arming it."

He shrugged, his eyes clouded with his concern. "Maybe you forgot this time."

Frustrated, scared, and exhausted beyond belief, she placed her hands on her hips. "I did *not* forget to arm it."

Her phone buzzed and zombie-like, she pulled it from the back pocket of her jean shorts.

"Camille stopped by to let me know to call you and tell you that she was living with her father again, but they had a fight. I just checked and she's gone again," Mrs. Lamb said.

Serena made an attempt to pull her thoughts together. "I'm not surprised. Sad to hear it, but not surprised." She was relieved that Camille seemed all right, but why hadn't she called or texted?

"I fed her a hot meal and gave her some prenatal vitamins."

"Thank you." Serena bit her lip and thought. "All right, if she comes back, tell her I really need to talk to her and let me know, will you?"

"Sure thing. Sorry, love."

"Me too."

She hung up, her mind still buzzing, the ebbing adrenaline making her feel light-headed.

"Are you all right?"

"Yes. I think. I need to get to the hospital so I can be there when my mom wakes up."

"I'll take you."

She stared at Dominic, unsure whether she wanted him to drive her or not. "You shouldn't have done that today."

He didn't have to ask what she meant. Instead, he dropped his head, then looked up at her. "Maybe not. I wanted to protect you."

"You took away my choice."

A frown flickered in his eyes. "I didn't realize that's what I was doing."

Serena sighed and looked away. Was she making too big a deal out of this?

Probably. But she was worried, tired, and cranky . . . and just plain scared out of her wits. "It doesn't matter now, I guess."

"Then can I drive you?"

"Sure."

Serena moved with him toward the door.

Dominic said, "I'll have someone stay on the house until everyone is finished up here. I don't think the guy will be back, but . . ."

"Right."

As she stepped off the porch, Serena looked up to see Colton and Hunter standing next to Colton's car. Twin grim expressions graced their faces and Serena felt her stomach twist.

"There's another one, isn't there?" she whispered.

Colton nodded.

"She was found in the same park as Leslie, but sitting under a tree."

"Did she have a package?"

Hunter nodded. "Rick's already out there."

Serena firmed her jaw. "Then I guess we need to join him."

Dominic frowned. "Hey, what about your mom?"

"My mother will be fine. She just needs to sleep it off. I don't want anyone else working on these bodies. If you have two different MEs working, something might be missed."

"Or one might see something the other one didn't."

Serena narrowed her eyes at Colton's statement. "True. But I want this one. If you think you need to have someone go behind me, then you take that up with my boss."

Colton held up a hand. "I didn't mean that, Serena."

Some of her anger deflated. "Sorry. I'm a little tense right now." She looked at the men. "But I'm still going." She paused. "Hold on a second. I want to get the yearbook." She stomped back inside to grab the book from the shelf.

Back outside, she asked Dominic, "Are you driving or do I need to take my own car?"

29

The killer watched from the sidelines and frowned. What was he doing? This wasn't supposed to happen. Tension swirled. Someone was messing with a plan that had already started spiraling out of control.

This latest problem was not going to go over well.

At all.

———■———

Serena and Dominic arrived at the crime scene after stopping off at the hospital for Serena to grab the items she needed to process the body.

Serena had called her father on the way to explain this new development, and he'd assured them that all was under control at the hospital and she was to do her job without worrying about her mother. "She's sleeping comfortably. They just want to keep an eye on her and will probably release her later this evening if nothing else develops."

Rick looked up and motioned her and Dominic over. Colton and Hunter brought up the rear. Serena placed her kit off to the side, not wanting to put it on the ground near the body in case the killer had left some trace evidence there.

To Rick, she said, "Why don't you go over this area and then I'll move on to the body."

He nodded and got busy. Thirty minutes later, he said, "I didn't get much, but maybe there'll be something in there we can use."

Serena moved to the dead girl. Curly blond hair that looked natural, not bottled, blue eyes, late twenties. A pretty girl Serena didn't need her yearbook to identify. "Hilary Meyer, head cheerleader and president of the debate team."

"Talented girl."

Serena felt grief nearly choke her. She'd known Hilary well, and while they hadn't spoken in several years, seeing her like this was hard. All deaths were hard, but this one . . .

Gathering her emotions together, she shoved them into a spot in her mind where she could pull them out later and deal with them. Right now, she needed to do her job.

As she worked on Hilary, Dominic stood at her side. Silent and thoughtful. And watching. Finally, she looked up. "What is it?"

"What's her TOD?"

Serena rubbed her nose with the back of her wrist. "I really hate to give out a time of death at the scene, but if you're going to twist my arm, I would say it was anywhere from three to seven hours ago. Probably closer to four and a half to five. Her core temp is 97.9, but if she's been sitting out here awhile, it would take longer for her to cool off in this heat. Her eyes aren't cloudy yet, so that's definitely less than twelve hours dead. No rigor yet, faint lividity on her hands, calves, and back, suggesting she was lying in a prone position on her back for a while after she died. Which probably was sometime between 8:30 this morning and 2:00 this afternoon."

Dominic frowned and gave an exasperated growl. "How is that possible?"

"What do you mean?"

"I mean how was she being murdered at the same time your mother is disappearing? Both at the hands of the same person?"

Serena frowned and tried to follow the timeline in her head. "I don't know. It's possible Hilary was killed around 8:30, then the killer went to my parents' house, grabbed my mother, and took her to my house, then went back to get Hilary wherever he'd left her and . . ." She trailed off and shook her head. "We won't know how long my mom was at my house until she wakes up and can tell us what happened."

Dominic rubbed his chin and Serena could feel the tension and stress emanating from him. "No, this just proves our killer has help. An accomplice. I was hoping that was wrong, but this nails it."

"Hey, Dominic, we've got a witness."

———■———

Dominic spun on his heel, his mind still working on the math, the timetable of events that had unfolded today. They still didn't make sense.

Hunter ushered a teenage boy off to the side, out of sight of the victim. Once again, the police had set up a barricade to keep the gawkers from being able to see much, but the news trucks had arrived and had their high-powered cameras aimed his way.

Biting back words he'd quit saying years ago, he motioned that he was coming.

Hunter kept the witness out of sight of the television cameras too. No sense in having the kid swarmed after he told Hunter and Dominic what they wanted to know.

"What do you have?"

"This is Corey Sims. He said he might have seen a bit of what happened over there by the tree."

Hunter took in the kid's bobbing Adam's apple and nervous licking of his lips. But he seemed willing to talk. "Tell me what you saw, son."

"I . . . um . . . I was meeting a friend here. We were going to toss the Frisbee awhile. Anyway, this dude wearing jeans and a

254

long-sleeved shirt rides by on a bicycle with this chick hanging on his back. I noticed him because I thought that he must be crazy to have on those kind of clothes in this heat."

"Did you get a look at his face?"

Corey shook his head. "No, he had on like a motorcycle helmet or something." He shrugged. "But some people are weird. Whatever."

"What else?"

"He stopped his bike and the girl just kind of slid off his back and slumped against the tree like she didn't feel good. He got off the bike and sat down beside her."

"Did he ever take off the helmet?"

"No. I almost went over and asked if they were okay, but there was just something kind of creepy about it all."

"Good instincts," Dominic murmured.

"Then he put a package in her lap and her head dropped down to look at it. He got up, said something to her, then got back on his bike and left. My friend got here and we started playing Frisbee. The next thing you know, some girl starts screaming that the woman was dead and you guys arrived."

"What time would you say you saw this guy put the girl under the tree?"

Corey's brow furrowed as he thought. He glanced at his watch. "Probably 1:00. The guy got here around 1:15. We've been here ever since." A flush darkened his already sun-pinked cheeks. "When we saw all the action going on, we stayed. I figured I'd better tell someone what I saw, so I waited until you started asking questions."

"Thanks, Corey." Hunter slapped the teen on his shoulder. "Can you give me a number in case I need to reach you?"

"Sure." Corey rattled it off and Hunter wrote it in the little black notebook he carried.

Dominic had one just like it. He looked over at Rick and Serena, who now had the package in front of them. With gloved hands, Rick worked the top off and reached inside.

Dominic moved closer. "What does it say?"

"'Eenie meenie miney moe, I like this game, I love it so. I'll be the winner, I'll come out on top, I play to win. You, I'll stop.'"

"More bad poetry." Dominic gave a disgusted grunt and watched as Serena directed the loading of Hilary's body into the body bag and then the back of the ambulance. They would transport her to the morgue where Serena would take over.

"I'm really beginning to hate the stuff," Serena agreed.

Dominic stood beside her as they watched the ambulance pull away. "That's four. Five, with Howard."

She bit her lip. "We have to stop him, Dominic. Now."

"I know, Serena, I know." He tightened his jaw. "Let's go see what we can find out from your mother."

They rode to the hospital in silence, each lost in thought.

———■———

By the time Serena found herself standing in front of her mother's door, she had a plan. A really bad, dangerous plan. One that she kept to herself because she knew exactly what Dominic would say about it. However, the only way to stop the next victim from dying was to stop the killer.

Even if she had to set herself up as bait to do it.

———■———

Serena's silence worried him. The little vertical crease in the middle of her forehead told him she was thinking about something. Something serious. And she wasn't sharing it with him. Yet.

Serena knocked on the door.

"Come in." The voice sounded weak. Tired. But at least the woman was alive.

They stepped into the room to find Mrs. Hopkins propped into a sitting position. Her eyes drooped, but she seemed coherent.

Serena rushed to the woman's side while Dominic shook Joel's hand. "How's she doing?"

"Pretty good. Of course she's going to be woozy awhile, but they gave her something to counteract the drug. She woke up about thirty minutes ago."

The two women hugged. Then Serena sat on the bed beside her mother.

Dominic stepped over and said, "I'm glad you're all right, Mrs. Hopkins."

She gave him a small smile. "Thank you."

"Can you tell us what happened?"

The woman lifted a hand to her eyes and brushed aside a stray hair. "I don't really remember much. I remember the doorbell ringing and letting the alarm system person in."

"What time was that?" Serena asked.

Mrs. Hopkins' brow furrowed. "Hmm . . . probably around 11:00 or so."

Dominic caught Serena's glance and knew what she was thinking. That was right there in the range of Hilary's time of death.

"Then what happened?"

"I turned to point to the alarm panel and felt a sting in the back of my neck. The next thing I know I'm waking up here." She cast a frantic glance at her husband, who hovered in the background. "Were we robbed?"

"No, darling," Serena's father hastened to reassure his traumatized wife. "No, we weren't."

"Then why—"

Serena's father cleared his throat and motioned to Serena not to say anything.

Dominic could see Serena's concern. "I'm sorry, Mom. It was probably someone who just got his kicks out of hurting people. I'm sure the police will catch whoever did this."

Her mother's sharp eyes said she wasn't buying that, but then her glance landed on Serena's father and she held her tongue.

Dominic watched the interaction between the couple. Interesting.

Joel hadn't told the woman she could have been the serial killer's next victim.

"What did this person look like?"

"He looked like . . ." She trailed off. "I don't really know. He had on a blue jumpsuit with the security logo on the back and a matching baseball cap. Short hair." She shrugged and bit her lip, looking so much like Serena, he almost smiled. Except there was nothing about the subject matter that was amusing. She said, "You know, I just had a glimpse. He pretty much kept his head down, looking at his clipboard when he talked." Her voice quivered. "I guess that was so I wouldn't get a good look at him."

They visited a bit longer, but Mrs. Hopkins didn't have anything more to add no matter how cleverly Dominic phrased the questions. She'd been unconscious almost the entire time. He'd gotten all he was going to get.

"Thank you for your help."

Her lips twisted. "I don't think I was much help, but I sure hope you catch him."

Dominic waited for Serena to say her goodbyes, then ushered her out the door.

"There's two of them working together," he said. "It has to be."

"Just like you thought by the way things went down with the car accident." She paused. "But it wasn't an accident. What do you call a car wreck that's done on purpose?"

"Vehicular assault," he muttered.

She shivered and he placed an arm around her shoulders, tucking her up against him. He liked the way she fit there.

"I need to do the autopsy on Hilary," she said.

"We both know what you'll find."

"I know. She'll be just like the others."

"She can wait until tomorrow," Dominic insisted. "Rick's processing the evidence gathered from her. The work is still going on. But you're exhausted and I am too."

"Okay. So . . . what are we going to do now?" she asked.

Before he could answer, his phone rang. He glanced at the caller ID and said, "It's Terry. Let's hope he has something for us on Gwendolyn Lindell." He tucked the phone against his ear. "Hello?"

"Your Ms. Lindell is a slippery thing," Terry grunted.

"But not too slippery for the great Special Agent Terry O'Donnell, I'm sure."

A sigh reached Dominic's ear. "Actually, I'm at a loss. I did manage to track her from the States, to Canada, to Ecuador, back to the States about a year ago. And then she vanished. Nothing with the credit cards, couldn't find a fake ID, nothing. She's staying low, working a job that doesn't require prints, and is paying cash."

"Or she's dead and no one's found the body yet."

"Or that."

"All right, let me know if you find something concrete."

"Will do."

Dominic hung up and frowned as he glanced around the area leading into the parking garage. Looked clear. His eyes probed, seeking any immediate danger or threat. He kept Serena close to him, not just because he liked her there, which he did, but he wanted to use his own body as a shield. If someone decided to take a shot at her, he wanted her as hard to see as possible.

When nothing happened by the time they entered the darker, cooler interior of the parking garage, he still wouldn't let himself relax. His eyes scanned in an arc, his ears in tune with the sounds around them.

"Are you all right?"

"Just fine."

"You're about to squeeze me in half."

He loosened his grip. "Oops, sorry."

They arrived at his car and she looked at him. "Why did you park in here when you could've parked right outside the hospital?"

Once inside the vehicle, he answered, "Because I didn't want to draw attention to the fact that I was here. If someone followed us," he shrugged, "there's not much I can do about that. But my car sitting right out front would be like a neon sign."

"Oh. True. Just wondered."

He nodded to the pole he'd parked beside. "See that?"

"The camera?"

"Right. That one is trained on this area." He nodded to the one across the garage. "And that one is also aimed this way. There's one behind me too."

Realization dawned. "Ah. So if anyone tried anything, you'd have a really good picture of it."

"Exactly."

Her stomach gurgled and she clasped a hand over it, embarrassment staining her cheeks.

He lifted a brow. "Hungry?"

The embarrassment faded and she drawled, "What gave you that idea?"

"Come on, I'll feed you. Katie's on your house tonight. I'll let her know she doesn't need to get there until around 11:00. Does that work for you?"

"Sure." The soft smile she shot him couldn't hide the fear she was feeling—or the bone-deep weariness.

"Hey," he said, reaching over to grasp her left hand in his. He squeezed her fingers. "We're going to get this guy."

"I know."

"What's that verse? Isaiah 40:31?"

She closed her eyes and quoted, "'But those who hope in the LORD will renew their strength. They will soar on wings like eagles; they will run and not grow weary, they will walk and not be faint.'"

"Don't give up, Serena. God's with us in this. He wants the killing to stop too."

She pulled in a deep breath and opened her eyes to look at him.

"Then why doesn't he just lead us to the killer," she grumbled. Bit her lip and looked up, staring out the window. "I'm not giving up. You don't have to worry about that."

He glanced at her, troubled by the sudden hard look in her eyes. "What? What are you thinking?"

She blinked. "I'm worried about Camille. I just wish she would call or text or something."

"You want me to put a BOLO out on her?"

Serena bit her lip. "Let's give it one more day. If I haven't heard from her by tomorrow night, you can do that. Let me check with her father first."

"Sure, if you think that's what you need to do."

"Tomorrow's Sunday."

"A day of rest."

She snorted. "Not for the weary."

He nodded to a local fast-food place. "How about a burger?" She wrinkled her nose and he laughed. "I'm just kidding."

"Cute." Her eyes brightened. "How about one of my pizzas?"

"You really like pizza, don't you?"

"I have to confess, it's my absolute favorite meal ever."

"It's not really a meal, you realize that, right?"

She pursed her lips. "Take me home, Mr. Special Agent FBI man, and I'll whip us up a *meal* of a pizza."

He felt a smile curve his lips and thought about that. He discovered he smiled a lot whenever Serena was around. That is, when she wasn't making him frown with worry and exasperation. And outright fear for her life.

Dominic pulled into Serena's driveway. Once inside, he made her wait while he cleared the place. Thankfully, it didn't appear that anyone had been inside. He made the call to Katie while Serena got busy in her kitchen.

"So you're going to stay there awhile? Till 11:00?"

He heard something in her voice but couldn't identify it. "Yes.

I've got her covered until then." He frowned. Was Hunter right? Was Katie interested in him as more than a fellow cop and friend?

"All right. I'll be there at 11:00."

"Thanks, Katie."

"Right." She hung up and Dominic just sat there for a minute.

"Everything all right?"

He looked up to see Serena in the doorway. Her beauty took his breath for a moment. He smiled. "Yeah. Fine. Katie will be here at 11:00." Serena bit her lip and looked away. Dominic frowned. "What is it?"

"She's in love with you," she said softly.

He froze. First Hunter, now Serena. "What makes you say that?"

She let out a puff of laughter. "I'm a woman, we notice these things."

He stood and walked over to her, took her hands in his, and said, "I'm not in love with her."

"I know."

He lifted a brow. "You do?"

"I'm a woman, we notice those things too."

"Really?" He had no doubt she was observant.

"Really. Besides, you wouldn't have kissed me on the boat if you were in love with Katie. You're not that kind of man."

"You're absolutely right. I wouldn't have kissed you on the boat. Or now." He pulled her closer and leaned over to capture her lips with his. She returned the kiss, lifting her hands to cup his face. When he pulled back, he said, "I want you to be safe, Serena. I don't want to lose you now that I've found you."

Tears misted her eyes. "I know."

"So," he cleared his throat and backed up a step, "would you like to go to church with me in the morning?"

"I would love to."

30

SUNDAY, 8:30 A.M.

Serena glanced in the mirror one more time, satisfied that she'd done a pretty good makeup job. The bruise on her cheek was only slightly noticeable. She padded into the kitchen and opened the drawer where she'd shoved Jillian's package.

Tomorrow she'd take it to the bank and put it in a safe deposit box.

Her doorbell rang and her heart flipped as she pulled the package from the drawer. She really needed to put it someplace safer.

Rushing into the foyer, she spied the small table and mirror her grandmother had passed down to her. Slipping the package behind the mirror, she let it rest against the bottom piece of wood that protruded to hold the mirror slightly off the wall.

Stepping back, she looked at the mirror and decided it was a good hiding place for now.

She opened the door to find Dominic standing on her porch. "You're the most punctual person I know," she said.

He laughed. "Come on. I'm going to enjoy going to church with you."

Serena smiled. "Yeah. It'll be nice to worship and totally focus on God for a while." She sobered. "And pray for the capture of a killer."

Dominic's smile slid. "I've been praying that for a long time now."

As they climbed into his car, her phone rang. She snatched it from the side pocket of her purse.

Covenant House.

"Hello?"

"Serena? This is Mrs. Lamb. Camille is here and said she had to talk to you. She said the guilt is eating her up inside."

Guilt? Concerned, Serena said, "Tell her I'll be right there."

Dominic lifted a brow when she hung up. "We're not going to church, are we?"

"I'm not." She frowned. "I'm sorry. Camille's at Covenant House and I really need to talk to her. Why don't you let me get my car and I'll meet you at church after I finish with her."

"You're kidding, right?"

She read the look in his eyes. "You're going to take me, huh?"

He simply lifted a brow.

Ten minutes later, Dominic pulled into the parking lot. "I'll walk you up and then come back out to make a few phone calls."

"That's fine. There's a security officer on campus at all times and the entrances and exits are monitored. Visitors have to be buzzed in, so if you decide to come in, press the white button by the door."

He looked relieved. "Sounds like you'll be secure."

"Secure enough."

They walked to the building and Serena showed her ID. After being buzzed in, she headed toward the family room, stopping several times to speak to the girls who recognized her.

"Hey, Ms. Serena, I got a job!" Serena turned to give a too-skinny black girl a hug.

"Good for you, Amanda. I'm proud of you."

The girl frowned. "You won't kick me out of here yet, will you?"

264

"No way. You know you're welcome here until you can save some money and find a place to live."

The girl's brow smoothed. "I know, but I just wanted to make sure."

"Relax, you're doing great."

Serena gave her another hug, finished her trek down the hall, and entered the family room.

Camille had staked out her spot in the corner of the couch. Her eyes were on the television screen, but Serena didn't think the girl was paying any attention to what played there. Serena spoke to several of the other girls who recognized her and smiled.

"Camille?"

Camille jumped and swiveled her head. Then she popped up and threw herself into Serena's surprised arms.

"Hey." She hugged the thin teen and pulled back with a smile. "Now that's what I call a greeting."

A flush crept into Camille's cheeks. "Sorry."

"Don't be sorry at all." Serena gave her another quick hug, then motioned for her to sit. Camille did and Serena sat beside her. "Where have you been? Why didn't you answer my texts and calls?"

Camille's eyes darted to the window then back to Serena. "It doesn't matter. I . . . um . . . I just had some things I had to work through."

"You want to talk about them?"

"Not really."

Serena decided to change the subject. "Have you seen a doctor?"

"No." Camille let out a mournful sigh. "What am I going to do?"

Serena studied the teen. "I don't know, Camille, I guess that's really up to you."

A long pause filled the silence, then Camille whispered, "I almost had an abortion."

Serena's breath hitched and she felt her stomach tilt. "But you didn't."

"I just couldn't. I . . . kept picturing the ultrasound that woman did at the pregnancy center and seeing the beating heart and . . . ," tears welled and spilled over before she finally finished, "I couldn't. I wanted to, but . . . I couldn't."

Serena reached over and gathered Camille into her arms. "I'm so glad you couldn't do it."

"Yeah." Camille rose and walked to the window. Standing off to the side, she pushed the curtain to look out.

"Is something wrong?"

Camille jumped. "No. I just . . . no."

But the nervous flicker of her eyes said she was lying.

"Camille, Mrs. Lamb said something about the guilt killing you. What did you mean by that?"

Licking her lips, Camille turned her gaze back toward the window. Then she said, "You've done so much for me."

"Honey, I care about you. A lot. You know that, right?"

Camille finally lifted her eyes to Serena's. "You've done more for me in the last year than any member of my family's done my whole life. Yeah, I believe you care about me, that's why—" She bit her lip and began to pace.

"Camille, I need to ask you a question and I need you to be honest with me."

Camille stopped her jerky stride. She looked at Serena, wariness flickering in her eyes. "What?"

"Were you at my house Thursday night when the alarm went off?"

She flinched. "At your house?"

"Yes." Why did Camille feel the need to repeat the question unless she was stalling, trying to think of an answer? "Don't lie to me, don't do that. At least tell me the truth. This is important."

The girl snapped her lips together and looked back toward the window. Fear shadowed her face. "Yes. I was there. That's why I came here. To tell you about . . ." She twisted her fingers and bit her lip. "I was looking for you."

"Tell me about what?"

Camille bit her lip and looked away, her expression so tortured Serena actually felt the girl's pain. "Did you try to get in the house and accidentally set the alarm off?"

Camille crossed her arms in front of her stomach and leaned forward. "No, I was . . . no, someone was already in your house."

"What? Why didn't you tell me this before now?"

"Because," she licked her lips, "I was scared."

"Scared of what?"

"She saw me . . . um . . . looking in the window. She looked right at me and the look in her eyes was . . . crazy." Camille shuddered and gulped in a breath. "She . . . uh . . . came after me, so I ran and she yelled she'd find me."

Serena stared. "She?"

"A woman. A tall woman dressed like a man with a baseball cap and everything. She had on those clothes they wear in the army."

"Army fatigues?"

"Yes. Camouflage."

Serena leaned back against the couch and stared at the ceiling. "A woman?" She'd have to pass that information on to Dominic. "But I don't understand how my alarm went off." She looked back at the girl. "I need you to talk to a friend of mine about the break-in and what you saw. He's an FBI agent investigating something, and the break-in may be related."

"Talk to the cops? No way!" Camille stood and started an antsy, restless pacing.

Serena frowned. "Why not? You haven't done anything wrong."

"Because . . . because if they come looking for me at my house, my dad will have a fit!" She edged toward the door.

Serena stood. "No, not at your house. You can talk to him here. He's right outside waiting on me to finish up here."

"Here?" Her voice squeaked.

267

"Camille, what are you so afraid of?"

Camille lifted a hand to her head and burst into tears. Shocked at the overreaction, Serena simply grabbed a tissue from the box on the end table and handed it to Camille.

"I'm sorry. My emotions are just so out of whack these days."

"I hear that's normal."

"Ugh. It's awful."

"So, will you talk to him? Tell him what you saw and everything that happened Thursday night? You could save someone's life."

Camille sniffed. "Save a life? How?"

"We think this person is after a friend of mine and if he—she—catches up to her, she'll hurt her . . . or kill her. We're not sure why she's after her, just that she is."

Camille hesitated, then gave a slow nod. "Okay."

Serena pulled her phone out to call Dominic. When he answered, she said, "Hey, can you come in for a minute? I have someone you need to talk to."

"Sure." She could hear the curiosity in his voice, but he didn't question her. "I'm on the way in."

"I'll let the guard know you're coming."

Camille stood. "I'm going to clean myself up some." She headed down the hall to the bathroom.

Serena walked over to the security officer and told him to let Dominic in. Then she stepped over to the window and looked out. From her vantage point, she could see Dominic climb out of the car and sprint across the parking lot toward the building.

Two minutes later, she felt her phone buzz as he strode down the hall toward her, a question mark on his face. "What's up?"

She looked at her phone and frowned. Then she looked up and answered him. "I had a long talk with Camille. She was definitely the teenager my neighbor spotted running across the yard."

Dominic's brows dipped. "Did she say why she was trying to break into your house?"

"She said she wasn't. Someone was already in the house when Camille got there."

He lifted a brow. "Who?"

"A woman."

The other brow followed the first. "What? A woman? Did Camille recognize her?"

"No. She said she was dressed in army fatigues and had a baseball cap on, but she was definitely a woman."

"And she was in your house."

"Right."

His mind clicked. He had an idea. Probably a far-fetched one, but he had to see how it panned out. "I need to look at one of those files from Howard's house again. After we finish here, do you mind if we stop by my office?"

"Sure." She nodded. "You do that and I'll go in to my office. I got a text. There's an emergency autopsy a family is paying for and Daniel asked if I could come do it. They want to bury the body tomorrow. While I'm there, I'm going to go ahead and do Hilary's too."

He frowned. "Is this a usual thing?"

She shrugged. "Sometimes. We try to honor a family's requests. If it falls on a Sunday, so be it."

"I don't want you there alone."

"I won't be. Paul is supposed to be there as well as Daniel. He's really stressing about the cuts that are getting ready to happen." She looked at her phone again, then down the hall. "Where did that girl go?" Serena tapped her foot, then narrowed her eyes. "Let me just see if I can find her."

Dominic watched Serena head down the hall, but his mind churned. He really wanted to get his hands on the file sitting on his desk. Impatience twisted inside him. First he had to make sure Serena was safe.

"She's gone!"

At her frustrated shout, Dominic strode toward her. Serena stood in the middle of the hall, hands on her hips.

"What?"

"She's gone. She went out the other bathroom door, down the hall parallel to this one, and out of the house." A young girl came around the corner and Serena pounced. "Helen, did you see Camille?"

"She went out the door a few minutes ago."

Serena raced for the door and Dominic took off after her. Serena skidded to a halt when she got to the security guard's desk. "Which way did she go? The girl who just left?"

He nodded toward the door. "Shot out of here like she had a snake on her tail."

Dominic followed Serena out the door and down the steps. She stopped and looked left, then right. "She's gone. Where would she go?"

"Probably the neighborhood that's right behind this place. If she's wanting to get away from you, she'll go where you can't follow."

Serena planted her hands on her hips. "But why would she want to get away?"

"She didn't want to talk to me."

Serena stomped her foot.

In spite of the seriousness of the situation, Dominic let out a surprised laugh. "I've never seen you do that before."

The flush that crept into her olive-complected cheeks made him grin. Her embarrassment was cute. She rolled her eyes and said, "It's a habit from childhood." Then she turned serious, pulled out her phone, fingers flying. "I'm sending her a text telling her to get in touch with me or . . . or . . . I'm going to cut her phone off."

"You're going to make a great mom."

She looked up, her cheeks still red. Then her eyes crinkled as her brow furrowed. "I'm worried about her, Dominic. She's pregnant."

270

"Ah. Oh boy."

"Yeah." Serena paced toward the subdivision, then back toward Dominic. "I think that's part of the problem."

"What?" He was confused.

"I have come to think of her as . . . mine. And she's not."

"But you want her to be?"

She sighed and whispered, "Maybe," as she stared in the direction Dominic thought Camille went.

He pulled her toward his car. "She seems to be a pretty resourceful kid. Give her a chance to text you back. She's obviously reaching out for some help or she wouldn't have come back to Covenant House. Let her think about it."

Serena allowed him to open the door for her, but he could see her reluctance. He had a feeling if she didn't have an autopsy to do, she would have been chasing right after the wayward teen.

While Serena sat staring at her phone as though she could will Camille to text or call, Dominic turned his thoughts to Howard's folder. He itched to get another look at it. Because if he was right, he was getting ready to blow this whole case wide open.

31

As Serena rode toward the hospital with Dominic, her mind chugged through everything. Jillian had sent her a package. Someone wanted that package. Camille saw someone, a woman, in her house possibly looking for that package.

If Serena gave it up, would the person leave her alone or kill her because of what he—or she—thought she knew? Should she open the package and read the contents in spite of Jillian's wishes? Or would that be betraying a friend? Then again, was that package putting her life in danger? The lives of those close to her?

Obviously.

Frustration pounded through her. *Lord, what do I do?*

"What are you thinking about?" Dominic's voice cut through her thoughts.

"Looking at what's in that package Jillian sent me."

He glanced at her. "You haven't yet?"

"No. I don't feel right doing it, but Jillian wouldn't want me or anyone else in danger because of it."

"Then it might be time to open it."

"You're right. It is. I probably should have done it a couple of

272

days ago." She paused. "In fact, I almost did. But how is knowing what's inside going to help? I mean, I know it's something someone wants. I'm not going to give it to that someone regardless of what's in it, so does it really matter if I look or not?"

"All good points, but if the contents will point us to the person doing this to you, then it would help in that respect."

"True." She bit her lip. "But after I look at it, tomorrow, I'm going to the bank and put that thing in a safe deposit box."

"I think that's a good idea."

She smiled. "Thanks. I probably should have done it as soon as I realized someone was after it. Maybe once it's in the box, I'll tape a note to my door or make an announcement on the six o'clock news that it's no longer in my house."

He chuckled. "Might not be a bad idea." Then he turned serious. "I'll escort you to the bank. I don't want you carrying that package around without protection."

"I won't say no to that."

Ten minutes later, Dominic pulled into the hospital parking lot and drove around to the morgue entrance. He pulled up beside her designated parking space. He said, "I'll come back. What time will you be ready to leave?"

"I'll call you, but probably around 5:00 or so."

"I'll be back."

She could feel him watching her as she walked to the door. Turning, she looked over her shoulder and gave him a little wave. From the corner of her eye, she caught movement to her left and froze.

"Who's there?" she called.

No one answered.

Dominic still watched from his car. The frown on his face said he noticed her hesitation.

Serena pointed to the dumpster to her left. She heard a scrape and another noise she couldn't identify—a small cry? Backing toward the door, she watched Dominic approach the dumpster, hand on his weapon.

He stayed to the side, the dumpster at his back. In one smooth move, he pulled his weapon and rounded the corner. "FBI! Get out here! Now!"

32

Dominic came face-to-face with Paul, Serena's assistant. The man's wide, scared eyes and uplifted arms had Dominic lowering his gun a fraction. "What are you doing?"

"I . . . uh . . . well . . ."

"Paul?" Serena's voice interrupted the man's stutter.

Paul flushed a deep red and took a breath. "Hold on a second. Can I put my arms down?"

"Step out here first," Dominic ordered.

Paul shuffled out from behind the dumpster, arms still raised. A mewling cry followed after him.

Serena asked, "What's back there?"

Dominic motioned for Paul to lower his arms. He did and ran a hand down his lab coat before closing his eyes briefly. "Okay, Dorie, game's up."

Dorie popped out, her hair now a bright orange, a sheepish smile gracing her lips. "We've been . . . um . . . feeding these kittens." She held up a small ball of kitten that had just started getting its fur.

Eyes wide, Serena stepped around them to peer behind the dumpster. Reaching into the small box, she cupped her hand under one of the gray and black kittens. "Aw, how precious."

Dominic put his weapon away, his adrenaline rush returning to somewhere near normal. "Kittens?"

Paul gave an embarrassed shrug as he shared a glance with Dorie. "I saw the mama cat get hit by a car two days ago as I was leaving the morgue. When I bent over her to see if there was anything I could do for her, I spotted the babies under the dumpster."

"Why didn't you just take them to the shelter?"

His jaw tightened. "I called the shelter and they said they were so overrun with kittens, they would probably have to put them down. I didn't want that to happen and I can't take them home because my roommate's allergic. So," he held up a teeny bottle filled with milk and smirked, "just call me—and Dorie—mom and dad."

Serena placed a hand over her heart. "You two nearly scared me to death. Why didn't you answer when I called out?"

He flushed again. "I was hoping you would just think it was a mouse or something you heard and keep going." He lasered a glare at Dominic. "I didn't know we'd nearly get shot."

"Sorry, we've been a little jumpy lately," she said.

"You won't tell anyone what we've been doing, will you?" Dorie frowned at her. "We're using our break times to do this, not work time."

Serena held up a hand. "I won't say a word, I promise."

Dominic asked Paul, "Will you see she gets inside safely?"

"Sure. I was finished up here anyway."

Dominic had asked Paul to see Serena inside, but he waited until they entered the building before heading for his car. His nerves gave one last shudder before settling down.

They were jumping at shadows. Her nerves were just as tight as his.

Kittens.

If only all of his "scares" would turn out to be so harmless.

As he slid into the driver's seat, his phone rang and he snatched it, praying someone had a lead somewhere.

Special Agent Jeff Brown said, "I think I've tracked your father to a shelter in Rock Hill, South Carolina."

"Give me the address." He headed toward the office while he processed this new information. Another lead on his father. A real one or another dead end? His gut clenched even as he told himself there was no sense in getting worked up about it now. He had other things to worry about first.

After Dominic hung up with Jeff, he placed a call to Hunter and gave him the information. "I want to go with you. When are you leaving?"

"Let me check with Alexia and get back to you. It'll be fast, though—if that's really him, I don't want to miss him. He moves frequently."

"I'll have a couple of agents pick him up."

Hunter hesitated. "We don't really have a reason to do that."

"He's a possible suspect in a kidnapping and attempted murder. I think we have reason."

"Fine. Have your agents bring him to the office. I'll be there for the next several hours."

Dominic pulled into the parking lot and shut off the engine. He called the FBI office in Charlotte, North Carolina, as he made his way to his desk. He told them what he needed and they promised to dispatch someone immediately to pick the man up.

Dominic felt his adrenaline pushing his concentration levels through the floor, but he forced himself to focus on the task at hand. He found Howard's file and opened it, looking for what he suspected. This was the whole reason he wanted to come into the office on this Sunday.

What interested him the most were the letters from Allison Kingston. A woman who seemed to have disappeared from the face of the earth. The post office box had been closed with no forwarding address. He looked at the writing, read the analysis from the expert one more time.

Could it be?

He scrambled for his phone and punched in the number for Rick's personal cell.

"Why are you calling me on my day off?"

"I need a favor."

"Of course you do."

"Seriously. Can you fax over a copy of the serial killer's notes? I want to compare them to the handwriting of a woman who's been visiting Drake in prison."

Rick said, "Well, I guess you'd better be glad that I decided to come into the office on my day off. I'll have it to you in less than five minutes."

"Thanks, buddy."

Dominic hung up the phone and walked over to the fax machine. His mind hummed and his blood spun in his veins. What if he was right?

What if he was wrong?

He'd know in a few minutes.

The fax machine purred to life and Dominic waited with an impatient tapping of his fingers against his left thigh. Finally, the paper spit into the tray and he snatched it. Looked at it, then raced back to his office to confirm what he already knew.

Allison Kingston was the one leaving the packages. Allison Kingston was their serial killer.

But who was her partner?

Serena made the Y-incision, her blade effortlessly gliding through the upper torso of the fifty-seven-year-old female who'd been found dead in her apartment last night. An empty bottle of pain pills told the story, but the woman's sister insisted it had to be murder—by the deceased woman's husband.

Serena would provide the official diagnosis after the autopsy.

Paul hovered to her left.

Dorie emptied the trash by the door, her gaze fixed on the action on the table.

"Can you tell me what you're doing? I'm taking an anatomy class on Saturdays. So far I have a hundred average."

Serena looked up and nodded. Dorie pulled out her ever-present pen and slid over to take notes as Serena walked her through the autopsy.

Two and a half hours later, Serena slipped off her gloves and washed her hands. Dorie hadn't been able to stay for the whole autopsy, but each time she was able to watch a little, she learned something that would help her in her future profession. It made Serena feel good she could help someone who wanted to advance in life and was willing to work hard to do so.

Paul said, "I heard they let Chuck Walker go." Chuck was one of the other assistants.

Serena looked at Paul and frowned. "When did that happen?"

"Late yesterday afternoon. I heard about it this morning. I didn't want to say anything in front of Dorie. I know she's worried just like the rest of us."

"Anyone else?"

"Just Chuck. But rumor has it there are more cuts coming from every department."

Grimacing, Serena stepped on the brake release and rolled Mrs. Hines into the freezer. Cause of death—overdose of Oxycontin. No signs of foul play, nothing to indicate that her death wasn't self-inflicted. Her heart hurt for the pain the woman must have been in and wondered what her story was. She sent up a silent prayer for her family.

Paul scrubbed the area around the sink with force.

"It's okay, Paul." She laid a hand on his shoulder, trying to offer a small measure of comfort. "I'll talk to Daniel and see if I can find out anything."

He shrugged her off. "Don't bother. If it's going to happen, it's going to happen. Nothing you can do about it."

A knock on the door grabbed her attention and she turned to see Dominic standing there. The look on his face sent a dart of apprehension through her. "Hi. What's going on?"

"I've only got a minute but wanted to talk to you about something."

"Sure."

His phone rang and he shot her an apologetic look as he stepped back in the hall. Serena exited the autopsy room where Paul stayed to clean up. In her office, she sat in front of her computer and glanced at the clock. An average autopsy case took about four hours. That was including all the paperwork. She still had the paperwork to do and Hilary's autopsy. It was turning into a long day.

Thankfully, the suicide was an uncomplicated case and hadn't taken her terribly long. The murdered Doll Maker Killer copycat victims took longer. Hilary's could last anywhere from four to six hours depending upon what Serena found.

However, it might not take her that long since she knew what to expect.

"Hey, Serena. I've got some news."

She turned to find Dominic standing in the doorway. "What is it?"

"We have a name for our killer."

"Who?"

"Allison Kingston."

She frowned and then lifted her brows as the name registered. "The woman who was writing Drake those letters?"

"Yes. We also pulled everything we could find on visitors he had. No one came to see him for an entire year the first year he was incarcerated. Then he had his first visitor on his one-year anniversary in prison. And every anniversary after that."

"Allison?"

"Yes. That was the name she signed in with."

"But you don't think it was her?"

"Nope. Rick got a print off Hilary's box and just called to tell me that he found a match for it."

"Who?"

"Gwendolyn Lindell."

"Drake's daughter," she breathed. "So, she found the guts to come visit him? Sounds like she forgave him." She blinked. "So she's the serial killer? Are you serious?"

"Sounds like. Drake's phone calls have also picked up. He used to make one every once in a while. To his lawyer, to the newspapers, to anyone who would listen to him cry his innocence. Recently, he's been calling two numbers we can't trace."

"Prepaid phones?"

"Probably. The calls never last more than ten, fifteen seconds."

She wrinkled her nose. "How weird."

"Tell me about it. We now have a tap on every phone he's used and someone monitoring it. I want to hear his next conversation."

Serena shivered at the look in his eye.

———■———

Gwendolyn checked her phone and saw that her contact had tried to reach her. Frustration bit at her. She didn't need his constant calls and texts. She'd call him when she was ready.

Unfortunately, he wasn't very good at waiting. If she knew who he was or had any way to trace him, she'd be tempted to put a bullet in that sweet spot in his forehead.

But he paid well and she needed the money.

Besides, the assignment had turned into an amazingly entertaining game and she wasn't ready for it to come to an end.

She hadn't realized how everything would happen. How the past and the present would collide. Maybe it was fate. Maybe it was just one more chance to prove to everyone that she was the one who mattered. She was the important one. The old feelings welled up in her. Pride that her father had chosen her. Happiness that she was the one he loved. Drake Lindell had taught her that everything she could ever want was hers. He taught her that if she wanted something someone else had, she could take it. He taught her that life was meant to be lived to the fullest and that everything was all about her.

He taught her to be a winner. To play the game and win no matter what the cost.

He'd taught her well.

33

I NEED UR HELP. I NEED U 2 COME GET ME.

A text from Camille. The girl's phone had been silent for so long, Serena was almost shocked to see her message pop up on the screen. Serena took another bite of her late lunch—a ham and cheese sandwich on whole wheat.

WHAT'S WRONG? She texted back.

I JUST NEED HELP. HAD A FIGHT WITH MY DAD. WILL U COME GET ME?

Serena looked at Paul. "I've got to go."

"What's wrong?"

"Camille needs me. She's texting me, asking me to come get her."

He frowned. "You think that's wise? Is she with her father?"

"I don't know." Serena texted, WHERE ARE U?

A pause. Then, I HAD TO DO IT.

Serena's blood chilled and her stomach twisted. Had Camille gone ahead with the abortion?

DO WHAT? Anxiety swirled. TELL ME WHERE U ARE.

AT MY DAD'S.

IS HE THERE?

NO. HE LEFT. PLEASE JUST COME GET ME AND TAKE ME TO COVENANT HOUSE. I'LL STAY THERE, I PROMISE.

Paul frowned. "You said her dad was a violent man. Maybe you shouldn't go."

Serena rubbed her forehead as she thought, reasoned it out. "She says her father's not there."

PLS COME GET ME BEFORE HE GETS BACK!

"I probably shouldn't, but I have to. She needs me." Serena texted. START WALKING. I'LL MEET YOU.

A long pause then, I CAN'T. HE WARNED ME I'D BETTER BE HERE WHEN HE GOT BACK. IF I LEAVE AND HE'S ON HIS WAY BACK, HE'LL SEE ME. PLS SERENA! I'M SCARED.

Serena's heart thudded. She should just call the cops and send them out there, but what if her father was there and the cops showed up? He'd take his wrath out on Camille.

She couldn't do that to the girl.

Paul nodded. "I'd go with you, but I have a date with a possible kitten owner." He paused. "But this is more important. I'll go with you."

She smiled at her co-worker. "You're a good man, Paul."

A flush crept up his neck and he snorted. "I don't know about that. A sucker for cute kittens, yeah, but . . ." He shrugged.

"But you can't go with me. I can't drag you into this. If her father comes back . . . no, I'll call Dominic."

She grabbed her purse and texted, I'M COMING.

Then stopped. "I don't have a car."

He tossed her his keys. "Here. Take mine. I'll get Dorie to bring me by your house to get it later." He looked at the schedule posted on the wall. "She'll be here in a couple of hours."

"You're sure?" She clutched the keys in one hand, her phone in the other.

"Go. The possible kitten owner is meeting me here."

"At the dumpster?"

Paul grimaced and nodded.

284

"Great. Thanks, Paul."

"Sure."

Serena punched in Dominic's speed dial number as she headed out of the hospital toward Paul's car. Dominic would be horribly upset with her for leaving the safety of the hospital, but Camille needed her and she'd promised the girl she'd be there for her.

She had no choice. She had to go.

Dominic's phone went to voice mail. "Hey, I got a text from Camille. She's at her father's house. 114 Bolton Drive. I'm headed over there to pick her up. Her father has a violent temper and I wanted you to go with me. But she said he wasn't there, so I'm just going to pop over real fast and get her before he gets back. Maybe you can meet me there. Call me."

She hung up and climbed into Paul's Jeep Cherokee. Then thought about what she was doing. She called Colton and got his voice mail. He and Dominic were probably together working on something and couldn't be interrupted.

Her fingers hovered over the 911 button she'd programmed. But if Camille's father came back and saw the police there, Camille would suffer for it.

What do I do? What do I do?

The screen blinked. R U COMING? PLS SERENA, I'M SCARED.

Serena set her jaw and sent up a prayer.

YES. ON THE WAY.

———————■———————

Dominic looked up to see Hunter followed by two federal agents escort a man in his fifties toward his office.

His father.

Not that the man deserved the title, but nevertheless, that's the one he had. He gave a nod toward the conference room. "More privacy."

Hunter nodded and escorted them down the hall. Dominic rose and followed. He stopped in the door and stared. His heart thudded, then slowed. David Allen didn't look like the man Dominic remembered from childhood. He was withered and stooped, looking twenty years older than he was.

The consequences of too much alcohol, drugs, and prison. He supposed that would do it to a person.

Dominic waited for the emotions to hit him like they had a little over two months ago when he'd tracked his father down to find him in prison. Hate, love, anger, resentment, bitterness. He'd run the whole range. Today, he simply felt . . . pity.

A broken shell of a man stood before him.

A broken shell that needed a shower and a shave.

He looked at Hunter.

Hunter nodded. "I've got to go. Let me know if you need anything else."

Dominic rubbed a hand down his face. "I've got it from here. Appreciate it."

Hunter left and Dominic turned to his fellow agents. "He cooperate?"

The one who appeared to be the elder partner shook Dominic's hand. "Sure thing. He didn't give us any trouble. Said he was hungry and would we mind feeding him. We got him a double cheeseburger and shake on the way over."

Kindhearted agents.

Once again Dominic nodded his thanks and the agents left.

Dominic looked at his father who stood before him, head still bowed, shoulders stooped.

And all of his dreams of confronting the man with accusations and recriminations flew out the window. "Have a seat."

The man sat, his eyes still on the floor.

"Do you know why you're here?" *Do you know who I am?* That was the question he wanted to ask.

"No." The quiet word came out on a grunt.

Dominic rubbed his eyes. "I need to ask you a few questions."

"'Bout what?"

His phone buzzed, but he didn't take his eyes off the pathetic figure in front of him. "About some things that have been happening around here. I know you were found at a homeless shelter in Rock Hill, South Carolina. How long were you there?"

"I don't know."

The man rocked back and looked up at Dominic. "Where am I?"

Dominic frowned. "I'm an FBI agent and you're wanted in the possible kidnapping of your daughter, Alexia Allen."

A befuddled look crossed the man's face. "What?"

"Dad . . ."

"Dad? Why are you calling me Dad? Who are you? Who's Alexia?"

■

Serena pulled into the driveway of the rundown house. From Camille's description, Serena knew it was a two-bedroom, one-bath house. Camille was an only child. Her mother had died when Camille was nine, leaving behind a devastated husband and a grieving child.

The husband turned violent, taking his grief out on the little girl who learned to walk on eggshells and stay out of his way. Camille said as long as she stayed in her room, her father seemed to forget she was in the house.

Serena wondered if she felt so connected to Camille because the girl reminded her so much of Alexia and her childhood.

Whatever the reason, she was here. Since Dominic wasn't answering his phone, she finally just texted him to let him know where she was and then texted Camille to tell her to come on out. And to make sure her father wasn't back yet.

His beat-up red truck wasn't in the driveway. A good sign.

But her nerves stretched tight as she thought about the man coming home and finding Serena spiriting his daughter off to Covenant House.

He'd have a fit. A violent, life-endangering fit.

Her phone buzzed. Colton. "Hello?"

"I got your message. Please tell me you didn't go out there by yourself. Dominic will have a conniption."

"Um . . . okay, I won't tell you that."

"Stay there. I'm on the way."

"Where's Dominic?"

"He's tied up with his father. Stay put. You hear?"

"I hear."

She hung up, feeling better about her safety since Colton was on the way. It wouldn't take him long to get here. She texted Camille again to come get in the car.

When Camille didn't appear in the door or text her back right away, a slow dread started to build in the pit of Serena's stomach. She tapped the steering wheel and waited. Finally, she got out of the car and knocked on the door.

And waited.

Nothing.

The dread turned to fear. Fear for Camille. Was Serena too late? Should she have called the cops?

She dialed 911 and held her finger over the Send button.

With her other hand, she tried the doorknob. It twisted in a smooth move. Her internal alarm bells clamored for her attention. She ignored them and stepped inside the house. Knowing Colton was only a few minutes away made her feel better.

Shutting the door behind her, she took a tentative step forward into the living area of the house. "Camille?" She called softly. It didn't seem right to raise her voice. Odors from the kitchen directly in front of her saturated the air, stimulating her gag reflex. Covenant House wasn't a better option than this?

As she walked into the den, she spied a small hallway to her left. The bedrooms.

"Camille? Are you here?"

A noise sounded. A scuffling sound, a shuffle or a scraping shoe. "Camille?"

Worried the girl might be hurt or in trouble, that her father had finally snapped and done something awful, Serena threw caution to the wind and hurried down the hallway. The first room on her right held a twin bed, a Justin Bieber poster, and a scattering of clothing across the floor.

Her stomach in knots, but unable to leave without making sure Camille was all right, Serena gathered her meager courage and pressed forward. She wished she had her father's Glock, but she didn't have a concealed weapons permit.

Maybe she should have gotten one.

———■———

Dominic glanced at his watch. 3:30. He'd promised to pick Serena up at 5:00. After the doctor finished with his father, he'd walk down to the morgue and check in with her. Concerned about the confusion his father had exhibited at the office, Dominic realized the man was either having some kind of psychotic break or he was ill. He'd managed to talk him into seeing a doctor, got him in the car and to the hospital without incident.

Dr. Eileen Travis exited the room, her brow furrowed. Dominic pounced. "What's wrong with him?"

"Without further testing, it's hard to say, but I would hazard a guess that he's in the early stages of Alzheimer's."

The word struck a blow to Dominic's heart. As much as he'd hated the man growing up, knowing the kind of death he was going to face gave him no satisfaction.

"I see."

"We've given him some medication to calm him down, but he really needs a full workup of tests. If it is Alzheimer's, we need to get him on the right regimen of medication."

"Do what you have to do. He doesn't have insurance and I don't know if he even has Medicaid. It doesn't matter. I'll make sure you get your money."

Dr. Travis nodded and left to write her orders.

Dominic pulled in a deep breath and thought about what he needed to do first. He had to call Alexia and Hunter and let them know what was going on.

Then he'd go down and see Serena.

He pulled out his phone and saw he had three missed calls and four texts. He checked Serena's first and felt his heart drop into his shoes.

———■———

Serena believed in evil. She'd seen it in action on a daily basis. Shootings, beatings, child abuse, suicide. Evil existed. And right now, she felt evil hovering around her.

Immediately, she started to pray.

A sound to her left.

She whirled to face the danger head on, saw Camille's father, mouth gagged, hands and feet tied. His terror-filled eyes stared at something behind her. She pressed her thumb on the Send button before she whirled . . .

. . . and felt a prick in the back of her neck, then knew no more.

34

Dominic tried Serena again and still she didn't answer. He hung up, fear crawling through his gut. He kept his car headed toward the address she'd left on his phone and kicked himself for not keeping his phone on ring. But she'd been safe. If she'd stayed at the hospital, she would *still* be safe.

"You're panicking for nothing," he reassured himself out loud. "She's fine. She's just left her phone in the car or something."

She was fine.

She probably was.

But he needed to see that for himself.

"Answer your phone," he muttered as he gunned the car to pass a slower moving truck. He turned his lights on and they flashed, getting instant results. People moved out of his way.

He could be there in less than ten minutes.

Keeping his eyes open for those who might not be paying attention, he zipped through the traffic as fast as he dared.

Soon, he turned onto Bolton Drive.

And then he was in the driveway. Colton's vehicle was parked against the curb. Dominic relaxed a fraction. Had Serena called Colton when she couldn't get him? Why hadn't Colton called him?

The whole thing looked weird, the feeling that trouble waited just behind the front door.

With everything in him, he wanted to shoot out of the car and burst through the door. Instead, he waited, watched, kept his eyes on the house, the surrounding area. Were there any neighbors home? And if Serena were here, how did she get here? Rick still had her car, he'd dropped her off at the morgue, so what had she driven? Had she taken a cab?

Dominic dialed Colton's phone and waited.

His nerves twitched. His instincts shouted at him. Something was wrong.

But before he called it in, he had to make sure. Climbing out of the vehicle, he stared at the front door. Then started toward it. He'd picked up no immediate threat in the area around him.

No immediate threat.

That didn't mean one wasn't waiting behind the door.

Or causing Colton not to answer his phone.

Dominic shoved the phone in his pocket and drew his weapon. With the other hand, he twisted the knob. It swung inward and Dominic stood to the side while he took in the small interior of the house.

His gut said he needed to call for backup. And yet . . .

"FBI! Come out and show me your hands!"

He waited.

"She's not here."

Dominic froze. "Colton?"

The man came from the kitchen. "Yeah. I just got here about thirty seconds ago. Kitchen's clear." His jaw worked. "Let's clear the rest of the house."

"Something wrong with your phone?"

"I felt it buzzing but hadn't cleared the area yet, so couldn't answer. Sorry. Still have to clear the rest of the place."

"Let's do it then."

Slowly, Dominic made his way through the den, stopping at the side of the door that led into the kitchen. Rounding it, his gun held ready, he cleared the room and continued down the hall. Colton had his back.

His pulse pounded, senses sharp.

Where was Serena? Or Camille?

At the first bedroom, he repeated his actions to clear the room and stepped inside.

Checked behind the door and froze.

Nash stared sightlessly from his bound position on the floor. The bullet hole in the middle of his forehead told the story. "Oh man."

Colton stepped past him, walked down the hall. "Clear!"

There was nothing he could do for the man now. Quickly and efficiently, Dominic and Colton cleared the last room and bathroom, then got on the phone. He called CSU and reported his find to Rick.

His next call was to Hunter and Katie. "Get out to 114 Bolton Drive. We've got a dead body and a missing teen." He prayed Serena had arrived, grabbed Camille, and left before the killer had shown up, but he had a bad feeling that wasn't the way it had gone down.

He didn't want to wait on the others, but he also didn't want the scene contaminated in any way. Back on the phone with Hunter, he asked, "Where are you?"

"Five minutes out."

"Rick's on the way. I don't know where Serena or Camille are, but this dead body's not making me feel very good about things." In fact, he'd never reacted this way with a case before.

But Serena was more than a case. She was the woman—

He cut that train of thought off and said, "No sign of forced entry."

"Someone let the killer in."

"It's her, Hunter. The Doll Maker Killer's copycat." His gaze dropped to the floor as he paced and watched Colton grab a pool stick from the corner of the room and use it to dislodge an item under Mr. Nash's left leg. "You recognize that?"

Dominic looked down to see Serena's phone with the purple and pink cover lying on the floor. "She's got her."

The pounding in her head was her first clue that she was still alive.

Quiet sobs reached her ears.

Serena forced her eyes open. They fell shut. With effort, she shoved them open. And began to register her surroundings.

A table with a green covering and cards spread out over it. Blue, red, and white chips. Dice.

A casino?

She blinked again.

"Serena?" A bare whisper that she almost didn't hear.

She turned her head and her eyes landed on Camille. With her ankle cuffed to the steel chair, the girl sat huddled on the floor, her terror stamped plainly in her eyes. Serena tried to talk and found her throat dry and scratchy. She managed to force out a hoarse, "Are you okay?"

"No. What's going on? I think I'm going to puke."

"Did you see who did this? What happened?"

"I saw her."

"Her?"

"Yes. Her."

Serena turned at the voice. Slowly, so as not to aggravate the dizziness making her head spin and stomach churn.

But when she laid eyes on the woman in the doorway, she gaped. "Dorie?"

"Hmm. Yes, but you can call me Gwendolyn."

Dominic was on the phone rounding up everyone he could think of to help with the search for Serena and Camille. "Ping their phones. I want tower locations, text message transcripts, phone calls. Everything you can dig up."

Terry's computer began clicking and Dominic used his Bluetooth in order to have both hands free. He hung up with Terry and dialed Hunter. "I need a SWAT team on standby in case this turns into a hostage situation."

"Roger that," Hunter said. "I'll put the call in."

"And check with the taxi services to see if they let a woman off anywhere near Nash's address."

Dominic hung up with Hunter and placed a call to Nate Lindell.

The man answered on the second ring and Dominic got right to it. "This is Special Agent Dominic Allen again."

A pause. "I believe I've answered all the questions I can."

"Last time we met, you said you'd been wondering if your sister could somehow be involved in the killings. You were right."

"It doesn't surprise me."

"And right now, she's got Serena Hopkins and possibly a young girl by the name of Camille Nash. Where would she take them?"

"I . . . I don't know. I haven't seen my sister in twenty years."

"Think, man! I need a location. Did your father own any other real estate property? Anything?"

"She would take her somewhere she wouldn't be interrupted." He spoke slowly, as though he were talking to himself. "The old place? No, she couldn't do that . . ."

"We already checked the old place, the shed is gone, as is the room that was under it. The bank repossessed the house and a young family bought it and has been living there for the past twelve years."

"I know."

Nate sounded distracted and Dominic wanted to scream at the man to pay attention. "Hey, Nate. Come on, think."

"I don't want to think. That's not a part of my life I want to revisit. Now leave me alone."

Click.

Nate had hung up.

Dominic clenched his hand around the wheel. *God, I need your help. Please let me find her.*

———■———

Serena let her eyes follow the woman as she crossed the room. "You lost weight."

The inane words helped her try to put everything together. The pistol in her hand terrified her. Dorie King was Allison Kingston. Who was Gwendolyn Lindell. Daughter of the Doll Maker Killer.

The woman laughed, surprise flickering across her face. "I've lost weight? That's the first thing you can say?" She glanced down at her now slender form. "Yeah, I knew once the girls started dying, the cops would be doing all kinds of research on the Doll Maker Killer. Figured my picture would come up as the daughter of Drake Lindell. Couldn't take a chance on anyone recognizing me from those."

Serena blurted, "You killed Howard?"

Gwendolyn's brow furrowed. "Yes. He'd pretty much outlived his usefulness."

Confusion riddled Serena. Maybe when her mind cleared a bit she would be able to figure it all out. "You were in my house," she whispered. Darkness wanted to claim her once again, but she resisted. What had Dorie . . . Gwendolyn . . . used on her?

"You have something someone wants," Gwendolyn said.

"The package. That's what you were looking for."

Gwendolyn smiled, a cold, cruel smile. "Yes, the package. Thank you for not playing like you don't know what I mean. As much as I love games, that's not one I want to play."

Serena swallowed. "Can I have some water?"

Her question seemed to throw Gwendolyn off for a moment. The woman frowned, then turned and disappeared into a small room behind Serena. She heard water running, then a cup was shoved into her hand. "Feel like you have cotton mouth, huh? A side effect of the drug."

Serena took a small swallow and tasted the sweetness of the water. "What did you use?"

"Scopolamine, of course. Compliments of my uncle in Ecuador. It makes one very compliant. You were even kind enough to drive Paul's jeep for me."

Serena frowned. She had no memory of that.

Camille's eyes bounced back and forth between her and Gwendolyn. All Serena could think was to keep her talking. Would Dominic get her message?

"How did you get past my alarm system?"

Gwendolyn lifted a pink tinted brow. "Through your doggie door. By the way, you have a loose board on that fence in the back. Might want to get that checked." She laughed, a hard, cold sound that sent terror shuddering through her.

The doggie door. Serena shivered at the simplicity of it. Then anger pushed its way through her terror. "Why did you attack my mother?"

Gwendolyn frowned and shrugged. "I didn't do that."

Serena didn't believe her, but why would she lie? "Then who did? And why?"

"I have an idea, but it doesn't matter."

The memory of her wreck came back to her and she looked around, her eyes probing the room, the shadows and corners. "Wait a minute. You have a partner. It took two of you to do what you did when you rammed me with your car and killed the officer."

Gwendolyn stood and laughed. "Oh Serena, this whole thing has just been an amazing game. A game." She shook her head and muttered, "A game. *My* game. No one else's game, you understand?"

"No. What do you mean? Who was the other person helping you?"

Could she keep Gwendolyn talking long enough for Dominic to figure out where she was? Did the woman have her cell phone? Could they trace Camille's?

"No one was helping me. He just came out of nowhere and . . . helped me. I don't know why, but I'm not going to question fate."

A thought occurred to Serena. "How did you know I'd be at Camille's house? She texted me, telling me she needed help. How did you know?"

Gwendolyn laughed again. "Camille didn't tell you?"

"Tell me what?"

"She lost her phone the night she broke into your house."

"She broke—" Serena blinked, her gaze landing on her friend still huddled in the corner. Clarity reigned. "Oh. You found the phone and texted me. It was a setup."

"Exactly," the woman drawled.

"I didn't break into her house." The quiet words grabbed their attention. Camille pulled herself up into the chair and stared at them, her gaze dull. With a hint of defiance. "I didn't break into her house. I was in the garage, and when I saw a light flashing inside, I looked through the garage door window. I saw you snooping around. You had her alarm turned off."

"Yes, when you have friends in high places, it's not hard to get a simple alarm code." Gwendolyn smirked.

"But the alarm went off that night," Serena whispered.

Gwendolyn's smirk faded. "Your sneaky little friend caused that to happen."

Camille narrowed her eyes, swallowed hard. She lowered her eyes, then looked back up at Serena. "I lied to you at Covenant House. I didn't want to talk to the FBI guy because I was afraid I'd get in trouble for being in your garage."

"Oh Camille," Serena breathed.

The girl looked up, a defiant light smoldering as she stared at Gwendolyn. "But I couldn't let you hurt Serena." She made a good effort at an I-don't-care shrug. "And I sure couldn't call the cops. The only thing I could think to do was set off the alarm. So I armed it and then ran out the front door when you had your back turned." Satisfaction momentarily blotted out the girl's terror and Serena's heart filled with the knowledge that Camille wanted to help protect her, had put herself in danger to get a killer out of Serena's house. So that's why she ran. She didn't want to admit to Dominic, a cop, that she'd been trespassing in Serena's garage.

"Camille, hon . . ."

Keep everyone talking was the only thing Serena could think of at the moment. Give Dominic time to get his text and realize something was wrong. "Wait a minute, how did you get in my garage without setting off the alarm? And how did you know my code?"

Averting her eyes, Camille offered a little shrug. "I used to hide in your boat to get away from my dad. Your window in the storage room is unlocked. I just climbed in, unlocked the storage room door, and crawled under the tarp."

Serena pictured Camille doing exactly what she said. The storage room locked from the inside. Once in the room, she would just have to open the door to step into the garage. Simple enough. "And your alarm panel is easy to see from there. I just watched you punch it in. Even got the new code when you changed it. When it got too hot in the boat and you weren't home, I'd turn the alarm off and go inside."

Which explained why the person who had snatched her mother hadn't set off the alarm. They'd probably surprised Camille, who hadn't had time to arm the alarm before getting out of the house.

So her safely alarmed home wasn't so safe. And people in high places? What had Gwendolyn meant by that? She'd been living with a false sense of security for years. Her stomach twisted and she offered up a silent prayer. *Please, God, please, deliver us from this evil.*

299

35

Terry called and Dominic touched his Bluetooth to answer. "What do you have?"

"I pulled the text messages from Camille's phone and Serena's. They exchanged texts. Camille was probably at her house when she texted, because they came from the tower closest to her house. Same for Serena."

"We found Serena's phone at Camille's house. Keep trying to locate Camille's phone."

More tapping in the background, then Terry said, "Nothing is showing up. Either her phone is off or the batteries have been pulled."

How was he going to find her?

He still kept coming back to Nate.

"Get someone to pick up Nate Lindell. I'm going to pay a visit to Drake. If anyone knows where they would be, it's him."

Dominic hung up and aimed the vehicle for the prison while dialing a number he'd memorized the day he'd met Serena again at the first crime scene.

"Columbia Hospital Morgue. Paul Hamilton. How can I help you?"

"Paul, this is Dominic Allen. Serena's missing and I need to know if you've talked to her lately."

"Missing? What do you mean missing?"

Dominic gave the man a short explanation. "So I need to know the last time you talked to her."

"When she borrowed my jeep a couple of hours ago."

So that's how Serena had gotten to Camille's house. But where was the jeep? Had the killer taken it? But then how had the killer gotten to Camille's house? Walked? Taken a cab?

"Anything else you can tell me?"

"No. Nothing. Sorry." Worry riddled his voice. "Please let me know when you find her."

"Will do."

Dominic wheeled into the parking lot of the prison and bolted for the building. Hunter arrived right on his tail.

Ten long minutes later, they were in the room with Drake Lindell. "I know your daughter, Gwendolyn, aka Allison Kingston, was in on the killings with you twenty years ago, you sick—" Dominic broke off and got himself under control while Drake looked at him. The sympathetic expression on the man's face made him want to put his fist through it.

Hunter took over. "We've already checked your old torture chamber, but it's gone. Where would Gwendolyn take Serena and Camille?"

His brow lifted. "She took the medical examiner?" Amusement danced in his eyes for a split second before he shuttered them again. "I wonder why."

Dominic leaned in, invading the man's space. Unfortunately, it didn't seem to faze him. "I think you know exactly why." He slapped down a paper with two phone numbers on it. "We're also in the process of tracing these calls. Why don't you make things easier on all of us and just tell us who the numbers belong to."

Hunter rubbed his chin. "I'm betting one belongs to Daddy's little girl, Gwen."

"Where would she take her, Lindell?" Dominic's voice was low, demanding.

"I don't know what you're talking about. Now, I'm ready to go back to my cell." He stood and motioned to the guard.

Dominic rose to stop him, but Hunter's hand on his forearm made him pause.

"Let him go. He's not going to tell us anything."

Dominic slammed a fist onto the table.

Hunter said, "Let's get back to the office, go through every shred of information we have, and figure this out."

Dominic shook his head. "We don't have time for that."

"Okay, you have another suggestion?"

He didn't. Pacing, he thought, racking his brain, searching for an answer, praying to the Almighty to provide one. Nothing came to him.

Then, "It's the missing girls."

"What is?" Hunter asked.

"I don't know. I keep thinking about the girls that are still missing. You know as well as I do that if they haven't turned up yet, they were probably killed twenty years ago."

"Yeah. I know."

He walked to the door. "Come on. I want to look at those files again. Our answer is there."

Hunter followed him out the door.

Serena yanked at the cuffs. Gwendolyn had left the room a few minutes ago. "Camille, we've got to figure out how to get out of here."

Camille sniffled, then whispered, "We're going to die, aren't we?"

"Not if we get out."

"We're not going to get out." Camille looked at her cuffed ankle. "How do you get out of handcuffs?"

"You pick them."

Hopelessness stared back at Serena. "Camille. Look around. You can get up and move from the chair a bit. See if there's anything small and sharp."

Camille simply stared at her.

"Camille! Do it!" She felt bad for yelling at her when the girl jerked and frowned, but at least it got her out of the chair and searching the floor.

Serena did the best she could from her spot at the other end of the table.

And then the search was over when the door opened again and Dor—Gwendolyn walked back into the room. She still held a weapon, but it was a different one.

Gwendolyn lifted a brow when she saw Camille out of the chair and on the floor. "What are you doing, brat?"

Camille froze, then slunk back to her chair, shooting a glance at Serena as she muttered, "I felt sick."

"Well, stay put. It'll be time to move in just a minute." Gwendolyn lifted the gun and Serena tensed. But the woman simply opened the cylinder on the revolver and inserted a bullet. She left the other chambers empty.

"What kind of gun is that?" Serena asked, although she figured she probably knew.

The woman lifted a brow. "You care what kind of gun this is?"

"Satisfy my curiosity, will you?" she snapped. Terror and anger were battling it out inside of her.

"Hmm. Why don't I just answer the question you're dying to know?" Her eyes narrowed and took on a dangerous glint.

Fear spiked in Serena—the fear that had never left her since waking up in this room with a killer.

Gwendolyn shot her a satisfied smile. "Yes, it's the same gun that killed Leslie and Kelly. And Patricia and Briann. And Kelsey and—"

"Wait. Stop. Who are Kelly and Briann?" Serena tugged at the handcuff once more. To no avail. Her stomach heaved and she swallowed hard. Keep her talking.

"Oh, that's right. You never found them. And you won't."

"Why not?"

She shrugged. "Because those are the rules." A wicked grin crossed her face. "Now let me tell you about the other rules."

Gwendolyn stepped forward and placed the gun into a clip on the steel rod that was attached to Serena's end of the table. "Rule number one. Don't try to get the gun out. You won't be able to. If you try to get the gun out, I will immediately shoot you with this one." The woman pulled another gun from the waistband of her shorts. It was a twin to the other. "These are the best guns ever. Daddy taught me to shoot when I was just a little girl. I'm a crack shot." She looked at Camille, who cowered and buried her face in her hands. "In other words, I don't miss."

Serena flashed to her father teaching her to do the same.

Gwendolyn turned the gun over and studied it. "It's a .32 caliber IOF Revolver MK1. Lightweight, but deadly."

Camille started to shake, her eyes lifting from her hands and flicking from Gwendolyn to the door, to the blind-covered window, then back to Serena.

"Now," Gwendolyn grabbed a deck of cards and dealt a few, "what's your game? Texas hold 'em? Twenty-one?"

"What are you talking about?"

As though Serena hadn't spoken, Gwendolyn went on, "I like the roulette table myself." She walked over to the other end of the table near Camille and pulled the cover from a roulette wheel. With a professional flick of her hand, she gave the wheel a spin.

Clicking filled the room as the little ball went round and round. "Pick a number, Serena. And a color. Red or black?"

"What?"

"A number! A color! Are you stupid?"

"Um . . . four. Black." What was going on? What was she doing?

The clicking continued.

"When it falls on a number, if it's not the number and color you picked, then you lose."

Click. Click. Click. The little ball fell into one of the slots. Gwendolyn watched it jump, then land in another.

"Seven red." She looked up and smirked. "You lose." She waved the other gun and pointed it at Camille. The girl shrieked and ducked her head.

"No! Don't!" Serena pleaded.

Gwendolyn laughed and lowered the gun. "I'm just kidding. I'm not going to shoot her."

"You're not?" Serena didn't allow herself to feel relief; she knew the woman was up to something.

Gwendolyn stood next to Serena and reached over to make sure the gun attached to the steel rod was aimed at the girl at the end of the table.

Slowly, it dawned on Serena what Gwendolyn had in mind. The woman confirmed it when she said, "You are."

———■———

Dominic shoved the files aside and stood. Terror had his adrenaline flowing. They weren't going to find her in time. "How long did the other victims live before she killed them?"

"A couple of days."

He looked at his watch. "It's been three hours. What if Gwendolyn doesn't follow her MO? After all, she changed it from the original killings."

Colton leaned forward. The task force was gathered around the table, each studying various aspects of the case. Detectives questioned the girls from the home. A BOLO had been issued for Paul's Jeep Cherokee. Newscasts ran missing persons reports for Camille and Serena.

For the next six hours, they worked and searched, following up leads that led straight to one dead end after another.

305

Dominic rubbed his eyes, swigged another sip of his now cold coffee, and grimaced.

He reached for the file containing the pictures of the missing girls again. The file that had grown exponentially with added information about each girl.

"Each one had a best friend," he whispered.

Colton looked up. "What?"

"Best friend. Each dead girl had a best friend. They disappeared within hours of each other."

"But Camille's not Serena's best friend," Hunter pointed out.

"No." Dominic stood to pace, his thoughts racing. "No, she's not, but she's someone Serena cares about. And she was there. She was probably also a convenience thing, but . . ." He thought about what he just said. "She's someone Serena cares about."

"You said that already."

Dominic looked at Colton. "So who did Gwendolyn care about as a child?"

Hunter leaned forward, his eyes taking on a brighter hue. "Her father."

"No, it has to be someone else. Female. Who was her best friend, besides her father?"

Colton looked at Hunter, then back at Dominic. "I don't know, but I see what you're getting at. We need to find out. Who can we ask?"

"Nathan Lindell."

◼

Hours had passed and Serena's stomach rumbled even as she knew if she tried to eat anything, she'd throw up. Gwendolyn had dropped her bomb about Serena being the one to shoot Camille, looked at her watch, and then said, "I'll explain more of the rules when I get back. Gotta run." Then she'd laughed and unclipped the gun, saying, "I guess I'd better take this with me. I'd hate for you to have a tragic accident."

Then she'd left.

Hours ago.

Serena wondered if she was at work. When she thought about it, Gwendolyn hadn't missed a shift since she started working at the hospital.

She thought of the many times Gwendolyn could have snatched her from work. The times Serena had worked late, the only one in the lab, and Gwendolyn had been there cleaning.

And yet, she'd waited until now. Why?

She knew Gwendolyn wanted the package from Jillian. But still . . . if Gwendolyn was going to kidnap her over the package, she could have done it long before now.

She scanned the area one more time, looking for something, anything, that could be used to pick the handcuff lock. She searched as though she hadn't looked for the last few hours.

Of course there was nothing there.

She yanked at the cuff attached to the chain.

The door rattled and Serena tensed.

Camille jerked from her light doze, whimpered, and shuddered. Her eyes met Serena's.

Gwendolyn stepped through the door still dressed in her work uniform, fingers clutching two brown paper bags. The padding around her middle and hips reshaped her into the Dorie/Gwendolyn that Serena knew. "Well, hello there. And how are my friends today?"

Serena had lost track of time. She didn't know if it was light or dark outside. But if Gwendolyn had been at work and she worked third shift, it was probably around 7:30 in the morning.

"Hmm . . . nothing to say?"

"Camille needs a bathroom and something to eat. She's pregnant." Serena wouldn't mind a bathroom break herself.

The woman flinched. "What?" She looked at Camille. "You didn't tell me you were pregnant."

Would that make a difference somehow? Or had she just made matters worse?

307

Camille's eyes darted between her captor and Serena. "It didn't come up."

"Well, you're lucky I ran through a drive-thru." She held up the bags, then smirked at Serena. "It's not your usual froufrou fare, but if you're hungry, you'll eat it."

She tossed a bag in Serena's direction. Serena caught it, the smell of the burger causing her stomach to rumble once again. She simply held the bag as she watched Gwendolyn uncuff Camille.

Gwendolyn gave Camille a little shove. "No funny stuff. You try anything and I put a bullet in your friend—and I'd really hate to do that this early."

Shuffling, keeping her head down, Camille disappeared behind Serena into the small bathroom.

Soon, Serena heard the toilet flush and Camille reappeared. The girl's gaze shot to the door and Gwendolyn lifted the gun. "Please don't."

Tears tracked down the teen's cheeks as she walked back to the chair and allowed Gwendolyn to reattach the cuff to her ankle without protest.

Gwendolyn looked at Serena. "Your turn."

Free of the cuff, Serena paid her visit to the restroom. And looked for anything that would be useful as a handcuff pick.

Gwendolyn banged on the door. "Hurry up!" Serena flinched and moved faster. As silently as possible, she lifted the lid of the water tank and worked quickly.

Just as she slid the tank lid back on and turned around, the door slammed open. "Did you fall in? What's taking you so long? I'm ready to start the game."

Serena didn't bother to answer, she just walked back to the chair at the table and let the woman cuff her ankle.

"Now," Gwendolyn said as she reattached the gun to the steel bar. "Pick a number and a color."

"What are the rules of the game?" Serena asked.

Gwendolyn circled the table. "You pick a number and color. I spin the wheel. If you're right, one of you lives. If you're wrong, one of you dies." She giggled, her delight in the game clear.

Serena felt terror choke her again as she looked at Gwendolyn's hand poised above the wheel. Not good odds. "I thought you wanted the package."

The woman paused and frowned. Cocking her head, she laughed. A sound that grated across Serena's already snapping nerves.

Gwendolyn tapped her chin with the barrel of the gun. "I almost forgot. I was so excited to begin the game I forgot all about it. Yes, I need the package. So where is it?"

"At my house."

Gwendolyn lifted the gun and pointed it casually at Camille. "Where?"

"In a place you'll never find it."

"Don't try to get the upper hand!" she screamed, her demeanor changing in a blink. "You won't win! I always win! Now tell me where it is or I kill her."

Serena's heart thudded as she kept her face neutral. Was she gambling with Camille's life? "If you kill her, you can be sure that I will die right along with her and you'll never have the package. You said you have friends in high places. I'm guessing they're the ones who want the package."

Gwendolyn didn't deny it. In fact, she seemed stunned at Serena's gall to try and bargain with her.

Encouraged, Serena said, "Let her go and I'll take you to get the package."

"Let her go, huh?"

"Yes."

"And you'd die to protect that package?"

Serena met Camille's fearful gaze. "I'd die to protect my friend."

The door slammed open and Serena jumped as Gwendolyn spun to face the newcomer. Her jaw dropped and she said, "Nate?"

36

"Hello, little sister. Time for a little family reunion."

Looking completely nonplussed, Gwendolyn gaped, snapped her jaw shut, then said, "What are you doing here?" She glared at him. "You nearly scared the life out of me at the morgue. I told you to stay out of my game."

Serena watched this new development play out between brother and sister.

Gwendolyn demanded, "How did you find this place?"

"The cops told me where it was."

Hope leaped inside Serena even as Gwendolyn narrowed her eyes. "Then where are they?"

"Oh, they're around. But they won't be coming here." His gaze took in the table, the room. The occupants.

Serena's hope faded at his words. And the look on his face.

Nate said, "You have a nice little setup here, don't you? Looks a lot like what I found the night I called the cops."

"You? You!" Gwendolyn screeched. "I thought it was our mother! I blamed her and all this time—"

A cruel grin spread across Nate's lips and Serena couldn't tear her gaze from the two of them. And she couldn't help the small

310

hope that they'd shoot each other and she and Camille could get out of here. She leaned over to fumble with the cuff while Gwendolyn was occupied. The hope that had spiked at Nate's arrival disappeared as fast as it had risen. The man wasn't here to help her and Camille, that much was obvious.

"What do you want?" Gwendolyn snapped. "I've got unfinished business."

"As do I." Nate walked to the table and examined the steel rod with the gun now attached. "Shall we play?"

"You weren't invited. You were never invited," Gwendolyn sneered.

Nate's eyes turned as cold as his father's had the last time Serena had seen him. "I didn't need an invitation this time. I invited myself."

Gwendolyn pouted. "That's against the rules."

"I don't care what the rules are." He looked around. "I think I know how this game works and I'm playing this time."

"No, you're not."

Lightning fast, Nate's hand flipped up to reveal a gun. Before Gwendolyn could react, Nate fired and his sister fell to the floor, a bullet in her chest.

Serena couldn't help the scream that slipped out. Camille let out a piercing wail as Gwendolyn stared up at her brother through shocked blue eyes and gasped, "Nate? Why?"

He stared down at her. "Because it's my turn to play."

———■———

Nate had sworn he had no idea who his sister had been friends with as a child. "I'm sorry, I just don't know. I avoided her and my dad like the plague. If she had a friend other than my dad, then I never met her."

So now they were knocking on doors in the Lindells' old neighborhood as Terry narrowed the list to just residents who'd lived in the neighborhood when the Lindells did.

So far, they were batting a big fat zero.

Everyone knew the story of the house that had belonged to the Doll Maker Killer, but very few residents had lived there when the Lindells had.

And when they came across a neighbor who wasn't home, Dominic simply had Terry find the person and get him on the phone.

Soaked in sweat and more frustrated than he could remember, Dominic was ready to throw in the towel and retreat to look elsewhere for a hint about where Serena might be.

Until they came across the Martins. "Do you remember Gwendolyn Lindell?"

Mrs. Martin, a woman in her early sixties, pursed her lips. "The daughter of the Doll Maker Killer. Yes, I remember her. Pretty little thing with a mean streak a mile long."

Dominic tamped down his excitement. Finally they were getting somewhere. "Do you remember who her best friend was when she was a child? Or even as a teen?"

"Sure. It was a girl from our church youth group. She lived two doors up from me." Mrs. Martin pointed to the light brown ranch-style house with black shutters. "Her name was LuAnne Rose. She and Gwendolyn became inseparable for about six months. Then LuAnne disappeared. Police never found her."

Dominic exchanged a look with Hunter. "Who lives there now, Mrs. Martin?"

"A young single woman who keeps to herself. Seems friendly enough and waves when she sees me, but I've never had a conversation with her, come to think of it."

"When did she move in?"

"Oh, a few months ago. I remember the house being on the market for about a week, then it sold. I thought that was amazing in this economy."

"Amazing, all right," Hunter muttered.

"She's a musician, I think."

"Why do you say that?"

"There was some work going on when she first moved in. I asked one of the workers what she was doing." She flushed. "So I was nosey. Sue me."

"It's all right. What did he say?"

"Said she was soundproofing her basement so she didn't disturb the neighbors with her music."

Or her victims' cries for help, he thought grimly. He nodded to Mrs. Martin. "Thanks so much. That helps."

Dominic shook the woman's hand and pulled out his phone. "I need the SWAT team and backup to 312 Hovarth Avenue. Possible hostage situation. Suspect is armed."

"We don't know she's there," Hunter said.

Dominic looked at the quiet house and pointed. "That vehicle wasn't there on our last pass." He rubbed a hand across his eyes. "She's there."

"What's the matter, Gwenie, that wasn't in the rules?" Nate mocked his dying sister and all Serena could do was watch.

Camille's sobs reached her and she wished she could comfort Camille and help Gwendolyn. No matter what the woman had done, Serena couldn't just sit there and watch her die. "Let me help her."

Nate turned his eyes on her and she froze at the malevolence there.

"What are you going to do, Nate? Let her die?"

He looked at his sister. "That was sort of the point in shooting her," he muttered.

His coldness made Serena shudder. "Let me help her."

"No." He looked around and took in a deep breath. "So this is the playing field."

"Nate, you haven't done anything really wrong. You protected

313

us," she said. "You can be the hero. You saved us from the serial killer."

Nate seemed to ponder her words, then shook his head. "No, I didn't."

"What do you mean? Of course you did."

"I wanted to play." He looked down at Gwendolyn, who'd drawn a ragged breath two seconds earlier. But now, Serena noticed, her chest remained still.

He was as warped as his sister. The relief that she'd felt previously seeped away to be replaced with a familiar fear.

"You want us to die, Nate?"

His brow furrowed. "No."

"Oh good."

He smiled. "Not yet anyway. Not until after we've played the game."

———■———

Dominic and Hunter watched the SWAT team disperse around the home while officers went door to door, evacuating the residents who were home.

He checked his weapon and Hunter did the same. Colton and Katie had arrived and were awaiting instructions.

Dominic pushed his earpiece in a little further and said to the SWAT team leader, "What do you have, Mac?"

Mac had some serious equipment that allowed him to see through cement walls. Vaguely Dominic remembered the man going with Rick to some conference and learning all about it. Dominic wished he'd paid better attention to Rick when he was all excited about telling him about it. Something about a TWR-S Through the Wall radar system.

Mac was saying, "No security system. No booby traps found. Basement is soundproof, but we have visibility of four people with the radar system. One person is on the floor unmoving. Two others appear to be seated. The fourth one is moving around, walking between the two who are sitting down."

"Weapons?"

"A pistol in the hand of the one walking around. And one appears to be attached to a pole at the end of the table."

Technology was a wonderful thing.

"Okay, let's figure out a plan."

——■——

Serena gulped. "What are you doing?"

Nate opened the gun and spun the cylinder. "One bullet." He grinned. "Russian roulette."

Camille seemed almost catatonic at this point.

Nate shook his head. "I knew Gwen was after you. I followed her to your house so many times I lost count. She had chosen you to be her next toy, the next player." His jaw hardened and a malicious look came into his eyes.

His comment seemed random, but she had a feeling he was going somewhere with it.

"I even tried to help her catch you one time."

"Wha—the car wreck," Serena whispered.

"I saw Gwen ram your car. And then the cop behind you was going to interfere."

"*You* killed him?"

"I did. I thought Gwen would be happy for my help. That she would let me play when she realized I was the one that helped her get away."

"But she wasn't happy for your help, was she?"

His lips tightened. "No, she wasn't."

"Why not?"

"She didn't want me to play." His eyes turned mean. "They never wanted me to play. 'Go back inside, Nate, this is Daddy-daughter time.'" He singsonged the words and gave a vicious kick to one of

315

the chairs not bolted to the floor. It careened over and slammed against the cement floor with a crash.

Camille didn't even flinch.

Serena cringed but held back her scream.

Nate spun the roulette wheel much like Gwendolyn had done. He watched the little ball jump and land, jump and land. "So, who's going to go first?"

"What do you mean?" Serena asked.

"Well, after Gwendolyn and I saw each other at the morgue, she came to me and warned me away from her business."

A thought hit her. "The notes the killer—Gwendolyn—left in the boxes. They weren't for me or the authorities, were they?"

He smirked. "No. Your FBI friend let me see all of the notes on his second visit. That's when I was sure that some of them were meant for me. Her snarky little way of telling me to back off. That I wasn't *allowed* to play. I wasn't *invited* to play." His grip tightened on the gun and Serena drew in a steadying breath, trying to keep the clamoring terror at bay.

She looked at Gwendolyn. One killer down, one to go. The inane thought crossed her mind and she nearly giggled. And realized hysteria was going to set in soon.

"Nate, don't do this, please."

"Shut up." Then, conversationally, he asked, "You know who used to live here?"

"No. Who?" *Keep him talking. Steady, be steady.*

"Gwen's best friend."

"Oh. What happened to her?"

"Dad made Gwen kill her."

Serena felt nausea well up. "Why?" she whispered.

"Because Gwen was getting too close, too friendly, with Rose, and Dad wouldn't have that. Because she was his."

Nate paced from one end of the room to the other. Then back to the terrified Camille. He stooped in front of her and ran a hand over the girl's hair. Camille cringed as tears leaked down her cheeks. Nate frowned.

"How do you know that, Nate?" she persisted. "If you didn't get to play the game, how do you know this?" Serena tried to think of something, anything, to get his attention off Camille and back on her.

It worked. For the moment. He cocked his head, stood, and spun the roulette wheel again. "Because they made me bury the body. And all of the ones that came later." He smirked. "See, the police only had half of the bodies." At her horrified expression, he lifted a brow. "Oh yeah. The winner got to be found, all cleaned up and posed. Dad was very gracious about giving the winner's family closure."

He stuck his gun in the waistband of his pants and settled his hands on Serena's shoulders. She wanted to scream at him to get his hands off her, but she bit her tongue. As long as his attention was on her, it wasn't on Camille.

He said, "Look at the other end of the table. Look at Camille."

Serena did as she was told. The girl lifted terrified eyes, her breath hitching as she struggled not to hyperventilate. Serena could relate to the feeling.

"Now," his breath tickled her ear and she swallowed the urge to vomit, "let's pick up where Gwen left off. Pick a number and a color."

"No."

He raised his gun and aimed it at Camille in one smooth move. Serena gasped, "Okay, four red."

He let the gun drop to his side. "Four red. That's more like it."

The little ball started its never-ending journey once again and Nate watched it, seeming to be captivated by it. "Four red, four red," he intoned.

Serena leaned over and worked on her cuff once again. And felt it click. The little piece of wire she'd snitched from the toilet had done its job.

"Hey, what are you doing?"

She sat up. "Trying not to be sick."

He grinned at her. "No time to be sick, darling, you just lost the bet."

He walked to Camille and pulled her up closer to the table. The girl jumped up and shoved him. Nate stumbled from her. Serena shot to her feet, and the clasp of the handcuff tripped her. She fell back into the chair as Nate whipped the gun around and slammed it into Camille's stomach.

The girl went down, gagging and groaning.

"Camille!" Serena placed her hands on the gun in front of her and tried to yank it from the clasp, but she didn't know the trick to release it and didn't have time to figure it out. And if she pulled the trigger now, she'd hit Camille.

Nate slammed Camille back against the chair, whipped her hands behind her back, and pulled on her arms until she arched her back and screamed. Then he said, "Do anything like that again before the game is over and I'll end it now, you understand?"

Sobs wrenched from Camille's throat and Serena clenched her fists, silently begging God to intervene. "Don't, Camille, don't fight him, honey."

Camille gave up with a wail, leaned her head back, and cried.

Nate jerked her head up. "Now, now, that's no way to behave at my table." He walked to Serena, the gun held in front of him. With his left hand, he motioned for her to sit. "Now, put your hands back on the gun. You lost. You get to shoot your friend."

"What?" she gasped. "I'm not going to shoot her."

"You will or I'll shoot her. Then I'll shoot you. Then I'll go find your mother—again—and shoot her. And before you ask, yes, your mother was a message to Gwen that I was going to play the game whether she liked it or not."

"A message?" Stunned, Serena simply gaped. "Why didn't you just kill her?"

He barked a laugh. "You would have preferred that?"

"Of course not! I just don't—"

"Understand."

"Yes, I don't understand."

He shrugged. "I didn't want you grieving your mother. Grief does crazy things to people. You might not have functioned for days, weeks, months. I needed you functioning. It was the only way to get at Gwendolyn. When she took you, I'd simply take you away from her." He looked at his sister's now lifeless body on the floor. "And that's what I did."

He was insane.

He was also in control at the moment.

Nate spun the cylinder again. "So if you don't play, I'll go after your father, then your pretty little friends at Covenant House and see how many of those sweet young things like to play games. It's your choice. Taking one life for the good of many. If you don't want to be responsible for the people you love dying, shoot her."

Camille shook like a tree in a hurricane. Serena stared down the gun at the girl and knew she couldn't even shoot to miss. The gun was held and aimed firmly in its holder. She looked back at Nate. "And what happens to me if I shoot her?"

"You get to live."

Visions of the dead girls, the victims of the Doll Maker Killer, came to mind. "Somehow I doubt that. You just said the winners got a bullet in the forehead and were placed on display for all to see."

Confusion riddled his gaze for a moment, then he said, "Well, then I guess I can change the rules, right? After all, Drake's in prison and Gwen's dead. So the rules can change." Satisfaction gleamed as he waved the gun. "So, I'll let you live. But if you don't shoot her, you'll definitely die. And if you don't pull the trigger, she gets a turn. If she kills you, then she lives. It's as simple as that."

"That's the dumbest game I ever heard of," Camille whispered.

Chills swept over Serena. One hard tug and she'd be free of the

319

cuff around her ankle. But where would she go? Could she get to the door and get it open before Nate put a bullet in her back?

No, she couldn't.

She released the gun and said, "Then let Camille take a turn because there's no way I'm going to pull that trigger." She dropped into the chair and stared defiantly at the man.

Camille jerked. "I can't shoot you!"

Serena turned her gaze to Nate. "What do you do when the players won't play?"

Cold, soulless eyes stared back at her. "Kill them and find new ones. Just like Dad and Gwen used to do."

37

Dominic's heart chilled as he heard Nate's emotionless statement. A member of the SWAT team had managed to place a listening device on the window. Fortunately, it worked even through the thick glass. The one area Gwendolyn had cut corners. It was thick but not soundproof. He looked at Hunter. "We've got to get in there now."

Hunter asked, "Does the door open inward or outward?"

Dominic had Mac check for hinges.

"In," Mac said.

"Let me know when he's in front of the door."

"Copy that," Mac's voice came through his earpiece clearly.

———◼———

Serena watched Nate's cruel eyes. He paced as he waited for her to pick up the gun. She desperately tried to think of a way out and came to the sickening conclusion that there was none.

Nate gestured with his gun. "I don't have all day. I have a job to get back to. Now let's go."

"Who's going to bury the bodies this time, Nate?" she whispered.

He frowned. "I'll worry about that later. Shut up and pull the trigger." He walked up to her and placed the gun against the side of her head. Serena settled her hands on the weapon in front of her, felt the coldness of the butt of the gun against her palm.

Sweat slid from her temple and she swallowed.

"Do it!" His scream shattered the silence broken only by harsh breaths. She flinched and stared at Camille. Where could she aim? How could she communicate with the girl to move left or right—

"May I pray first?" she blurted.

"What?" He stilled and looked at her, disbelief stamped on his features. "Pray?"

Serena bowed her head and reached down, pulled the cuff open.

"Pray!" he screamed. "No, you can't pray! Now take the gun!"

"I'll go first!" Camille cried. "I'll do it!"

Nate swiveled and moved to the girl. He backhanded her and Camille's head snapped back. She spat blood and glared at him.

"It's not your turn," he sneered.

Nate moved back to Serena and grabbed the back of her hair. She cried out as he lowered his head next to hers. "You're ruining my game! Do I have to do everything?" He wrapped his hand around the gun.

"No!" With all of her strength, she shoved back with her elbow and caught him in the stomach. Air whooshed from him as he stumbled back.

Then the door exploded inward, clipping him in the shoulder. He went down, his gun sliding across the floor, and Serena raced around the table to grab Camille and push her down. Choking gas filled the room and she figured someone had tossed a flash bang into the room as they knocked the door down.

"Freeze! FBI!" Shouts and screams filled the air.

Camille clutched at her and Serena nearly cried her relief when Dominic appeared at the door, weapon drawn, eyes searching.

They landed on her and she saw the instant relief fill them.

Nate Lindell fought his captors as they did their best to subdue him in the small space. With a yell and a twist, he brought a hand up and broke the nose of the officer nearest to him. Blood spurted from the man as he fell back with a harsh cry.

His partner tackled the man. Dominic added his weight and together they worked to subdue him. Serena pulled Camille around to the other end of the table, out of harm's way.

Another harsh cry sounded. She whirled to see a large knife Nate managed to procure flash in the dim light of the room.

"Dominic! Be careful!"

Nate went down, clipped behind the knees by another officer. Then incredibly, he was back up, as was Dominic.

A gunshot sounded.

Nate's eyes went wide and blood bloomed across the chest of his starched white shirt.

Serena's ears rang as she spun to focus on Camille, who sat at the table, staring, wide-eyed and frozen, her hands locked around the weapon.

Dominic tackled the man once again and this time he stayed down.

More officers swarmed inside. Camille remained still as stone, her eyes on the man who had added his own short reign of terror to their day.

"We're fine now, Camille. We're fine."

"He was going to kill Dominic."

"I know." Serena pulled the girl's hands from the weapon and wrapped her in a hug as an officer uncuffed Camille's ankle from the leg of the chair.

Together, they walked toward the exit.

Serena tried to shield Camille from the two bodies on the floor, but the girl pulled away. Dominic's arms wrapped around Serena as Camille looked into Nate's lifeless eyes and whispered, "You lose."

38

Serena looked at Dominic. "So, when Nate came to the morgue looking for Leslie, he recognized Gwendolyn and contacted her, wanted to know what her game was."

Dominic nodded. "She told him to butt out of her business, and he thought that by helping her get you, she'd finally let him play."

"Which is why he killed the police officer and gave her a chance at you," Colton said and shook his head. "Sick dude."

Dominic said, "But neither of them knew I was just a few minutes behind you. Nate took off and Gwen grabbed your briefcase and fled."

"And the notes she started leaving were directed toward Nate."

"And we let him know that by telling him what they entailed."

"I'm sure that was just fuel to his fire." Katie smirked, then sobered. "But he was a sicko anyway, just like the rest of his family."

Alexia sighed. "I wonder why some kids who are abused turn out so awful like Nate and Gwen, and other kids, like Dom and me, I think we turned out okay. I mean, we're not perfect, but at least we don't go around killing people. We actually want to help people."

Serena shook her head. "I don't know. It could be the influences

324

in a child's life. Not just family, but teachers, church people, friends, et cetera. You know?"

Alexia looked at Serena. "Yeah, I know. You were one of those influences. Even though your dad wasn't always around and he frustrated you a lot, I could tell you loved him and he loved you."

Serena blinked against the rush of tears. "Yeah. You're right about that."

"And Marcus Porter was there for me," Dominic said.

Serena leaned forward in her seat. "That's why I want to be so involved with the girls at Covenant House. I want to see them grow into the people God meant for them to be. To move past their mistakes and build something from their lives."

"How's Camille?"

Serena glanced down the hall. "Asleep, I think."

"How's the baby?" Hunter asked.

"No damage from the blow to her stomach. She had an ultrasound after they brought her in."

"Is she going to keep it?"

Serena drew in a deep breath. "She's not sure yet. She's for sure not aborting, so that's good. If she wants to give it up for adoption, I told her I'd help her find a family who would give it a blessed childhood."

"The childhood she never had," Alexia murmured.

"Right. But until then, I told her if she would stay in school, she could stay with me."

Dominic gazed at her. "You're amazing."

Colton stood. "I'll see you guys later. I'm going to see if I can do anything to locate Jillian."

He left and Hunter and Alexia stood too.

Hunter said, "We're going to see your dad at the hospital. The psych meds seem to be working and he's having a better day today."

Alexia shook her head. "He's been an undiagnosed schizophrenic all these years. No wonder he couldn't keep it together when we were younger."

Hunter squeezed her hand. "He's getting the help he needs now."

Alexia looked at Serena and Dominic. "He asked to sign the divorce papers. Said he could do one good thing and give Mom her freedom to find some happiness in her life while she still had some time."

"What did Mom say about that?" Dominic asked.

"She seemed okay with it after she realized Dad wasn't changing his mind about it."

Hunter wrapped an arm around Alexia's shoulders. "I'm sorry, hon."

She shrugged, looked at Dominic, and said, "It's for the best, right?"

"Dad's adamant. And in his right mind right now, so, yeah . . ."

Alexia slipped out from under Hunter's protective arm and gave Serena a hug. "I'm so glad you're okay."

"Me too."

"See you later."

Serena watched them leave. She looked at Dominic and said, "It's time."

"For what?"

"To look in that package."

"Are you sure?"

"Yes. I'd already made up my mind to look, but by the time I did, everything was already going crazy and I simply didn't get a chance. And I don't think Jillian had any clue the trouble she'd spark with this thing." She took a deep breath and walked to the small table in the foyer. Reaching behind the mirror just above the table, she pulled the package out.

Walking back into the den, she opened it, and slid the envelopes out. Bypassing the one she'd already read, she sat on the couch and opened the second one.

"Wait a minute," Dominic said, reaching over to place his hand on hers. "Before you get into that, I need to tell you something."

Surprised at the intensity of his tone, she let the envelope fall to the couch beside her. "What is it?"

"I'm falling in love with you."

She blinked. Then smiled. "Well, that's good news."

He huffed a laugh. "That's it? That's all you have to say after I worked up the nerve to tell you?"

Trembling on the inside, her heart filled with a tender love for the man sitting next to her. "It's only been a short time, Dominic, but I've come to care about you so much. We've been through some pretty intense times and I think that just sort of heightens all the emotions—"

He placed a finger over her lips. "Put your doctor persona away for now. How does the woman feel?"

"She's falling in love with you too," she whispered.

"Good." He settled his lips over hers.

As she settled into the kiss, she decided he was right. Too much analyzing wasn't good. Right now, she simply wanted to feel. Feel loved and safe and right where she wanted to be. Right in Dominic's arms.

He lifted his head, eyes narrowed, and said, "How long do I have to give you before you would say yes?"

She lifted a brow. "Why don't you ask me and find out."

He laughed. "Okay. I will. When you least expect it."

She smacked his arm and he kissed her again. Then said, "Okay, let's look at the package."

"Oh. Right. The package."

She lifted the envelope from the sofa, pulled out the letter.

And started to read.

39

"So, what's the next failure of a plan?" Frank couldn't help the snide question.

Silence echoed over the line.

Then the voice said, "It was a good plan."

"Not good enough."

"If Serena had been killed by Gwendolyn Lindell, no one would have been the wiser. She would have simply been another victim of a serial killer. No one would have been able to connect her with us."

"We still don't have the package."

"That's all right, we have something better."

"What's that?"

"A lead on Jillian. Her plane lands tomorrow at 10:50 a.m."

Frank stilled. "She's coming here?"

"She is."

"Don't let her leave the airport alive."

"That's the plan."

ACKNOWLEDGMENTS

There are always so many people involved in putting a book together that I'm afraid to start thanking them because I don't want to forget anyone! But I'm going to give it a shot.

Thanks to my awesome editor, Andrea Doering, who believes in me and my work—even when I have my doubts!

To Tamela Hancock Murray of the Steve Laube Agency for all your hard work on my behalf and for believing in me too!

I can't say thank you enough to Officer James (Jim) Hall and Retired FBI Agent Wayne Smith, who proof my law enforcement details. Any inaccuracies are mine and mine alone. You guys never charge me enough!

Also, a big thanks to Ruthie Owens at Spartanburg Regional Hospital for answering all of my many autopsy questions about a year ago.

And of course, I can't forget the rest of the amazing and talented Revell team. Michele Misiak, Claudia Marsh, Barb Barnes, and the art design team—you guys rock and I love working with you all. I know there are more of you who are behind the scenes, so I'm thanking you too!

One person I also want to thank is Taylor Bevil, a young lady I'm proud to call friend. She's an insightful, detail-oriented reader who caught a couple of mistakes when I asked her to read the story. She also offered excellent suggestions on how to make the story better! Thanks for your input, Taylor!

And last, but never least, I want to thank you readers who buy my books and support what I do. I definitely couldn't do this without you!

Lynette Eason is the author of several romantic suspense novels, including *Too Close to Home, Don't Look Back*, and *A Killer Among Us*. She is a member of American Christian Fiction Writers and Romance Writers of America. Lynette graduated from the University of South Carolina and went on to earn her master's degree in education from Converse College. She lives in South Carolina with her husband and two children.

Come meet
Lynette Eason at
www.LynetteEason.com

Follow her on

facebook   Lynette Barker Eason

twitter   LynetteEason

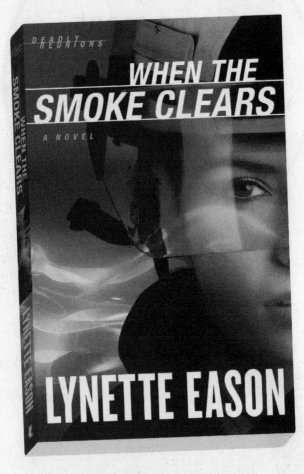

Women of JUSTICE Series